MAX AND THE CORPORATE TAKEOVER

D.P. BOWKETT

Dippy Bee

First published in 2025 by Dippy Bee Publishing

While the book may reference historical figures, the portrayals of these individuals are fictional and not intended to constitute definitive biographies. Any similarity between these fictional depictions and actual historical persons or aliens, living or dead, is entirely coincidental.

Cover illustration by Alex at IndieBubble
Interior Formatting by Kelley at Sleepy Fox Studio

A very special *thank you* to my beta readers who encouraged me to get this far.

eBook ISBN: 978-1-7395583-5-2
Print ISBN: 978-1-7395583-4-5
Thema codes YFHH, YFG, YFC
BISAC codes YAF019040, YAF056010, YAF001000

Also by D.P. Bowkett

Max Janus – The Bobby Years

Modern-Day Young Adult Science Fiction Fantasy

Max and the Hidden Visitor

Max Janus – It's My History

Young Adult Science Fiction Fantasy History

Max and the Regent Supreme

PROLOGUE

Dear Friend,

If you've read my first two biographies, you'll know why I came to your planet over two thousand years ago and why I'm currently being hosted inside an eighteen-year-old Londoner called Bobby Morris.

If you haven't, then *why not*? Just kidding. But seriously, *Max and the Regent Supreme* explains why I left my dystopian home planet of Zephyrion and ended up in the house of Julius Caesar. *Max and the Hidden Visitor* brings my story up to date and tells how I ended up being a part of the Morris family and surrounded by some eccentric but incredibly loyal friends.

Back on my home planet, I was what you might describe as a specialist law enforcer, with the investigation and prevention of corruption being one of my main duties. Not only was my job part of the reason why I came to your planet, but it's also something I've been doing ever since.

However, I've always tried to avoid human politics and concentrated on catching Deceptors from Zephyrion. Deceptors are what we call criminal Shadowers, and Shadowers are what the most significant race of people on Zephyrion were called until the rebranding to Zephyrions after the Grand Formation, when the planet unified under one government. Before you ask, I am a Shadower, I don't have any desire to be rebranded, thank you very much.

Since I encountered Bobby, his family and his friends, life has been a little crazy. But I'm pleased to say things have finally returned to some semblance of normal.

Then again normal is relative. Humans can't hum while pinching their noses closed. Shadowers can, so it's strange you can't. On Earth you have days, weeks, months and years, but on Venus a year is 225 Earth days, while a day is 243 Earth days, so a day is longer than a year. And have you ever realised the word queue is just one letter doing all the work, while the others stand silently in a line behind it. So what really is normal?

Max

P.S. Have you stopped pinching your nose and trying to hum yet?

1
SUMMER JOB

'Hey, Bob. What're you doing here?' Dazza asked as he waited for his sausage and omelette roll. 'Are you meeting someone by Saint Paul's?'

'Hi, Dazza,' Bobby replied. 'Nah, Danny's dad arranged an interview for me at some investment bank around the corner, but I'm a bit early.'

'I always thought you were a bit of a banker,' Dazza laughed as his order was called.

Bobby stared at his smoothie, knowing he didn't want it, in the same way he didn't want to be here. If he were just one year younger, he'd be chilling out with his mates during the summer holidays.

'*Welcome to adulthood,*' Max thought.

'*Can I choose the hybrid model? I get to make all the decisions as an adult and have my own money, but I can still enjoy long summer holidays?*' Bobby replied with a smile.

'*If you find a way to achieve that, trademark it because so many would love that way of life,*' Max laughed.

'Budge up,' Dazza said, squeezing onto the stool next to Bobby, who was looking out onto the busy street.

Bobby loved living in London. For all of its issues with crime, which he felt weren't a lot different from those of many other major cities, he loved the diversity of life teeming past the coffee shop's window. Bobby smiled at the young boy skipping along behind the boy's father. The boy was of an age where he should be at school, but whether it was due to an illness, medical appointment, or whatever, he was enjoying his time out of the educational establishment.

'What's with the grey suit?' Dazza asked, crumbs of his roll falling onto the counter. 'Is it a posh job?'

'What?' Bobby asked, dragged back from observing the world.

'The job Danny's dad's arranged. What's it doing?' Dazza asked, taking another bite of his roll.

'I'm not sure. It's some sort of student thing. They take students every year after the exam results are out and use them to analyse stuff,' Bobby replied.

'*I told you I could get you a better job,*' Max thought.

'*Yeah, okay, Cowboy, but if I get this job, I get to work with Danny,*' Bobby replied.

'*But you can't base your career on working with friends,*' Max said.

'*I know that, but having a friend there will make it a bit easier,*' Bobby snapped.

'Why are you over here?' Max asked Dazza, changing the subject.

'Business Inside Out saw my college portfolio and asked me to come in,' Dazza replied.

'Who?' Bobby said.

'Business Inside Out. They report on business and financial news and expose corruption,' Dazza said before gulping down the last of his roll.

'What do you know about business and corruption, big man?' Bobby laughed.

'They don't want me as an investigator. They want me as a photographer,' Dazza replied.

'Does it feel weird that we're job-hunting now, and yet not long ago, we were simple students?' Bobby asked.

'You're kidding, right?' Dazza laughed, draining his smoothie.

'What?' Bobby challenged.

'Not long ago, we were fighting a Daxson, a corrupt copper and one of Max's planet's criminal Deceptors,' Dazza replied.

'Fairs,' Bobby smiled.

'Excuse me, gentlemen, but have you seen a couple of dullards looking for jobs?' a voice said behind them.

Max and Dazza turned to see a familiar face.

'Just when you think today is stressful enough, Danny arrives,' Dazza laughed.

Bobby looked at Danny, noting how he was almost standing. His wheelchair lifted him upward and forward while the straps held him firmly in place.

'Danny, you look amazing. How's the new wheelchair?' Max asked.

'New Dawn 2 is doing well, Chief,' Danny replied. 'Instead of lifting me in a seat, it helps me get into a more natural standing position.'

'That's amazing, but where are your control glasses?' Max queried.

'They were too unreliable. I've developed a contact lens control. It picks up not only the direction I'm looking in but what I'm focussing on,' Danny replied.

'That's incredible,' Bobby said.

'I know. Some people would say I'm a genius,' Danny laughed.

'Not a chance,' Dazza laughed.

'Only because they're jealous,' Danny chuckled. 'Are you ready for your interview, Bobster?'

'Yeah, I guess so,' Bobby replied, a mix of nerves and excitement.

'I need to shoot,' Dazza said, standing.

'Yeah, I need to head off too. I'm seeing a Mr Swancott in fifteen minutes,' Bobby replied.

'Swancott? You mean Dad didn't get you an interview with Big Bill?' Danny laughed.

'Big who?' Bobby asked.

'Big Bill. William J Pierce, WestFi's CEO,' Danny replied.

'WestFi as in Westbridge Enterprise Finance?' Dazza asked, turning back to face Danny.

'Yeah. Have you heard of them, big man?' Danny asked.

'Of course I have. BIO's been reporting on them as a major investment bank who came from Asia into Europe,' Dazza replied.

'Who's BIO?' Danny asked.

Dazza smiled proudly, 'Business Inside and Out. They want me as a lead photographer.'

'Well, I wouldn't brag too much, big man. They're like the gossip tabloid of the business world,' Danny laughed.

'Hey, chill it, Danny. Not everyone has family connections,' Max said. 'Some people have to grab whatever opportunities they can get.'

'Sorry, big man, the chief is right. If you have a passion, any job in that direction is a good choice,' Danny replied.

'Thanks, guys. Good luck, Bob,' Dazza replied, heading towards the door. 'Are we still meeting up later?'

'Yeah. Adam suggested meeting up in Winnett Street around eight,' Bobby replied.

'Well, come on, dude, we'd better get moving. Can't keep Mr Swannedoff waiting,' Danny laughed.

'You mean Swancott,' Bobby replied, heading towards the door.

'Yeah, him too,' Danny chuckled.

Twenty minutes later, Bobby is sitting in the office of Bruce Swancott's secretary.

'I'm sorry, but Mr Swancott is on a call and running late. Can I get you a drink?' his secretary asked.

'*I'll have a malt whiskey and ice,*' Max thought.

'*I don't drink,*' Bobby replied.

'*I know,*' Max sighed. '*But a two-thousand-year-old alien can dream, can't I?*'

'Can I have a water, please?' Bobby asked.

The secretary wandered off to a small kitchen area and returned carrying a glass of water.

'He shouldn't be much longer,' the secretary said, handing Bobby the water.

A few minutes later, the door opened, releasing a young, exuberant black Labrador, who spotted Bobby and dove towards him, spilling the glass of water over Bobby's lap.

'Chris, send in the candidate,' Bruce Swancott said from the doorway before spotting his dog jumping around. 'Buster, come here. I'm so sorry Mr...'

'Bobby Morris, Sir. I think I'm your candidate,' Bobby replied.

'Come in, Bobby,' Bruce replied. 'I'm sorry about Buster; he just gets excited meeting people.'

Bobby stood up and handed the empty glass to the secretary, pretending his trousers weren't soaked. As he walked into Bruce's office, he said, 'It's fine, sir. I know how excitable puppies can be.'

Bruce grabbed Buster's collar, pulled him into the office, and closed the door. 'That's good. Some people struggle with dogs, you know.'

'My mum always says trust a person who loves dogs or a dog who hates a person,' Bobby said.

'*No, she doesn't,*' Max thought.

'*Yeah, but he doesn't know that,*' Bobby protested.

'Your mum sounds very wise, Barry,' Bruce replied.

'*See. Love me, love my dog,*' Bobby smiled.

'I see Paul White has recommended you. Have you worked for him?' Bruce asked.

'Not exactly. I've worked with his son, Danny,' Bobby replied.

'Oh, Danny, yes,' Bruce replied, leaning back in his chair. 'He's a...hmm...an enthusiastic lad.'

'Yes, sir,' Bobby replied, desperately trying to hold down Buster, who seemed intent on jumping onto his lap.

'I'm sorry, is Buster bothering you?' Bruce asked before adding, 'Buster, leave Barry alone.'

'Erm, it's Bobby, sir.'

'No, he's called Buster. I've only had him six months,' Bruce replied.

'No, sir. I mean, my name is Bobby.'

'Sorry, of course, Bobby. I see you can start on Monday, and has someone in my Personnel Support team taken you through the role?' Bruce asked, walking over to a coffee machine, putting a capsule in the top before pressing the start button.

'Someone called Jess from Human Resources took me through it on a video interview,' Bobby replied. 'I understand it's putting data into some software and —'

'Oh, for goodness' sake,' Bruce huffed, walking over to his office door and opening it. 'Chris! Did that memo go out about the department rebranding?'

'Yes, Bruce. We've been officially Personnel Support since Monday,' Chris replied, looking up from his screen.

'Then tell Jess I want to see her in five minutes,' Bruce shouted before shutting the door.

Bruce's raised voice caused Buster to finally leave Bobby alone. He ran over to a blanket near the floor-to-ceiling window, where he lay down.

Bruce picked up his espresso from the coffee machine, walked over to Buster, and started fussing with him. 'Do you have any more questions, Barry?'

'When will I hear if I've got the job?'

Bruce stood up and turned towards Bobby with a frown. 'You've already got the role. Mr White's recommendation and the fact that you match some of our diversity requirements meant I just needed to meet you to ensure your personality fits. Anything else, Barry?'

'Bobby, sir. Well, I don't think so. Except, where do I go on Monday?'

'You'll get an email later today with details of where to report and confirming the terms of your employment. Now, excuse me, I have another meeting,' Bruce replied, downing his coffee and opening the office door.

Bobby stood up and started walking towards the open door, holding out his hand to shake Bruce's. Before Bruce could reciprocate, Buster flew off his blanket, barking excitedly and lunged at Bobby's back, knocking him flat on his face and licking Bobby's neck excitedly.

Bobby felt Bruce dragging Buster off him before he saw a hand in front of him and a soft female voice say, 'I'm so sorry about his dog. Let me help you up.'

Bobby looked up into the smiling, familiar face of the woman who had done his video interview. 'Thanks.'

'Oh, flipping hell! Chris, hand me some tissues,' Jess said.

Bobby got to his feet and looked down as blood dripped to the floor. 'Umm...'

'Jess, get in here,' Bruce shouted from his office.

'Chris, take care of Bobby. I think it looks worse than it is,' Jess said. 'I'll check on you after I've sorted Bruce out.'

'I think he may have broken your nose,' Chris said, holding a tissue against Bobby's nose.

'No, it's okay, he's just got a few burst blood vessels,' Max replied, grabbing the tissue off Chris.

'What was that?' Chris asked.

'Dunno what you mean?' Bobby replied. 'Has the bleeding stopped?'

'Yeah, it looks like it has, but why did you talk about yourself in the third person?'

'I didn't. I just asked if the bleeding had stopped.'

'Before that. You said, "he's just got a few burst blood vessels" like you were talking about someone else,' Chris said, frowning.

'Umm, no, I meant the dog had just burst some of my blood vessels,' Bobby replied, smiling weakly.

'That flipping dog. He's so lovable, but Bruce hasn't got a clue about training him,' Chris said, dipping a tissue into a glass of water and wiping the drying blood off Bobby's face.

Bobby looked down at his bloodstained suit and shirt. 'Mum's going to kill me. She only got me these last weekend.'

'*I'll get you a new suit. I said I would last time,*' Max thought.

'*Look, Cowboy, I know you've got the money, but we've got our principles and pride,*' Bobby replied.

'...company will pay,' Chris said.

Bobby looked at Chris quizzically. 'Sorry, I was distracted. What did you say?'

'I said don't worry about your clothes, the company will pay,' Chris smiled, wiping the last of the drying blood off Bobby's face. 'I'm afraid your handsome looks can't be fixed as easily. You'll look bruised and battered for a few days, but we can sort out your clothing this afternoon.'

'*He's flirting with you,*' Max thought.

'*Don't be daft. He's just doing his job,*' Bobby replied.

'*I'm telling you, he is one hundred percent flirting,*' Max insisted.

'*I'm not listening,*' Bobby said.

'Are you alright, Bobby? You don't seem totally here,' Chris asked.

Bobby smiled. 'Sorry, yeah—'

Bruce's office door flew open, crashing against the table behind it.

'So we agree, I'll use the new department name, and you'll get Buster trained,' Jess barked, slamming the door behind her.

Bobby stood up to meet Jess. 'I'm so sorry. I seem to have caused a bit of a mess.'

'Nonsense. It's Swannedoff's inability to train his dog that's to blame,' Jess replied, examining Bobby's face and clothes as Bobby burst out laughing.

Chris tilted his head to one side. 'What's so funny?'

'It's just my friend, Danny called Mr Swancott that too,' Bobby chuckled.

'Of course he did. He was the one who came up with the name,' Chris replied.

'It fits him too. No matter what the meeting, he mentally swans off,' Jess laughed. 'It's such a shame about Buster, he's such a loving dog.'

'Yeah. Now he's used to me; he just comes up for a fuss or a treat and then lies under my desk. Maybe it's Bruce that needs training,' Chris said.

'I think Bruce is untrainable!' Jess smiled, 'So, how long have you known Mr White and Danny?'

'I met Danny gaming online about three years ago. I only really know his Dad from visiting Danny at home. I know he did something in the city and got me this job, but I don't know anything more than that,' Bobby replied.

Chris looked at Jess and shrugged.

'What?' Bobby challenged.

'You honestly don't know who Paul White is?' Chris asked.

'Well, I know he's Danny's dad.'

Jess laughed. 'Yeah, he is, but he's also brought in tens of billions of pounds of business in the last year alone. Everyone in the city knows Paul White. If Paul says "jump," even Big Bill asks, "How high?"'

'I think even Jay is scared of him,' Chris laughed.

'Who's Jay?' Bobby queried.

'Zara Shah. Her family own WestFi,' Jess replied.

'But you said her name was Jay,' Bobby replied, frowning.

'Everyone calls her Jay. Her grandfather, Sanjay Shah, started the business and was known as Jay. He always called her his mini-Jay,' Jess explained. 'She used to be known as Jay Junior, but now she's just known as Jay.'

'Oh,' Bobby replied, losing interest.

'*The Paul White is Danny's dad,*' Max thought.

'*If you knew, why didn't you say before?*' Bobby replied.

'*Because I never linked the two people. Obviously, I've met Danny's dad, but I've never met Paul White, "The White Shark", or even seen pictures of him,*' Max said defensively.

'The White Shark!' Bobby said out loud.

'That's right. So you do know him then?' Jess said.

'What? Oh, uh, no, sorry, I remember hearing the name somewhere,' Bobby replied.

Jess looked down at Bobby's bloodstained suit. 'We need to get you some new clothing. We can't let Mr White's protégé leave with bloodied clothes.'

'I'll be okay. Mum is good with getting stains out,' Bobby replied.

'Nonsense. I've got the afternoon off, so I can take you to get some replacements, all paid with Bruce's corporate credit card,' Chris laughed.

'Make sure you go to one of the high-end shops. It's only fair Bobby gets a like-for-like replacement,' Jess insisted.

Bobby started to protest, 'But Mum got me this fr—'

Jess held her hand up. 'Your mother clearly shops at the best stores, Bobby. Chris, I know I can trust you to do the right thing. I need to go now, but I'm pleased you're joining the company, Bobby. I'll see you on Monday. Come to reception at 9:30 and ask for Chris Medici; he'll sort you out.'

'Does he work for you?' Bobby asked.

'Not directly. Chris works for Bruce, but he supports the whole department, and he's been cleaning you up for the last half-hour,' Jess smiled, nodding towards Chris.

'At your service,' Chris jokingly replied. 'Now let's go and max out Bruce's card.'

2
A Night on the Town

'This is too much,' Bobby protested.

'Nonsense. Bruce spends way more on his suits,' Chris replied as they sat in a wine bar behind the Gielgud Theatre.

'But I could buy an old car for the same price,' Bobby said.

'But you wouldn't look half as good in it,' Chris smiled.

'But I only ruined my shirt and suit. Why did you insist on getting me these jeans and top?' Bobby asked.

'Because you said you were meeting some friends, and I can't let the reputation of WestFi down by having you meet them in clothes bloodied on our premises,' Chris laughed.

'Won't you get into trouble?'

'No. It's become a joke that Buster needs his own company credit card to pay for all the damage he causes. Are you sure you don't want an alcoholic drink?'

'I don't drink,' Bobby replied. 'It disagrees with me.'

'*You've brought us to a wine bar to drink soft drinks,*' Max moaned.

'*You know what happened the last time I had a lot to drink at Agathe and Michael's house,*' Bobby replied. '*I fell down the stairs and woke up the next morning with no memory of anything.*'

'*You had two small whiskies,*' Max groaned. '*That's hardly a lot.*'

'*It is when you don't drink,*' Bobby protested.

'Bobby, are you alright?' Chris asked.

'Hi, Chris. Don't worry about Bobby; he's probably talking to Max,' Danny chirped.

'Oh, hi, Danny. What do you fancy?' Chris asked.

'I'll have a virgin mojito, please,' Danny replied before glancing up, which made his wheelchair lift him into a standing position against the bar.

'So, who's the Max you reckon Bobby is talking to? Is it some form of imaginary friend?' Chris asked with a puzzled look.

'Ah, awks,' Danny said sheepishly.

'Don't tell me he's a little strange?' Chris asked, tapping the side of his head.

'Blimey, no. Max and Bobby aren't a little strange at all,' Danny replied.

'That's a relief. I like him,' Chris said.

'No, they're well beyond a little strange; it's more like major league strange,' Danny laughed. 'And as for you likin—'

'Who's strange?' Bobby challenged.

'I was just saying to Chris that this bar is a bit, uh, unusual and strange,' Danny flustered.

Chris smiled, 'Danny was just about to explain who Max is.'

'Oh. Well, this will sound strange, but Max is an alien currently living inside me until his DNA shell is complete,' Bobby replied.

'That's not strange at all. I've lived with an alien all my life; she's called my sister,' Chris laughed. 'Seriously though, who is Max?'

'What Bobby just said,' Max replied.

'Haha. Nice try with the voice change. Come on, who is he?' Chris chuckled.

'My name is Maxohal, and I was born approximately 2,100 years ago on a planet called Zephyrion, many light years away,' Max replied.

'And he likes bananas and salad cream sandwiches,' Dazza said, joining them.

'Hey, Dazza, this is Chris. He works with us at WestFi,' Danny said.

'Banana and salad cream sandwiches are strange,' Chris laughed. 'Nice to meet you, Dazza.'

'You too, Chris. Flipping hell, Bob, what happened to you?' Dazza asked.

'I got Bustered,' Bobby smiled.

'Huh?'

'Bobby got steamrollered by our HR Director's dog,' Chris explained.

'Wow, can I get a picture?' Dazza asked.

'You got the paps job then?' Danny said.

'We're not paparazzi; BIO is a serious business magazine,' Dazza replied.

'Never mind that, who's Max?' Chris pressed.

'Like I said, I'm from another planet, and I've lived on Earth since 45 BC,' Max replied.

'Yeah, sure.' Chris replied. 'So, who was our King then?'

'There wasn't a King. It was different tribes ruling this country,' Max replied.

'Okay, well, what about in, erm, 1482?' Chris challenged.

'Edward the Fourth, of course, but what happened to his son Edward the Fifth is a bit unpleasant,' Max replied.

Chris mulled this over, then said, 'Okay, what about 1651?'

'In 1651, there wasn't a king. The country was under the control of the Commonwealth of England,' Max replied. 'Although I still don't forgive the Cavaliers for shooting me for selling chickens to Cromwell's lot,' Max said.

'What about in 1553?' a woman said, joining the group.

'Hi, sis,' Chris said. 'Guys, this is my sister Mercedes. She works in the actuary department.'

'I don't start until Monday, actually,' Mercedes replied.

'Hey there,' the group replied.

'So come on. Whoever is talking about our kings, who was the king in 1553?' Mercedes asked.

'At the start of the year, it was, erm, Edward the Sixth until he died, then Lady Jane Grey succeeded him for just over a week before being replaced by Mary,' Max replied.

'You're good at historical English monarchs,' Mercedes said. 'What about in 1789? What happened globally?'

'In 1789, the French Revolution started with the storming of the Bastille. In April, the mutiny on the Bounty occurred in the South Pacific Ocean. In the same month, George Washington was inaugurated as the first President of the United States,' Max answered.

'What changed in 1953?' Dazza asked.

'Dazza, you know who we are,' Bobby protested.

'It's okay,' Max replied. 'But there were quite a few changes, like the coronation of Queen Elizabeth the Second. Mount Everest was conquered, and two humans finally discovered DNA, describing the double-helix structure of DNA in a paper.'

'You mean James Watson and Francis Crick,' Mercedes said, sipping a spritzer Chris had ordered for her.

'Looks like you're not the only smarty pants, Max,' Danny smirked.

'I mean with regards to printing,' Dazza said.

'I think he's referring to the rule that until 1953, publishing or possessing a detailed map of the country was illegal. It was a law brought in during World War Two and continued during the Cold War,' Mercedes said, giving Danny a side glance.

'Someone's been spending too long on the internet,' Danny laughed.

'Actually, I did a degree in Actuarial Science and one in the History and Philosophy of Science,' Mercedes smiled.

'If you've done two degrees already, you must be older than you look because you look younger than Chris,' Danny challenged.

'I'm nineteen,' Mercedes replied, sipping her drink. 'Chris is twenty.'

'If you're such a genius, why are you joining WestFi?' Danny asked.

'From what Chris has told me about you, I should be asking you the same question,' Mercedes replied confidently. 'Isn't your dad the super wealthy Paul White?'

'Says a member of the Medici family!' Danny fumed.

'Come on guys, play nicely,' Chris laughed. 'And our family's wealth is long gone.'

Max looked at Danny before glancing between Chris and Mercedes. 'I didn't register the name earlier when Jess said it, but are you two members of the Medici family of Florence?'

Chris laughed. 'According to our Nonna, we are. She loves to tell stories about our ancestors.'

'They're not stories. They're true,' Mercedes protested.

'What's a nonna?' Dazza asked.

'It's what we call our grandmother,' Chris replied.

'Do you speak Italian?' Max asked.

'Not much,' Chris laughed. 'I speak a little and understand a bit more. But of course, my triple S can.'

'Whats a triple S?' Max queried.

'He's trying to be funny, calling me his super smart sister,' Mercedes replied. 'Sì, ovviamente parlo italiano fluentemente. E tu?'

'Complimenti per il tuo italiano perfetto. Quando sono arrivato sulla Terra, ho imparato il latino, ma ora che è quasi estinto, uso l'italiano,' Max replied.

'What are they saying?' Dazza asked.

Chris sighed, 'Mercedes was showing off how she can speak it fluently, and Max complimented her and said something about speaking Latin when he arrived on Earth but now speaks Italian.'

'Never mind them. Did someone say Danny's dad was super wealthy and called Paul White?' Dazza challenged.

'You know my dad's called Paul,' Danny replied, glowering at Mercedes. 'And that we're wealthy.'

'Yeah, but...Paul White, as in the White Shark?' Dazza asked.

'That's right,' Chris replied.

Dazza lifted his camera, 'Can I get a picture? White Shark's disabled son drinking with friend assaulted by WestFi director's dog?'

'Yeah, of course,' Danny snapped. 'Followed by Paul White's differently-abled son decks pap photographer.'

Dazza lowered his camera. 'On second thought, maybe not.'

Bobby's phone pinged, and he read the message

Adam

> Sorry, boo. Coach has insisted we travel up tonight. I'll see you tomorrow x.

'Are you okay, Bob?' Dazza asked, noticing the look on his friend's face.

'Yeah, it's just Adam. He can't come. They've got to travel up tonight for tomorrow's game,' Bobby sighed.

'Who's Adam?' Chris asked.

'Adam Lee, you know, Watford's new midfielder,' Dazza replied. 'He's Bob's boyf—'

'Best friend,' Bobby interrupted.

'Yeah, but he's also—' Dazza started.

'All our friend,' Bobby added, glowering at Dazza.

Danny elbowed Dazza discreetly, but Dazza shouted, 'Oww, what was that for?'

'I assume they're trying to stop you saying he's Bobby's boyfriend,' Mercedes said.

'Shh,' Bobby hissed.

'What's wrong with him dating a man?' Mercedes asked.

'He's a professional footballer. They have to stay closeted because of their career,' Bobby said. 'Can we stop talking about it.'

'Sounds ridiculous to me,' Mercedes replied.

'It's fine. We just need to keep it quiet that we're dating,' Bobby insisted.

'Well, I'd shout it out loud if you were my boyfriend,' Chris smiled. 'Even if that means I'm dating two for the price of one.'

'Sorry, Chris, but I've got a girlfriend called Avery,' Max replied.

'But you're gay?' Chris challenged.

'Bobby's gay, but I'm person-oriented, so I like individuals based on who they are, not their gender or sexual orientation,' Max replied.

'So you really are two people in one body, like a multiple personality disorder?' Chris asked.

'Duh. No, it's our friend Bobby, and he's been inhabited by our alien friend until Max can build his DNA shell,' Danny replied. 'There's no disorder.'

'It sounds more like a folie à plusieurs, a madness of many or shared delusion to me,' Mercedes said.

'Nobody is forcing you to stay,' Danny snapped.

'It's okay, I find it interesting,' Mercedes smiled.

'You guys really believe Bobby is two people?' Chris asked.

'I'm not two people. I'm Bobby Morris, son of Simon and Pat Morris, and my little sister is Lily. Max is an ancient alien who has been sharing my body for a few months and will soon move into his own body,' Bobby replied.

'It's true. The chief is sharing Bobby's body for a while,' Danny replied.

'Show them how fast you can move, Bob,' Dazza said.

'I'm not a circus act, Dazza.'

'Well, you weren't faster than Buster,' Chris laughed.

'Seeing behind me isn't a skill I have,' Max replied as they moved from the bar to a high table surrounded by tall stools.

A glass smashed across the other side of the bar, followed by a cheer.

Chris turned and groaned. 'That's Terry, one of our trading directors.'

'He seems very friendly with that other guy,' Danny observed.

'You mean Stephen Marchent the third,' Mercedes replied.

'How do you know him?' Bobby asked.

'He owns one of Mr White's target companies,' Mercedes said.

'My dad won't appreciate you publicly announcing a business he's secretly trying to buy,' Danny huffed.

'It's hardly top secret,' Dazza replied, lifting his camera and taking some pictures of Stephen and Terry laughing and hugging. 'BIO reported on that last week. They reckon his business, M Bank Research, has found a new mineral while studying an archaeological site near Rome.'

'What do you mean?' Danny asked. 'And will you put that camera down? We're supposed to be enjoying a night out.'

Dazza glanced at Danny, then lifted his camera back up. 'Yeah, okay, just a coup—'

'Sorry, sir, but we don't allow paparazzi in here,' a large muscular bouncer said, pushing Dazza's camera down. 'Would you mind leaving, please.'

'But I'm not paps; I'm having a drink with friends,' Dazza protested. 'I just heard that noise and took some jokey pictures.'

'Well, you can either leave or give me your camera and bag, and we'll keep it safe behind the bar,' the bouncer said.

'But papa...I mean, a good photographer is never without his camera,' Dazza protested. 'It's like his best friend.'

'Then I suggest you and your best friend leave,' the bouncer replied, moving uncomfortably close and standing imposingly with his arms folded.

Despite the bouncer's build, Dazza's six foot four inches meant he was still around five inches taller than the bouncer. Dazza glanced down and felt that, for the first time, his height gave him no advantage, and he sighed, put his camera in his bag, and handed it over to the bouncer. 'If that gets damaged, I'm suing this place.'

'Thank you, sir,' the bouncer replied, heading behind the bar and into a room where he left the bag.

'What're you laughing at, Danny?' Dazza challenged.

Danny wiped the tears from his eyes. 'Sorry, mate. It was like a ginger Eiffel Tower met a huge, immovable, short mountain.'

'If he was a ginger Eiffel Tower, wouldn't that mean he'd gone rusty,' Mercedes laughed.

Dazza chuckled. 'She got you there, Danny.'

'A bit like that bouncer got you,' Danny snapped back. 'Never argue with someone whose biceps have their own weather system.'

'*I've never seen Danny so tetchy,*' Max thought.

'*Nor me. Mercedes seems to push his buttons,*' Bobby replied.

'*I think he might fancy her,*' Max said.

'*Uh, how do you draw that conclusion, Cowboy?*' Bobby laughed. '*I'd say it's more like he hates her.*'

'*Love and hate are a fine line, and I think Danny is on the love side, with a good dose of denial,*' Max said.

'*So you reckon Chris might be flirting with me, and Danny fancies Mercedes,*' Bobby chuckled. '*Don't launch a dating app 'cos your matchmaking sucks.*'

'*I'd bet a banana and salad cream sandwich on it,*' Max replied.

'*I'll match your bet and raise you a packet of cheese and onion crisps for breakfast,*' Bobby laughed.

'Hello, Earth to Bobby,' Chris said, waving his hand in front of Bobby's face. 'I asked if you wanted another drink?'

'Can I have one of those virgin mojitos Danny is drinking,' Bobby asked.

'Good choice, Bobster,' Danny replied. 'I'll have the same, please, cos I—'

'I never drink and drive,' Dazza and Bobby said in unison while pretending to tap their wheelchairs.

Danny looked between Dazza and Bobby, 'Whaaat?'

'You're always saying it,' Bobby laughed.

'Saying what?' Danny protested.

'I think they're claiming your drinking and driving joke is one you say a lot,' Mercedes explained.

Danny glowered at Mercedes. 'Well, at least I try to be funny.'

'I wonder what Terry and the other guy are talking about?' Chris pondered.

'Terry's asking if Stephen wants another bottle of champers?' Max said. 'And Stephen replied, "This time next week, it'll be the good stuff."'

'How do you know that?' Mercedes asked, peering over her shoulder. 'I'm sitting closer to them than you, and I can't hear them over the noise in here.'

'I'm just zoning out the others and can hear them. Can't you guys do that?' Max replied.

'It's way too loud in here,' Danny insisted as another loud song played through the bar's speakers. 'I can barely hear you guys.'

'Stephen is saying he needs an extra fifteen percent and if Terry gets it, he'll give him three percent, but Terry's saying he needs eight percent as he has to pay the boss,' Max added.

'Whose Terry's boss?' Danny asked. 'My dad'll want to know if someone in WestFi is secretly skimming money off his deal.'

'He reports to Big Bill. Terry's in charge of medium-sized investments,' Chris explained.

'You've had it now, Chief. They've moved to the far side of the room,' Dazza laughed.

'Stephen's told Terry six percent is as high as he'll go,' Max said.

'You can't possibly hear them now,' Mercedes insisted.

'I can't, but I can read their lips,' Max replied.

'How are we doing this? I've never known you read lips or zone into certain voices before,' Bobby thought.

'That's because I've never been able to do this before,' Max replied.

'Why can you do it now?' Bobby asked.

'That's an excellent question. I wish I had an equally excellent answer,' Max laughed. *'All I know is that you're the first host I've had where I'm gaining new skills. Normally, I leave a host with extra skills, not gain them myself.'*

3
THE PRICE OF LOVE

'It's time to get up, Bobby. Mummy sent me to wake you,' Lily said excitedly, jumping up and down on the bed.

'It's Sunday morning, Lily. Go away,' Bobby replied.

'Mummy said dinner will be ready soon. Is Adam still coming?' Lily asked.

'Adam!' Bobby exclaimed, sitting upright.

'*You forget about Adam coming for lunch,*' Max laughed.

'Why *didn't you remind me*?' Bobby huffed.

'*He's your boyfriend,*' Max replied.

Bobby grabbed his phone and started typing,

Bobby

Morning sweetheart xx.

Adam

Hey Boo. Hope you didn't miss me too much. I'll be at yours in 30.

Bobby

Ok. Mum's cooking lunch.

There was no reply as Bobby stared at his phone. *'He's left me on read.'*

'He's probably getting ready,' Max said.

'Gettin ready for what?' Lily asked.

'How do you do that?' Bobby said.

'Whatya mean?' Lily replied, scowling.

'How can you reply to something I've thought?' Bobby queried.

'You didn't think it, silly. Max did,' Lily laughed, jumping off the bed and heading to the door.

'Lily, who am I?' Max thought.

'You're Max, of course. You were Daddy's friend,' Lily replied, skipping out of the bedroom.

'You knew my dad?' Bobby challenged.

'No. Well, I don't think so. Didn't you say your dad worked in the car industry, and he was Australian?' Max asked.

'I seem to remember you once moaned about hosts asking questions they can answer by reading your mind,' Bobby retorted.

'Okay, fairs. I was more thinking aloud than actually asking,' Max huffed.

'You said fairs?' Bobby laughed, heading towards the bathroom.

'And?'

'That means you're finally talking properly, not like some old dude. Welcome to the twenty-first century, Cowboy,' Bobby chuckled.

'Haha! It just means you're infecting my speech,' Max replied sarcastically. 'But back to Lily, I've never met an Australian car engineer, let alone been friends with one.'

After a quick shower, Bobby picked up a can of deodorant and started spraying himself liberally. 'Lily seemed certain you were friends with Dad, which is weird considering she wasn't born until after he died in that car accident.'

'She's probably just imagining things like most five-year-olds,' Max replied dismissively. 'Take it easy with the Love L'Amour. You want to smell nice for Adam, not render him unconscious by the smell of aftershave!'

Bobby strolled back into his bedroom, picked up a t-shirt, and read its logo: 'Too alien for Earth. Too human for outer space.'

'Your mum's idea of a joke when we told her about me. She's an incredible woman,' Max said.

'And she loves Dad so much,' Bobby replied, putting on the top and pulling on the joggers he'd borrowed from Adam months ago.

'I hope she can find another man to care about so much,' Max sighed.

'She doesn't need another man. She's got me and Lily,' Bobby replied tersely.

'Of course she has, but she needs to find someone to share her life with. She's still young, and you and Lily will grow up and live your own lives.'

'Mum has everything she needs. We'll take care of her,' Bobby insisted, heading downstairs.

As Bobby walked into the kitchen, his mum, Pat Morris, was checking the meat in the oven. 'Morning, sleepyhead. I assume by how sweet you smell that Adam is still coming for lunch?'

'Morning, Mum. Yeah, he said he'd be here soon,' Bobby replied, grabbing a glass and filling it with tap water.

'You two look so nice together. I'm doing roast chicken for lunch. Is that okay?'

'Yeah, Adam loves chicken.' Bobby pulled out his phone and sighed in relief to see Adam had replied.

Adam

> I forgot to say we're going out for lunch.
> The club has laid on a function for our

new sponsors. I've checked, and they said it's okay for your mum and Lily to come. They like the family vibe.

'Are you okay, Champ?' Pat asked.

'It's Adam,' Bobby sighed before turning his phone so Pat could read the message.

'It's okay. You go with Adam and have a lovely time,' Pat smiled.

'No. You've spent ages cooking all this food,' Bobby protested.

'Besides,' Max added, 'Adam said you and Lily can come too. The chicken's done, so we can always turn everything else off and have it tomorrow evening.'

Pat never ceased to be amazed at how quickly she learned to distinguish between Max and Bobby talking in the same body. 'And I bet you've got a recipe for cold chicken and vegetables, Max?'

'I might have,' Max laughed. 'Now go and get Lily. You need to change, and so do we.'

Pat knew resistance would be futile. 'Fine, but I've not got anything—'

The doorbell rang twice.

'Get the door, Champ. I'll get Lily and give her a wash,' Pat said, rushing into the living room.

Bobby rushed past his mother, opened the front door and was greeted by a tall, thin man in a black sequinned suit with a lime green t-shirt and cream trainers.

'Are you Adam Lee?' the man asked nervously.

'No. I'm his friend, Bobby. But Adam is on the way,' Bobby replied.

'Oh, thank goodness for that,' the man said, sweeping Bobby aside and walking into the house. He turned and shouted to the small group behind him, 'Chop, chop. Come on, this is the right house…' He paused and looked Bobby up and down before adding, 'And we have a lot to do.'

Pat picked up Lily, turned, and then screamed as half a dozen people marched into her living room with garment bags and a rail. They started taking clothes from the bags and hanging them on the rail.

'What are you doing in my house?' Pat demanded, staring at the sequinned man.

'You must be Mrs Morris. It's a pleasure to meet you,' the sequinned man said, bowing with a flourish. 'Now we must hurry. Mr Lee said he was inviting you and how important you were to him. So we've come to dress you for his big day.'

'I can dress myself, thank you, and now I'm off to wash my daughter,' Pat retorted.

The sequinned man held out his arms. 'Let me. Jessica, take this little angel upstairs and help her wash.'

A young woman stepped forward but stopped in her tracks as Pat glowered.

'No stranger is taking any of my children anywhere, ever again. Do I make myself clear?' Pat said firmly and with the death stare of a parent.

Jessica looked at the sequinned man nervously, and he shook his head.

'Of course, Mrs Morris. You take care of your daughter, and we'll get Bobby dressed while we're waiting,' the sequinned man said.

After three different outfits on Bobby and even more on Lily at her insistence, Pat finished trying another dress.

'I'm not sure. What about those dresses?' Pat sighed.

'You look fabulous, Mrs Morris. Besides, those dresses are for Mr Lee's other guest,' the sequinned man replied.

'What other guest?' Bobby challenged.

'Me,' Avery said, walking into the room with Adam.

'Blimey. You look stunning,' Adam said, walking over to Bobby and kissing him.

'That'll be my Max's influence,' Avery laughed, also kissing him.

The sequinned man looked puzzled as he tried to understand how this boy was called Bobby and Max and seemed to have a boyfriend and a girlfriend before muttering to himself, 'I thought my relationships were complicated.'

'Adam,' Lily screamed, running into the room from the kitchen.

Adam bent and swept her up, causing Lily to giggle. 'How's my favourite young lady? You're looking almost as radiant as your mum.'

'I'm really good. These people turned up and dressed me in lots of clothes, and then they did Mummy and—'

'That'll do, young lady. Poor Adam will go deaf if you keep going at that rate,' Pat laughed.

Before long, Adam and Avery had been dressed, and they were all heading to the football stadium in a stretched limousine.

'What's this all about?' Bobby asked as Pat tried to stop Lily from pressing every button she could reach.

'I'm not supposed to say, but I guess you'll hear it when we get there. We've got a new major sponsor who is going to build us a new ground, and I'm being presented as their new first team signing as part of the deal,' Adam smiled. 'I guess my fifteen goals in twelve games helped.'

Bobby threw his arms around Adam, 'That's fantastic, hun. I'm going to be so proud walking out there on your arm.'

'Erm, thanks, boo, but we need to be careful in public,' Adam squirmed.

'Oh, yeah, of course,' Bobby replied.

'What do you mean by "careful"?' Pat asked.

'Nobody can know I'm gay,' Adam replied. 'We need to make it look like Avery's my girlfriend and Bobby's my best friend.'

'But that's not true or fair?' Pat protested.

'It's fine, Mum,' Bobby replied. 'We always knew we'd have to be discreet if Adam became successful.'

'Granny says you should just be you,' Lily muttered as she found a new cubby hole to investigate.

'What does she mean?' Bobby asked.

'Who knows? Lily's been mumbling about Granny this and Granny that for weeks,' Pat replied. 'Okay, I'll accept this as long as Bobby is happy.'

'I am, Mum. Honest,' Bobby replied forlornly.

The car pulled up outside the football stadium, and Adam stepped out to shouts of, "Adam," "Over here, Adam," "This way goal wonder," "Oi, dude. Over here, loser."

Adam smiled at Dazza's familiar voice. He held out his hand to help Avery out of the car and turned towards Dazza, standing amongst the photographers but towering over them.

As Bobby exited the car and helped his mother and Lily out, he glanced at Adam, noting his arm around Avery's waist.

'*It's just a show, Bobby,*' Max thought. '*Adam loves you, and Avery loves me.*'

'*I know. I was just looking around,*' Bobby snapped back.

'*Even after all this time, you still forget. I'm inside you, buddy. So I know what you're thinking and see what you see,* ' Max replied.

'*Fine, yes, I'm jealous. Are you happy now?*'

'*It's not about me being happy; it's about you not letting jealousy ruin what you've got with Adam.*'

'*Sorry, I'm not perfect like you!*' Bobby huffed.

'*I'm not perfect. I'm just ridiculously old, and I've loved and lost so many over the centuries because of my emotions,*' Max sighed.

'Come on, we're going in,' Pat replied, grabbing Bobby's arm.

As they entered the stadium, Bobby looked at all the banners emblazoned with M Bank Research logos.

'I've heard of that company,' Bobby said.

'Sorry, Champ, what did you say?' Pat asked.

'I was just thinking that I've heard of M Bank Research,' Bobby replied.

Adam turned and said, 'Yeah, I told you earlier. They're our new sponsor.'

'No, you never mentioned their name. You just...' Bobby trailed off as he noted Adam heading off with Avery on his arm towards a group of young men dressed in identical suits.

'*This is his moment,*' Max said.

'*I know,*' Bobby snapped.

'*But as far as M Bank Research is concerned, it was Dazza who mentioned it and said—*'

'Mr Marchent, this is my closest friend, Bobby, his sister Lily and his mum Patricia,' Adam said, interrupting Bobby and Max's internal discussion.

'Please call me Pat,' Pat blushed.

'What a lovely family you have, Pat,' Stephen Marchent replied. 'And Adam is such a talented player. I'm pleased to be a part of making his future a part of this club along with those he loves.'

'Are you really going to give the club a new ground?' Bobby asked.

'Bobby, I told you that in confidence,' Adam replied firmly.

'It's okay, Adam. Your friend is just being inquisitive. Yes, Bobby, that's the plan, unless we can find a way to redevelop this ground into something more worthy of Premier League status,' Stephen replied.

'How can you afford to fund this? I've been told you are trying to sell your business based on discovering a new mineral near Rome,' Max said. 'And yet you're investing in a football club and sponsoring the formal signing of their leading goal scorer into a long-term contract.'

'Ma—I mean Bobby, that's so rude,' Adam protested.

'Nonsense, Adam, your friend clearly cares about you,' Stephen replied. 'You are almost correct, Bobby. I'm not seeking to sell my business; I'm looking for an investment angel to further our research. If our analysis is correct, this new mineral could make it possible to travel across space in seconds instead of years.'

'Oh, I'm off to Rome soon on holiday with my family and some friends,' Avery said. 'Maybe we could go and see your discovery?'

'I'm sure we can arrange that, but let's get the formalities of today sorted and we can talk a bit more about it. In the meantime, Pat, how about we leave these youngsters to mingle, and we get a drink and show your little munchkin around,' Stephen replied.

'I'm not a munchkin. My name is Lily.'

'Then we should give Lily the grand tour,' Stephen smiled.

'Granny says you're a very nice man,' Lily replied.

'Well, your granny sounds like a wonderful woman,' Stephen replied, escorting Pat and Lily away.

'He's creepy,' Bobby said.

'He seems charming to me,' Avery replied.

'Me too,' Adam confirmed.

'He was in a gay bar Friday night negotiating a cut on the sale of his business with a guy from WestFi,' Bobby replied.

'So you're saying because he might be gay or bi, and he might be seeking the best price for his business, he's creepy,' Adam laughed.

'Don't laugh at me. I know what I saw and heard,' Bobby protested.

'I can't talk to you when you're like this,' Adam replied.

'Like what?' Bobby huffed.

'Like you are right now. In a mood about something and moaning about everything,' Adam replied. 'Come on, Avery. I'll introduce you to some of the team.'

'That's right, go off with your girlfriend and leave me alone,' Bobby hissed.

'*What's wrong with you? I've never known you behave like this,*' Max thought.

Bobby noticed a room off to the side of the corporate suite and headed over to it. He peered inside and saw a large desk with pictures of former managers, players, and trophies around three walls and a glass wall looking down at the pitch. Most importantly, the room was empty, so he walked inside, shut the door, collapsed onto a sofa and started sobbing.

'I don't know what's going on, Max. Help me,' Bobby cried.

'How can I help? You're blackwalling me, so I can't see what you're thinking,' Max replied.

'As I've said before, I don't know how to blackwall you. Can't you break through? All I know is I can't cope with my emotions. Why am I pushing Adam away and being nasty about him and Avery putting on a show? I know he loves me, and she loves you, so why am I jealous?' Bobby moaned with his head in his hands, tears streaming down his face and dripping to the floor. 'And why am I so angry about that Marchent guy? He was being charming to Mum and Lily, but...'

There was a pause as Bobby's thoughts trailed off, interrupted by the occasional loud ripple of laughter from the guests in the main suite next door.

'It could be something to do with my transmuting. Sometimes, the process can clash with my host's hormones. When that combines with someone your age, whose hormones are already changing because of your age, it can get quite messy,' Max sighed.

'Messy in what way?'

'Well, my first host was around your age, and Gaius just collapsed. But others have slept for a week or more, some tried to fight everyone they know, and one didn't sleep for a week as he was full of energy. Although that was a few centuries ago, and the village loved the wooden church hall he built almost single-handedly,' Max replied.

'But after you've gone, they're okay?' Bobby sniffed.

'That's it!'

'What is?'

'Your blackwall dropped while I was talking. You're scared of being left alone,' Max said.

'That's daft.'

'Is it? You're worried that Adam's success will mean he'll have to choose between you and football with pretend girlfriends.'

'Well, today's shown which he'll choose,' Bobby replied, as he started to cry again.

'Today has shown that he's willing to put on a front, but he wants you here no matter what,' Max replied. 'I'm flattered that you also don't want me to leave.'

'Ha, I can't wait to get my freedom back,' Bobby lied.

'You forgot to put your wall back up, I can see that's not true.'

'Even if I am worried about Adam and you, why can't I stop crying,' Bobby replied as tears started streaming down his face again.

'Because the thing you dread most is your mum leaving.'

The tears increased more as Bobby started sobbing. 'But Mum would never leave me. How does that even make sense? She's always going to be my mum.'

'Your fear is more about your mum leaving your old life behind. You're scared that one day she'll find someone she wants to be with and remarry, and this Marchent guy represents that risk. What if she does like him, and he likes her?'

'But she's already married to my dad.'

'Bobby, you know your dad died over five years ago before Lily was born. Doesn't your mum deserve to find happiness and someone to share her life with?' Max asked.

'She's already got me and Lily,' Bobby wailed.

The door creaked open, and Avery's head appeared. 'Bobby, are you okay?'

Bobby looked up and tried to speak, but he just croaked.

Pat pushed past Avery, followed by Stephen Marchent and Adam. As Avery followed them, she shut the door behind her.

Pat crouched in front of her son and placed her hands on his knees. 'Bobby, what's wrong?'

Adam sat down beside Bobby and placed his arm around Bobby's shoulder. 'Boo, what's up, sweetheart?'

Bobby looked up into the loving face of his mum. He wanted to tell her how much he loved her but knew the words wouldn't come out. Then he turned to look at Adam. He'd often looked into Adam's face since they first became a couple. He'd seen Adam look happy, sad, angry and almost every emotion in between, but this time Adam looked scared and worried. How could he ever think this man would leave him?

'I, uh, just got a bit emotional about everything. Max thinks it might be the transmuting process,' Bobby said, wiping his eyes.

'Do you all need to go home? We can make the announcement about Adam as a separate press release,' Stephen suggested. 'My driver will take you.'

Bobby looked up at Stephen, who was genuinely concerned. 'No, it's...' Bobby held back the tears and started again. 'No, this is Adam's and your day, Stephen. I'm not going to spoil it. I'll stay here out of the way,' Bobby replied firmly, choking back his emotions.

'I'm not going out there without the man I love,' Adam insisted.

Stephen looked at Adam in shock. 'You're gay?'

'Yes, I am, and I'm not going to hide it anymore if this is what it does to my boyfriend,' Adam replied standing up.

'How about we announce three things today? M Bank Research's sponsorship and our support in signing the club's leading goalscorer to a long contract, a goalscorer who is gay and proud?' Stephen suggested.

Adam looked at Bobby, and they smiled at each other conspiratorially. 'Let's not mention the gay part. Our sexuality is irrelevant. But if someone asks about the man on my arm when I walk out from here, I won't deny who I am or who Bobby is.'

The door flew open, and an athletic man in his late thirties with short-cropped hair faded at the sides barged in. 'What the hell is going on in my office?'

Adam turned to face the man. 'Coach, I'm so sorry. My friend was really upset, so we brought him in here.'

'Are you alright, lad?' the coach said, looking at Bobby and noting the young girl by the side of the woman crouching down.

'I'm good, sir. Just had to sort some stuff out in my head,' Bobby replied.

'Good lad. Wouldn't want my top scorer's boyfriend upset,' the coach laughed.

Adam's mouth dropped open in shock.

'You knew he was gay?' Stephen challenged.

'Aye. Is that a problem? Mr Marchent,' the coach replied.

Adam started mumbling, 'Does, uh, anyone... well, who else—'

'Everyone at the club knows, lad,' the coach said, slapping Adam on the shoulder.

'I didn't know,' Stephen replied.

'You're our new sponsor, not a club staff member,' the coach said. 'Does it matter if he likes cheese and onion or salt and vinegar crisps?'

'No, of course not. My best friend Terry likes a bit of both. I don't care, but it would have been nice to know,' Stephen replied.

'Is everyone okay about it?' Adam asked.

'Course they are lad. Some of the squad started talking about you when you came for that trial a few months back,' the coach replied. 'But they were more worried about if you could play that well in a full game rather than which crisps you like.'

'Where are the crisps? I want some,' Lily moaned.

They all turned to look at Lily and started laughing.

'Then, little princess, you shall have crisps,' the coach said, crouching down to her level. 'Tell this lot to cheer up and follow us back to the buffet where there are lots of crisps,' the coach whispered conspiratorially.

'Cheer up and follow us for crisps,' Lily said. Then, looking up at Pat, she added, 'Come on, Mummy.'

4
ANOTHER DAY AT THE OFFICE

I wish they'd turn that alarm off?' Bobby grumbled, pulling the pillow over his ears.

'*It's your alarm,*' Max replied.

'*Well, turn it off then,*' Bobby moaned.

Max rolled over and hit the cancel button on the phone.

'*Oh, thanks. Now I'm awake,*' Bobby complained.

'*Well, we are sharing one body, so I can't turn your phone off without moving us,*' Max replied, yawning.

'*How much longer are we sharing MY body,*' Bobby queried.

'*Well, it's been around five months since the power station incident. So I'd say it's only a few weeks until I finish transmuting,*' Max replied.

Bobby sat up and swung his legs out of bed. '*It's only six thirty. Why are we up so early?*'

'*Because you need to go to work,*' Max replied. '*Let's grab a shower.*'

'*I had one yesterday,*' Bobby protested.

'*Two days ago, actually,*' Max replied, moving Bobby towards the bathroom.

'*Well, that means I'm still clean,*' Bobby grumbled.

After a quick shower, with Bobby protesting the whole time, he dressed and wandered downstairs to an empty kitchen.

'*I'm not hungry,*' Bobby thought as Max looked in the fridge.

'*How about a bacon and egg frittata?*' Max suggested.

'Okay, maybe I'm a little hungry,' Bobby replied.

A short while later, Bobby sat eating his breakfast. His mother wandered into the kitchen, checked the water level in the kettle, and turned it on.

'Morning, Champ,' Pat said, kissing Bobby on the forehead.

'Morning, Mum. You were in bed early last night. I got in at ten, and the house was in darkness,' Bobby replied.

Pat blushed. 'Lily and I spent the day at Legoland.'

'Oh, you never mentioned yesterday morning that you were going there,' Bobby challenged.

'It wasn't planned. Stephen rang and asked if we wanted to go. He's been so kind since we met at Adam's football thing two months ago,' Pat replied.

'*Don't say it,*' Max thought.

'*I wasn't going to say anything,*' Bobby protested.

'*Good. It's your mum's life, and Lily seems to like him too,*' Max replied.

'Morning, Bobby,' Stephen said, walking into the kitchen. Stephen walked over to Pat and kissed her briefly, 'Morning, Pat, I never heard you get up.'

'Morning, Stephen,' Max replied as Bobby stood up and strutted towards the living room, leaving his half-eaten breakfast on the table.

'Morning, Stephen,' Pat sighed. 'I'm sorry Bobby ignored you. I guess I should have warned him that you stopped the night.'

Stephen smiled. 'It's fine. He said good morning at least before storming out.'

'No, that was...' Pat trailed off, remembering Stephen knew nothing about Max. 'I mean, that was still rude of him.'

'You told me about his dad,' Stephen replied. 'Have you seen anyone else since Simon died?'

'I had a drink with someone once, but he didn't like children, and Bobby and Lily will always come first in any relationship,' Pat replied.

'Exactly as it should be, and if I'm the first person Bobby's seen you with since his dad died, it's bound to be awkward,' Stephen replied.

'*Why did you do that?*' Max demanded as Bobby stomped upstairs.

'*Done what?*' Bobby snapped.

'*Ignored Stephen and stormed out of the kitchen?*'

'*I said good morning. What more do you want? Besides, I need to clean my teeth.*'

'*I said good morning, not you, and I had to fight you to say that, and when has oral hygiene been your priority?*'

'*Well, it's wrong. Mum's married to my dad.*'

'*Bobby, you know your dad died in that car accident over five years ago.*'

'No, he didn't,' Lily said, wandering out of her bedroom.

'Shut up, Lily. Dad died before you were even born,' Bobby snapped.

'But Daddy's not dead. Granny said he can't escape,' Lily replied, heading towards the stairs.

'Granny Mosley's dead too,' Bobby growled as he opened his bedroom door. He slammed the door behind him and slumped onto his bed.

Lily skipped down the stairs, 'Bobby's so silly isn't he.'

Bobby picked up his phone and messaged Danny.

Bobby went to clean his teeth. As he walked out of the bathroom, he saw his mum leaning against the wall by his bedroom door and sighed.

'You might well sigh, young man. What's with the attitude?' Pat asked.

Bobby shrugged. 'What attitude?'

'Robert Christopher Morris, don't you dare give me that. You know full well what I mean. You ignored Stephen downstairs and stormed off,' Pat said sternly.

'I said hell—'

'Max said good morning, not you,' Pat interrupted, folding her arms.

'Come on, Pat. You know it's bound to be difficult for Bobby to accept a new man in your life,' Max said.

'Max, you may be sharing Bobby's body, but this is a mother-son thing, so butt out,' Pat replied.

'Are we done? Danny's picking me up soon,' Bobby replied.

'Stephen said he can take you to work as he's got a meeting with them this morning.'

'That's good, but Danny is coming for me.'

'I just said Stephen is taking you in.'

'Hey both, it's fine; Danny's doing me a favour. I need to go home first to pick up some papers, so I'd make Bobby late anyway,' Stephen said, coming up the stairs.

'Well, if you're sure, Stephen,' Pat replied.

Stephen hugged Pat and winked at Bobby. 'Of course, hun.'

Bobby cringed when he heard Stephen use the same hun word for his mum that he used for Adam.

Half an hour later, Bobby sat in Danny's car, heading towards WestFi.

'Spill the beans guys. It's been two months since you started at WestFi, and you've never asked for a lift before,' Danny asked.

'Stephen Marchent offered to give me a lift and —'

'Stop the bus. Stephen, as in M Bank's CEO?'

'Yeah,' Bobby sighed.

'I'd heard rumours he was seeing someone, but your mum!' Danny exclaimed.

'What's wrong with my mum?'

'Nothing. I just thought...'

'You thought it'd be some glamorous young model, didn't you?'

'No, of course not,' Danny protested before adding, 'Yeah, okay, I did.'

'You rich lot all stick together,' Bobby laughed, playfully punching his friend in the arm.

'Oi, don't interfere with the driver,' Danny chuckled.

After a short silence, as Danny drove through the streets of London, Bobby asked, 'What's going on with you and Mercedes then?'

Danny turned to glower at Bobby, causing the car to swerve to the left.

'Watch out,' Bobby shouted.

Danny straightened the car, 'That was your fault.'

'You're driving,' Bobby protested.

'Yeah, well, you mentioned her name,' Danny snapped.

'But I heard you're going to Italy together,' Bobby challenged.

'It's not a holiday. We're being sent as part of the due diligence team on your mum's boyfriend's business. Their

Italian subsidiary uncovered this mineral that lets you send energy across vast distances in seconds,' Danny huffed.

'He's not Mum's boyfriend,' Bobby protested as Danny parked in the underground car park.

'How come his car was parked next to your mum's this morning? Did he pop in for an early morning coffee?' Danny smirked.

'Will you two behave,' Max said. 'You're supposed to be friends.'

'We are, Chief,' Danny replied. 'But to be real friends, you need regular bants?'

'Why is everything about banter?' Max sighed.

'Hey, Danny, it looks like we've got the cowboy on the ropes now,' Bobby laughed.

'Hope you've beefed up your computer security, Chief,' Danny said.

'Yes, very funny, Danny. There's no more ID 10 T issues, thank you,' Max replied. 'Anyway, you've reversed into your parking spot.'

'Yeah,' Danny said.

'Well, how can you get your wheelchair out of the boot?' Max queried.

Danny pressed a button on the driver's door, and it opened. Then he pushed a button on his chair, and there was a clunking sound, before his wheelchair turned, lowered some legs and walked out of the car. The chair lowered back onto its wheels, and Danny closed the door.

'Blimey, I hadn't noticed you were driving in your wheelchair,' Max replied.

'Yeah, it was annoying to keep switching from my chair to the car seat, so I decided to get rid of the car seat,' Danny said proudly.

Max smiled. 'Is there anything you don't think you can fix as a disabled person—'

'As a differently-abled person,' Danny corrected. 'And no, I don't think there is. Apart from your love of banana and salad cream sandwiches, that is incurable.'

'That needs embracing, not curing,' Max laughed. 'Anyway, we need to go.'

'Me too. Catch you later, losers,' Danny replied, heading towards the lifts near him as Bobby walked towards the opposing set of lifts.'

After setting up his laptop at his desk, which informed him that it needed an important update, Bobby sighed before wandering to the small kitchen area. He opened a cupboard and grabbed a glass before filling it with water. Then, glancing at the basket of free fruit provided daily for staff to help themselves, he grabbed a banana.

'Just need the salad cream, bread, and butter now.' Max laughed.

'I wish I'd never introduced you to that sandwich; you're addicted to it,' Bobby replied, as he turned back towards his desk and walked straight into Mercedes, spilling water over her.

'You seem to have a talent for spilling drinks,' Mercedes said, brushing the water off her.

'Oh, I'm so sorry. I was distracted.' Bobby apologised profusely as he grabbed some paper towels and started trying to pat the water off Mercedes.

Mercedes grabbed Bobby's towels and took over trying to soak up the water. 'I'll do it, and don't worry; at least it's only water.'

'I'm so clumsy at the moment,' Bobby replied. 'Are you okay if I leave you to it? I've got a meeting with my boss in ten minutes.'

'That's why I've come looking for you. We've just been meeting about the due diligence work for M Bank, and your name came up,' Mercedes said. 'You weren't at your desk, so I spoke to your manager, Nigel, and he said you might be here. You "have a routine" apparently.'

'Do I? Oh,' Bobby replied. 'What do they want me for? I don't know anything about due dilithingy.'

'Due diligence,' Mercedes corrected. 'It's where a company being bought is checked out by the potential buyer and their advisors to ensure everything they've claimed about their profits, operations, customer processes, etcetera, is true.'

'Will I need to analyse stuff then? According to Nigel, I'm getting quite good,' Bobby replied proudly. 'Did he recommend me?'

'Not exactly. I mentioned that you spoke Italian fluently, which will help the DD team,' Mercedes explained.

'DD team?'

'Sorry, I forget how easy it is to slip into jargon. I mean the due diligence team.'

'So they just want me as a translator?' Bobby asked dejectedly.

'That's an important job because a lot of the DD team only speak English—well, except for Danny, who also speaks techiedegoop.'

'*She likes Danny*,' Max said. '*Did you notice how her face softened when she mentioned his name.*'

'*I didn't notice anything*,' Bobby replied.

'Are you talking to him again?' Mercedes asked.

'Huh?'

'That alien, Mark,' Mercedes said.

'You mean Max. Yes, I was, sorry,' Bobby replied.

'Does it feel weird having him inside you?'

'It was to start with, but now it's like having a friend with you all the time,' Bobby said.

'*That's a lovely thing to say*,' Max thought.

'*I meant an annoying friend*,' Bobby laughed.

'I'm inside you, buddy. I know what you meant,' Max replied.

'I think it would drive me mad,' Mercedes said. 'My brain constantly goes a hundred miles an hour about things. Having another person inside me thinking simultaneously is just argh.'

'Danny's like that,' Max replied. 'He is constantly thinking about how to make his life better.'

'Oh, wow. That's you, Max, isn't it?'

'Yeah.'

'I noticed the change in your voice.'

'The more people get to know us, the more they notice the difference.'

'What's it like for you inside Bobby?' Mercedes asked.

'Different. I must have had around seventy to eighty hosts over the last two thousand years, and generally, it's been the same pattern. They are either scared, angry or puzzled. Then once they get used to being able to read my memories and thoughts, they relax,' Max replied.

'Why is it different in Bobby?'

'It's hard to describe. I'm developing skills I've never had before. I can move very quickly, read people's lips and tune into people's voices in crowded rooms,' Max said.

'Excuse me, but I am here, and this is *my* body,' Bobby protested.

'Sorry, Bobby,' Mercedes said. 'Oh, hell, come on, I was supposed to fetch you and take you to the boardroom.'

Bobby noticed Mercedes hitting the fiftieth floor as they got into the lift. 'I thought you said our boardroom?'

'No, I said *THE* boardroom.'

The lift opened, and the glare of glass, silver, and mirrored surfaces bounced light around the foyer, only softened by an abundance of plants, including a stunning twelve-metre-square, glass-bound room in the central area of the fiftieth floor that looked like a tropical jungle. To the right, Bobby noticed a large boardroom where he could see shadows through the frosted glass.

'*This sends a cold shiver down my spine,*' Max said.

'*I know it's incredible, isn't it,*' Bobby replied.

'*No, it's too reminiscent of a world I left behind long ago,*' Max shuddered. '*It's also a bit dazzling as my aura is bouncing around on all those reflective surfaces. What's wrong with good old wood.*'

Mercedes headed toward the boardroom door and stopped in front of a sign seemingly projected onto the opaque glass door, reading, 'Occupied. Identify to enter.'

'Mercedes Medici with...' Mercedes turned to Bobby, widened her eyes, and tilted her head.

'Oh, um, Bobby Morris.'

The glass door turned transparent and opened.

'Mercedes, we thought you'd sent out a search party for that gentleman,' a large man in his mid-fifties with grey receding hair laughed.

'Sorry, Mr Martin and everyone, we had an accident with some water,' Mercedes explained as she escorted Bobby towards two empty chairs by a wall covered with an ornate mirrored mosaic of a Phoenix rising from an erupting volcano.

'*More flipping mirrors. At least because it's a mosaic, the pieces are at different angles, so it's not dazzling. And all the glass here has an anti-reflective coating, thankfully,*' Max moaned.

As they sat beside Danny, Bobby noted around forty people in the room and hissed to Danny, 'What's going on?'

Danny held his finger to his lips to indicate Bobby should be quiet. 'That's Big Bill.'

A thin, wiry man in his late sixties dressed in an expensive dark blue suit sat at the opposite end of the imposing granite table. He leaned back in his chair and looked around the room. His pure silver hair looked as perfectly tailored as his suit, and Bobby swore it glistened in the sunlight streaming through the window.

'What I'm about to tell y'all must stay in this room. Is that clear?' Bill asked.

The room erupted into a chorus of, 'Yes, Bill.'

'Chris, pull up the deck,' Bill said in his soft American drawl.

The glass wall, which Bobby had noted as opaque when they came out of the lift, suddenly became a screen showing a presentation. Bobby spotted Mercedes's brother, Chris, in the opposite corner of the room and smiled at him.

'This is M Bank,' Bill explained as Chris flicked through some slides. 'It's fifty-six percent owned by the Marchent family, and this is the current CEO, Stephen Marchent the third.'

The presentation showed a picture of Stephen, which made Bobby squirm.

'You okay, Bobster?' Danny whispered.

'Not really, considering he was kissing Mum in my kitchen this morning,' Bobby replied.

Bill glanced at Bobby and Danny, frowning before he continued. 'M Bank has been around for three hundred and fifty years, born from one of the remnants of the long-gone Medici Bank. The irony of having two descendants of the Medici family here with us ain't lost on me.'

'Only by adoption. Our dad adopted me and Chris when he married Mum,' Mercedes hissed.

'Thing is, M Bank and its Research subsidiary, which the current CEO started, were just about done for until they stumbled on that new mineral,' Bill continued.

The boardroom door opened, and Danny's dad, Paul, entered. He was wearing a black T-shirt, dark flannel trousers and a grey tweed jacket. While the look was casual, there was no doubt that his clothes were expensive.

'Morning, Bill,' Paul said. 'Sorry I'm late, but I've just met with Mr Marchent.'

'Mornin', Paul,' Bill replied.

'It looks like I've arrived at the right time,' Paul said, glancing at the presentation. He looked around the room and said, 'Hi, son. Hey, Bobby.'

Danny and Bobby acknowledged Paul with a nod and a wave.

Paul pulled a chair from against the wall and sat at the large granite table. 'Have you mentioned M Bank's financial situation, Bill?'

'I've just said they were on the brink of collapse until they found this new mineral,' Bill replied.

'I'm afraid things have moved on. Innovest has tested this material and confirmed it can send energy over incredible distances and extract energy from living things,' Paul said. 'They say their tests on mice were successful.'

'In what way does it extract energy?' Max asked.

The room went silent as everyone turned to look at this young upstart.

Paul smiled, 'That's an excellent question, Bobby. Innovest isn't sure how it works, but in their tests, it seems to extract the energy in a mouse-like shape. The mouse's body remains behind as a dead shell, and the energy shape seems to contain their personality and behave like them.'

'So it's like extracting their soul from their body?' Nigel asked.

'They're not sure what it is, but the energy shape evaporates quite quickly,' Paul explained.

'*We have to stop this,*' Max said.

'*Why? This sounds like an incredible discovery,*' Bobby replied.

'*Because it's cruel and because I think they've discovered luminae. It was one of the discoveries on my planet that ultimately led to its demise.*'

'*Oh yes, I can see now. They used luminae to extract your energy souls from your body and novasium to stabilise it,*' Bobby said.

'*Exactly. Then they decided if we were all energy souls, it would remove the pollution caused by agriculture and stop—*'

'Global hunger,' Bill said. 'The owner of this technology can wipe it out— and end all human diseases and death if they can stabilise this energy shape.'

'And that's why Spearhead and Bluestone are already sniffing around. Marchent got Innovest onboard to prove this mineral was special, and now he's willing to sell to the highest bidder.'

'This can't happen,' Max shouted as he stood up.

'Well said, Bobby,' Paul replied as Danny yanked Bobby back into his seat. 'We need to get control of M Bank before Spearhead, Bluestone or any other.'

Bill leant forward and looked around the room before stopping at Paul. 'I've known you a long time, Paul, and we both know we can't compete with Bluestone. So, you wouldn't be here unless you've got a plan.'

'First of all, the mineral seam they've found is small, and I mean very small...' Paul paused as his phone pinged. He picked it up and smiled. 'And as of two minutes ago, you are now looking at the majority shareholder of Innovest.'

'What's up with you, Chief?' Danny hissed.

'This is so bad. We have to destroy this,' Max replied.

'I've never known you so emotional.'

'Because I've lost one home planet and the people I loved. I can't do it again.'

5
DD Day

'Mum, stop fussing,' Bobby protested.

'I'm just making sure you've got everything,' Pat replied.

'I'm only going for ten days. I've got three days of due diligence work, and then I'm meeting Avery's family for a holiday,' Bobby groaned.

'But you've never been abroad before,' Pat protested.

'But I have,' Max replied. 'And don't forget Bobby's work is coordinating the travel.'

'Well, you'd better take care of my boy, Max. I love him,' Pat replied.

'And I love you more,' Bobby replied.

The doorbell rang, and a minute or so later, Lily came running upstairs. 'Someone called Kiss wants Bobby.'

Bobby ran to the window in his mum's bedroom and then ran back. 'It's Chris. He's taking us to Heathrow.'

'He said he was called Kiss,' Lily protested.

'It's okay, sweetie,' Pat said, kissing her daughter on the forehead. 'Bobby, do you have your passport?'

'Yes, Mum. I need to go,' Bobby replied, grabbing his laptop bag and picking up his suitcase.

Pat grabbed her son and hugged him. She didn't want to admit it, but this was the first time he'd ever been away for more than a sleepover, and she hated it. 'Call me when you get to Rome, and I want a message or something every day while you're there.'

'Mum. I gotta go,' Bobby squirmed.

Pat released Bobby and followed him downstairs. As he walked out of the house towards the car, she shouted, 'Love you.'

Bobby turned and replied, 'Love you more.' He opened the boot of Chris's car and put his case and laptop bag inside before closing it and heading towards the passenger door.

'Morning, Bobby,' Chris and Mercedes said in unison.

'Hiya,' Bobby replied before glancing back at his mother and trying to wave discreetly.

'Why are you wearing a jumper?' Mercedes asked.

'It's a bit chilly this morning,' Bobby replied.

'But it'll be roasting in Rome,' Mercedes said.

'I feel the cold. So I'll keep it on, thanks,' Bobby replied.

'Bobby, you know she's right. Check my memories,' Max insisted.

'I'm fine, thank you. Just because you think it's warm doesn't mean I will,' Bobby replied.

An hour later, they sat in one of Heathrow Airport's business departure lounges.

'How long before we get there?' Bobby asked as he sat drinking water.

'The flight is about two and a half hours,' Chris replied.

'The first time I made this journey back in the reign of Emperor Vespasian, it involved riding a horse to Dover, or Portus Dubris as we called it. Then, a sailboat across the channel and several horses down to Massilia, sorry, I mean Marseille, and then another boat to Ostia and finally Rome.' Max said.

'Blimey, how long did that take?' Bobby asked.

'Only about thirty-five to forty days,' Max laughed.

'What's so funny,' Chris asked, noticing Bobby chuckling.

'It's just Max saying it used to take him around forty days to make the same journey back in Roman times,' Bobby laughed.

'I wish I'd lived back then,' Mercedes said.

'Yeah, I was thinking the same,' Danny replied, smirking as he joined them. 'How are you dullards doing?'

'Hey Danny,' Bobby said, fist-bumping his friend.

'Good to see you guys enjoying my dad's hospitality,' Danny smiled.

'If your dad is funding this, how come he didn't charter a plane to take us to Rome?' Chris asked.

'Because Mr White overruled it and said it was business class and the airport lounge only for Danny and his friends, and the rest go economy.' Mercedes said.

'I bet Big Bill and Mr White are on a private jet,' Chris replied.

'Of course they are,' Danny said. 'Dad invited me too, but I wanted to travel with you guys.'

'Aww, thanks, Danny. This is my first time on a plane. I'm so excited,' Bobby said.

'You're a disabled person, and you turned down a private jet to travel on a commercial flight?' Mercedes challenged.

'I'm not disabled. I'm differently-abled, thank you. Have you got a problem with that?' Danny bristled.

'I couldn't care less how abled you are. I don't believe you voluntarily chose not to fly on a private jet,' Mercedes replied.

'Whatevs, I don't care what you think. Anyway, come on, our flight's boarding, and I've got priority,' Danny said, heading off in his wheelchair.

'He's only a priority board because of his chair,' Mercedes said as they hurried after Danny.

Before long, they were sitting on the plane, taxiing towards the runway.

'I don't get Mercedes. She's so full of herself. She forgets my dad is the boss of this deal,' Danny moaned.

'I disagree,' Max replied. 'She knows your dad is the boss, and she also knows you're not.'

'Yeah, but I am his son, Chief,' Danny protested.

'Exactly. You're his son, but people like Paul White know where to draw the line between business and family,' Max replied.

Three rows back, on the other side of the aisle, Chris looked towards Bobby, and Danny then said to Mercedes, 'Do you think I stand a chance with Bobby? He's so cute.'

'He's dating that goal-machine footballer. I don't think he'll be interested in you,' Mercedes replied as she watched the plane accelerate down the runway.

'Perhaps the four of us could go to a romantic restaurant in Rome?' Chris suggested.

Mercedes slowly turned and stared at her brother. 'If you think I'm spending a second of my free time with that ego on wheels, let alone double-dating with him, you can dream on.'

The flight passed quickly, and before long, Danny was complaining as the airline staff helped him into a narrow airline wheelchair and then wheeled him off the plane and into a standard wheelchair being pushed by a member of the airport crew.

'You go and get your chair, and we'll collect the luggage,' Bobby told Danny. 'What's your case look like?'

'You'll know mine,' Danny laughed as he was wheeled away.

When Bobby, Mercedes, and Chris found the right luggage carousel, there was luggage already flowing around.

Bobby was the first to grab his large gold, ribbed shell case.

'You know we're only here for three days?' Mercedes asked as she bent and collected her small black case.

'You are, but Danny and I are here for ten days as we're meeting with some friends for a holiday,' Bobby replied.

Chris picked up his large duffel bag and said, 'Just Danny's bag now. Why couldn't he tell us what it looked like?'

'He did, and here it is,' Bobby laughed as a large bright blue case headed towards them with a sticker saying "Danny's case" splashed across it.

'Hey, peeps. Thanks for getting my case,' Danny said, heading toward them.

Chris glanced at his watch. 'Come on, guys. We've got a meeting at the hotel at one thirty, and it's already noon.'

'Oh, flipping hell,' Danny moaned.

'What's up, buddy?' Max asked.

'My chair won't go into standing mode.'

Bobby crouched down and checked the wiring.

'Ah, I can see your problem; one of your cables has pulled out, dragging a circuit board with it,' Max said.

'Looks like I've got ten days of staring at belly buttons,' Danny sighed.

'M Bank Research has a technology centre, so you might be able to get some spares,' Chris said as they walked through the customs channel.

'Hey guys, there's someone over there with a WestFi sign,' Bobby said.

'At least Dad's laid on transport,' Danny muttered, heading towards the man with the sign.

As the others caught up with Danny, he turned and said, 'The executive travel is this way.'

They followed the sign man outside, and as they hit the wall of heat, Bobby groaned, pulling off his jumper, 'It's quite warm here.'

Mercedes looked at Chris and smiled.

'Where's the limousine?' Danny asked the sign man.

The man looked at Danny and pointed towards a black minibus.

Danny glanced back at his colleagues before saying, 'Oh, that's perfect for my chair.'

As they reached the minibus, the driver opened the side door, pulled out a ramp, and indicated that Danny should enter the vehicle.

As Danny got to the top of the ramp, he looked around for the anchor points for a wheelchair.

'You, slide into the seat,' the sign man explained in stilted English.

'Oops, Daddy's not read the memo,' Mercedes whispered to Chris.

Danny half slid and half fumbled into a seat before the sign man grabbed the wheelchair and loaded it into a trailer behind the minibus, along with the suitcases.

'I guess you're used to this sort of luxury travel,' Mercedes smiled as she slid into the seats behind Danny.

'Don't rise to it,' Max whispered as he sat beside Danny.

A few hours later, everyone had checked into the hotel and had the due diligence briefing covering the agenda for the next two days. A break before the second half of the meeting meant they could relax with refreshments and a buffet.

'How's it going with Innovest, Dad?' Danny asked.

'It's fine. They've issued a statement saying the data they released on that mineral may have been contaminated, so they need to rerun them, which could take several weeks,' Paul White replied. 'Sorry about the commercial flight and hotel room, but this is business, and I didn't want others to accuse me of favouritism.'

'It's okay. The transfer minibus was a pain, and the airline damaged my chair,' Danny sighed. 'But the junior suite works well.'

Paul laughed. 'You've got the hotel to thank for your room. They were told someone was in a wheelchair and said the junior suite was the only suitable option. What's wrong with your chair? We can—'

'Paul, how's it going?' Big Bill asked, walking towards them.

'Oh, hi, Bill. I heard your flight had been delayed. I said you should have jumped on our charter plane,' Paul replied, shaking Bill's hand.

'I couldn't make it. I had a meetin' with the new Prime Minister and Jay,' Bill replied. 'Hi, Danny. Did I hear Paul sayin' there was somethin' wrong with your chair?'

'Hey, Big Bill. Yeah, some airport klutz ripped out a wire, pulling a circuit board with it,' Danny moaned. 'Max spotted it.'

'Max? Does he work for us?' Bill asked.

'Sorry, err, I meant Bobby,' Danny replied.

'Bobby? Oh, the translator,' Bill laughed in his soft drawl.

Hearing his name mentioned, Bobby joined Danny, Paul, and Bill.

'Hello, Mr White, Mr Pierce,' Bobby said respectfully.

'I think we've known each other long enough for you to call me Paul.'

'Yes, uh, of course, Paul,' Bobby replied awkwardly.

'And you can call me Mr Pierce,' Bill laughed, slapping Bobby across the back jovially. 'Just kiddin', Bill, or Big Bill will do just fine.'

'Thank you, Mr... Bill,' Bobby said as his face started to glow red in embarrassment.

'About your chair, Danny. Can you fix it?' Bill asked.

'Yeah, it should only take a couple of hours, but I didn't bring my tools or spares,' Danny replied.

'Well you're here to review M Bank's systems and technology. So, why don't you head over to their technology centre in the mornin' to check it out and take Bobby to translate for you?' Bill suggested. 'You should be able to get what you need to fix that chair of yours.'

'Cheers, Bill,' Danny replied.

'Puoi assicurarti che Danny si comporti bene?' Bill asked.

'Farò del mio meglio, padrone,' Bobby replied.

Danny glanced at his dad, and the father-son language was clear: it was time to go. 'Come on, Bobster, I need some food.'

Bobby smiled at Paul and Big Bill and headed off with Danny.

'What did you say to Bobby?' Paul asked.

'I just asked if he could make sure Danny behaves,' Bill replied.

'How was Bobby's reply?' Paul said.

'Perfect, but strange,' Bill replied. 'He said he'll do his best, but...'

'But what?'

'He sounded more like my Italian grandfather, using padrone instead of signore for sir to show respect. Are you sure he's the same age as Danny?' Bill laughed.

'I'm not even sure Danny is the same age as Danny.' Paul chuckled.

'You and me tomorrow then, Chief,' Danny said as he loaded his plate with caprese skewers, bruschetta and frittata slices.'

'Whoever made these frittatas needs to try a bit harder,' Max grumbled as they reached the buffet.

A catering staff member walked past with more frittatas on a tray. He overheard Max and muttered, 'I ragazzi di oggi non hanno rispetto per i vecchi.'

Danny turned to the server, noting his greying, thick, wavy hair, which made him look like he was in his early fifties, and challenged him, 'What did you say?'

'Sorry, sir. I was moaning about young'uns having no respect for their elders. Just an issue in the kitchen,' the server said.

'Well, I hope they learn some respect for eggs,' Max replied. 'They'd get a roasting for serving these to Caesar back in the day.'

'I wouldn't know sir, although my brother might have a view on that,' the server replied.

'Is your brother some hotshot chef then?' Danny challenged. 'Maybe I've heard of him.'

'I doubt it, sir,' the server said, placing the frittatas on the table.

'I've eaten at some of the best restaurants in the world. What's your brother's name? I could get him a job if he's that good,' Danny insisted.

'I'm not sure where he is, sir. We lost touch a few years ago,' the server replied before checking the rest of the buffet and turning towards the kitchen.

Danny smiled and said, 'Family issues, huh? I've got friends like that who haven't spoken for weeks or months. What do you think, Bobster?'

Bobby and Max had been watching Danny and the server with interest. Several questions and discussions took place between them before Max said, 'You may not know how Caesar may have felt about these frittatas, but would Cicero have liked them?'

The server stopped and turned to face Bobby. 'Cicero, sir?'

'Yes, Cicero. I remember him being a very learned man who could see beyond the image in front of him and see the true person underneath,' Max replied.

'I think Cicero would have liked anything Maxohal had cooked,' the server said, smiling.

'Maxohal doesn't sound like a very Italian name,' Danny queried.

'Is that you, Zym?' Max asked.

'Maxo?' the server queried.

Max grabbed the server and hugged him.

'Err, guys, this is awks. What's happening?' Danny asked.

'Danny, I'd like to introduce my brother Zym,' Max replied.

'Zym? Who the heck is he? My name's Bruno,' the server replied.

'And my name's Bobby,' Max said.

'Excuse me, but *my* name is Bobby,' Bobby insisted.

'Ah, you're in a new host,' the server replied.

'Yes, Zym. Is Bruno your host's name, or have you transmuted?' Max asked.

'No, my host left for a life in the UK years ago. This is all me, Junior,' Zym said. 'Bruno Morelli at your service.'

Danny frowned as the last few minutes of conversation registered. 'Chief, are you saying this is your brother as in another alien?'

'Yes, but more than that, he is my brother, as in we have the same parents,' Max replied.

'No way!' Danny insisted. 'That makes him over two thousand years old too.'

'I think I'm around two thousand one hundred years old, but who's counting?' Zym replied.

'So what are you doing here?' Danny asked.

'Is your friend always this obtuse?' Zym asked Max, pointing down at his own uniform.

'Hey, my dad is funding this,' Danny protested.

'Well, Daddy's funding means I'm one of your servers,' Zym replied with a smile.

'This is my worst nightmare. The genius with an ego meets the wisdom with an attitude,' Max sighed.

'Should I thank you or hit you?' Danny asked.

'Personally, I think we should both hit him,' Zym laughed.

'I could say I've really missed these *pick on Max days*, but I'd be lying.'

'Admit it, you've missed me,' Zym smiled.

'Only when I needed someone to blame things on.'

'How long has it been since you guys last met?' Danny asked.

'I'm not sure,' Max mused.

'I am, it was 1858!' Zym exclaimed.

'Oh,' Danny replied before realising what Zym had said. '1858?'

'Yeah, you know how it is. As you get older, you sometimes lose touch with family and friends for a while,' Max explained.

'Maybe for a few months or a year or two, but almost a hundred and seventy years,' Danny replied. 'Come on, Chief, I know you can be a bit forgetful, but forgetting your brother for almost two centuries.'

'I didn't forget him; he just disappeared without any explanation,' Max protested.

'I didn't disappear; my last host, Felice Orsini, decided he wanted to unify Italy and free it from Austrian rule. Looking exactly like the man who tried to assassinate Napoleon III meant I had to flee to the Americas,' Zym said.

'And when I found out you were there, I came after you in 1860, but I got caught up in the civil war,' Max explained. 'After that, life just rolled on.'

'Bruno, dai, ce serve sapè che n'ato c'ha da esse rifornito,' another server shouted.

'What did she say?' Danny asked.

'Sorry, they're waiting for me to say what food needs topping up,' Zym said, turning to leave.

Max grabbed Zym's arm. 'It's good to see you, Zym.'

Zym turned and smiled. 'You too, Junior.'

'Zym, we're meeting in reception at seven before going for dinner,' Danny said. 'Why not join us?'

'I'd love to, but I'm working tonight. How about tomorrow evening?' Zym replied.

'I'd like that,' Max replied. 'I'm in room 326. Just let me know what time you're free.'

Danny rolled his eyes. 'Guys it's not the dark ages. Get your phones out and unlock them.'

Max and Zym did as instructed before Danny grabbed the phones, tapped a few buttons, and handed them back. 'There, you've got each other's contact details now.'

'Is he always like this with technology?' Zym asked.

'Oh no,' Max replied.

'Thanks, Chief,' Danny said proudly.

'No, normally he's a hell of a lot worse,' Max replied as Zym headed towards the kitchen laughing.

6
Help Me, Bro

'The coach will be outside at eight-thirty for those going to M Bank Research's Italian Headquarters. For those going to the technology centre, the car will be outside at eight-fifteen,' Big Bill announced over breakfast.

'That's us, Bobster,' Danny said.

'How come you're not coming with us?' Mercedes asked.

'Because we're special,' Danny replied.

'It's because Danny needs some parts to fix his chair, and Big Bill and Paul said it would be a good opportunity to check out their technology centre,' Bobby added.

'I'd love to come with you,' Chris said.

Bobby's phone pinged.

Zym

Max, I need to see you in reception in 5 mins

'Are you okay?' Danny whispered. 'You look worried.'

'It's Zym. He wants to see Max, and it sounds urgent,' Bobby replied, showing Danny the text.

'Let's go,' Danny said.

'He wants to see me, buddy. You wait here, I'll be back in a bit,' Max said, standing and heading towards reception.

Max walked into reception and could see Zym by a door marked "Personale autorizzato."

'Max, I checked your hotel booking this morning, and it says you're with M Bank,' Zym said with concern.

'Sort of. We're working with an investor looking to acquire them,' Max replied. 'What's the problem?'

'That's why I'm doing this job,' Zym said. 'I heard they were using this hotel for their executives, so I thought I might hear something about it if I got a job here.'

'Hear something about what?' Max asked.

'I've been following a lead about Shadowers going missing for the last seven years, and it brought me back to Rome,' Zym said.

'Do you mean they've been killed?' Max asked.

'No. Well, I don't think so. It started when I came across someone in a hospital in South Africa who survived what looked like a fatal car crash. She'd got bank cards and ID that said she was someone else. When she started to recover, she said the false name belonged to a Shadower she had hosted a few years before.'

'That's odd. Have you come across any others?'

'At least ten instances. Almost all involved car crashes, and in every case, the victim had been the host to a Shadower and had the Shadower's ID,' Zym said.

'Were they all in South Africa?' Max asked.

'No. They've been everywhere. One in China, two in the USA, another in Brazil, several across Europe.'

'My dad was killed in a car crash just over five years ago,' Bobby said.

'Was he a Shadower as well?' Zym asked.

'No, he was an engineer in the motor industry, but he was very talented,' Bobby replied.

'I'm sorry to hear that lad, but this definitely involves Shadowers, not humans,' Zym said.

'But if you've identified ten former hosts who survived attempts to kill them but with ID trying to pass them off as a Shadower, how many were killed?' Max asked.

'I don't know. Without the hosts surviving, how can we tell? It would just be a human killed in a car accident,' Zym replied.

'I've got an idea, but I need to speak to Danny,' Max said.

'Danny? Who the hell is Danny?' Zym asked.

'The ego on wheels you met last night,' Max laughed.

'Oh, him. Seems like a nice guy, but a bit of a 'Daddy's boy' and a 'don't you know who I am' sort,' Zym grumbled.

'Yeah, that's Danny,' Bobby laughed.

'But putting that aside, he's a genius with technology,' Max replied.

'Sounds like he can help us,' Zym replied. 'Where are you going today?'

'Danny and I are off to their technology centre,' Max said.

'I've been trying to get in there for ages. See what you can discover because that place is shrouded in secrecy.'

'Do you think it's linked to the missing Shadowers?' Max asked.

'All I know is everything leads back to Rome and M Bank Research. But of all their facilities, that one is the most secretive.'

'Zym, sir, can I ask you something?' Bobby asked.

'Of course, Bobby,' Zym smiled.

'Is Stephen Marchent dangerous?'

'Well, he's the major shareholder and CEO of M Bank who owns M Bank Research, but I've not found any direct links of Shadowers or deceptors to him. Why?' Zym queried.

'Because he's dating my mum,' Bobby explained.

'I suggest you're careful around him. There's nothing to say he's controlling it, but he does run the company involved, so he must know something,' Zym said.

'Hey, Bobster, Chief, our wheels are here,' Danny shouted as he headed towards them. 'Hey, Bruno, how's things?'

'Ciao, Danny,' Zym replied.

'We need to go. I'll talk to Danny today and see if he can help,' Max said before turning and heading off.

Zym headed towards the restaurant when a woman stopped him.

'Excuse me, sir. I was wondering if you know where the M Bank people are?'

'Si, signora. Some have gone to their offices,' Zym replied.

'Did you notice if my partner, Stephen Marchent, was with them?' the woman asked.

'Signor Marchent is your partner, Signora...?'

'I'm Mrs Morris, Patricia Morris.'

'Mu scusi, Signora Morris. I haven't seen Signor Marchent today.'

'Oh, well, thank you anyway,' Pat said, heading towards reception.

A thirty-minute car journey later, Bobby and Danny are waiting in the reception of M Bank Research's Technology Centre.

'Why does everything on this trip remind me of my arrival on your planet,' Max sighed, looking at the centre's name on a sign above reception, the Cicero Centre.

The reception felt like a homage to Ancient Rome. Marble columns bookended the marble reception deck, and statues of Roman Emperors were dotted around the room. In the centre was a square pool filled with plants and water cascading down like steady rainfall.

'That's wrong,' Max grumbled.

'What's up, Chief?' Danny asked.

'They've tried to make it look like an impluvium. But why would you have plants polluting your household water,' Max moaned.

'I don't think they're interested in accuracy,' Danny replied. 'It's more about the aesthetics.'

A woman in her early thirties in a fashionable black and white outfit walked into the reception. 'Buongiorno! Welcome to our office. You must be Mr White and Mr Morris?'

'That's right,' Danny said, shooting forward in his wheelchair.

'My name is Alessia, and I will be your host to ensure you have everything you need. But, ah, there is a problem. It seems we did not receive, how do you say... an advance copy of your questions or what you would like to see.'

'That's because we prefer to ask questions as we go along,' Danny said.

'I see. Let me take you to our boardroom. We've laid on some refreshments, and some of our senior managers will come in during the day to take you through what they do,' Alessia said.

'Actually, could we start with a tour of your facility,' Danny asked.

Alessia looked awkwardly and then smiled. 'Of course. Let me get you some passes.'

As Alessia headed towards the reception desk, Danny turned to Bobby. 'Is it me, or does our host seem a little nervous?'

Alessia leant over the reception desk and whispered to the security guard, 'Mi può dare due pass per tutte le aree, tranne la zona Q? Inoltre, avvisi il Signor Ferruzzi che i nostri ospiti sono fuori controllo,'

'That's rude,' Max said.

'What did she say?' Danny asked.

'Well, first of all, she's asked for passes that let us in everywhere except in zone Q,' Max said. 'And then she told the guard to tell Mr Ferruzzi that we are out of control.'

'Out of control?' Danny queried.

'Yeah, like we're a bit dangerous,' Max replied.

'If anyone asks, pretend you can't speak the lingo, or at least you only speak a little bit,' Danny said.

'Okay, but what have you—' Max stopped talking as Alessia rejoined them.

'Mr White, here is your pass and yours, Mr Morris. As instructed, it gives you full access to the facility,' Alessia said.

'Who is Mr Ferruzzi?' Bobby asked, incurring a glower from Danny.

'Who?' Alessia asked.

'Mr Ferruzzi. I heard you mention a Signor Ferruzzi, but I only speak a little Italian, so I couldn't understand the rest,' Bobby said.

'Oh, ah, no, the guard is called Ferruzzi,' Alessia smiled disarmingly.

'*She's good. That was a very smooth reply*,' Max thought.

'*But she lied*,' Bobby replied.

'*Exactly. She lied, but she barely lost her rhythm and the smile at the end, which made you feel like you could trust her*,' Max said. '*She's very experienced at deceit.*'

'Oh yeah, that explains it,' Bobby replied to Alessia.

'Shall, ah, we start the tour?' Alessia asked. 'Where would you like to start?'

'Actually, my wheelchair's circuit board is damaged. Do you have a department for components and spare parts?' Danny asked.

Alessia looked confused before saying, 'Yes, of course. If you head down that corridor I just need to speak to reception. I will catch up with you.'

'Oh, you mean you want to talk to Mr Ferruzzi,' Bobby said, smiling.

'No, just the security—ah, sorry, yes, of course, Mr Ferruzzi. Yes, I need to speak to Mr Ferruzzi on security,' Alessia replied.

As they headed towards the corridor Alessia had indicated, Danny hissed at Bobby, 'Why did you say that? She'll guess we suspect her.'

As they turned round a corner into the corridor, Max replied, 'Shh, I'm listening.'

'No, Signor Ferruzzi, non possono entrare nella zona Q... Li sto portando al reparto ricambi... uno di loro ha bisogno di pezzi per la sua sedia a rotelle. Devo addebitarglieli?— Sì, signore, qualunque cosa voglia e senza addebito. Ho capito... No, signore, li terrò lontani dalla zona Q e da tutto il personale di zona Q. Devo and are, signore, in questo momento sono incustoditi. Sì, signore, mi scusi, arrivederci.'

'You can't hear her from here. That background music is too loud,' Danny protested.

'She's just confirmed to Ferruzzi that we can't get to zone Q, and she'll keep us away from Q personnel. She also asked if she should charge you for parts for your wheelchair,' Max replied.

'Charge me? Perhaps she doesn't know who—'

'I think the world knows who your dad is, Danny,' Max laughed. 'The good news is Alessia was told you can have whatever you want at no charge.'

'I should think so too,' Danny laughed. 'Come on, we need to be down by those doors before she catches us.'

As Alessia turned the corner, she saw her guests waiting by a frosted glass door. 'Signori, you didn't need to wait for me.'

'It's fine, we didn't want to wander too far without you,' Danny replied, smiling.

'Besides, I get lost in a supermarket,' Bobby added.

'Ah, yes, English humour,' Alessia replied, tapping her card against a device on the wall, causing the door to slide open.

As Alessia marched ahead, leading the way down a corridor, Danny and Bobby tried unsuccessfully to see into the rooms they passed, but the glass walls were heavily frosted.

As they passed a crossroads with another corridor, Danny looked left and noticed another glass door at the far end. Bobby spotted a solid metal door to the right and slowed down to study it.

'What's behind that metal door?' Max asked.

'Scusi?' Alessia said, increasing her walking pace.

'That metal door back there?' Max said.

'Metal?' Alessia asked.

'Sì, la porta di metallo,' Max replied.

'Ah, that's just the fire exit,' Alessia replied as she tapped her card against another card reader and rushed through.

'*Strange. Don't fire exits normally have a push bar or similar,*' Bobby thought.

'*Yep. I think that door is anything but a fire door,*' Max replied. '*We'd better hurry up; they're getting ahead of us.*'

'The parts department is just here,' Alessia said to Danny.

As Bobby caught up with Alessia and Danny he tripped and collided with Alessia. 'I'm so sorry.'

'It's fine, Mr Morris. No harm done,' Alessia replied. 'Now, if you tell them what you want, they should be able to help.'

'Thank you, Alessia,' Danny said. 'We may be a while, so if you have anything else you need to do, go right ahead.'

Alessia smiled. 'It is fine, Mr White. My day is to—'

Alessia's phone pinged, and she glanced at it.

Capo

> Torna qui subito! Dì al team dei ricambi di tenerli lì e assicurati che non ci siano Shadowers in giro.

'Excuse me. I need to leave you for a while. Our team will take care of you while I'm gone, but if you want to continue the tour, let them know, and they'll contact me,' Alessia explained before heading off.

Danny was talking to the parts team about components to fix his chair when Max whispered to him, 'I'm going back to that metal door. Keep them busy here.'

'Sure, Chief. Do you know why our tour guide has abandoned us?' Danny asked.

'Yeah, I saw her message. Someone has ordered her to see them and instructed her to make sure the parts team keep us here,' Max replied.

'And the rest? I know when you're holding back,' Danny said.

'Okay, she was told to make sure there are no Shadowers around,' Max said.

'Wow, so there are Shadowers here. But our passes are limited. You won't get past that metal door,' Danny said. 'Well, unless you give me time to reprogram it.'

'No need, buddy. I've used an older technique to give me access,' Max replied. 'I swapped my card for hers.'

'The old switcheroo, huh,' Danny smiled. 'Remind me to keep my hand on my wallet when you're around.'

'I've seen your wallet. It's full of doodles on scraps of paper, a credit card in your dad's name and a black card for a fast-food joint,' Max laughed. 'Can you cause a distraction so I can slip away?'

'Leave it to me, Chief. In a few seconds, nobody will notice you've gone,' Danny winked.

Danny's wheelchair suddenly shot forward, colliding with some racking, which fell backwards, unloading its contents onto the floor.

'I'm so sorry,' Danny said as he glanced to his right, and his chair set off again, knocking more shelves over.

A few minutes later, Bobby was standing in front of the metal door. He took a deep breath and tapped Alessia's card against the card reader, opening the door.

'*Which way do we go, Cowboy?*' Bobby asked with corridors leading away to the left, right and straight ahead.

'*Your guess is as good as mine,*' Max replied. '*Let's go left. Straight ahead seems so predictable.*'

As they wandered down the corridor, they noticed the number of doors on both sides increased.

'I wonder what's inside,' Bobby said, tapping Alessia's card against another card pad.

The door opened to reveal a bed, a small desk and, to the right, a small bathroom. Bobby moved down to the next room and saw the same layout again.

'*This is bad,*' Max said.

'*It just looks like sleeping quarters,*' Bobby replied.

'*Did you notice anything missing in the bathrooms?*' Max asked.

'*Like wh..., ah yeah, I've just seen it in your thoughts. There's no toilets,*' Bobby said.' *But when you transmute into your own shell, you need to eat, which means you need toilets.*'

'*Which means these quarters are designed for Shadowers, not in their shells,*' Max said.

'*But that's impossible with Earth's atmosphere,*' Bobby challenged.

'*Now you mention it, it does feel more oppressive here like the atmosphere is denser,*' Max said as they reached another metal door. He tapped Alessia's card against the card reader, and the door opened.

7
Time to Leave

Max looked up at the machine in front of him and shuddered. The air inside the massive, clinically clean cavernous room was cool and still, with a faint hum coming from the machine, which almost seemed to vibrate into the very fabric of the building.

'*Are you okay?*' Bobby asked.

'*Absolutely not. Can't you see it in my memories?*' Max replied.

'*I can't make out anything clearly. It's such a blur of images and emotions. All I know is you've seen something like this before, and you're angry, scared, frightened, no not frightened, you're terrified,*' Bobby said, staring at the giant machine in front of him.

'It's an—' Max froze as he heard footsteps rapidly approaching.

He turned quickly to see a tall man marching towards them, with black slicked-back hair and a dark Mediterranean complexion, dressed in a sharp black and green uniform bearing the M Bank Research emblem. He looked angry, and his eyes were cold and piercing.

'Che ci fai qui? Chi sei tu? Questo è un luogo riservato!' The guard said sternly.

Bobby flinched at the speed and intensity of the man's speech. The guard stepped closer, his hand resting on the sidearm at his waist, as his eyes narrowed with suspicion.

'He's just asking who we are and why we are in this restricted area,' Max explained.

The guard stepped closer and repeated more forcefully, 'Che ci fai qui? Chi sei tu? Questo è un luogo riservato!'

Max stammered, 'Sono... Sono qui per errore. Non volevo... Non volevo disturbare nulla.'

The guard's eyes widened slightly, but his expression remained one of controlled authority. He responded, his voice softer but still filled with caution. 'English?'

'Yes, thank you, uh, I mean sorry. As I said, I'm here by mistake. I didn't mean to disturb anyone,' Bobby replied.

The guard tilted his head in a mix of curiosity and confusion about how this person was in this area.

Bobby looked at the machine and asked, 'What is that thing?'

'That is not something you need to be concerned about,' the guard replied. 'So, why are you here?'

Bobby swallowed, feeling the tension in the room thicken. 'I just used the toilet and was trying to get back to the parts department and my colleague.'

'Come with me,' the guard said, motioning with a sharp flick of his wrist, indicating that Bobby should follow. 'We need to confirm your identity and why you are here.'

'I told you, I got lost coming back from the toilet. My name is Bobby Morris, and I'm part of WestFi's due diligence team,' Bobby protested.

However, the guard's firm grip on Bobby's arm made it clear he wasn't interested in a debate. As Bobby was led away, the machine's hum grew fainter.

'*What is that machine?*' Bobby thought.

'*It's an Exodus machine,*' Max replied, fear tinging every word.

'Mr Morris. How did you get into that secure area?' Alessia demanded.

Bobby glanced around the small, stark room and gulped. The blank grey walls were only broken up by the single chair he was sitting on. 'I nipped to the toilet and got confused about my way back.'

'But how did you get through the secure doors?' Alessia demanded.

'I just tapped my card like you showed us,' Bobby replied sheepishly.

'But your card doesn't give you access to that area,' Alessia replied.

'Really? Let me make a note of that. You assured Danny and I that our cards gave us full access to the facility. I'll have to tell my bosses you were hiding areas from us,' Max said firmly, standing up. 'Now, if you'll excuse me, I need to rejoin my colleague.'

'*You can't demand that, we sneaked in there,*' Bobby thought.

'*Shh, in cases like this, it's five percent facts and ninety-five percent confidence,*' Max replied.

The guard looked shocked at this sudden change in this trespasser from guilty and sheepish to assured and demanding. He glanced at Alessia, but she shrugged, equally confused.

'Wait here,' Alessia said as she left the room and pulled out her phone.

'*Any second now,*' Max replied. '*From what I could hear through that door, she's been told to release us.*'

The door flew open, and Alessia walked in, her face red and angry. 'I am taking you back to your colleague. He can finish collecting his parts, and then you will come with me to the boardroom. We will go through the presentations as originally planned.'

Twenty minutes later, Danny and Bobby were alone inside the boardroom. Bobby and Max had explained everything they had seen to Danny, and they were now looking around the room. The modern wood and chrome table, the frosted glass door with large black vertical pull handles on each side, and the black surround clashed with the traditional wood panelling around the walls and the heavy black leather and wood chairs.

'Are you sure that couldn't have been some sort of telescope or weapon?' Danny asked as he inspected the food along the wall to the one side of the frosted glass door.

'I know an Exodus machine when I see it,' Max grumbled.

'You'd think they could've made an effort,' Danny grumbled. 'Ugh, they've got olives. They're just grapes that gave up on life. Nature's way of saying, "Not everything needs to be edible."'

'They've got pizza and pasta,' Bobby added, wandering over to the drinks and pouring some sparkling water.

Danny picked up a slice of cold pizza, held it up to eye level, and squinted at it as if trying to decipher some ancient code. 'It looks like the perfect incentive to go on a diet, and as for the pasta, they seem to think "al dente" means "still raw." You could use it to repair the Colosseum—it might last longer, too.'

'Do you want a drink? The fizzy water is nice,' Bobby suggested.

'I need coffee,' Danny moaned. 'Do they have a double espresso on that thing?"

Bobby selected the double espresso on the hot drinks dispenser, and when it finished filling the small cup, he handed it across to Danny.

Danny took a sip of the lukewarm coffee and grimaced. 'This espresso's so weak it should come with a motivational speech. I'm sure it just apologised for existing.'

As Danny and Bobby returned to the boardroom table, the door opened.

'Mr Morris and Mr White. These are the department heads at this technology centre. They'll take you through everything we are doing here and explain our exciting plans for the future,' Alessia said curtly as several other smartly dressed executives filed into the room and sat down.

'*Bet they don't mention the Exodus machine,*' Max thought.

'*We could ask them,*' Bobby suggested.

'*No point, they'd only lie.*'

'Two of our department heads are dialling in from our London office. If you could hit the meeting acceptance button on that pad in front of you, they'll join us on one of the screens,' Alessia said.

Danny leant over to Bobby and whispered, 'Have you seen this VoIP? It's prehistoric.'

'What's a VoIP?' Bobby asked.

'It stands for voice over internet protocol. It's how video calls work,' Danny replied.

Five hours of presentations later, Danny was lost in his thoughts as he doodled away on his digital notepad while Bobby was still trying to be enthusiastic.

'Alessia, your team have put on an impressive display, but if everything is going so well, why do you support WestFi's takeover?' Bobby asked.

'Well, in our case, it's not so much a takeover; it's more like a consolidation into WestFi,' one of the department heads said. 'It'll open up more funds to support our research.'

Danny perked up and looked towards the man. 'How is it a consolidation? WestFi doesn't own any part of M Bank.'

'No, but M Bank Research is a joint venture with one of WestFi's subsidiaries,' the man said.

'Why weren't we told that?' Danny demanded.

The department heads looked awkwardly at each other.

'I took you through the organisational structure,' Alessia replied, scrolling back through her presentation. 'M Bank Research was founded fifteen years ago to study new minerals discovered by M Bank. It was formed as a joint venture between M Bank, who took fifty-five percent of the business and WJ Futures, who have the remaining forty-five percent.'

'Who owns WJ?' Danny asked.

'Its structure is complicated as it's based in the Cayman Islands, but it's part of WestFi. That's why it isn't part of the full due diligence review,' Alessia said.

Bobby leant over to Danny and whispered, 'She's showed us this already.'

'I was busy working on how this mineral could be used to transmit energy over short distances. It would mean an end to wiring,' Danny replied.

'Is that good?' Bobby asked.

'It would mean no energy loss between its storage or production point and where it's used,' Danny said.

'Tesla was looking at doing something similar, but I'm more concerned about its use in an Exodus machine,' Max said.

'Signori?' Alessia said loudly.

'I'm sorry, Alessia. Danny was discussing some ideas for this new mineral,' Bobby replied.

'We think it has transformational properties,' one of the department heads said excitedly.

'So do we,' Max grumbled.

'Do you need anything else from my colleagues or me?' Alessia asked.

'A tour would still be nice, and Bobby, I mean Mr Morris, promises not to wander off this time.' Danny smiled at Alessia.

'Very well. Let's allow my colleagues to return to their jobs, and I'll show you the rest of the facility,' Alessia replied.

'Of course,' Danny said. 'Thank you everyone for your time.'

'Yes, thank you,' Max added. As the department heads started to leave, Max looked at the one who talked about transformational powers. 'Oh, Signor...'

'Michele Carbone, Signor Morris,' the man replied.

'Signor Carbone, I should have guessed. Some of your experiments are legendary in the field of science,' Max said, smiling.

Michele blushed. 'Thank you, Signore. Did you want to ask something?'

'I was just wondering if you've named the mineral you've discovered?' Max asked.

'I didn't discover or name the mineral, Signore. But it's been registered with the International Mineralogical Association based on the mystical way it extracts energy and transmits it as light particles.'

'Oh, that's interesting,' Max replied. 'So what's it called.'

'Luminae, Signore,' Michele replied.

As the department heads left the room, Alessia followed them, but she stopped by the door. 'Mr White and Mr Morris. I need a comfort break. I do not expect to have to come looking for you when I return.'

As the door closed behind Alessia, Danny turned to Bobby. 'Are you two okay? Bobby looks very pale.'

'They've got an Exodus machine, which you could argue that science and technology in any advanced civilisation might create. But to name the mineral in it luminae, the same name we used on Zephyrion, isn't a coincidence. A Deceptor is controlling this,' Max insisted.

'But Stephen Marchent owns M Bank. Do you mean my mum's in danger again?' Bobby exclaimed.

'I don't know anything at the moment,' Max replied.

Bobby pulled out his phone and tapped in a message.

'Everything okay back home, Bobster?' Danny asked.

'Yeah, it's fine,' Bobby replied.

'But we shouldn't just suspect Marchent,' Max said.

Danny frowned. 'Whaddya mean, Chief?'

'WJ Futures owns forty-five percent of this research division, but who within WestFi owns or controls WJ?' Max asked.

'Big Bill's name is William J Pierce, so he could be the WJ,' Danny said.

'What about Jay?' Bobby suggested. 'It could be Big Bill and Jay run it together.'

'That makes sense, Bobster. You're not as daft as you look.'

'I'm not as weak as I look either if you're looking for a fight.'

'Guys, we don't have time for banter. This is serious,' Max said.

'Yes, sir. Sorry, sir,' Danny laughed, pretending to doff an imaginary cap.

'There is one other person who fits those initials,' Max said.

'Well, come on, Chief. Don't keep us waiting. Who's the other suspect?' Danny asked like a detective closing in on a case.

'Isn't your dad named after your grandad?'

'Yeah, and?'

'So he is Paul White Junior,' Max replied.

'Woah, stop right there. My dad makes his money from buying and selling businesses, not through technology research,' Danny insisted.

Max went to reply, but the boardroom door opened, and Alessia came through with Paul White by her side.

'Afternoon, guys,' Paul said. He turned and looked at the food drying out and curling up. 'I love Italian food, but you can't beat bacon butties at a corporate event.'

'Dad, what're you doing here?'

'I've heard you've had an eventful day,' Paul laughed.

'I didn't mean to wander off, Mr White. Sorry, I mean Paul,' Bobby stammered.

'It's fine, Bobby. Alessia explained that she was just worried about you. They were conducting tests in that room, and they still don't know if it's dangerous, like radioactive,' Paul replied.

'*That's rubbish*,' Max thought angrily.

'Did Alessia call you?' Danny asked.

Paul looked at Alessia with a puzzled expression. 'No. I just bumped into Alessia in reception, and she was telling me about Bobby's escapades on the way here.'

'So why are you here?' Danny challenged.

'Stephen has flown over and offered to show me around this place. I didn't even know it existed until Big Bill showed me the timetable for the due diligence,' Paul replied.

'Alessia was just about to do the same,' Max said. 'Maybe we could combine both tours?'

'Nice idea, Bobby. But Stephen and I have some confidential stuff to discuss.'

'Mr White and Mr Morris, let's leave Mr White for his meeting with Mr Marchent. This way for the tour,' Alessia said.

'Hey, Danny,' Paul shouted after them.

Danny spun around in his chair. 'Yeah, Dad?'

'Did you get the spares for your chair?'

'Yeah, I did, thanks. Why?'

'I think you dropped something.' Paul said, holding up a box.

Danny went back to Paul and took the box. 'I don't th—'

'Shhh,' Paul whispered. 'Just take this with you and under no circumstances open it until I see you this evening.'

'Okay, thanks, Dad,' Danny said a little too theatrically. 'I would have had trouble fixing my chair without this.'

As Danny rejoined Bobby and Alessia, Paul smiled and thought, 'My lad's a genius, but sometimes he's as subtle as a brick.'

8
COULD IT BE?

'R-R-Remind m-m-me to u-upgrade my s-s-suspension. These f-f-flipping c-c-cobbles are m-m-murder in a chair,' Danny grumbled as they crossed the area by the Colosseum.

'You chose the restaurant,' Mercedes replied. Then, in a mocking Danny voice, she added, 'Trust me, dullards. I know a place to eat with great views.'

'It does have g-g-great views. B-B-But why'd we have to c-c-come this w-w-way? There's a smooth p-p-pathway round the other s-s-side,' Danny muttered.

'Because Bobby's never seen the Colosseum,' Chris said, watching Bobby snap pictures in all directions.

'He's never seen M-M-M-Milton K-K-K-Keynes either, but at least there's no c-c-cobbles there,' Danny juddered.

'Stop moaning. Look, he's loving it. One minute he's pointing and muttering, and the next he's off like an excited child on holiday,' Chris replied.

Bobby ran back to his friends. 'This is amazing. Max has told me so much about Rome, but seeing his memories and then seeing it for real is incredible.'

'Can we go to the restaurant now?' Danny grumbled. 'And we're going that way. There's less cobbles and no steps.'

'Okay. I can get a great picture from over there,' Bobby agreed. 'The road is higher, so it'll be perfect.'

'*You know it was flat around the Colosseum when it was built,*' Max said.

'It's amazing,' Bobby said enthusiastically.

'Have you really never been abroad?' Mercedes asked.

'No, not since 1925,' Bobby replied. Bobby rubbed his head and added, 'Sorry, I mean no, never. Max was last here in 1925, but I've never been outside the UK.'

'You've never been outside the M25,' Danny laughed as they crossed the Piazza del Colosseo.

'That used to be a gladiator training base. The Ludus Magnus,' Max replied, pointing towards some excavated ruins.

'I bet you trained there,' Danny said.

'Actually, I trained gladiators there for a while,' Max replied.

Twenty minutes later, they sat at a table outside the restaurant, looking up at the Colosseum.

'It's impressive,' Chris said.

'I can't believe I'm here again,' Bobby added excitedly.

'I thought you said you'd never been abroad?' Chris challenged.

'I haven't,' Bobby replied.

'But you just said you can't believe you're back here again,' Chris said.

'No, I said Max, um, he said he can't believe he's here again,' Bobby replied.

Mercedes leaned across to Danny and whispered, 'Is Bobby okay? He seems to be a bit confused tonight.'

'Maybe it's jet lag. We are an hour ahead of the UK,' Danny laughed.

'Who ordered the frittata?' a familiar voice said.

Bobby turned to see Zym holding a plate. 'Zym, what are you doing here?'

'Max said to meet you here, and as I know the owner, I thought I'd bring your meals out,' Zym smiled.

After they'd eaten, they started discussing the events of the day as Bobby and Danny went through what had happened at the research centre.

'Are you sure it was an Exodus machine?' Zym asked.

'I've hung off one of them,' Max replied. 'I'm never going to forget what they look like.'

'That's true,' Zym laughed.

'If it wasn't for Simo and that stretchy tarpaulin, I'd never have made it', Max said.

'Actually, it was Jeric who suggested it,' Zym replied.

'Don't mention his name,' Max replied tersely. 'It's been over two thousand years since I last saw him being stabbed by that gladiator.'

'Sounds like you had quite a day. Mine was boring,' Mercedes said.

'What were you guys doing?' Bobby asked.

'I was with Chris going through the personnel records,' Mercedes replied.

Chris laughed. 'Yeah, our day got as exciting as being unable to find the personnel files for the likes of Kalin Thomas, Rodrigo Valazquez, Juli Fellowes and Simon Morris.'

'And the only machinery we saw were printers and laptops,' Mercedes sighed. 'Although it was fun teaching their HR Director how to get into her system.'

'Blimey. How do you guys in Personnel Support cope with so much drama and excitement?' Danny chuckled.

'My dad was called Simon Morris,' Bobby said.

'Was he?' Chris replied. 'I guess it's a fairly common name.'

'Maybe he did some work for M Bank,' Mercedes suggested. 'A group of people with missing files started around five or six years ago. Apparently, they joined following an acquisition of a small business.'

'It wouldn't be my dad. He died around that time,' Bobby sighed wistfully.

'Were they the only ones whose files were missing?' Zym asked.

'No, there's quite a lot,' Chris replied.

'Perhaps you could get a copy tomorrow?' Max suggested.

'I'd have taken a copy already,' Danny said.

'I already have,' Mercedes replied as she pulled off her ring and flipped out a small USB connector from the inside of the ring.

Danny pulled out his tablet from one of his chair pockets, then looked at the ring and laughed, 'That connector is so last year. Hang on, I might have an adaptor for it.'

Mercedes put her ring back on and tapped it against her watch. She flicked through a couple of screens and then groaned. 'Genius 2!'

'What?' Max asked.

'Danny, is your computer tablet called Genius 2?' Mercedes demanded.

'Yeah, so,' Danny replied, still rummaging through the pockets in his chair for an adaptor.

'Then I've AirShared it to you already,' Mercedes said.

Danny stopped looking for the adaptor and picked up his tablet, 'Hah, looks like it didn't work. There's no file to accept.'

'Oh, I bypassed that and put it in a new folder called Rome. It's a subfolder to My Clever Ideas,' Mercedes replied. 'It's the file called missing data.'

Danny laughed. 'Nice try, but my security protocols would have...'

Mercedes smiled demurely. 'Have you found it?'

'Yes,' Danny snapped. He started flicking through the file and whistled before saying, 'There's almost a hundred names on here.'

'Can I see,' Zym asked, holding out his hand.

Danny handed over his tablet, and Zym started skimming through the file.

'Is there anyone linked to the missing Shadowers?' Max asked.

'It's hard to say. Some of us use variations of our original names, and others change their human names with each host like I do,' Zym replied.

'So that's not telling us anything, then?' Max said.

'I didn't say that. There's a Paulie Lace, a Kendra Tailor, and a couple of others whose first names match those who came with us. What did you say your dad's name was?' Zym asked, looking at Bobby.

'Simon Morris, Sir.'

'Here he is. Simon Morris, aged forty-three, from South Yarra, Melbourne, Australia,' Zym said.

'Bobby, are you okay?' Chris asked.

'Bobster, what's wrong? You've gone white,' Danny said, looking concerned.

'Where does it say he's working?' Bobby demanded.

'It doesn't say anything more than what I've said' Zym replied.

'Pass my tablet,' Danny demanded, holding out his hands.

Zym passed it over, and Danny started studying the file. He looked at Mercedes and said, 'What are the other files you sent me?'

'I've not gone through them all. I just did a data grab. I know the one was a list of experts they said they were trying to get to join the company. Having industry experts can boost a company's value, but it must also be flagged during due diligence as a potential risk, as they might not agree to work for the new owners,' Mercedes explained.

Danny started flicking through some files but then paused. 'Chief, what was your first name on Earth, and what is your real name?'

'I was Maxoraxin, sorry, I mean Maxohal, when I left Zephyrion, then I was Gaius when I arrived on your planet,' Max said.

'There's no Gaius on here,' Danny said. 'What was your full name?'

'Gaius was your host's name, not yours,' Zym insisted

'Sorry, I thought that's what Danny wanted. My first name in a shell was Maximus Janus.'

'What was yours, Zym?' Danny asked.

'Xymenos Fabius,' Zym replied. 'The first name is Greek, but it was the closest I could find. After that, I gave up using names like mine and started using names I liked. Oh, and my Zephyrion name was Zymraxin.'

'Then you guys are in trouble,' Danny said, turning his tablet around.

Max grabbed the tablet and started reading it. 'It's got Maxohal, Maximus Janus, Maxwell Thomas and several other names I've used. The last entry says "Lost near Cambridge," and it's in the last twelve months!'

'What does it say about me?' Zym asked.

'Zymraxin, waste of time,' Max laughed.

'Hilarious, Junior. Give me that,' Zym said, grabbing Danny's tablet.

'Obviously changing names helps. It's got Zymraxin and then Xymenos, but besides Sir William Hamilton and Felice Orsini, they don't have any other names I've used,' Zym said. 'Max, what was Lucraxin's earth name?'

'Lucius Balbus, I think.'

'He's here too,' Zym said. 'Whoever wrote this list knows everyone who came to this planet when we did, and they have others with Zephyrion names, too.'

'Excuse me,' Mercedes said to Zym. 'Did you say you were Sir William Hamilton? As in one of Lord Nelson's closest friends?'

'Yeah. Harry was a good lad. He liked a glass or six of wine and enjoyed a spot of gambling, but I never lost a game of cards to him,' Zym replied.

'Between you and Max, you could write a whole set of bestselling books on the history of mankind since Roman times,' Chris said.

'Now, why didn't I think of that?' Max laughed, winking at Danny.

'Look, this may be funny to you guys, but can we get back to my dad?' Bobby demanded. 'How can he be working for M Bank Research when he died more than five years ago?'

'It might not be your dad, lad,' Zym said.

'Oh no, of course, silly me. There are hundreds or thousands of forty-three-year-old men called Simon Morris who come from South Yarra, right?'said Bobby sarcastically.

'Zym, does the file with Bobby's dad's name have a Zephyrion name against his?' Max asked.

'Nope. That file just gives the name, age and where they're from. Like Juli Fellowes, thirty-six years old, Rhode Island, USA.'

'So where do we go from here?' Chris asked.

'We need to break into that technology centre and go through their files,' Zym said. 'There must be some clues in there.'

'Chief, you did say Zym is your older brother, didn't you?' Danny asked.

'Yeah, why?'

'That would explain why he thinks it's the last century,' Danny replied. 'Who breaks into buildings nowadays to check out a company's data?'

'So what do you suggest, Wheels?' Zym grumbled.

Danny held up his tablet, 'Hacking, of course. Although hacking is such a nasty word—'

'And illegal,' Mercedes added.

'Exactly,' Danny replied. 'I prefer calling it a gentle stroll through their systems to test their security.'

'That sounds like hacking with a pretty bow on it,' Max replied.

'How dare you, Chief. I'm duty-bound as part of my due diligence work to test their systems,' Danny laughed.

'How do we do it then, Wheels?' Zym asked.

'Well, since you asked. I—' Danny started to say.

Max kicked Zym under the table. 'Never, ever ask Danny how to do something unless you want your brain to melt.'

'I was only going to say we could use a secure VPN and hunt for a vulnerable access point which we enter via the Tor network. I've done it before, haven't I, Chief?' Danny said. 'It's low risk, and our IP is untraceable. We'll be in and out without leaving a trace.'

'An interesting but overly simplistic approach,' Mercedes said.

'Oh, I'm sorry. I forgot to check with our translating actuary,' Danny smirked.

Mercedes paused, leant back in her chair, and stared at Danny.

Danny squirmed; he was expecting a verbal fight, and the silence unnerved him. 'What do you suggest then?'

Mercedes smiled and leaned forward. She sipped her drink and put her glass back on the table. 'While helping their HR Director, I briefly looked at their security protocols and network architecture. They've got a multi-layered security approach, and their edge routers use strict access controls and stateful packet inspection.'

Danny laughed, 'Oh, give me something challenging. Their VoIP is running an old version of Asterisk, which everyone knows is vulnerable.'

'That's good to know, but they use an AI-driven SIEM with behavioural analytics. There'd be sirens going off if there were any unusual traffic patterns,' Mercedes replied.

'What about exploiting a zero-day in their SCADA systems? I've been working on a rootkit which could do it. But how can we deliver it?'

'Their HR software is from a third-party supplier using an outdated certificate validation in their VPN,' Mercedes said.

Zym frowned. 'Isn't a VPN a visible pant—'

'No, it's not,' Max said quickly. 'It's a virtual private network. It keeps data sent over the internet secure. Now hush.'

'Brilliant. I could write a polymorphic code that alters its signature on each transmission,' Danny said. 'It'll avoid triggering their intrusion systems.'

'We'll need to include a dead man's switch and a self-destruct routine,' Mercedes added.

'How about setting up a simpler routine that double backs on itself?' Danny suggested.

'That's the most intelligent suggestion you've made. We keep their security team focused elsewhere,' Mercedes replied.

'So come on then,' Zym said. 'Let's do it now.'

'Blimey, you're as bad as your brother. It'll take a few days to set this up,' Danny replied.

'But we've only got two more days of due diligence,' Chris said.

'Chris is right. It'll be a lot easier to get this onto their network from the inside, even if that HR software has an out-of-date certificate,' Danny said.

'If we work through tonight and maybe tomorrow night, I could upload it on our last day,' Mercedes suggested.

'You can't work for three days without sleep,' Max insisted.

'We can always sleep and work in shifts,' Mercedes said.

'I've got a suite, so that could work,' Danny replied.

'Come on then,' Mercedes said, standing up.

'Blimey, Chris. Your sister is so bossy,' Danny said, reversing his chair and heading after Mercedes.

'You've only known her a few months. Try putting up with that your entire life,' Chris moaned as the rest of the group headed after Mercedes and Danny.

9
BREAKFAST ANYONE?

'Guys, it's seven thirty; we need to grab some breakfast,' Chris said as he and Bobby walked into the suite's living room after showering.

'Yeah, um, go without me. I'm not hungry,' Danny insisted, tapping away on his laptop.

'Mercedes, are you coming?' Bobby asked.

'Yes, no, grab me a ham or cheese bagel or something,' Mercedes said, staring at her screen.

Ten minutes later, Bobby and Chris sat in the hotel restaurant. Bobby was tucking into his fruit bowl while Chris ate a full English breakfast.

'Why can't anyone other than the Danes or English make proper bacon,' Chris moaned.

'What I'd give for a proper fry-up,' Max replied.

'I need to watch my figure,' Bobby replied. 'I used to have a swimmer's physique. But I'm getting fat.'

'Bobby, if you get any skinnier, you'll fall down a drain,' Max said.

'I don't think I'll ever get used to you two conversing in the same body,' Chris laughed.

'I've never got used to anything Maxo has to say,' a voice said behind Chris.

Chris turned to see a familiar face. 'Hi, Zym.'

'What's happening with our computer experts?' Zym asked. 'Actually, where are they?'

'Morning Zym. They're glued to their screens,' Max replied.

'Have they hacked into the system then?'

'Not yet. You'll know when Danny succeeds as he'll want to tell you how clever he was,' Max laughed.

'Unless Mercedes gets in first. I swear, since she first met Danny, her mission has been to beat him,' Chris said.

'They do seem like a competitive pair,' Zym agreed. 'Anyway, I can't stop; I'm the duty chef this morning.'

'When the hell did you learn to cook? You used to burn water back on Zephyrion,' Max asked.

'A great chef inspired me.'

'That's nice, but I wouldn't call myself a great chef. Maybe a good one, but not great,' Max replied.

'Not you, you numpty. I mean Jean Parmentier, the sixteenth-century French chef. He always said to use fresh local ingredients for the season. I used to supply him with vegetables, and one day, he got me cooking, and it went from there. Anyway, let me know if they manage to hack in and get anything,' Zym said, rushing off.

'You look a bit crushed,' Chris said, looking at Bobby's face.

'No, I'm fine,' Max replied quickly, watching his brother head through the kitchen doors.

A while later, Bobby and Chris headed back to Danny's suite, with Chris carrying a bacon roll wrapped in serviettes and a wrapped ham and cheese bagel.

'Maybe this coffee will stop Danny complaining,' Bobby said.

'The look on that waiter's face when you asked for two double espressos in one disposable cup,' Chris laughed.

As they reached the entrance to Danny's suite, Bobby tapped the card, opened the door, and heard a scream. He rushed into the suite, followed by Chris, and saw Danny and Mercedes hugging and screaming excitedly.

'Hey, are we interrupting something?' Chris asked, putting the food down on the coffee table.

Danny and Mercedes turned to see Chris and Bobby staring at them with their mouths open. Then they turned back and looked at each other for what seemed like an eternity but was barely a second, their faces only an inch or so apart.

Mercedes let go of her embrace of Danny and backed away, while Danny moved his chair back into sitting mode.

'Oh, uh, we've cracked it,' Mercedes said.

Danny coughed awkwardly and then added, 'Yeah, we've found a way in using the coding we've done.'

'It looks like that's not the only thing you've found,' Chris said, looking at Danny and Mercedes, who were both getting redder in the face.

'Bobster, is that my coffee? And will you shut your mouth,' Danny muttered.

'Yeah, but, uh, you and Mercedes were...' Bobby mumbled as he handed the drinks to Danny and Mercedes.

'No, we weren't,' Danny insisted as he took the lid off his drink, realised it was hot chocolate with cream on, and swapped it with the one Mercedes was holding.

'No, you weren't, what?' Chris asked.

'We weren't whatever it was Bobby thought we were,' Danny protested.

'*I told you they fancied each other*,' Max thought smugly.

'*Alright, Cowboy. You were right,*' Bobby conceded.

Chris turned to Bobby, 'What were you thinking they were doing?'

'Never mind that. Why do you look smug, Bobste...no, sorry, that's the Chief looking smug, isn't it?' Danny said, crossing his arms.

'Me?' Max replied. 'I'm just observing events.'

'Well, there's nothing to see here. We were just celebrating cracking the coding,' Danny huffed.

'Of course you were,' Max smiled.

'Besides, me and Mercedes? Really? Yuck, no way,' Danny grimaced.

Mercedes glowered at Danny. 'I'm sorry, but I think you'll find you're no catch.'

'Oh, here it comes. Because I'm differently-abled, nobody would want me,' Danny snapped.

'I couldn't care less if you could walk, run or bloody fly,' Mercedes growled, placing her hands on her hips.

'Liar,' Danny shot back. 'Loads of people fancy me. I'm smart, funny and rich. So it must be the wheelchair.'

'You're irritating and spend more time tinkering with gadgets than washing, which means **you stink**. And as for funny, your jokes would make most dads cringe,' Mercedes retorted.

'But I am rich and dress in fashionable clothes,' Danny replied, straightening his shirt.

'No, your dad is rich. Your clothes need a wash more than you do, and when did you last comb your hair?'

Danny ran his fingers through his wild hair, trying to flatten it and smiled. 'There, is that better?'

Mercedes raised an eyebrow, her tone softening. 'A little. But you still stink.'

'If I go for a shower, will you wash my back?' Danny asked, grinning cheekily.

'In your dreams, Mr Perfect.' Mercedes smirked.

'Mr Perfect Genius, actually,' Danny replied, laughing.

'Go and shower, Mr Far From Perfect,' Mercedes replied. 'I'm off to my room to clean up and change.'

As Danny headed towards the bathroom and the suite door slammed behind Mercedes, Chris looked at Bobby.

'Was that an argument, or were they flirting?'

'I'm over two thousand of your Earth years old, and I still can't understand humans.'

Half an hour later, Danny returned to the room to find Bobby and Chris lounging on a sofa.

'Come on, dullards, we need to get moving.'

'Is that a silk shirt?' Bobby asked, noting Danny wore a tailored blue shirt and black designer jeans.

'This old thing?' Danny replied nonchalantly. 'Yeah, I've had it ages.'

'Also, does your shower use water or aftershave?' Chris asked.

'Oh, is it too much? Mum got me it for Christmas. It's popular with catwalk models, apparently.'

'You smell and look great. I'm sure it'll be appreciated,' Bobby smiled.

The buzzer to the suite went off, and Bobby answered it.

'Are you guys ready?' Mercedes said, striding into the room.

'Oh, blimey. Mercedes looks stunning. That tailored black suit and white top with her red hair is a stunning look,' Max thought.

'She smells divine. If I wasn't gay, I could even fancy her.'

'Well, come on, guys. The coach is due downstairs in ten minutes,' Mercedes said confidently. She looked at Danny, but her expression barely flickered. 'Have you loaded the code onto a stick?'

Danny stopped staring at Mercedes and headed to his laptop. 'Give me thirty seconds.'

Mercedes walked over to her laptop, took off her ring, flipped out the USB connector and said, 'I'll do it. It'll be easier if it's on my ring.'

'Okay,' Danny replied, closing his laptop and sliding it into a pocket on his chair.

'Just distract the HR Director for five minutes,' Mercedes said.

'How?' Chris asked.

'I don't know,' Mercedes snapped. 'Tell her you love her. Say you need to speak to her in private or something.'

'I'm gay!'

'I'm hungry, so what! Just get her out of the room for a few minutes.'

'What if I pretend to be ill?'

'Fine, just get her out of here.'

'How do I say I'm ill in Italian? Is it, Io no bene?'

Mercedes sighed and walked over to the HR Director. 'Mi scusi, ma mio fratello non si sente bene perché ha mangiato troppo. Potrebbe gentilmente portarlo dal medico aziendale?'

She walked back to Chris and said, 'Pretend you have stomach cramps.'

Chris held his stomach, and as the HR Director approached, he started groaning.

'Come this way,' the HR Director said, helping Chris to stand.

'Ohhh... my stomach hurts so bad.'

All the way to the door, Chris kept making loud noises. 'It's like knives—ohhh, it's so—ah.'

The HR Director kept encouraging Chris to stand up straight, but he let out another exaggerated moan. Chris clutched his stomach again as they reached the door and bent forward.

Chris turned to look at Mercedes and winked before disappearing through the door, assisted by the HR Director.

Mercedes rolled her eyes. *And the award for the worst performance in a starring role goes to Chris Medici,* she thought.

Mercedes walked over to the HR Director's desk, pulled off her ring, and flipped out the connector, putting it into the laptop. A box popped up on the screen, showing the time to upload. After a minute she thought, '*Why is this taking so long?*'

Mercedes heard voices and footsteps coming down the corridor. She looked around desperately and spotted one of the paper files she was working on with the list of key personnel. She rushed to her desk and grabbed it, but the office door started to open. Mercedes tried to run back to the HR Director's desk but tripped and flew across the room, knocking over a chair.

'Mercedes, are you okay?' Bobby asked.

'Oh, flipping hell. I thought you were Antonella. She's taken Chris to see the company medic,' Mercedes said as she stood up and brushed herself down.

'Is he okay?'

'Yeah, it's just a distraction so I can upload our code. Why are you here?'

'Danny's dad has asked all the due diligence team to meet in the boardroom at noon,' Bobby said. 'I offered to let everyone know.'

Mercedes glanced at Antonella's laptop and saw the upload was at seventy-eight percent. 'I think the code we put in to prevent detection is slowing down the upload.'

'Never mind that your nose is bleeding, and you've cut your head,' Bobby replied.

A voice behind Bobby said, 'Scusi, questo è il mio ufficio. Posso aiutarla?'

Bobby heard Max thinking, '*Excuse me, that is my office? Can I help you?*'

Turning to face Antonella, Max replied, 'Mi scusi, faccio parte del team di due diligence e stavo informando Mercedes.'

'*That's quick thinking, saying, "We're part of the due diligence team and briefing Mercedes",*' Bobby said.

'*What do you mean, buddy? We are part of the DD team briefing Mercedes about the boardroom meeting,*' Max replied.

'*Oh, yeah.*'

Mercedes glanced at the laptop screen, which said the upload was at eighty-nine percent. 'Hi, Antonella. How's Chris?'

'The dok-tore is looking after him.'

Mercedes looked at Bobby, then down at the laptop, before staring back at him, her eyes widening in a silent plea.

'Um, Antonella, Mr White was wondering if you have data on how many, erm, what the breakdown of, uh, employee diversity is?' Bobby stuttered.

'Sì, sì, certo. I mean, yes, of course,' Antonella replied. 'I'll upload it on my laptop.'

The laptop screen showed ninety-seven percent.

Mercedes moved in front of Antonella and started picking up the paperwork she had dropped when she tripped.

'Mercedes, can I get to my laptop to get the data for Mr White, please?'

'Yes, of course. I just need to get these papers. Oh, can you grab those papers over there?' Mercedes asked.

Antonella picked up the stray papers behind her and handed them to Mercedes. 'Now, please, I need my laptop,' she insisted.

Mercedes dumped the papers onto the laptop keyboard and noticed it had changed from uploading to finalising. 'Of course, Antonella,' Mercedes said, knocking a pen onto the floor.

Antonella bent to pick up the pen as the laptop screen said, 'Upload Complete.'

Mercedes sighed, hit return on the keyboard to remove the message, and then lifted the papers while discreetly removing her ring from the laptop.

'Let me get out of your way,' Mercedes said, smiling and stepping away from Antonella's desk.

'Thank you,' Antonella said. She tapped on her computer and said, 'Here it is. Shall I email it to you?'

'Yeah, sure, it's BobbyMorrisMax@gmail.com,' Bobby replied.

'It's on the way,' Antonella replied.

'Thanks. Come on, Mercedes, we need to go,' Bobby said.

A few minutes later, Bobby and Mercedes were heading towards the boardroom.

'You should have given your WestFi email,' Mercedes said.

'Paul didn't even ask for the data, so giving my personal email is the least of our problems.'

Ahead of them, they spot Chris walking towards them.

'Don't ever ask me to do that again!' Chris said, looking at Mercedes.

'I just said act like you've got stomach cramps,' Mercedes replied.

'Why couldn't you say I had a migraine? I've had a doctor put his finger in a place neither of us wanted it, followed by tablets which... well... as soon as they kicked in, I thought my insides were being dumped into the loo,' Chris said.

'TMI, mate,' Bobby replied.

'Huh?' Chris said.

'Too much information,' Bobby said.

'Besides, you did overact the stomach pains,' Mercedes insisted.

'You told me to be a distraction with stomach cramps,' Chris protested.

'Yes, a distraction. You acted like you were dying,' Mercedes said.

'Never mind that. Did the upload work?' Max asked.

Mercedes checked her phone and smiled. 'It looks like we have full access.'

Everyone's phone bleeped.

'Who the heck are "The Halfwits plus one?"' Chris asked.

'That'll be a Dannyism,' Bobby replied as he opened the group message.

Danny

> Hey dullards. Connection confirmed.
> I'm stalking their data

Bobby

> We're coming to the boardroom. C U in 2

Danny

> I'm not gonna be there. Dad's got me
> working on something

A few minutes later, they sat in the depressingly dull boardroom.

'I thought Italians were all about style?' Chris moaned as he looked around the magnolia-painted room with a large antique wooden table dominating the centre of it.

'I know, not a single picture, mirror, or decoration in here. Not even a television. Just a projector onto a blank wall,' Mercedes agreed.

'Who's the woman between Big Bill and Paul White?' Bobby whispered to Chris.

'That's Jay.'

'As in, the owner of WestFi?' Bobby asked with surprise.

'Yeah, this must be big if she's here.'

Over the next two hours, Paul and Big Bill reviewed the latest due diligence reports, with Jay sitting quietly listening.

'Thank you everyone. Y'all have done some fantastic work,' Big Bill said. 'Normally, I'd be sayin' we're halfway through, so get back to it, but our friend here has an announcement,' Bill continued, gesturing for Paul to stand.

As Paul stood, he said, 'Thanks, Bill. I want to echo Bill's appreciation for your hard work to everyone here. However, events have taken a new twist, and we can end this part of the process early.'

There was a groan from the DD team.

Paul raised his hands. 'It's not bad news, my friends. The deal is very much on, but it means you get this afternoon...' Paul glanced at his watch, 'Okay, you get the last couple of hours of today and all of tomorrow until your evening flights as free time to explore Rome.'

The groan turned into a cheer.

Paul looked around the room, smiling. 'Don't worry, we'll let you make up the time when we complete the deal. It's going to get crazy.'

The room burst into laughter.

Paul reached into his pocket and pulled out a scrap of paper. 'Now for the bad news. As some of you may have noticed, there has been a remarkable absence of heckling from our resident computer expert, also known as my son, Danny.'

'Thought I'd gone deaf,' someone in the team shouted as the room burst into laughter again.

'Indeed,' Paul replied. Paul glanced down at his son's scrawled list of names, 'Danny is working on some technology for me, and he's asked for help from the following three people. So, I'm sorry, Bobby Morris, Mercedes Medici and Chris Medici, you'll have to explore Rome some other time.'

Paul bent and whispered something to Jay, and she shook her head, clearly unwilling to do whatever Paul had asked.

Paul straightened up, 'Thank you, everyone. Enjoy the rest of your time in Rome. Bobby, Mercedes, and Chris, there's a car waiting outside the reception to take you to Danny.'

10
THE TAKOVER

'Mr White, Mr Marchent is here,' the secretary said.

'Thank you, Erzsébet,' Paul replied. 'Show him in.'

'Mr White will see you now,' Erzsébet said, escorting Stephen Marchent into the meeting room.

'Paul, good to see you. Oh, you have company,' Stephen said.

'Sorry, Stephen, I should have warned you. You know Big Bill, and this is Zara Shah. Her family own WestFi,' Paul replied.

'Please call me Jay. My grandfather was called Jay, and he used to call me Jay Junior.'

'I'm very pleased to meet you, Jay, and Bill; it's always a pleasure,' Stephen said.

'Good to see ya, Stephen,' Bill drawled. 'I hear you've got yourself a new lady?'

'Yes. I met her at a football event. She's lovely, and she's got two adorable children. Especially her five-year-old daughter.'

'Is that all, Mr White?' Erzsébet asked.

'Thank you, Erzsébet. I'll let you know if we need anything.'

'Can I get you a drink?' Paul asked, walking across the room.

'I'll have an espresso and a water, please.'

After sorting out the drinks, Paul sat down and said, 'Terry tells me that you're looking for a twenty-five percent increase in our offer.'

'Even at that price, you're getting a bargain. Bluestone is here next week, and Spearhead have already made an improved offer,' Stephen insisted.

'But if Spearhead has already made a better offer, why are we here?' Paul challenged.

'Because I'm confident in what we've discovered, and I knew that once you saw it, you'd realise its potential,' Stephen replied.

'Really? I heard that Spearhead said they'd take a minority shareholding until you can prove the technology, and Bluestone was spooked by Innovest backtracking on their research, claiming it may have been contaminated,' Paul said assuredly.

'That's just a communication error. I'm waiting to speak to Innovest's new CEO. But there's been no announcement about who that is since they were taken over,' Stephen said hesitantly.

'Then our offer stands,' Paul replied.

'But luminae will transform the energy industry. No more national grids or expensive infrastructure,' Stephen insisted.

'Stephen, you're a good guy and believe in the business, but M Bank's a busted flush. If it weren't for that mineral discovery by the M Bank Research folks, it'd be done for,' Big Bill said.

'But it's not just the energy we can transform. If we can stabilise the energy extraction, we could turn humans into energy, ending illness and mortality.'

Jay leant forward and smiled. 'Mr Marchent, my Dada, sorry, I mean my grandfather, built this business on facts, not hopes. Ifs don't pay the bills. If I could see the future, I wouldn't need to manage risks. I can only base my valuation on what I can see.'

Paul's phone pinged, and he checked the message.

Danny

Dad it works

Paul sighed and looked at Stephen. 'It seems Innovest are even more unsure of the mineral's ability. Plus, you've found such a small quantity of it; it'll soon run out.'

Stephen glanced at his phone. The wallpaper picture of Pat and Lily was a comfort but also a pressure on him to secure their future. 'Okay, my final offer is fifteen percent more.'

'Stephen, you're not listening. I should be saying twenty percent less,' Paul insisted.

'Come on, Paul. Despite what Innovest might be saying, you know this will transform the world.'

'Stephen, I like you, and I know Bobby's mum has had a rough time since her first husband died. I'll up our offer by two percent,' Paul smiled.

Paul's phone pinged again.

Danny

It's powering everything

Paul glanced at his phone, shook his head and whispered the message to Bill.

'Five percent, and we have a deal,' Stephen said.

Paul smiled. 'Stephen, I don't want to argue over the last nickel and dime, so I'll meet you in the middle. Three percent, and we're done.'

'Okay, we have a deal,' Stephen replied.

'Great. I'll get the paperwork drawn up,' Paul said, standing and shaking hands with Stephen.

'Stephen, always a pleasure,' Bill said with a nod.

Jay stood up and shook Stephen's hand. 'Mr Marchent, welcome to the WestFi family. I look forward to working with you.'

'Well, if I'm part of the family, you should call me Stephen.'

'Of course, Stephen. Now, don't let us keep you. I'm sure you have much to do,' Jay replied.

Once Stephen had left the room, Bill exclaimed, 'Hotdog, Paul! I was convinced you'd have to go twenty percent higher.'

Jay looked equally impressed. 'Even by your standards, that was some deal. How did you know he'd drop the inflated price?'

'I had some help from my son and his friends,' Paul laughed. 'Bobby overheard Stephen offering Terry a payoff if he managed to get an extra fifteen percent.'

'Loose lips lose deals,' Bill said with a smile. 'But how'd you get wind of Spearhead's offer?'

'The reason Marchent couldn't speak to Innovest's new CEO, me until midnight tomorrow night, is because I've been organising its sale,' Paul said.

'I don't understand,' Jay said.

'I bought Innovest for two reasons. The first was obviously to prevent the news of M Bank's discovery being corroborated,' Paul answered.

'And the second reason?' Jay asked.

'Because Bluestone and Spearhead have been after it for years. That's why Marchent chose them. He's clever, I'll give him that. He knew if Innovest confirmed his claims, the news would get to Bluestone and Spearhead.'

'But how did you get them to agree to sell to you?' Jay asked.

'I did a deal with the previous owners to buy a fifty-one percent share on the promise of a fifty-fifty split of any profits I make on a subsequent sale in the next two years,' Paul said. 'I started talking to Bluestone and Spearhead the same day I took control of Innovest. In the end, they agreed to use a special-purpose vehicle to acquire Innovest, and they'll split ownership of the SPV with some of their investors. I think a ten percent return on my eleven-day investment isn't too shabby.'

'And knowin' you, Paul, you casually got 'em to spill the beans about their interest in M Bank,' Bill laughed.

'I think that's what they call insider trading,' Jay said.

'Merely bending the rules in our favour,' Paul replied. 'Talking of which, how did your meeting with the Prime Minister go?'

'He agrees that having the International Federation for Fiscal Security approving UK budgets would prevent the financial markets from bringing down his government as it has done previously,' Jay replied.

'So, that means the IFFS's runnin' the UK? Well, your PM did say he prefers Zermatt to Westminster,' Bill said.

'Another country that sees sense in letting us manage their risks,' Jay laughed.

'I'm off to Innovest to see how Danny's getting on. What are you up to?' Paul asked

'We've got a meeting with the Deputy Chair of the IFFS, Andrew Daks. He's been chosen to replace Pietr Van den Berg as Chair,' Jay replied.

'We're headin' to Switzerland in a couple hours to break the news to him,' Bill said.

'He doesn't know?' Paul asked, surprised.

'Nah. He knew Pietr was retirin' 'cause of health problems, but we picked Andrew since he'll do the right thing,' Bill said.

'He will—unless he wants his husband and the world to see those pictures,' Jay grinned.

'Still managing those risks, huh, guys,' Paul smiled. 'I'd better get to Innovest before Danny blows the place up.'

'Always,' Bill replied. 'And say howdy to your boy. I like his spirit.'

'Go to reception and ask for my driver. Grace will take you wherever you need to go,' Jay offered. 'Just make sure she's heading to Munich in the morning.'

'Don't you need her to take you to the airport?' Paul asked.

'We've got a chopper pickin' us up and takin' us to the airport,' Bill laughed.

As soon as Paul had left the room, Bill asked, 'Why're you lettin' him outsmart Bluestone and Spearhead? Don't get me wrong, I want WestFi to succeed, but you own us and are the major shareholder in the other two.'

Jay laughed. 'It's a fun sport watching my companies try to outsmart each other. Besides, Paul's one of us now.'

* * *

'Why does everything have to be glass and mirrors?' Max sighed as he glanced around the reception. *'Don't architects have any imagination nowadays? What's wrong with wood, stone and marble?'*

'There are marble statues. Look, there's two either side of the main entrance, and they're more than fifteen feet tall. Why do I keep using your old measurements,' Bobby fumed. *'I mean around five metres tall.'*

'Nothing wrong with imperial measurements, buddy. But as for those statues, they're so predictable. Minerva for craftsmanship, skills, innovation and war, and Mercury for commerce, trade, and profit.'

'I like the slogan above reception, "Innovest: Let us innovate your investment,"' Chris said.

'It probably cost them thousands of pounds to pay a marketing agency to come up with their name and that slogan,' Max grumbled.

Ten minutes later, they were escorted to a laboratory. As the door opened, they saw Danny racing around the room in his chair, and all their phones pinged.

Mercedes pulled out her phone. 'My phone says it's charging.'

'And mine,' Bobby said.

'Hey, dullards. Notice anything missing?' Danny asked.

Mercedes paused and looked around the room. 'Aside from your modesty, decorum and manners, there seems to be a lot of devices like lamps and computers working even though they're unplugged.'

'Give that person a medal,' Danny replied.

'Danny, where's your chair battery?' Bobby asked.

'On that counter, Bobster,' Danny said.

'How is this possible?' Chris asked.

'I don't understand how it works, but I know it does,' Danny laughed. 'I just need to text Dad to say it's powering everything.'

'What is the "it" you're saying is doing this?' Mercedes asked.

Danny shot across to a desk in the middle of the room where a stone about the size of a small fist was glowing a pale red. Attached to it were wires leading to two small towers at either end of the room, each topped by a metal dome.

'*I'm sure I've seen one of those before*,' Bobby said, staring at the towers. 'But it was bigger.'

'*We have. Claudia had one to transmit energy through the air for her Daxson*,' Max replied flatly.

'It's that mineral M Bank Research has found—luminae,' Danny said.

'How did you get some?' Chris asked. 'It's kept under heavy security.'

'My dad handed me a small package when Bobster and I were at their technology centre.'

'That still doesn't explain what it's doing,' Mercedes insisted.

'I've connected this luminae rock to a Tesla Tower. It seems to extract electricity and send it across the room,' Danny said.

'It's actually called a Wardenclyffe Tower. Tesla designed it to transmit electricity wirelessly,' Mercedes said.

'I know. I researched it a few months ago after...' Danny glanced at Bobby.

'After a little incident at a power station near Cambridge,' Max sighed.

'That was you guys?' Chris replied. 'You caused a huge explosion, from what I heard.'

'It wasn't that big,' Max said.

'Never mind that. Transmitting energy without wires isn't new, but where is that energy coming from?' Mercedes asked.

'That's the magic,' Danny replied. 'As soon as I wired the luminae up, it started glowing. I assume it has stored electricity like a battery.'

Mercedes rolled her eyes in contempt. 'That makes no sense. I'd say it's more likely that it's extracting radiant energy.'

'That's exactly what it's doing,' Max replied.

'You seem very certain,' Mercedes said.

'I am, and we need to destroy all trace of it,' Max insisted.

'No chance, Chief,' Danny replied. 'This will change everything. Electricity for all.'

'Your dad'll become the richest person in the world,' Chris said.

'This is only going to end one way. The death of so many living things,' Max insisted. 'And the end of your planet.'

'Come on, Chief. Just because your home planet was destroyed, it doesn't mean this technology will be abused on ours,' Danny replied.

'But you and Mercedes have already said, "Electricity for all," and "It's extracting radiant energy," which is just the start,' Max said.

'But radiant energy is almost limitless,' Mercedes protested.

'Yes, but if it starts to farm the electricity too efficiently in concentrated areas, it'll impact natural processes like photosynthesis. Before long, plant growth will slow down and may die. Then it'll be the animals who live off those plants dying.'

'How about we extract it from the atmosphere instead? That way, it could be done evenly across the planet,' Danny suggested.

'Even I can see that's a bad idea,' Mercedes replied. 'That'll interfere with weather patterns and atmospheric chemistry.'

'Exactly,' Bobby said. 'It could cool the planet down to disastrous levels.'

'Err, when did you become an expert on the climate, Bobster?' Danny asked.

'Oh, um, well, I saw it in Max's thoughts,' Bobby said, rubbing his head.

'Are you okay?' Chris asked.

'No, yes, um, I think so... Sorry, I just keep getting confused, and my head hurts.'

'Here, sit down. You look so pale,' Mercedes said, pulling up a chair.

'Can we shut the luminae down? The electromagnetic fields aren't helping,' Max groaned.

'Okay, Chief. Just let me hook my chair—'

Bobby stood up and stumbled over to the glowing luminae, pulling it off the table and throwing it across the room before bellowing, 'I SAID SHUT IT DOWN.'

Bobby collapsed to the floor as Mercedes and Chris ran over to him.

'Is Bobby okay?' Danny asked, still connecting his wheelchair battery.

'I'm not sure. His breathing sounds okay, but his pulse is slow,' Mercedes said, holding Bobby's wrist between her fingers.

Danny powered up his chair and shot across the room. 'Bobby, wake up, please.'

Danny bent over, holding his friend's hand, and noticed it felt hot. He turned Bobby's hand over and noted the burn mark on the palm in the shape of the luminae rock.

'Do we need to get a doctor?' Chris asked.

'I'm a doctor,' Bobby groaned, his eyes flickering open. 'Mr Michael Thoma...'

'He's passed out again,' Mercedes said.

'Who's that doctor he claimed to be?' Chris asked.

'Michael Thomas. He's a lovely guy, and his wife's cooking is amazing,' Danny said.

'So, he's a real person? Why is Bobby saying it's him?' Chris said.

Danny shrugged his shoulders, 'I dunno. Michael was Max's last host. Maybe it's—'

'Where am I?'

'Bobby, lie there for a minute. I'm here with Danny and Chris. You got angry about the luminae, threw it across the room and then collapsed.'

Bobby put his hand to his face in embarrassment. 'Oh, I'm so sorry.'

'Bobster, you got us worried for a minute,' Danny sighed in relief.

Bobby sat up, rubbed his head, and looked around the room. 'Why is it so quiet in here?'

'Someone pulled the plug out,' Danny laughed. 'And I mean, you literally pulled the plug out when you threw the luminae at that TV.'

'I did that?' Bobby asked, looking at the smashed television screen and the lump of dull grey rock on the floor.

'You sure did. Your aim was dead centre of the screen. It never stood a chance,' Chris replied with a smile.

Bobby put his hand across his mouth, embarrassed about what he'd done. 'I hope nobody was hurt?'

'Only you, Bobster. The luminae was hot and burnt your hand.'

Bobby looked down at his hands and turned them over. 'Where was it burned?'

'Blimey, you must have...' Danny's voice trailed off as he turned Bobby's hands over and back again. 'But...I don't understand. You had a bad burn on your right hand, but it's gone. Chief, did you fix it from inside?'

'Not that I know of, Danny,' Max replied. 'Bobby and I were out cold. The last thing I remember was asking you to shut down the luminae.'

'So his body just healed itself?' Mercedes asked.

'Uh, possibly,' Max said. 'When Shadowers first come to Earth, they often don't understand how to control their host's or their shell's DNA. As soon as it gets injured, they'd repair it. It's like a natural defence mechanism. But it also draws attention to you, leading to accusations of witchcraft and sorcery. It can take some Shadowers a while to realise it's not automatic and it's their mind subconsciously doing it. Once they realise that, they learn to stop doing it subconsciously and let the injuries heal naturally. I learnt that lesson when I was an enforcer tracking down Deceptors on other planets.'

'I'd love to hear more about your life. You've seen so much,' Mercedes said.

Max slowly got to his feet. 'Maybe another time. We need to clean this mess up.'

'It's fine. My dad owns Innovest. The cleaners can do it,' Danny replied as he went across the room to retrieve the luminae.

'You know, Danny, for a nice guy, sometimes you really sound like a privileged arse,' Max said as he spotted a vacuum cleaner in the corner of the room and used it to start cleaning up.

'Excuse me, I think you'll find I'm a genius privileged arse, actually,' Danny laughed as he inspected the luminae. 'I can't see any damage done.'

Mercedes started checking some of the computers by plugging them in and switching them on. 'These seem okay. Which machine were you using to link to M Bank?'

'My dad,' Bobby shouted. 'Have you found him?'

'I haven't had chance to start viewing the data yet. Dad needed me to test the luminae first.'

'Which computer were you using, Danny? I'll have a look,' Mercedes said.

'I didn't use any of their computers. I used my laptop over there,' Danny replied, waving towards a desk at the far end of the room.

'They must have found our code as the link has been terminated,' Mercedes said, looking at the laptop screen.

'That's okay; I ran a data download into my secure cloud safe,' Danny said smugly. 'I'll come and log you in.'

'It's fine, I'm in,' Mercedes replied.

Danny shot across the room and pushed Mercedes out of the way. 'How the heck?'

'It wasn't difficult. You left the access open to do the download,' Mercedes laughed.

'I've waited ages to say this,' Max laughed. 'You've got an ID ten T fault.'

'Very flipping funny,' Danny snapped.

'What's an ID ten thingy?' Chris asked.

Max wrote ID10T on a whiteboard.

'I'm using that,' Chris chuckled.

'Can we shut up and find my dad,' Bobby insisted.

'I am looking, Bobster,' Danny replied.

'Here's a folder called "Project ET." The files refer to the acquisition of a small business called TransEnergi. There's an employee list,' Danny said.

'Who's on there?' Chris asked.

'Hang on, the list isn't alphabetical, and it contains a lot of rubbish about potential integration or duplication with existing M Bank employees,' Danny replied.

'Like what?' Max asked.

'Well, there's a Juli Fellowes. It says she is a scientist with specialist skills in advanced laser projection,' Danny said. 'It says she was hired due to no matching skills in M Bank and is now based in Zermatt.'

'But M Bank don't have offices in Zermatt,' Mercedes said.

'Yes they do. They have a team supporting the IFFS there,' Chris replied.

'I never saw anything about that,' Mercedes insisted.

'Yeah, it was in one of the due diligence reports I worked on.' Chris said.

'Sorry, I'm sure Juli is a very nice person, but what about my dad?' Bobby said firmly.

'He's here, Bobster. Simon Morris, a senior engineer from South Yarra, Melbourne. Skill set duplicates multiple M Bank senior engineers and not offered employment,' Danny said. 'Sorry, mate. It seems he wasn't taken on.'

'Maybe that's why he was involved in a car accident. He was losing his job following the takeover of his employer, and he was distracted when the car hit him,' Chris suggested.

'I guess,' Bobby sighed. 'I was sure he was still alive.'

'*I'm sorry, buddy. I wish he was still alive, too. I'd have loved to meet him,*' Max thought.

'It says he was offered a significant settlement. Whatever that means,' Danny said.

'That's company speak for him being offered more to leave than his contract or the law entitled him to,' Chris said.

'I can hear voices,' Max said. 'It's Paul saying, "He'll be thrilled to see you."'

'Who's he talking to?' Danny asked.

'My mum!' Bobby replied in shock.

The door to the room opened, and Paul White and Pat Morris walked in.

'Hey, Champ. How's your trip been?'

'Mum, what're you doing here?' Bobby said in mock surprise.

'Stephen said he was coming to Rome and thought we could join him and make a family holiday out of it.'

'But why are you *here*?'

'I ran into your mum in our hotel foyer and asked if she fancied seeing you working,' Paul said.

'Where's Lily?' Bobby asked, glancing around.

'Stephen took her to the Villa Borghese for ice cream and the rides,' Pat said. 'I'm going there after seeing you. Come with me.'

'I'm working,' Bobby protested, wishing he could spend time with her.

Paul smiled. 'I'm sure we can spare you, Bobby.'

Bobby hesitated. The thought of exploring Rome with his mum and sister, with Max as his internal guide, was so tempting.

But the idea of Stephen being there, especially after just discussing his father, was too much. 'Thank you, Mr—Paul. But we have some things to finish off. I'll catch up with Mum tomorrow when I'm on holiday.'

'Well, if you're sure,' Paul replied before turning to Danny. 'The luminae works then, son?'

'Better than we thought, Dad.' Danny replied before explaining everything that had happened, while Paul confirmed he had sealed the deal to acquire M Bank.

'It seems your dad and my Stephen are going into business together, which makes us one big family,' Pat said to Danny.

The phrase "my Stephen" made Bobby cringe.

'I need to go and, err, get some papers,' Bobby said. 'Love you, Mum.'

Pat watched her son all but run out of the room. 'Love you more, Champ.'

11
HOLIDAY

'Max, how are you, sweetheart?' Avery asked, running towards Bobby and throwing her arms around him at Rome's Fiumicino airport arrivals.

'Hi, Avery. I'm doing well, but it's been a crazy time,' Max replied.

'Bobby, how wonderful to see you!' Mrs Moore said warmly as Avery's parents caught up with her.

'Err, hello, Mrs Moore,' Bobby replied sheepishly.

Avery's father leaned forward, lowered his voice and half-whispered conspiratorially, 'We're glad she's seeing you again. Her last boyfriend... well, he wasn't quite right for her.'

'Dad! Rahul was only twenty-three,' Avery protested.

'Exactly, beta. He was too old for you. You're only eighteen,' Mr. Moore said firmly. 'Bobby is much more suitable.'

'*If only she knew, huh, Cowboy,*' Bobby said.

'*Physically, I'm the same age as you. I admit mentally I'm almost two thousand one hundred years old, but Avery is mature for her age,*' Max replied.

'Queen Elizabeth the First could be mature for her age, but you'd still be ancient to her,' Bobby laughed.

'You can hardly take the high ground. You used to date Avery even though you're gay!'

'I was bisexual at the time, actually.'

'Of course you were,' Max laughed.

'Where's the rest of the gang?' Avery asked.

'Danny is doing some work for his dad. Adam can't make it because of his football team, and Abi has gone backpacking across Australia, but Dazza is coming,' Bobby replied.

'Is Dazza still dating Abi? I've not caught up with them for weeks,' Avery asked.

'Yeah, he's besotted. He wanted to go with her, but his new job meant he couldn't get a month off.'

'I think your friend is coming,' Mr Moore said.

'But you've never seen him, Baba,' Avery said.

'From how you've described him, beta, I can't imagine many six-foot-four men with ginger hair towering over everyone else in the airport,' her father smiled.

Avery and Bobby turned to see Dazza scanning over the heads of the other travellers.

Avery started waving. 'Dazza, over here.'

Dazza spotted Avery and came marching through the crowd. 'Hey, Avery. Howdy, Bob. How's things?' Dazza asked.

'I'm good,' Bobby replied.

Avery hugged Dazza, 'Great to see you, Dazza. How's Abi?'

'She's loving Australia. She's done the Sunshine Coast, Brisbane and Byron Bay, and now she's in Sydney before heading to Melbourne in a day or two,' Dazza explained.

Avery's dad coughed.

'Oh, sorry, Dazza. These are my parents.'

Dazza held out his hand. 'Mr Moore, Mrs Moore, I'm pleased to meet you.'

'You too, Dazza. Please call us Ravi and Anjali,' Ravi replied, shaking Danny's hand.

'Is there anywhere to eat around here? I'm starving,' Dazza said.

'Our apartment is near the Villa Borghese on the Piazza di Spagna. So we can drop our bags off and walk into town for lunch,' Ravi said.

'Ravi, let the youngsters go on their own. They don't need us oldies tagging along, yaar,' Anjali replied.

A short while later, they stood by the windows of the rented apartment, looking out at the bustling piazza.

'Where's the swimming pool?' Avery asked.

'Arre, Anjali, did you hear our daughter? She has a six-bedroom apartment overlooking the Spanish Steps, and now she wants a swimming pool too!' Ravi sighed.

'Sorry, Pappa. I just thought it had a pool. But this is beautiful,' Avery said, hugging her father. 'Thank you.'

'You know we're only here for a week, beta? This isn't our new home,' Ravi laughed.

'I don't understand,' Dazza said, looking out of the window with Bobby beside him.

'Don't understand what, big man?' Bobby asked.

'I thought Rome was in Italy,' Dazza said, frowning.

'It is, buddy,' Max replied.

'But Ravi said they're the Spanish Steps. Is Rome on the border of Spain and Italy? Are the steps the border?'

'No. They're named that because of the Spanish Embassy over there,' Max replied, pointing across the piazza.

'So Spain's not in Rome?'

'No, Dazza. Spain is a big country across the Med,' Max replied.

'Oh, it's in Africa—'

'Guys, come and choose your bedrooms,' Avery said.

'The boy's bedrooms are down that end, and ours are up this way,' Ravi said with a determined smile.

'Yes, Pappa Ji,' Avery replied, dragging Bobby and Dazza down the corridor.

'These bedrooms are huge,' Bobby said, looking around the third bedroom.

The eight-foot-high ceiling seemed to stretch away above them, exaggerated by the long dark columns of brown from the curtains, the tall windows and the chocolate brown feature wall contrasting against the other three pale cream walls. Opposite the bed was a four-foot-wide floor-to-ceiling mirror, further accentuating the room's height.

'I'm having this one,' Dazza said, kicking off his shoes and flopping onto the bed. 'This bed's huge. I can sleep without my feet hanging off.'

'Dazza, the other two rooms also have king-size beds, and if you haven't noticed, your feet are hanging off,' Avery laughed.

'Yeah, but look,' Dazza said, wriggling up to a pillow on one side and stretching diagonally. 'A bed that fits me. I'm staying here.'

'I thought you were hungry?' Bobby said.

'Oh, yeah. Come on then!' Dazza said, scrambling off the bed and putting his size fourteen shoes on. 'Which room are you having, Bob?'

'I'll have the red bedroom. It doesn't have an en-suite but it faces out onto the Piazza di Spagna.'

As Dazza marched towards the private lift, Avery grabbed Bobby's arm and pulled him back to her.

'I've missed you, sweetheart,' Avery said, wrapping her arms around Bobby and kissing him.

'I've missed you too, Avery,' Max replied. 'I think my transmutation is almost complete. It's not quite like any others I've had, but I'd say a few more weeks at the most before Bobby and I have our own bodies.'

'Oi, Cowboy. How many more times? I have a body. You're the squatter until your own is ready,' Bobby insisted.

'Come on. I'm hungry,' Dazza shouted.

'I'm sure even Caesar's Legionnaires couldn't get between Dazza and his food,' Max laughed.

As the trio crossed the piazza, Dazza spotted a restaurant. 'Hey, that'll do; they've got pictures of pizza.'

'I am not eating in a restaurant with pictures of the food on the menu,' Avery said firmly.

'It's okay, we can go to one of the restaurants the locals use,' Max replied.

'I'm not eating any foreign food,' Dazza insisted. 'Pasta, pizza or chips will do fine.'

Bobby and Avery looked at Dazza open-mouthed.

'What's up with you guys?' Dazza asked.

'You realise pizza and pasta are Italian?' Avery said.

'Yeah, course. But they're English-Italian, not foreign stuff like snails and things,' Dazza insisted.

'Snails are French cuisine, not Italian,' Max sighed.

'Yeah, well, I ain't eating none of that stuff,' Dazza said firmly. 'English food only—Hey, come on, there's a burger bar.'

As Dazza shot off, Avery turned to Bobby. 'Which one of us is going to point out they're an American burger chain?'

As Avery and Bobby caught up with Dazza, he was already standing by a terminal scrolling. 'Look, guys. They've got proper food.'

'Dazza, we're going to a restaurant,' Bobby pointed out.

'It's okay. This will keep me going until we get there. What do you guys want?'

'I'm fine, thanks,' Avery smiled.

'How about you, Bob?'

'No grazie, amico.'

'Huh?' Dazza frowned.

'I said no thanks, buddy,' Bobby replied.

'You said something foreign!' Dazza replied.

'No, non l'ho fatto!' Bobby insisted.

'He's doing it again,' Dazza said. 'And he called me a fatto.'

'Bobby, are you and Max okay?' Avery asked.

'What's wrong with you both? Dazza said I was talking foreign, and I just said, "No, I didn't." Don't you guys speak English?' Bobby replied in frustration. 'And come on, mate, I'd never call anyone a fatto. I've had enough name-calling and insults to last Max's lifetime. I'd never do it.'

'Okay, but I'm still having something to eat and I'm gonna try some local stuff,' Dazza replied as he completed his order.

'Hey Max, look, they've got some Roman ruins. Let's check them out while Dazza waits for his meal,' Avery suggested.

As they wandered downstairs, Max said, 'This is part of the Aqua Virgo, which was built during Augustus's reign.'

'Augustus? Wasn't he the son of your master when you first came to Earth?' Avery asked.

'Sort of. He was Caesar's nephew and then adopted son. He built the aqueduct to bring water to the centre of Rome from twelve miles away. In fact, it still feeds the Trevi Fountain,' Max replied distractedly.

'Max, sweetheart, are you okay?'

'I did speak Italian, didn't I?'

'Yeah, you did.'

'I don't understand what's happening. Either Bobby or I keep saying or doing strange things.'

'Is it your transmutation process?'

'No. I've transmuted seventy or maybe even a hundred times, and it's always the same when it comes to separation. My host will either be asleep or pass out, and we separate while they're unconscious. The only thing that varies is how long the last part takes. It can be hours or even a few weeks.'

They finished looking at the ruins, with Max explaining what they were seeing, before wandering back upstairs and saw Dazza sitting at a table finishing his meal.

'I'm sorry,' Bobby said as they reached Dazza.

'What for?' Dazza mumbled as he stuffed the last few fries into his mouth.

'Because you were right. I did speak Italian. Oh, and I didn't call you a "fatto," fatto is Italian for done,' Bobby explained.

'That's okay, Bob. And as for the meal, I'm fatto,' Dazza laughed. 'See, I can speak Italian too!'

'Thanks,' Bobby replied.

'Come on, guys. I'm hungry now,' Avery said.

'Me too,' Dazza agreed.

'But you've just had a burger meal,' Bobby said.

'Yeah, but they lied. I ordered some of their foreign food, the Gran Crispy Bacon, but it was just like our Large Crispy Bacon from home. There was no Gran stuff, whatever that is.'

'Gran means lar—actually, never mind, let's go and eat,' Max said. 'My brother has given me a few recommendations, but there's one by the Trevi Fountain that he said is amazing.'

'Do they do proper food?' Dazza asked.

'How does steak sound?'

'Lead on, dude.'

<hr>

'How's it going?' Paul asked.

'It's good, Dad,' Danny replied. 'The luminae pulls energy from the air and converts it into a form we can transmit without wires over long distances.'

'What about the energy extraction from living things?'

'We can't stabilise the structure when it's extracted,' Mercedes said. 'Within a few seconds to a minute, it vaporises.'

'Danny said Max mentioned another mineral they used,' Chris said.

'Alright, dullard, steal my thunder,' Danny laughed. 'Max said it was called something like novasium or novaseum. The luminae extracts the energy in an unstable form, but the novathingy makes it stable.'

'Which means every living thing would just be energy?' Paul asked. 'Immortal and disease-free.'

'Defo, Dad.'

'The IFFS would love this. They could use targeted selection to reduce the global population,' Paul replied. 'How can we get hold of this Nova mineral?'

'I don't know. Max said it was plentiful on Earth, whereas luminae is rare, but he still hasn't explained what it is,' Danny said.

'I think you need a holiday, son.'

'But what about our research?'

'Mercedes and Chris can keep you informed. Aren't Bobby and Max on holiday with some friends? You should join them and see what you can find out about this other mineral,' Paul suggested.

'I was going to join them three days ago when Avery and her family flew over, but we've been working on this,' Danny replied.

'Well, it's time you joined them and relaxed,' Paul replied. 'Are you supposed to be staying with them, or shall I get your hotel room extended?'

'Avery's Dad has booked a luxury villa where we were all supposed to stay,' Danny replied. 'I'll message Avery to say I'm coming. I might find out more if I stay with them.'

***

'Hey, Danny's coming,' Avery said.

'I'll ask the waiter to set another place,' Max said, calling a waiter over.

'Why's there a haircut on the menu?' Dazza asked.

'A haircut?' Avery asked, leaning over to look at Dazza's menu.

'Look, it says a "Mullet Bottarga" Can you get a trim while you eat?'

Avery sighed. 'It's not a mullet haircut. It's a food delicacy made from the mullet fish. The roe pouch is dried and cured before being thinly sliced.'

'Nah, I don't do fish unless it's cod and deep-fried in batter, let alone a fish's pouch. Is that like a kangaroo's pouch?'

'No, it's—actually, never mind,' Avery smiled. 'You wouldn't like it.'

'I'll have the ham and melon, followed by the sirloin steak and chips,' Dazza said. 'Oh, and the profiteroles. You're right, Max. This place does do proper food as well as foreign stuff.'

'It's my brother's recommendation,' Max replied. 'He knows the owner. Apparently, the owner trained under him.'

'I never knew your brother was—hang on, you don't have a brother!' Avery said with a start.

'Yes, I do, he's called Zym. Well, at the moment, he's called Bruno, but his real name is Zym,' Max replied.

'But...how...why... you've never mentioned him before,' Avery said.

'Well, I've not seen him for a while. I just forgot,' Max said.

'How do you forget your brother?' Avery asked.

'Easy when it's been almost two hundred years,' Danny laughed.

Avery stood up and hugged Danny, who was standing in his chair.

'Easy tiger, your man is present. I wouldn't want to have fight Max for your honour,' Danny said with a cheeky grin.

'You wouldn't stand a chance, buddy,' Max replied.

'At your age, I wouldn't be so sure, granddad,' Danny said, grinning.

'With age comes great wisdom, and with wisdom comes the knowledge of how to disconnect your battery,' Max laughed.

'Hey, big man, how was your flight?' Danny asked.

'Good, thanks, dude. How's corporate life treating you?' Dazza replied.

'It's good. I can't tell you what we're working on, but it's exciting,' Danny said, changing his chair into seating mode as he approached the table.

'Oh, you mean the takeover of M Bank by WestFi and your dad. Plus, the testing you've been doing on energy extraction and transmission, including on living things,' Dazza replied as he placed his order by pointing at the menu to the waiter.

Bobby and Avery placed their orders, which gave Danny time to scan the menu and place his.

'How do you know all that?' Danny challenged Dazza.

'We know everything at BIO. Besides, the final takeover announcement got filed this morning before the Borsa Italiana opened,' Dazza replied, glancing around the room at the food on other tables.

'But how did you know about the energy extraction?' Danny challenged.

'A good journalist never reveals his sources,' Dazza said with a smile.

12
MEMORIES

'What are you and your friends doing today?' Ravi asked.

'We've booked tickets to see the Colosseum and the Roman Forum, Pappa. What are you and Maa doing?' Avery replied.

'We're off to see the Sistine Chapel,' Anjali said. 'I hear it's so beautiful.'

'Guys, I can't do those cobbles again. You go to the Colosseum, and I'll check in with the guys at work,' Danny said.

'Come on, dude. Are you a man or a mouse?' Dazza challenged.

'Eek,' Danny squeaked.

'Yeah, come on. How often do you get to visit ancient monuments with someone who's lived there,' Avery said.

'A tour of ancient monuments narrated by an ancient monument,' Danny laughed.

'Watch it, buddy,' Max replied. 'We knew how to make things that last back then. Bigger, stronger and harder!'

'Okay, I'll come, but I need to message the DD team first.'

Bobby's phone pinged, and he read the message before sighing.

'What's up, Bob?' Dazza asked.

'We've got round two of the ego and the attitude,' Max replied.

'If Zym is coming, then I'm defo tagging along,' Danny said.

'We're going to meet your brother? Does he look like you?' Dazza asked.

'You still don't get this host and shell concept, do you?' Max laughed. 'Zym looks like his last host, a short, average-build Italian in his mid-fifties, with dark skin and salt and pepper hair.'

'Oh, okay. Anyway, where're we having breakfast?'

'We've just had it,' Avery said.

'But that was just bread and fruit. I mean a proper breakfast,' Dazza insisted.

'I'll message Zym on the way. He said to meet him by the giant typewriter,' Max replied.

Half an hour later, the four of them stood at the end of the Via del Corso, staring at the Victor Emmanuel II Monument.

'It looks more like a giant wedding cake to me,' Avery said, tilting her head to one side.

'That round bit at the front could be a fancy pork pie,' Danny added.

'Will you guys stop talking about food,' Dazza insisted.

'Did someone say they were hungry?' a man said behind him.

Dazza turned to face the man and said, 'Too right, dude. My mate's bro is supposed to be meeting us and taking us somewhere for breakfast.'

'Well, it seems like this is your lucky day,' the man said, peering up. 'I presume you're Dazza?'

'Yeah, how'd—'

'Morning, Zym,' Max said. 'I see you've met our giant, ginger, eating machine. This is Avery, and you've already met Danny.'

'Nice to meet you, Avery, and hello again, lad. I hope you're keeping Maxo in order.'

'Will you stop calling me that. It's Max, period.'

'Okay, Max period, no need to get stroppy,' Zym laughed.

'I see you've got Max's sense of humour,' Avery smiled.

'Yeah, sorry about that. I borrowed it years ago but forgot to give it back. I guess that's why he's always miserable.'

'Are we eating here?' Dazza asked, pointing at the restaurant they were standing in front of.

'No. Max told me you have a refined diet, so I'm taking you somewhere special,' Zym said.

A while later, Dazza leant back in his chair. 'That fry-up was almost as good as Mike's Café.'

'Only almost as good?' Zym asked in surprise.

'That is very high praise,' Danny laughed.

'You guys missed out,' Dazza sighed in satisfaction.

'Was that your phone, Dazza?' Avery asked.

Dazza pulled out his phone and said, 'Yeah, it's Abi. She's hooked up with some other backpackers, and they've only gone and hitched a ride with a guy flying to Melbourne.'

'I reckon if Abi fell in a sewer, she'd climb out with someone's diamond ring,' Avery chuckled.

'So, what's happening with getting M Bank Research's data?' Zym asked.

'I've done a data download of their personnel data, and I've got some of their research files, but I didn't have time to get everything,' Danny replied as he pulled out his tablet.

'This is impressive,' Zym said as he watched Danny scroll through the files, opening some to show the contents.

'Of course it is,' Danny replied, sipping some water.

'Did you find out anything more about Robbie's father?' Zym asked.

'I think you mean Bobby,' Danny replied. 'It turns out he worked for a company M Bank acquired, but he was one of many they let go.'

'Sorry, Bobby. I'm terrible with names,' Zym said. 'I'm also sorry there weren't more details about your father.'

'It's okay. I guess just hearing his name again gave me a glimmer of hope.'

'Talking of names, I think I may have found another Shadower in that file your friend hid in her ring,' Zym said.

'She's no friend of mine. I just work for the same company as Mercedes,' Danny grumbled.

'Well, never mind that; take a look at this,' Zym said, pulling up an image of a newspaper column.

Max looked at the image and read the headline, 'Family beg missing sister to come home. It says she's been missing for almost two years.'

Zym scrolled the screen to show the newspaper picture of an olive-to-dark-skinned slim female with a thin oval face, wide eyes and long wavy hair. 'Remember that face,' he instructed.

'Hang on, I'll take a photo,' Max said, pulling out Bobby's phone.

'Too late, Chief. I've already pulled a copy onto my tablet,' Danny said.

Zym tapped away on his screen, saying, 'Now look at this report from the RI Beacon, dated two years earlier.'

Max grabbed Zym's phone and read aloud, 'Local Laser Scientist Killed in Tragic Crash Near Airport. Residents are mourning the loss of Dr. Juli Fellowes, 36, a respected figure in the laser technology field and a familiar face in the community. Dr. Fellowes was tragically killed yesterday evening in a multi-vehicle accident along a particularly hazardous stretch of I-95, just south of the T.F. Green Airport. The crash, which involved several cars during peak traffic hours, marks another fatality at this notorious section of the interstate.'

'Is there a picture of her?' Avery asked.

'It looks a bit like the other one, but the glasses and pulled-back hair...hmm, actually yeah, look,' Max said, turning the phone around.

'Blimey. Look at this,' Danny said, showing his tablet screen. 'I took the picture of the doc, removed her glasses, and gave her a similar hairstyle to the missing woman.'

'They must be twins,' Dazza said, studying the images. 'That's some impressive picture manipulation, dude.'

'Thanks, I'll take that as high praise from a newspaper pap,' Danny teased.

'I'm not paparazzi,' Dazza growled.

'Calm down, youngsters,' Zym insisted. 'They could be twins or one of them—'

'Is a Shadower, and the other was her host,' Max said.

'I'm confused,' Bobby said.

'No change there, Bobmeister,' Danny replied. Before adding, 'Oww. My arm's gone numb.'

'It's okay. I'll punch the other one next time,' Bobby laughed. 'Seriously, though, if Juli Fellowes was killed in Rhode Island, how can she be on M Bank Research's records as working in Zermatt?'

'That's actually a good question,' Danny admitted. 'I'm running a script on the data download, but there's no images linked to personnel files. So we can't see if she looks the same.'

'I could have told you that. I searched every file your girlfriend got in her download,' Zym smiled.

'You manually opened every file? That's so lame,' Danny laughed. Then he realised what Zym had said, and his face dropped as he snapped, 'She's not my friend and definitely not my flipping girlfriend.'

'The more he denies it, the more I believe it,' Zym laughed.

'Zym, stop it,' Max said firmly.

'Spoilsport,' Zym chuckled.

'So, what next?' Avery asked.

'I'm off to Zermatt,' Zym replied.

'We'll come with you,' Danny said.

'Hey, I'm on holiday and won't get another for months,' Dazza protested. 'Besides, I've got to go to Zermatt in a couple of months for the IFFS conference. BIO is reporting on it.'

'That's okay, big fella. I need to go alone. It's easier for a jobbing chef to get into sensitive places by myself rather than show up with a team,' Zym said.

'But we can help with things?' Danny protested.

'You already have, lad. Besides, you've proved your skills are behind a keyboard. You can be more help doing that.'

'Well, you can't stop me coming,' Max insisted.

'Yes, I can, Junior. We agreed a long time ago not to put our hosts at risk. Besides, you're not far off transmuting from what you've said. I don't want to deal with that while trying to find Dr. Fellowes.'

'Fine, but keep me informed,' Max reluctantly agreed.

Avery glanced at her watch. 'We need to go soon if we're going to get into the Roman Forum at our timeslot.'

'Danny, can you send me your latest data download?' Zym asked.

'I've sent you the link to the files in my cloud storage,' Danny replied.

'Great, what's the password?'

'Your face.'

'Is that all one word and uppercase?'

'No, it's your face!'

'So it's not case sensitive?'

Danny rolled his eyes. 'When you click the link, it'll start up your camera and scan your face. As long as your face still looks like yours, the files will open.'

'Smart little devil, aren't you,' Zym laughed.

'Come on then,' Dazza said, standing.

'Yeah, okay,' Max replied as he stood up, his eyes rolled and he collapsed.

A few minutes later, Bobby looked up and saw four pairs of eyes staring down at him. 'Err, what happened?'

'You stood up and collapsed again,' Danny said.

'Has he done this before?' Avery asked with a concerned look.

'Yeah, at work,' Danny replied.

As Zym helped Bobby up and sat him on a chair, he asked, 'Are you transmuting? I normally just collapse once, but over time, I've learnt that some of us transmute differently.'

'He keeps speaking foreign, too,' Dazza said.

'Mainly Italian,' Avery added.

'I'm fine,' Bobby insisted.

'Actually, I think it might be because we haven't eaten enough,' Max said.

'I had a big bowl of fruit for breakfast,' Bobby replied firmly.

'You had one bite of a banana and three grapes,' Max said.

'I'm just trying to lose a bit of weight.'

'Robbie, sorry, I mean Bobby, if Max is close to transmuting, your body is burning through calories like a top athlete. If you don't eat properly, you're putting your life in danger,' Zym said.

'Fine, I'll have a big lunch.'

Zym walked over to a waiter, repeatedly pointing back to Bobby as he talked. The waiter nodded and ran off. A few minutes later, he reappeared carrying a cornetto, some yoghurt with fruit and muesli and some bread with jams and honey.

'I thought croissants were French?' Dazza asked.

'It's a cornetto. It's a bit like a croissant but filled with custard,' Avery explained.

'You can have it if you want, Dazza,' Bobby replied.

'Oh, cheers, I...' Dazza paused with his hand extended towards the plate as he noticed everyone's eyes on him. He pulled his hand back and said, 'Nah, it's okay, Bob. I'm full; besides, you need the energy.'

Bobby looked at the food and wished it would disappear. He glanced around at his friends and realised they wouldn't let him leave until he ate something. He stared at the plate, the scent of custard from the cornetto teasing his senses but also causing his stomach to knot, not from hunger but from the fear of losing control of the one thing in his life that he could manage.

His mind raced, searching for a way to satisfy his friends without giving in to the gnawing fear accompanying every bite.

He decided to go for the yoghurt first, stirring it to mix the muesli and fruit. He took a tiny spoonful, enough to appear like he was eating. 'Okay? I'm eating,' he said with a forced smile.

Zym looked at Danny and raised an eyebrow but didn't say anything. Bobby knew they weren't fooled, but he was determined to stay in control.

He started ripping the cornetto into small pieces, selected a piece and nibbled at the edge where the pastry was the thinnest, avoiding the custard filling. He made a show of chewing it repeatedly as if he'd stuffed a lot in. 'It's so nice, but I'm getting full,' he said, although it lacked sincerity to even himself.

Danny frowned. 'Bobster, you've hardly eaten anything. You'll pass out again if you don't eat something.'

'Bobby, I told you when we first met that I never forcefully take over my host unless I have to, but we're getting so weak. Please eat some more. If you die, my energy soul will move into a new host, but you'll be leaving behind all your loved ones,' Max thought. *'Including me.'*

Bobby forced down another small bite, cutting and pushing the food around the plate, making it look like he was making progress, but every bite felt like a battle.

'That's enough; I'll be fine now until lunchtime,' Bobby said, quieter this time, unsure who he was trying to convince more—his friends or himself.

'Bobby Morris, you listen to me,' Avery said, placing both hands on the table and leaning towards Bobby. 'I love that man inside you. Adam loves you, and your Mum and Lily have already lost a husband and a dad. I don't care if we stay here all day. But you're eating that food.'

Bobby glanced up at Avery briefly, but it was enough for her to see the tears in his eyes. She sat down beside him and grabbed his hand. 'Please, Bobby, we don't want to lose you.'

Bobby smiled meekly at Avery. He didn't want to hurt anyone, but over the last couple of months, this had become the one thing he could control. He went back to the yoghurt and muesli. Each spoonful felt like it would get stuck in his throat, but he knew his friends were right. As he was beginning to think about stopping again, his phone pinged.

Adam

> Hey sweetheart. Just finished training and I thought I'd remind my handsome man that I love him xxx

Bobby smiled as he read the message. If he ever needed to hear from Adam, it was right now. That feeling of one thing in his life being right was enough to persuade him to eat some more. He finished the yoghurt and sat back.

'Guys, I really am stuffed now.'

'It's true. I can feel Bobby's stomach, and after several weeks of little food, it can't take much more in one sitting,' Max confirmed.

'I never really thought about it before, but one of us having a conversation with our host when we're sharing a body is rather weird,' Zym said. 'Just make sure you eat some regular small meals, Bobby, for yours and Max's sake.'

'I'll try,' Bobby promised.

'I'll make sure you do more than try,' Avery insisted.

'Um, if Bob is full...does, uh, that mean no one wants that cornetto,' Dazza asked hesitantly.

Dazza's desire for food broke the tension, and everyone started laughing.

'Help yourself, big man,' Bobby laughed.

Avery glanced at her watch. 'We'll never get to the Colosseum for our allotted time for the Forum now.'

'You don't need to go through that way. There's a closer entrance by the Chiesa di Santa Maria di Loreto,' Zym said.

'I know where you mean. We came here on holiday a few years ago, but it's just an archaeological dig,' Danny replied.

'You're out of date, youngster. They opened it up ages ago, but everyone goes to the Colosseum entrance. That means this one is quiet, with minimal queues, and it goes all the way to the Roman Forum,' Zym said.

A while later, Avery, Dazza, Bobby, and Danny were wandering around the ruins of Ancient Rome as Max gave them a running commentary.

'Over there was the Temple of Mars, and through here should be... yep, this is the Forum of Julius Caesar. He started it, but Augustus finished some parts of it.'

'I was expecting those cobbles again. These walkways they've installed are great,' Danny said as he moved around with his chair in standing mode.

'Bobby, why are you on your phone instead of enjoying the views?' Avery scolded.

'It's not me,' Bobby protested.

'Sorry, hun. I'm posting on my socials,' Max laughed.

'When did you get all trendy?' Avery laughed.

'Danny helped me,' Max replied.

'And I've got access, just in case the chief messes up,' Danny laughed. 'You know how these oldies can be.'

'Don't you start,' Max chuckled. 'I posted those pictures from the top and bottom of the Spanish Steps yesterday, and one of my friend followers, Pauline, asked if my "knees hurt!"'

'Even your followers know you, Chief!' Danny replied, before he started cursing. 'We're back on those flipping cobbles again.'

'Welcome to Rome,' Max smiled. 'Having trouble with them, buddy?'

'It's a stupid surface; what's wrong with tarmac?' Danny said, wobbling along.

'Because they didn't have tarmac over two thousand years ago,' Max laughed as Danny staggered across the cobbles.

'I give up,' Danny grumbled as he changed his wheelchair from standing to sitting.

'It feels so weird being here,' Max said, staring at the ruins.

'Was it like this when you were last here?' Avery asked.

'Some of it had been revealed in 1925, but I wasn't here for sightseeing. This is the first time I've stood on the Via Sacra since around 150 AD,' Max sighed wistfully. 'And when I first came here, Gaius and I ran up that hill so many times.'

'Did you race to the arch?' Dazza asked.

'No, the Arch of Titus wasn't built until around 81 AD. Gaius died long before then.'

13
Domestic Disharmony

'How was Rome, Champ?' Pat asked.

'Yeah, it was great, thanks, Mum,' Bobby replied.

'I thought we might have seen you again while we were there.'

'Sorry, we were busy,' Bobby said, filling a glass with water.

'You looked so grown up when Danny's dad let me come and see you at work.'

'Yeah. I wish I had time to chat, but we were doing some important experiments.'

'That's okay,' Pat lied, not wanting him to know how much it hurt when he'd run off.

'Did you and Lily have a good time?'

'It was incredible. Your dad always promised to take me there. He said he'd been a long time ago, but we never made it.'

'That's nice.'

'I'm doing a fry up for us. Do you want some?'

'No, it's okay. I'm not hungry.'

'*You need to eat something, buddy,*' Max replied.

'*I'm fine. I ate loads on holiday. Besides...*'

'*Besides, Stephen is here?*' Max challenged.

'*Well, yeah, maybe.*'

'*How about we go into town? We could meet the gang in Mike's.*'

'*Yeah, okay.*'

Bobby typed a message into his phone and sent it. 'I'm off to town to meet the guys,' he told his mother.

'But we wanted to speak to you,' Pat replied.

'Who's we?' Bobby asked.

Pat looked down at her feet awkwardly. 'Stephen and I want to ask you and Lily something.'

Bobby started to rush out of the kitchen. 'Okay. I'll be back later.'

'Are you going to be home for tea? We could talk then,' Pat shouted after him.

'Sorry, I'll be late. Don't wait up,' Bobby shouted back.

As Bobby raced towards the front door, he collided with Lily, who had run down the stairs, giggling. He picked her up in his arms and swung her round playfully.

'Now, what's Mum said about running down the stairs?' Bobby said with a smile.

'I know, but Stephen was chasing me,' Lily laughed as Stephen came downstairs.

'Morning, Bobby. You're quite correct; I shouldn't have chased Lily down the stairs,' Stephen agreed.

'No, you shouldn't have,' Bobby replied.

'Paul tells me you did a fantastic job on the due diligence.'

'I was just doing my job.'

'He said Danny told him that you all had a great time on your holiday afterwards.'

'Yes, thank you, it was nice.'

'*Be polite, buddy,*' Max thought.

'*I am being polite. If I weren't, I'd ignore him,*' Bobby replied.

'*Mummy says it's rude to ignore peoples,*' Lily said.

'*Lily, how…I mean, I'm thinking things, how are you replying?*' Bobby thought.

'*You're not thinking, silly. You're talking to Max,*' Lily giggled.

Stephen noticed Lily giggling and staring at Bobby, and he frowned.

'*Is this because of what happened before?*' Max asked.

'*Whaddya mean? 'fore what?*'

'*You know the Daxson and everything,*' Max replied.

'*No,*' Lily chuckled as she started to squirm to get free.

Bobby kissed his sister on the cheek and dropped her slowly to the floor.

'Yucky,' Lily said, wiping her face.

'Did your mum mention us having a talk?' Stephen asked as Lily ran off towards the kitchen.

'Yeah, she said something. I've got to go. Bye, Lily,' Bobby said as he rushed out the front door.

'*Don't forget Daddy,*' Lily replied.

'*I'm not calling that man my dad,*' Bobby thought, slamming the door behind him.

Twenty minutes later, Bobby was inside Mike's Café. The familiar smell of fried food comforted him and gave him a pang of hunger.

'Whatcha want, mate?' Mike asked.

Bobby glanced at the handwritten blackboard menu on the wall, even though he knew it by heart. It hadn't changed in all the years he'd been coming here with his friends, but somehow, checking it felt like part of the routine—a small, familiar habit he couldn't avoid.

'Have you got any fresh fruit?'

'Course, lad. We got fresh tomatoes, fresh bananas, fresh… hang on a minute. Carol, is them 'shrooms still edible?'

'Aye, Mike, just about.'

'We got fresh 'shrooms too.'

'Tomatoes and mushrooms aren't fruit,' Bobby said.

'Okay, you got me, 'shrooms aren't fruit, but tomatoes are.'

'No, they're—'

'*Technically, they are, buddy*,' Max thought.

'Can I have a pancake with some chopped banana, please?' Bobby ordered.

'It's what's on the board or any mixture thereof. I recommend the fry-up,' Mike said.

Bobby pointed up at the board. 'It's up there under specials. Pancakes with fruit,' Bobby protested.

Mike glanced up at the board. 'That's the old specials.'

'What's the new specials then?'

'Hang on, let me check. Carol! You got any flour for pancakes?'

'Yeah. But they don't want them puffy American ones, do they? I ain't got baking powder.'

'Even though they're our old specials, we can accommodate sir's request. Would you like honey on it?'

'No thanks, just the banana and pancake, please.'

'You're missing out. It's fresh from the tin,' Mike said, holding a green and gold tin.

'That's golden syrup, not honey. It's just sugar,' Bobby protested.

'Yeah, but it's natural sugar, well, natural-ish. And it is fresh from the tin,' Mike replied.

'I'll pass.'

Just as Bobby sat at a table by the window, Dazza and Adam walked in. Bobby ran over to Adam and threw his arms around him.

'I've missed you, hun, so much,' Bobby said.

'I've missed you too, boo,' Adam replied.

'I'll have the fry-up, please, Mike, and can I swap the toast for fried bread?' Dazza said.

'For my best customer, that's not a problem,' Mike replied.

'Adam, what do you want?' Dazza asked.

'I'll have two poached eggs on toast,' Adam replied.

'Where's the ego on wheels?' Dazza asked as he sat down.

'Danny's at work. Mercedes said she'd found some data she wanted him to check,' Bobby replied.

'So, come on then. Why did you want to meet so urgently?' Dazza asked.

'It's Mum. I think she wants to marry that man,' Bobby replied with disgust.

'You mean Stephen Marchent?' Dazza asked.

'Yeah.'

'That's great, you can give me the inside news,' Dazza said as their food arrived.

'He did make things awkward the way he acted when he found out I was bisexual,' Adam said.

'He creeps me out. It's like Mum's forgotten about Dad,' Bobby replied, scrolling through the pictures on his phone.

'Would it be so bad if your mum did marry Marchent? Your dad died several years ago,' Dazza said.

'Five years ago, actually,' Bobby said, staring at a photo.

'Is that your dad?' Adam asked. 'You mention him a lot, but you've never shown me his picture.'

'Yeah. That's me and Dad at the seaside building sandcastles when I was about eight,' Bobby sighed.

'I've seen him,' Dazza said, glancing at Bobby's phone as he dipped the fried bread into his egg.

'I wish you had, but he died before we met,' Bobby replied.

'Nah, not back then. I've seen him online recently,' Dazza said, chomping on the fried bread.

'Dad didn't do socials. I wish he had so I could see and hear him again,' Bobby said remorsefully.

'No, it was something Abi saw in Australia. Some show called "They Ended Up Where?" It traces people's history from when they're young to where they ended up,' Dazza explained. 'It's mainly about where famous or rich people came from, but they also have a section called "Gone Missing" about successful people who've disappeared.'

Dazza scrolled through his phone and found the link to the show. 'Look, it's got that guy from those films and that musical about miserable people. Abi knows I like him.'

'Never mind that, what about this guy who looks like dad?'

'Here it is,' Dazza replied as he found the section on his phone.

'This is the sad story of Richard Roberts. A young man who had it all but then lost it all,' the presenter said.

'He does look a bit like Dad might look if he was worth millions, didn't have a beard and was a gym freak,' Bobby agreed, looking at a picture of the teenager on a yacht.

'Wait a bit,' Dazza said. 'He had a drinking and gambling problem. Let me fast forward it.'

'And that's how rich Richard Roberts, the young heir to a small fortune from South Yarra, went from a wealthy young socialite to a down and out,' the presenter said. 'What Richard never knew was that he had a son called Alex, who joins me now. Alex, you only found out about your father four years ago. Tell me about it.'

Alex proceeded to explain how his mother had a brief affair with Richard twenty-three years ago but called it off due to Richard's addiction.

'I only found out about my father when Mum was dying, but he was missing by then,' Alex said. 'This is the last picture I have of him from the hostel he lived in shortly before he disappeared.'

A picture of a dishevelled but well-fed Richard appeared on screen.

Bobby paused Dazza's phone, 'No, it's impossible. Dad moved to the UK twenty-five years ago, so he can't be that guy's dad.'

'He's probably just a look-alike. We all have them?' Max thought.

'Yeah, he looks a little like Dad. But we've all got look-alikes out there,' Bobby insisted. 'Actually, the more I look at him, the more differences I can see.'

'He does look older and heavier in that last picture than the one of your Dad with you on the beach,' Adam agreed.

'Hang on a minute, I'll screenshot the image and then put it through my imaging software,' Dazza said. 'I'll get it to make him thinner and add a beard.'

A minute later, Dazza finished tapping away at his phone and paused for a second, glancing between his phone and Bobby's.

'I'm missing out on a tasty breakfast at Mike's Café with the guys, so this had better be good, dullards,' Danny grumbled as he rolled into the laboratory WestFi had commandeered at M Bank Research's Cambridge campus.

'Look at this,' Chris said, putting an apple under a glass dome attached by a hinged arm to a machine. Two leads ran from the machine, one set connected to the lump of luminae and the other disappearing behind a screen.

'We need to stand back near the walls as we've had a few mishaps,' Mercedes said.

'Is that the separation machine that was used on those mice?' Danny asked.

'Yes, it is, but I'm not testing this on animals unless you want to volunteer?' Mercedes replied with a smile.

'I think I'll pass,' Danny replied, ignoring Mercedes's dig.

'Then get back against that wall with Chris,' Mercedes ordered. 'And put these dark goggles on.'

'I can barely see,' Danny moaned, lifting the goggles.

'If you don't wear them, you might not see again.'

'Fine, I'll wear them.'

'Doesn't matter to me if you do or don't,' Mercedes replied curtly before moving behind a screen.

As Danny and Chris stood against the wall facing the glass dome, Mercedes counted down from three, pressed a button and the room filled with an intense white light.

As the light subsided, Danny lifted off his goggles. 'Is that it?' he asked.

'Yes. It looks like it worked,' Mercedes replied, coming from behind the screen.

Danny rolled over to the dome and peered at the apple. 'It looks the same to me.'

'Lift off the dome and tap the apple with that stick,' Mercedes said.

Danny reached over to lift the arm holding the dome and screamed. 'Flipping hell, that's hot. You could have warned me.'

'You could have asked,' Mercedes replied. 'I did say lift off the dome and tap the apple with that stick.'

'You made it sound like I only used the stick to tap the apple!'

'Is it my fault you can't understand simple instructions? Now use the stick to lift the dome, then hit the apple with the stick.'

Danny tentatively picked up the stick, worried that Mercedes was setting him up again.

'It's just a piece of wood,' Mercedes laughed.

Danny used the stick to raise the arm of the machine, lifting the dome clear and tapping the apple, which rolled onto its side.

'Wow, this is amazing,' Danny said sarcastically. 'You made a big white light, and everything stayed the same.'

Mercedes walked over to the table. 'Look, there. I realise you struggle to pay attention to anything, but surely you can see that glow?'

'That's just the reflection of the light on the apple,' Danny muttered.

'Did you part-exchange your eyesight for your ego?' Mercedes asked, grabbing the stick out of Danny's hand and whacking the apple, which collided with the edge of the machine as another glowing apple rolled towards the edge of the table.

'Okay, so what's happened?' Danny asked.

Mercedes picked up the apple by the machine and threw it to Danny, who caught it.

'Taste it?'

'Is it going to kill me?' Danny asked nervously.

'Only if we're lucky,' Mercedes replied. 'It's fine; it won't hurt you, but you'll notice it's different.'

Danny bit into the apple and spat it out. 'That's disgusting. It's like chewing on wet, crunchy cardboard with no flavour.'

'All the flavour and nutrients have been removed,' Mercedes explained. She reached across to the glowing apple shape and held it out. 'Now try this, but be careful, it's very light.'

Danny picked it up gently. 'Wow, it's as light as a feather.'

'Bite it,' Chris said.

Danny bit into the apple, but without any resistance, his teeth clashed. He rubbed his mouth while subconsciously chewing before realising there wasn't anything in his mouth.

'That's weird. I know I bit into it, and I can see a bite-size piece missing, but there wasn't anything to chew on even though I can taste apple,' Danny said.

'Incredible, isn't it. The glowing apple seems to have all the properties of an apple without the organic material,' Chris said.

'I also feel like I've eaten something, but I still feel hungry,' Danny replied.

'It's still too soon to tell, but I think your physical body needs the organic part of the apple to digest, but it gets the flavour and energy boost from the glowing apple,' Mercedes explained.

'If we can prove that the body gets all the nutrients from this bit, it'll change our lives forever. Food with almost no weight, making it easy to transport but with all the good bits in,' Danny said. 'Hey, without the organic part, does it mean there's no calories either?'

'We don't know yet. We need to do some more tests and then get them analysed for nutritional content, but we need to find a specialist laboratory to do the testing,' Mercedes said.

'That won't be a problem, my Dad'll sort it.'

'He's not even noticed the biggest breakthrough,' Mercedes said to Chris with a sigh.

'Trust me, I can definitely see the big breakthrough in opportunities this will create,' Danny said, admiring the glowing apple.

'No, you're seeing the huge money-making opportunities while staring at the big breakthrough,' Mercedes said. 'Chris, how long has it been since we separated the apple from its energy and nutrients?'

'About five minutes so far.'

Danny frowned, and then his eyes widened. 'It's still exactly the same. It hasn't evaporated.'

'Energy dissipates, not evaporates,' Mercedes corrected.

Danny ignored the comment and said, 'How did you make it stable?'

'I remember you said Max talked about their machines using luminae and another mineral called novasium. The luminae obviously extracts the energy version of the object, and novasium must help stabilise it,' Chris said.

'Where did you find this novasium stuff?' Danny asked.

'You said that Max mentioned that luminae was rare, but there was a seam near Rome, which M Bank discovered. And that novasium was widespread but in small pockets,' Chris explained.

'So, we started going through minerals that matched that geographical pattern,' Mercedes added.

'But there must be more than a thousand minerals like that,' Danny challenged.

'True, but M Bank Research had already started testing and eliminating some. They spotted trends like minerals containing carbon, silicon, phosphorous, sulphur, halogens, and boron always failed,' Mercedes explained. 'But those with antimony and oxygen had varying degrees of success.'

'Which meant you could concentrate on those antimony oxide minerals,' Danny said.

'But we then narrowed it down even more by wondering why M Bank had a facility in Zermatt,' Chris said.

'Brilliant. How many antimony oxide minerals are there in that region of Switzerland?'

'Hardly any, but we did discover reports of cervantite being present as an oxidation of stibnite,' Mercedes explained.

'But stibnite is sulphur-based,' Danny challenged.

Yes, but the sulphur gets replaced by oxygen during the oxidation process, making it an antimony oxide,' Mercedes sighed. 'Don't you understand chemical reactions?'

***

'Well, that's the best I can do,' Dazza said, placing his phone on the table next to Bobby's phone.

'See, I said they didn't—' Bobby stopped talking as he glanced from his phone to Dazza's and back.

Adam looked at Bobby and put his arm around his shoulder. 'Are you okay?'

'He could almost be Dad, couldn't he?' Bobby said, confused by what he was looking at.

'*It certainly looks like him,*' Max thought.

'It could easily be his twin,' Adam agreed. 'Did your dad mention a twin?'

'Dad didn't like talking about his family. He said his mum died when he was young, and he was brought up in a care home,' Bobby said.

'What about brothers or aunts or uncles?' Dazza asked.

'I did ask once why I never had any aunts or uncles. Mum said she was an only child, and she thought Dad was too.'

'She didn't know for certain?' Adam asked.

'No. She said Dad always changed the subject when she asked about his family.'

'Who changed the subject,' a familiar voice said as the café door opened.

'Morning, Danny,' Dazza said.

'So, who's changing the subject,' Danny repeated as he headed to the counter.

'Bobby's dad whenever he was asked about his family,' Adam said.

'Whooohooo, a man of mystery, huh?' Danny laughed as he placed his order and joined them at the table.

'It's not funny,' Bobby protested.

'I'm sorry, Bobster. How come you're talking about your dad anyway? Is it because his name came up in M Bank's records?'

'No, it's a show Abi saw and sent to Dazza,' Bobby sighed.

'Is it safe to watch any show those two watch together?' Danny chuckled.

Adam scowled. 'Do you take anything seriously?'

'Only if it's something I can do anything about,' Danny replied. 'Otherwise, what's the point? If you can't change it, accept it and move on.'

'It is what it is, eh Danny?' Max said.

'Defo, Chief.'

'There are two types of people in the world to fear. The silent observers and those who accept the things they cannot change,' Max said. 'Put the two together, and that is someone you don't want to mess with.'

'Hear that, guys? The Chief described me as someone not to mess with,' Danny laughed.

'He said, a silent observer. I've played premier league teams where the crowd has been quieter than you,' Adam replied.

'Adam's right. Only one person fits both of Max's descriptions, and that's Max,' Dazza said.

'Alright, dullards. So, come on then, what's going on with Bobster's dad?'

14
Big House in the Country

'Cup of tea, Champ,' Pat said, placing a mug on a box beside Bobby's bed.

'Thanks, Mum,' Bobby replied groggily.

'You were home late last night.'

'Yeah. After meeting up with the guys at Mike's, we went into London and met Avery.'

'Sounds like you had a great time.'

'È stata una figata!'

'Um, did you learn some Italian on holiday?'

'No,' Bobby said with a frown. 'I just said it was awesome.'

Pat tilted her head to one side, studying her son. 'Sorry, I guess it's my hearing. The perils of getting older,' Pat lied with a smile. She knew she'd heard him clearly.

'You're not old, Mum,' Bobby said, sitting up and sipping the tea. 'Ugh, there's sugar in here.'

'Only one. I thought you'd complain because there weren't three,' Pat laughed.

'Me too, to be honest,' Max replied.

'Oh, morning, Max. I've hardly seen Bobby over the last few weeks, so I'd almost forgotten you were still inside him,' Pat laughed.

'Excuse me, but I am here, you know. I'm just cutting out sugar to get fitter,' Bobby explained.

'Talking of getting fit, we're having a day in the countryside, so we'll do plenty of walking,' Pat replied.

'Great. Are we having a picnic?' Bobby asked.

'No, Stephen is taking us to a country pub near his family home.'

'Oh, sorry, I forgot, I'm meeting Danny today.'

'Well, you can tell him you'll see him another day.'

'But we're investigating something.'

'It'll have to wait. We're having a family day and no arguments, young man,' Pat said firmly.

'But Mum, it's about Da—'

'No buts. You're coming, and you'll be nice to Stephen.'

'But—'

'Bobby!' Pat said firmly as she got up and walked to the bedroom door. 'You've got half an hour to get ready.'

'Fine!' Bobby grumbled.

As the door closed behind Pat, Max said, '*Come on, buddy. I admit Stephen doesn't always seem like the nicest of people, but—*'

'*But nothing, Cowboy. You heard the way he was when he found out Adam was gay.*'

'*Bisexual,*' Max corrected.

'*Adam's gay. I should know. He only says bisexual for the press,*' Bobby insisted.

'*Okay, and yes, Stephen handled that badly, but he seems to treat your mum and Lily well, and he's always nice to you.*'

Bobby swung his legs out of bed, stood up and stretched. '*He's only nice to us because he wants Mum.*'

Bobby grabbed a can of deodorant and started spraying it under his arms.

'*You need a shower, buddy. The spray is for after you've washed,*' Max said.

'*I don't care. If I'm spending the day with him in the country, I'll probably smell of manure anyway,*' Bobby grumbled, pulling on his jeans and a top.

'Lily, go and see why your brother is taking so long,' Pat said.

Lily scrambled up the stairs and pushed open the bedroom door to see Bobby lying on the floor. 'He's asleep again, Mummy,' she shouted down the stairs.

Pat sighed. 'I swear the older he gets, the more he sleeps,' she said to Stephen. 'Wake him up, Lily.'

'Bobby, wake up!' Lily shouted as she pushed his body.

'Huh,' Bobby groaned, looking up at his little sister.

'We're going now. Mummy sent me to get you.'

'What? Where am I?' Bobby asked groggily.

'You're in your bedroom, silly.'

'Why am I on the floor?'

'You were sleeping, lazy bones.'

Bobby grabbed the side of his bed and pulled himself up. '*What happened, cowboy?*'

'*I haven't got a clue. One minute we were talking; the next, Lily was waking us up.*'

'*Come on, you two,*' Lily said before running downstairs.

Bobby finished his cold tea. '*How much longer before she can't interact with us in my head?*'

'*I don't know that either. I've had children around three years old who seem to know I'm in a host, but Lily's ability is very odd.*'

Bobby half-walked and half-stumbled downstairs. As he reached the penultimate step, his legs gave way, and he fell forward into Stephen, who caught him before he could fall to the floor.

'Hey, Bobby. Are you okay?' Stephen asked.

'Yes, thank you. I just tripped on the last step,' Bobby replied.

'Thanks for catching me, though,' Max added in his best Bobby impression.

'*Why'd you do that*?' Bobby thought.

'*Because it's called being polite,*' Max answered.

'Hello, sleepyhead,' Pat said, entering the hallway. 'Here, I've got you an energy bar and a bottle of water as you're too late for breakfast, but don't spill it in Stephen's car.'

'Pat, it's just a car. Material things aren't important. I'd rather the kids were happy and enjoy themselves than be scared of spilling things,' Stephen replied. 'Let them have whatever they want; it's almost an hour's journey.'

'Mummy, I want a yogie drink,' Lily said.

'I'll have a yoghurt too, please, Mum,' Bobby said.

'*I'm not going to let you spill it in the car,*' Max said.

'*As if I would,*' Bobby smirked. '*Seriously though, I may not like him, but I don't do petty things.*'

As they walked outside, Bobby noticed the dark purple Bentley Flying Spur parked by his Mum's Focus ST.

'*What a flexer,*' Bobby thought.

'*A what? Oh yeah, a flexer is what we used to call a flash git,*' Max replied. '*I quite like it, it's a nice car.*'

An hour later, a few miles past Marlow and with no yoghurt spilt, Stephen pulled up to a large wrought iron gate, pressed a button on his keyring, and drove the car up a long curving gravel driveway as the gates quietly parted.

'Stephen, it's beautiful,' Pat said, gazing at the large three-storey brick and stone house.

'It's been in the family since my ancestor started building it in 1653.'

'*Almost a new build them,*' Max laughed.

'Mummy, what's a new build?' Lily asked.

'It's a house that's just been built, but this one is really old,' Pat replied. 'Why'd you ask, munchkin?'

'Max said it was a new b—. Oww, Mummy, Bobby hit me with his elbow.'

'Bobby, say sorry to your sister,' Pat said. After a short pause, she added, 'I'm not going to say it again, young man.'

'Sorry, Lily,' Bobby said begrudgingly, whispering, 'Snitch.'

Lily stuck her tongue out, smug that her brother had been told off.

As they pulled up outside the house, Stephen said, 'Who's Max?'

'Who?' Pat asked, trying to look innocent.

'Max. Lily said, "Max said," before Bobby elbowed her,' Stephen insisted, turning off the engine.

'Max is Bobby's friend,' Lily said proudly.

Pat waved her hand discreetly as if patting a child and whispered, 'Lily's imaginary friend.'

Unfortunately, Lily heard her mother and piped up, 'No, it's Bobby's friend. He's an alien from Zephyrion.'

Pat tried again to signal to Stephen that it was just a young child thing, and Stephen nodded, indicating that he understood.

They walked to the heavy-looking solid oak door with large iron studs, and Stephen said, 'Stephen Marchent.'

The door slowly opened.

'Oh, my. That door looks so old. I was waiting for you to pull out some gigantic iron key,' Pat laughed.

'When I inherited the house, it had that key on the wall,' Stephen said, pointing to a large key inside the doorway. 'But I didn't have a big enough pocket, so I installed a voice-activated door lock.'

'But the door's so old,' Pat gushed.

'They think the door was a replacement, but it's still around two hundred years old,' Stephen said as they walked into the grand hallway.

In front of them stood a grand oak-panelled room with an imposing oak double staircase. Large sets of stairs against each wall led up to a landing, looking back into the hallway.

'I'm sorry about the clutter, but the chandeliers are being cleaned,' Stephen said about the two huge crystal chandeliers dominating the hallway floor.

'*Is he seriously apologising about getting his la-di-da lights cleaned?*' Bobby huffed.

'*I'm actually impressed. So much of this hallway looks original,*' Max replied.

Stephen took them on a tour of the house and around the formal gardens. Lily kept running around, opening and closing doors and cupboards in the house and then running around the flower beds.

Bobby spent the whole time messaging Danny.

Bobby

> Have you found out anything about that Roberts guy?

A few minutes later, Danny replied.

Danny

> It's bizarre. His details came up on a flight to the UK a few days after he disappeared

Bobby

> But wouldn't the Australian police have checked things like that?

Danny

> The airline details say he never took the flight

> **Bobby**
>
> So that's a dead end?

> **Danny**
>
> Not quite. I've found a record of him arriving on a private flight to Farnborough

> **Bobby**
>
> I'm on my way

> **Danny**
>
> No point. That's all I've got so far. Come over when you get back. I should have more by then

'Everything okay?' Pat asked, noticing Bobby on his phone.

'Yeah, it's fine. Danny's been checking out some stuff. Can I go and see him soon?' Bobby asked.

'I'll do you a deal. If you put up with us today, you can drive to Danny's tonight,' Pat said.

'Very funny. I may have passed my test, but I don't have a car,' Bobby grumbled.

'It was supposed to be a surprise, but did you notice that black car parked near the house when we pulled up earlier?'

'That Golf? Yeah, it looked tidy,' Bobby replied, before adding in shocked realisation, 'You mean that's for me?'

'Yes, it's yours. Stephen helped me find it for you, and the insurance is paid for this year,' Pat smiled.

'Love you, Mum.'

'Love you more, Champ!'

They returned to the house, and Stephen said, 'Let me show you into the study while I check on the refreshments.'

As Stephen disappeared into the bowels of the house, Pat looked around the room. 'It's beautiful. That huge marble fireplace and the parquet flooring.'

'Shame the walls are banana yellow,' Bobby laughed.

'I think it's custard,' Lily said. 'I like custard. Are we having some?'

'It does look like custard, munchkin,' Pat replied.

'Have you seen all those shooting trophies in that cabinet?' Pat asked.

'Probably bought them,' Bobby sneered before sitting in the large, deep red leather mahogany captain's chair behind a desk, feeling an air of authority from how it made him sit. He slid his hands over the slender arms of the chair, noting the heavily polished but well-worn marks from the grip of hands over the years. Stephen's imposing antique oak desk was an even richer hue of deep, polished, aged wood. The centre of the desk was dominated by what looked like a recently replaced deep red leather insert, while a green-shaded brass desk lamp added to the feeling of importance Bobby felt sitting there.

Bobby noticed some files to his right with the M Bank logo and started leafing through them.

'Bobby, get up from there and leave Stephen's papers alone,' Pat said.

'He's not hurting,' Stephen said, carrying a tray of drinks, biscuits and small cakes and placing them on the coffee table by a grey sofa and chairs in front of the desk. 'Let me know if you find anything interesting in those documents. I fell asleep when I tried wading through them.'

'Now I know we are going out for lunch, so I got some treats nobody would like,' Stephen joked. 'I mean, nobody likes mini chocolate rolls, do they,' he added, winking at Lily.

'I do, don't I, Mummy,' Lily said excitedly.

'Just one, young lady,' Pat laughed.

'Bobby, would you like anything? I've got some protein bars you like,' Stephen offered.

'No thanks,' Bobby replied.

'We were just admiring all your shooting trophies,' Pat said.

'I was the school champion at clay pigeon shooting,' Stephen said proudly, pouring some tea from an expensive looking teapot into some bone china cups as Lily grabbed a fruit juice from the tray.

'Do I have to point my little finger out while I drink?' Pat laughed.

Stephen laughed. 'Of course, we have standards, you know. Bobby, would you like a drink?'

'Just water, please.'

'*Will you chill out? He's trying to be nice,*' Max thought.

'*I said pl-please, didn't I?*'

'If you grab the second handle up on that wooden filing cabinet behind you and pull, you can grab some water,' Stephen said.

Bobby turned and looked at the four-drawer cabinet. He grabbed the handle Stephen mentioned and pulled it, revealing a chiller drawer filled with water bottles and other soft drinks.

'Take whatever you want,' Stephen said.

Bobby pulled out a water bottle, noting it was as cold as any from his mother's fridge. Out of curiosity, he pulled one of the upper cabinet drawers, but this time, the top two drawers lowered in one piece, forming a shelf and revealing a well-stocked drinks cabinet and some glasses.

'That's if you fancy something stronger or just want a glass for your water,' Stephen laughed.

Bobby grabbed a glass. Surprised by its weight, he quickly put it on the desk before closing the cabinet door and pouring water into it.

As Pat and Stephen chatted and Lily sat colouring on the computer tablet Stephen had given her, Bobby continued to flick through the files on the desk.

'*Welcome to WestFi. A guide for new directors.*' Bobby read. '*I thought he'd sold out to WestFi?*'

'It's common for the previous owner to stay on to smooth over the transfer process,' Max explained. *'They often have an earn-out, like a bonus or part of the purchase price held back for a period of time until the transfer of staff and technology is complete or until certain targets are met.'*

'So, he won't be involved forever then?'

'He might be, sometimes there's a stock swap. So instead of getting cash for all his shares in M Bank, he might have been given shares in WestFi and a directorship,' Max explained.

'M Bank property portfolio,' Bobby read. *'Rome. M Bank headquarters, freehold. M Bank Research Technology Centre, leasehold. London, Bloomsbury, M Bank subsidiary headquarters, leasehold. Cambridge M Bank Research university facility, leasehold.'*

Bobby continued flicking through the file and paused, 'Stephen, where are the details regarding al vostro ufficio di Zermatt?'

'We don't have an office in Zermatt. Have you seen the cost of business premises in Switzerland,' Stephen laughed. 'Also, why did you say "regarding your Zermatt office" in Italian?'

'I didn't,' Bobby protested. 'But anyway, I was told some of your staff were based there. Something to do with the IFFS.'

'Not only do we not have an office or staff based in Switzerland, but I've never been involved with the IFFS.'

'Never mind that, Champ. Come over here. I want to talk to you,' Pat said.

Bobby went to protest, but his mother's look made it clear it was non-negotiable. He tidied the files up and walked around the desk. As he reached the chair nearest him, he leant forward to pick up a biscuit off the tray. He tumbled forward, catching the long edge of the table and rolling onto the floor, knocking a cup which crashed to the floor with him.

Pat jumped to her feet and rushed to help Bobby, but he was already getting up.

'Are you okay?'

'Yeah, I'm alright. Sorry, I just got a bit dizzy,' Bobby said as he stumbled into the nearest armchair.'

'*You feel so weak. I think we're still not eating enough,*' Max thought.

'*I'm fine.*'

Stephen held out the plate of biscuits. 'Here, have something to eat. You look pale.'

'And have some sweet tea,' Pat insisted, pouring some into a spare cup and adding sugar.

'*Why is everyone fussing?*' Bobby grumbled.

'*Because we all care about you,*' Max replied.

Bobby ate a biscuit and sipped the tea his mother had poured. 'I'm sorry I broke one of your cups.'

'Don't worry about it. It was an old one anyway,' Stephen replied.

Pat picked up the broken pieces and noticed the manufacturer's mark on the base of the broken cup. 'Stephen, it says Wedg—'

'Exactly, it's old. It's not even a complete set,' Stephen winked at Pat.

Pat put the broken pieces on the tray and smiled at Stephen. Sitting on the sofa beside him, she looked at Bobby and asked, 'How are you feeling now? Your colour is coming back a bit,' Pat said.

'I'm fine, Mum. I just stood up too quickly, and then bending made me dizzy,' Bobby replied.

'If you're sure, Champ,' Pat said.

'I'm okay, honest.'

'Lily, can you put that tablet down for a minute, please?' Pat asked.

'Minute, Mummy,' Lily replied.

'Now, please,' Pat said firmly.

'Fine,' Lily huffed, putting the tablet onto the table.

'What do you two think of the house?' Pat asked, looking at her two children lovingly.

'It's amazing,' Lily said.

'Bobby?' Pat asked.

'Yeah, it's alright.'

'How do you both fancy living here permanently?'

'But we live with you, Mummy,' Lily said, frowning.

Pat laughed. 'I mean, all of us live here, munchkin.'

'Yay,' Lily replied.

'Bobby?'

'You mean all four of us living here like a family?'

Pat looked at Stephen and smiled. 'Yes, a new family and a fresh start here.'

'It's okay. I'll stay in Haywood,' Bobby replied.

'You can't stay there alone. Besides, Stephen said he'll help me buy it, and we can rent that house out,' Pat said.

'Rent it to me then,' Bobby said stubbornly.

'You only turned eighteen a couple of months ago. Besides, you wouldn't be able to afford it,' Pat replied. 'It's not just the rent; you've got the energy bills, food, water rates, council tax, and lots more.'

'I don't feel the cold, and I don't eat much.'

'Talking of eating, you've been losing a lot of weight. You're not on some fad diet, are you?' Pat asked.

'No!' Bobby protested.

'So, we're agreed then. We'll come and live here with Stephen,' Pat said.

'Yay,' Lily said, jumping onto Stephen.

'But I don't want to live here. My friends all live in London, and this is hours away,' Bobby replied angrily.

'*It's only fifty minutes by car,*' Max thought.

'*Shut it. I don't want to live here with him.*'

'*That's mean,*' Lily said in Bobby's head.

'Butt out, Lily,' Bobby snapped as he stood up.

'Don't have a go at your sister,' Pat said firmly.

'It's actually under an hour back to your old house,' Stephen said.

'If you've got a car, maybe,' Bobby growled, walking back towards the drinks cabinet behind the desk.

Stephen smiled. 'We were keeping this as a surprise, but—'

Bobby turned angrily. 'Mum told me, and you can—'

Pat dived off the sofa to Bobby, who had collapsed. 'Bobby? Bobby, wake up!'

'Let me look,' Stephen said, kneeling beside her. 'I've done first aid. Call an ambulance.'

Pat picked up her phone and dialled, her hands shaking. 'I need an ambulance. It's my son, he's collapsed. He's only eighteen.'

Stephen quickly checked Bobby's pulse and breathing. 'Tell them his breathing is very shallow and his pulse is racing.'

'They've asked if his airway is clear,' Pat asked, as she gave the operator their address.

'Yes, it's clear,' Stephen replied, tilting Bobby's head back slightly.

'Mummy, is Bobby 'right?' Lily asked, clutching Pat.

'He's poorly, but he'll be fine, munchkin,' Pat lied reassuringly.

'How long?' Stephen asked.

'They're saying twenty minutes,' Pat replied. 'No, his lips and fingers aren't blue. Please hurry.'

'Mummy, Granny said it'll be okay.'

'Not now, munchkin. Stephen, they said, check his pupils and see if they react to the light.'

Stephen carefully lifted one of Bobby's eyelids. 'I can only see the white of his eyes. They've rolled back.'

'They said roll him onto his side and put him into the recovery position and monitor his breathing,' Pat said with fear as she held back the tears filling her eyes.

15
OVERLOAD

'Doctor, what's happening?' Pat asked desperately as the doctor emerged from the emergency room.

'We're still running tests, Mrs Morris,' the doctor replied hurriedly.

'Can we see him?' Stephen asked.

'I'm sorry, Mr Morris, your son is still unconscious. Until we know more, it's best if you wait here or in the relatives' room. We'll update you as soon as we can.'

'I'm not his...' Stephen started to say, but the doctor rushed away before he could finish.

A young male nurse approached them. 'Mr and Mrs Morris, the doctor asked me to take you to the relatives' room. Can I get you a drink?'

'This is Mrs Morris, but I'm not Mr Morris,' Stephen corrected. 'I'm here for his mother; my name is Marchent.'

'Sorry, Mr Marchent,' the nurse apologised, leading them into the relatives' room. 'Now, if you'd like to wait here, the doctor will be with you as soon as possible. There's some vending machines down the corridor with snacks and hot drinks.'

As the nurse turned to leave, Stephen asked, 'Nurse, how soon can we move him to a private hospital?'

'You need to ask the doctor. But our priority is making him stable and finding out why he's unconscious,' the nurse replied before leaving the room.

Pat slumped into a chair and put her head into her hands. Stephen sat beside her and wrapped his arm around her.

'He will be alright, won't he?' Pat lifted her head and looked at Stephen, her eyes welling up with tears.

'I'm going to ring some contacts and get the best neurosurgeon in here. In the meantime, why don't you ring your neighbour to make sure my housekeeper got Lily there safely? And do you have any of Bobby's friend's phone numbers?' Stephen asked reassuringly.

An hour or so later, the doctor walked into the relatives' room to be met by the couple he believed to be his patient's parents and half a dozen teenagers.

'Mrs Morris. Your son is in a stable condition, but we still don't know why he's unconscious. I'm sorry to ask this, but does he take any recreational drugs?'

'No, he does not,' Pat insisted.

'Has he got any allergies?'

'He used to be allergic to sticking plasters when he was young, but he's grown out of that,' Pat replied.

'What about medical conditions like diabetes?'

'No, nothing. There was nothing wrong with him. He's fit and healthy.'

Danny coughed, and the doctor turned to him. 'Do you know something, sir?'

'Could this be caused by anorexia?' Danny asked.

'At the moment, we'll take any possibilities, and yes, that could be a contributing factor to his condition,' the doctor said. 'I need to go and brief the team.'

Pat placed her hand on the doctor's arm. 'Doctor, he will be okay, won't he?'

The doctor smiled weakly. He seemed to spend so much time reassuring worried relatives, even when the odds were stacked against them. 'Mrs Morris, Bobby's vital signs are good. His blood pressure is a little high, which is unusual for an anorexic but not dangerously so. We need to run some other tests, but if this young man is correct about your son having anorexia, we have something to work on. Please try not to worry.'

Pat slumped back in her chair as the doctor hurried out of the room. As the door clicked shut, Pat looked up at Danny and then scanned the faces of Adam, Dazza, Mercedes, Avery and Chris. 'How long have you all known?'

'I got suspicious at the club event where you met Mr Marchent,' Adam replied, glancing at Stephen. 'I kept asking why he wasn't eating much, and he just said it was because of him getting upset. Whenever we were together, it looked like he was eating something.'

'But you seemed certain, Danny,' Pat said accusingly.

Danny looked down at his feet and mumbled, 'Well, it was, you know, when, uh...'

'I think what Danny is trying to say is that it was when we were in Rome,' Avery said. 'Bobby collapsed in a restaurant, and Max's brother insisted Bobby ate something.'

'Who's Max?' Stephen asked.

'Never mind that. Bobby collapsed in Rome, and nobody thought to tell me!' Pat replied angrily.

'Or me,' Adam snapped.

'Well, Zym made him eat some healthy food, and we kept an eye on him for the rest of the trip, and he did eat more than he was,' Dazza said.

'It's all my fault,' Adam said. 'I'm supposed to protect him and look after him.'

'No, I'm his mother. I knew he was losing weight, but he's been on diets before,' Pat sighed. 'I've been too busy with…things,' she added, looking at Stephen.

'Come on, Pat. You can't blame yourself,' Stephen said, wrapping his arm around her.

Pat shrugged his arm off and stood up. 'I'm sorry, Stephen, but this is all too fast. I need to put my children first.'

'Of course, love. We can postpone the move to Marlow. You need to look after Bobby,' Stephen replied, glancing back towards a commotion in the hallway outside the room.

Pat sighed. 'No, you're not listening to me. I need to—what the hell is going on out there?'

Dazza opened the door and looked out. 'We need to get out there.'

Pat rushed out of the room behind Dazza, followed by the others, and saw a figure with his back to her standing in the middle of the reception, talking loudly.

'Who's in charge here?' the man bellowed.

'Would you please keep your voice down,' the receptionist replied.

'I'll keep my voice down when I get to speak to the person treating my patient,' the man roared.

'Can you tell me the patient's name again?' the receptionist asked, visibly shaking. 'And your name, please.'

'I'm Mr Michael Thomas, and my patient is Bobby Morris. He was rushed in here an hour or so ago.'

Hearing her son's name, Pat rushed over to the man, quickly followed by Stephen and the others.

'Are you the neurosurgeon Dr Eyre recommended?' Stephen asked.

Michael turned and looked Stephen up and down. 'Who?'

'Dr Eyre. He said he knew a brilliant neurosurgeon who might be able to help,' Stephen said, holding out his hand.

Michael looked down at Stephen's hand before looking back into his face. 'I'm a neurological consultant, sir. I don't cut people open to deal with the issues of the mind.'

'Michael? What are you doing here?' Pat asked.

'Patricia, how lovely to see you despite the circumstances. Young Danny called me and told me about the developments with Bobby,' Michael replied. 'Catherine wanted to come, but she had an emergency at the hospital.'

'Do you think you can help?' Pat asked.

'I can't be sure until I check him, but I think it might be transmutation time,' Michael said.

'Money is no object,' Stephen said. 'Whatever it costs to help Bobby, I'll pay.'

Michael glanced back at Stephen. 'Who are you, sir?'

'I'm Stephen Marchent. I'm Pat's boyf—partner. But please call me Stephen.'

'Well, Mr Marchent, your money is no good when it comes to this family,' Michael replied.

'I'm sorry, but for Pat's son, just name your price.'

'Mr Marchent, there is not enough money in this world to come close to how much I owe this family and that young man. If you wish to splash your money around, I suggest getting young Dazza some food before he wastes away,' Michael said, winking at Dazza.

'Mr Thomas?' a doctor said. 'I'm Doctor Warner. I've been treating Bobby Morris.'

'Pleased to meet you, Warner. Now, if you can show me to my patient and update me on his condition,' Michael said. 'And drop the mister. Thomas will do fine.'

'I'm sorry, Mr Thomas, but I've checked the health service records, and you're not recorded as his physician,' Doctor Warner insisted.

'That's because Mrs Morris has only just contacted me, haven't you, Patricia.'

'Erm, yes, of course, Michael,' Pat confirmed.

'Oh, well, I'm afraid we need to ensure his condition is stable before we release him to a private hospital, Mr Thomas,' Doctor Warner insisted.

'For crying out loud, just call me Thomas. Don't they teach you simple etiquette in medical school nowadays, Warner? And never mind making decisions about his condition. Now stop wasting time, and let me see my patient. We can decide the best treatment afterwards,' Michael replied.

'I'm coming with you,' Pat said.

Michael leaned forward as if he was going to kiss Pat on the cheek and whispered, 'Patricia, if I'm to get Bobby somewhere safe, I need you to stay here. I'll take good care of your boy. I promise.'

Pat nodded in agreement.

'You, Marchent. Take very special care of this lady while I look after young Bobby,' Michael said before heading after Doctor Warner.

Michael strode into the emergency room, exuding the confidence of a senior consultant. His eyes scanned the unfamiliar surroundings, filled with familiar equipment and the unmistakable smell of antiseptic, mixing with the steady beeps of numerous machines. Around him, nurses and junior doctors were taking notes, checking charts, studying screens, and examining patients in various states of distress.

Warner stopped at a curtain surrounding a cubicle. 'We're still running tests, but he's hypoglycaemic, and his electrolytes are low, so we've got him on an intravenous drip to raise his glucose, potassium, and sodium levels, but—'

'Will you stop blithering around,' Michael said in frustration, pulling back the curtain. His eyes darted between the familiar face of Bobby, lying unconscious in the hospital bed, the monitors bleeping away as they tracked his vital signs and the nurse who was currently taking a blood sample.

An alarm went off as Bobby's heartbeat slowed dramatically.

'Not on my watch, young man,' Michael muttered under his breath. 'Warner, get the crash trolley,' he said firmly.

'But he's been doing this ever since he came in. It'll stabilise in a minute. It's fine.'

Michael glanced at the heart monitor and noticed it had gone very weak, but there was an echo of a stronger heart rhythm. 'I gave you an order, not asked for a diagnosis. This is far from normal. Get that crash trolley—now!' he barked, leaving no room for debate.

Warner rushed out of the cubicle, but another nurse had overheard the conversation, darted towards the crash trolley and was already heading back. As she hurried towards him, the wheels squeaked and the syringes, airways and other ephemera rattled.

When the nurse came through the curtain with the trolley, Michael moved quickly. 'Charge the defib to 200,' he ordered, his fingers checking Bobby's pulse as his eyes studied the heart monitor, which was now showing two heartbeats, one growing stronger and the other getting weaker.

'Charging,' a nurse said.

Michael watched the two heartbeats continue to separate. He knew what it meant. Bobby was dying, which was forcing Max to separate, either into his shell if it was ready or as an energy soul about to enter a new host.

Seconds stretched into what felt like minutes as Michael watched the medical team checking IV lines, squeezing the bag-valve-mask to fill Bobby's lungs with oxygen, and moving like a well-oiled machine.

'Clear,' Michael shouted with authority. The team stepped back as Michael held the paddles against Bobby's chest and the electrical charge surged through his body.

Michael held his breath and stared at the heart monitor, waiting for the beep of a single heartbeat, but the lower line had flatlined as the upper line had returned to normal. 'Come on, Bobby and Max. Stay together,' he whispered to himself.

The nurse started ventilation again, with each squeeze of the bag causing Bobby's chest to rise and fall.

'Get me one milligram of adrenaline on IV push and charge the defib to 300,' Michael ordered, as his eyes flicked between the heart monitor, the drugs being prepared and the status of the defibrillator.

'Clear,' Michael shouted for the second time before delivering a second charge into Bobby.

'Start compressions,' Warner said.

'No, wait,' Michael said sternly. As he studied the heart monitor, both heartbeats turned into a single flatline before kicking back into a slow but regular rhythm. 'Are you still inside him, Max?' Michael pondered.

A nurse appeared from behind the curtain and whispered something to Warner.

'Thank you, nurse,' Warner replied as he lifted his tablet. 'Mr Thomas, the blood test results are back, and the patient's glucose, potassium and sodium levels are almost normal.'

'Get Bobby up to a ward so he can be monitored,' Michael ordered.

'Uh, we've got a bit of a backlog on ward spaces,' Warner stuttered.

'No change there,' Michael replied. 'As long as he's kept under observation until he can be transferred. What's the current wait?'

'About six or seven,' Warner said.

'That's pretty impressive. I'll let the family know they can go up in thirty minutes,' Michael replied.

'Thirty minutes? I mean six or seven hours.'

'Whaat! Get him to a side cubicle. I want someone with him until I can arrange a hospital transfer,' Michael retorted. 'I'm going to see the family.'

A few minutes later, Michael walked into the relatives' room.

'How is he?' Pat said, springing to her feet as Michael walked in.

'Bobby's stabilised. His vital signs are good, and his heart rate's improving,' Michael replied cautiously but hopefully.

'What about Max?' Avery asked.

'Max is alive, but...' Michael hesitated.

'But what?' Avery pressed with concern.

'For a moment Bobby flatlined.'

'Flatlined?' Dazza asked, frowning.

'As in, he died, big man,' Danny replied bluntly.

'I know that, bonehead. I mean, what does it mean for Max and Bobby now?' Dazza snapped.

'Bobby's heart stopped, but we restarted it within seconds. He's stable now and should make a good recovery,' Michael explained. 'But I don't know if Max moved to another host.'

'Max wouldn't do that. He'd stay if there was any chance Bobby would make it,' Avery insisted firmly.

'I'm afraid it doesn't work like that. If the host dies, the Shadower's survival instincts take over, and their energy soul jumps to a new host,' Michael explained.

'But if the chief jumped, wouldn't you have seen the flash of his energy soul leaving Bobby?' Danny challenged.

'Only if he moved upwards. With all the chaos in there and so many people around, he could've easily shifted sidewards or downwards into someone else.'

'But he'd have let you know if he had,' Avery insisted with certainty.

'Jumping into a host nowadays seems to take Max a day or two to recover,' Michael said. 'We won't know until Bobby wakes up or Max comes round in his new host.'

'Adam, are you okay?' Stephen asked, noting Adam hadn't moved or spoken since Michael had returned.

Adam looked up, his face white as a sheet. 'I thought I'd lost him.'

Pat sat beside Adam and put her arm around him. 'We're not letting him go anywhere, agreed?'

Adam smiled weakly and nodded before he looked up at Michael. 'When can we see him?'

'I can take you and Patricia in to see him in a few minutes, but there's a long wait for a ward bed. I'm going to call around and get him into a private hospital.'

'I know the perfect place. A friend of mine is the CEO at the Oliver Clinic,' Stephen offered.

'Nooo,' the rest of the group groaned in unison.

Stephen looked shocked. 'What's wrong with the Oliver? It's got fantastic facilities.'

'Let's just say we've got some...bad history with that place,' Danny laughed.

A few minutes later, after several calls, Michael returned. 'The Royal Duke is preparing a room for him.'

'Thank you,' Pat and Adam both said.

'Yeah, thanks, Michael. Give them my details for the bills,' Stephen added.

'I already have,' Michael replied.

16
CHANGES

'Michael, how long have you been here?' Pat asked quietly, walking into the living room of the hospital suite between Bobby's hospital bedroom and the neighbouring family bedroom.

'Not long. Agathe will be here soon; she's just parking the car. She dropped me off so I could get an update on the patient, and it seems he's doing well.'

'Shh, not so loud,' Pat said, nodding towards a closed door.

'Oh, sorry, is Stephen still asleep?'

'No, not Stephen. It's Adam. He only leaves Bobby's side when I force him to go to bed,' Pat explained. 'Stephen has agreed to give me some space.'

'I'm sorry to hear that. Don't worry about the fees; there aren't going to be any as the hospital owes me a lot of favours,' Michael smiled.

'It's okay. We haven't split, but he's accepted we were going too fast,' Pat said. 'Hang on, you said last week that you'd given the hospital Stephen's details for the bills.'

'I did, didn't I,' Michael chuckled. 'Well, I thought he was getting a little flash with his cash.'

'Who's getting flash, Michael?' Agathe asked, carrying a large wicker basket.

'That Marchent fellow I told you about,' Michael said.

'Patricia, how are you coping, my dear?' Agathe asked, giving Patricia a tight hug.

'I'm okay under the circumstances,' Pat sighed, looking lovingly at her unconscious son through the open bedroom door.

'Michael told me young Bobby has recovered well with the intravenous drip.'

'That's what I've been told, but he's still unconscious.'

'I think Max is transmuting,' Michael said. 'With Bobby having anorexia, his body is burning through calories, and it just couldn't take any more.'

'Talking of eating, have you eaten anything this morning?' Agathe asked.

'Not yet. I'll get something later,' Pat replied.

Agathe picked up her bag and placed it on the table by the armchairs. 'I knew you'd be like that. I've got some patties. These are spicy beef and those are vegetable ones. I've got some buns and cheese and some coco bread with cheese. Oh, and some festival plus a bulla cake.'

Adam staggered into the room, wearing the same grey jogger bottoms and white t-shirt he'd worn all week. 'I heard a noise. Is Bobby awake?' he asked, rubbing his eyes.

'Adam, go back to bed. You've only been asleep for an hour,' Pat said.

'I'm fine,' Adam said, wandering into Bobby's room, sitting in a chair by the bed and holding Bobby's hand.

Agathe put some food on a plate, walked over to Adam and crouched. 'Adam, my dear. You need to keep up your strength. Please eat something?'

'I can't eat while Bobby's like this.'

'I remember sitting beside Michael many years ago, before you were born, and feeling the same. Everyone telling you the man you love is fine. "It's just the transmutation process of these aliens." But it's your loved one who's lying there, unconscious. They give you so many positive words, but you only see your soulmate's mental absence.'

'I just want him back, Agathe. I'd give up my football career if it'd bring him back to me.'

'He'll be back with you soon. I don't understand what happens, but when Max transmuted from Michael, Michael was different in a better way. All his anxiety and fear disappeared. It was like I got back a recharged Michael.'

'I don't care if I get back a recharged Bobby or my vulnerable, insecure Bobby; I just want him back. I can help him with his anorexia or anything.'

'Then eat. If you're going to persuade Bobby that eating is normal, you have to look healthy yourself.'

Adam looked at Agathe. 'Why do you care so much? I love that you do, but you only met us a few months ago.'

Agathe hugged Adam. 'My dear boy, Max taught me that we have a choice in life, to either make those we meet miserable or happy. The choice you make shows your true self.'

Adam smiled, taking one of the patties. 'Well, your true self is incredible.'

'I'll leave you and Bobby, but just shout if you need us,' Agathe said.

'Morning, peeps,' Danny said, barging into the living room. 'How's Bobster doing?'

'Hello, Danny,' Pat said. 'He's still asleep, but Michael said he's doing well.'

'Oh, sorry, Michael, I never saw you by the door,' Danny paused and sniffed the air a little too dramatically. 'Do I detect the presence of the world's greatest Caribbean chef? Where are you hiding Lady Agathe?'

'If it isn't my Danny,' Agathe laughed as she entered the living room.

'Hello, Danny. What have you been up to recently?' Michael asked.

'Not much, Doc. Helped Dad buy a business, discovered how to transmit energy, including animal souls, and wandered around Rome with an expert who lived there two thousand years ago,' Danny replied.

'Just normal things when Max is in your life, then?' Michael laughed.

'Very boring,' Danny chuckled. 'So what about that glorious food I can smell?'

'Help yourself. I've made plenty,' Agathe replied, pointing towards the food on the table.

Danny reached over and grabbed a pattie. 'Well, if you insist—'

Danny was cut short by an alarm and a scream from the bedroom. They rushed into the room and saw Adam leaning over the bed.

'Bobby, don't leave me,' Adam screamed.

Agathe ran to comfort Adam. 'It's okay, Adam. Bobby is still there; it's just Max transmuting out of him.'

'No, no,' Adam cried. 'Max has already transmuted. He's in the bathroom. It's Bobby's soul leaving him.'

Michael rushed past Agathe and stared at the bed. Bobby's body was motionless, and half emerging above it, almost like a double exposure picture, was a glowing white duplicate of Bobby.

'I've seen enough death to know that's not normal. That's like a Shadower's energy soul,' Michael said, slamming his palm against the emergency call button above the bed. 'Everyone, please stand back. Agathe grab that oxygen mask, put it snugly over his nose and mouth, then turn that valve to start the flow. You'll hear it hissing.'

As Agathe did as she was instructed, Michael started giving Bobby chest compressions. Michael's hands reached through the energy soul as he worked in a determined, rhythmic fashion on Bobby's chest. He counted in his head as he kept his eyes fixed on Bobby's lifeless face.

Pat and Adam held each other tightly as the monitors beeped frantically.

'Please don't let him die,' Pat begged.

'He's not going anywhere. I just need to keep his heart going,' Michael replied sharply as he pressed down on Bobby's chest.

'Michael, it's working. Look, the energy soul is lowering back into Bobby's body,' Agathe said.

A few seconds later, the door swung open as nurses and doctors rushed in and quickly assessed the scene.

'Mr Thomas, let me take over,' a doctor said.

Michael glanced to his left and recognised a former colleague. 'Harrison, what took you so long,' Michael said, stepping back and wiping his brow.

'Not now, Thomas,' Harrison replied as he took over the chest compressions and a nurse prepared the crash cart.

'I don't understand it. You told me he was doing well. What changed?' Pat demanded, tears rolling down her cheeks.

Michael stared at the medical team working on Bobby as he ran his hand through his hair. 'There's something else going on here—something we don't yet understand.'

'Do you mean Bobby won't recover from this?' Adam whispered.

'We won't know that until the team get him back,' Michael replied, nodding towards the medical team treating Bobby. 'But if Max is in the bathroom like you said, then whose energy soul is also inside Bobby? Two energy souls can't occupy the same host.'

'Max! I forgot with everything going on,' Agathe shouted.

'Who?' a voice said behind her.

Agathe turned to see a replica of Bobby standing in the bathroom doorway. 'Oh my lord, someone get me a gown before the poor lad catches his death of cold.'

Pat grabbed a fluffy white dressing gown from the back of the bedroom door and passed it to Agathe, who wrapped it around Max while looking away.

'Where am I?' Max asked.

'You're in hospital, my dear,' Agathe replied.

'Where's my brother?' Max asked.

Agathe smiled. 'Not here yet, Max.'

Pat went to speak, but Agathe indicated not to. 'He did the same when he transmuted from Michael. It's like he returns to being a child when he first emerges. It only lasts a short time.'

'Thomas, get here quick,' Harrison barked sharply.

Michael glanced at the monitors as he approached the bed. 'What's up Harrison? Has my patient worn you out?' Michael asked.

'How does he look?'

'His heart rate looks stable; in fact, I'd go as far as to say perfectly normal. His other vitals are also strong. Are you disappointed he's doing so well?'

'Not disappointed, amazed is probably a better term. Look at his skin tone,' Harrison said, pinching the skin on Bobby's hand to demonstrate how quickly the capillaries refilled.

'His blood circulation is impressive for someone close to death minutes ago,' Michael agreed. 'Aside from being asleep, he's almost glowing with health.'

Harrison stepped back. 'It's not just his skin that's glowing. Check his pupils.'

Michael reached over the bed and lifted one of Bobby's eyelids. 'Bloody hell.'

'Michael, mind your language,' Agathe scolded.

Michael lifted the other eyelid and took a sharp breath. 'Have you ever seen anything like this?'

'Not that intense. Could it be Leukocoria?' Harrison suggested.

'Do you have an ophthalmoscope?' Michael asked. He took the device from the doctor, lifted Bobby's left eyelid and peered into Bobby's eye. 'Nope, it's not white pupil. There's no sign of retinoblastoma, cataracts or retinal detachment. Aside from that glow, it looks normal.'

'Is he blind?' Adam asked nervously as he approached the bed, with Pat gripping his arm tightly.

'I don't believe so. His pupils reacted normally to the light from the ophthalmoscope,' Michael replied as the medical staff cleared away their equipment and stepped away to let the family approach the hospital bed.

Max looked around the room and scratched his head. 'Why's there so many pe—Bobby! How's Bobby,' Max said, rushing past a nurse towards the bed.

'Max is back,' Agathe laughed to herself.

'What's going on? Why are there so many nurses and doctors in here?' Max asked agitatedly.

'Hello, Max. Welcome back,' Michael smiled.

'Michael, no Thomas, no erm, what's your name? Hello,' Max replied.

'I'm Michael, although in your previous form, you used to call me by my surname, Thomas. I think my medical training rubbed off on you.'

'Oh yeah, Thom—no, that doesn't feel right, Michael,' Max replied. 'What's going on with Bobby then?'

'Your brother's heart stopped for a moment, but thanks to Mr Thomas's quick reactions, we managed to restart it quickly,' Harrison stated. 'He's stable for now, but we're going to monitor him and run some tests to identify what caused his cardiac arrest.'

'Cardiac arrest!' Danny exclaimed. 'Not another one.'

'You mean this lad's got a history of cardiac arrest? You should have told me, Thomas,' Harrison said firmly.

'I think Danny's referring to another friend who had one,' Michael replied. 'It's not related, Danny.'

'But the aura...' Danny hesitated.

'What aura?' Max asked.

'Come on, let's get out of here and let Mr Harrison complete his final checks,' Michael said, ushering everyone, bar the medical team, out of the bedroom.

'Can we stay?' Adam asked.

Michael glanced at Harrison, who nodded in approval.

'Okay, but only his mum and Adam,' Michael insisted.

Harrison smiled at Max, 'I think his twin brother might want to stay too.'

Danny burst out laughing. 'Max isn't Bobby's tw—'

'Max isn't properly dressed,' Michael interrupted.

'I've got some clean clothes for Bobby in the other bedroom that should fit,' Pat replied, holding Bobby's hand.

As Agathe took Max off to get the clothes and Danny entered the living room, Harrison grabbed Michael's arm. 'What's going on?'

Michael gulped nervously. 'I'm not sure what you mean. My patient had a cardiac arrest, and we've just saved his life.'

Harrison paused as the other medical staff left, adding, 'I'm not stupid. We've got a patient with glowing eyes like he's undergone some strange radiation or energy exposure and a naked duplicate coming out of the bathroom looking confused.'

Michael's brain went into overdrive as he tried to think of a logical explanation.

'You're not doing human cloning, are you?' Harrison demanded.

Michael laughed in relief. 'Human cloning! Good grief, no. The lad's twin works on a farm. He'd just gone into the bathroom for a shower when it all kicked off with Bobby.'

'So he didn't know his brother was in a bad way until he walked out to be confronted by all of us,' Harrison said. 'No wonder he seemed shocked.'

'Exactly. I'd have been shocked too, coming out of the bathroom naked to get dressed and find you've got an audience,' Michael laughed as he escorted Harrison out of the suite.

'Poor lad, he'll need treatment after that. Talking of treatment, keep checking on Bobby, especially his eyes; they are very strange,' Harrison chuckled. 'I'll let you know if his bloods tell us anything.'

'Thanks, Harrison, and great work in there,' Michael said as he shut the door behind the doctor.

As Michael returned to the living room, he saw Bobby sitting in a chair by the food table, shovelling it in. 'Bobby?'

'That's Max,' Agathe explained.

'Good grief. I'd forgotten how identical to his host Max is after transmuting,' Michael replied.

'Not entirely,' Danny added. 'Even before his eating problems, I've never seen Bobby eat that much.'

Max stopped eating momentarily, drank some water and said, 'What's going on with Bobby then, Michael?'

'I think his anorexia left him so weak your transmutation overloaded his heart. But he seems fine now,' Michael replied.

'But what about Bobby's aura?' Danny protested.

'I forgot about the aura. Hang on, what do you mean Bobby's aura?' Max challenged.

'When Bobby's heart stopped, an aura came out of him. It only went back when Michael restarted his heart,' Danny added.

'That's not quite what happened from a medical perspective, but Danny's right about the aura,' Michael confirmed.

Max stood up sharply. 'That's not possible. One Shadower per host. It's not just a rule; it's physically impossible for more than one. Besides, I'd have detected anything strange.'

'Are you sure? I mean, Bobby is pretty strange,' Danny laughed.

'Has anyone got a mirror?' Max asked.

'I've got a small one in my medical bag,' Michael replied, rummaging around before pulling out a small dental mirror.

'That'll do,' Max said, grabbing it and heading into Bobby's room, followed by the others.

'Well, Chief. Can you see anything?' Danny asked.

Max twisted around, trying to catch Bobby's reflection from multiple angles. 'Absolutely nothing. There's no aura. Are you sure you—'

'**Yes,**' Danny, Agathe and Michael said firmly.

'Well, he looks perfectly normal to me.'

'Lift his eyelids and check his pupils,' Michael said.

Max leaned over the bed and lifted Bobby's eyelid.

'Waah,' Bobby screamed, sitting up quickly and headbutting Max, who staggered backwards.

'Damn, that hurt,' Max said, rubbing his head.

Bobby looked towards Max and screamed again. 'Am I dead?'

'You were, but you're okay now,' Danny laughed.

Bobby glanced at Danny and then back to Max. 'But what, how, when?'

'You missed which, where and why,' Danny chuckled.

'Danny, behave. You can see young Bobby's confused,' Agathe scolded.

Pat ran across the room and flung her arms around her son. 'Champ, you're back. I've been so worried.'

'What happened? I remember something about you've got me a car, and I'm sure you said we were moving, but the next thing I remember is waking up here.'

'That's all changed now. You passed out, and then we rushed you to the hospital in an ambulance,' Pat explained.

'This looks more like a hotel than a hospital,' Bobby said, rubbing his forehead.

'You started in a normal hospital, but Danny called Michael, and he realised Max was transmuting and got you transferred here,' Pat explained.

Bobby looked at the red lump on Max's forehead and frowned. 'Did we bang our head when I fainted?'

'No, you flipping headbutted me when you woke up,' Max grumbled.

'Hang on. Why are you wearing my clothes?' Bobby asked.

'Your mum gave them to me after I transmuted,' Max replied.

'But I was wearing them when I fainted.'

'They've been washed since then,' Pat laughed. 'And yes, I've got some more...'

Pat trailed off as they heard a disturbance in the living room.

'He's my brother and I have to see him.'

'Sir, I don't mean to be rude, but you're old enough to be his grandfather. You need to leave. I've already called security.'

'You can call the Pope for all I care. Just get out of my way.'

Michael walked into the living room, followed by Agathe, to find a young male nurse arguing with an older man. 'Can I help you?'

'Si, si. I'm here to see...' the man glanced at something written on his hand. 'Bobby Morris.'

'And you are?' Michael asked firmly.

'I'm... sort of related to him.'

'Pat, can you come here, please? Do you recognise this man?' Michael shouted.

Pat walked to the bedroom door and studied the stranger. 'He does look familiar.'

'He says he's related—or sort of related—to Bobby.'

'I know I've seen him somewhere, but he's definitely not a relative of ours.'

'I think you'd better leave,' Michael said firmly.

'But I need to see him—and Max,' the man insisted.

'What do you know about Max?' Pat asked sharply.

The man sighed, 'I'm his brother, Zym.'

'You said your name was Bruno Moretti,' the nurse said.

'Bruno Morelli,' Zym corrected. 'But my friends call me Zym.'

'Zym? What are you doing here?' Max asked, entering the living room followed by Danny.

'Bobby and Max, I need to speak to you both,' Zym said, glancing at the others before adding, 'in private. Oh, and Wheels should come too.'

'Wheels! Hmm, I kinda like that,' Danny smiled.

'And I'm not Bobby and Max, I'm just Max—I've transmuted.'

'Where's Bobby? This concerns him too.'

17
THE BEGINNING

'I said I needed to talk to Max and Bobby alone,' Zym said.

'And I made it clear that I am not going anywhere if it involves Bobby,' Adam replied.

'What's so important you can't say it in front of the others?' Max asked.

'Because she's involved,' Zym replied, nodding towards the closed door leading to the living room.

'Who's "she"? Do you mean Agathe or my mum?' Bobby asked.

'The younger woman.'

'That's my mum. What do you mean involved? Involved in what?'

'I met her at the hotel in Rome. She's with Marchent,' Zym replied.

'Don't remind me,' Bobby grumbled.

'But you've still not explained what Pat is involved in,' Max said, sitting in a high-backed chair.

'M Bank Research's base is a forty-minute train ride from Zermatt, in Gornergrat,' Zym explained.

'And?' Bobby pressed.

'It's over three thousand metres high, with minimal light pollution and wide, clear views of the sky.'

'Sounds great if you like staring into space,' Bobby replied, his voice tinged with sarcasm.

'Funny you should say that. Their facility has a large observatory with a retractable dome,' Zym replied

Max thought momentarily before saying, 'It also sounds good for sending things across space.'

'I knew you'd get it, Junior,' Zym replied.

'I know I've been unconscious for a while, but I still don't get it,' Bobby said.

'Do you remember that Exodus machine we saw in Rome?' Max asked.

'You never told me that!' Zym exclaimed.

'I did,' Max insisted. 'Or I think I did. Anyway, Bobby, do you remember it?'

'Yeah, it was one of the few times I could feel you scared and angry,' Bobby confirmed.

'Those machines need a clear view into space to lock onto their target,' Max explained.

'And an observatory with a retractable dome is the perfect disguise,' Danny suggested.

'Exactly,' Max said.

Bobby picked up the glass of water by his bed and sipped it. 'I'm still confused. Those machines send energy not—'

'They send energy and also energy souls,' Zym interrupted.

Bobby glowered at Zym, then continued, 'Okay, so they send both, but that's the point they send, they don't receive. If someone wants to go to one of those planets, some Shadowers were evacuated to like...'

'You mean Astral 5, Noton 3 and Tascun 3?' Max said.

'Yeah, them. Why should we stop them if they want to go?' Bobby challenged.

'Because, my still-dazed friend, it isn't about them going. It's about creating the ability for them to come and go. Assuming those planets already have Exodus machines,' Danny said.

'Well done, Wheels. You're not as daft as you look, are you!' Zym laughed.

'Thanks, I try n—hey, what do you mean as daft as I look?' Danny challenged.

Max ignored Danny's protests and said, 'We've seen Shadowers coming to Earth for centuries, but it's tended to be in small numbers because it's always been a one-way trip.'

'Ah, I get it now. If someone travels back to those planets to show you can come or go, Earth could be swamped by Shadowers,' Bobby replied.

'That's one risk, but as a race, we were more advanced two thousand years ago than you are now,' Max explained.

'Which means the ones that come may not just swamp Earth but wipe your species out,' Zym added.

'That's nonsense. If your kind on those planets are more advanced than Shadowers on Earth, then whoever is doing this will be bringing in aliens who are so advanced they could wipe them out, too. They'd be idiots to do it,' Danny protested. 'It'd be a huge mistake.'

'Idiots make mistakes, egotists make huge mistakes,' Max replied.

'And this could be an off-the-scale mistake,' Zym agreed.

'Okay, I understand all this, but you told Max this involves Bobby. As in Bobby personally,' Adam said.

Zym pulled out his phone, opened a picture, and handed it to Danny. 'Do you guys recognise this?'

'Hmm,' Danny mused. 'It looks like a type of rice dish. Maybe a risotto with some meats. Going by the colour of the rice, I'd guess it has saffron—'

Zym snatched his phone and flicked past a couple of pictures. 'Not that one, this one?'

'Oh, yeah, that's a train,' Danny replied.

Zym rolled his eyes in frustration. 'And the logo on the carriage door?'

'That's M Bank's logo,' Danny said, showing it to Adam by his side and then turning the phone around so Max and Bobby could see.

'But Stephen said M Bank didn't have a facility in Switzerland,' Bobby protested.

'It looks like he lied,' Max replied.

'Now scroll through the pictures and tell me if you recognise anyone,' Zym said.

Danny moved his chair into standing mode, moved across to the television, and turned it on. He pulled out his phone, tapped a few buttons, and then returned to Zym's phone, which was now streaming to the television. As he started flicking through the pictures, everyone kept shaking their heads as each image flicked by.

'Stop!' Max said. 'Go back to that last picture.'

Danny scrolled back and zoomed into the face of the person. 'That's Dr Fellowes,' Max said.

'Well spotted, Junior,' Zym replied. 'Keep going, Danny.'

A few images later, Bobby yelled, 'Stop.'

'Do you recognise him?' Zym asked.

'Yeah, it's that guy who looks like Dad.'

'Oh yeah, Richard, something,' Adam replied.

'Richard Roberts,' Danny said.

'If you go to the next picture, I got one as he looked straight at me,' Zym said.

Danny flicked to the following image.

Adam said, 'Yep, that's defo him from that Australian show Dazza showed us. How did he end up there?'

'I think the real question is *why* did he end up there?' Max said.

'I think he's a Shadower. I'm sorry, Bobby, but I think your dad was a host, and whoever is behind M Bank killed him to get to Richard Roberts,' Zym said. 'It's the same method they used for others like Dr Fellowes.'

'Then I'm gonna kill them,' Bobby said, flinging back his bedcovers and swinging his legs over the side of the bed.

'Oh, for crying out loud, what is it with you and Max strutting around naked?' Danny groaned.

Adam opened a drawer, saw some clothes, and passed them to Bobby.

Bobby quickly dressed and said, 'Come on then. I'm going to avenge my dad's death.'

While the others had been busy with Bobby, Max had walked over to the television screen. 'Danny, zoom into that person on the right-hand side of the screen.'

Danny zoomed in and said, 'It looks like a woman, but half her face is obscured by her phone.'

'Is this a live picture?' Max asked.

Danny looked at Zym's phone and said, 'Yeah, let me scroll through the images to see if there is a clear view of her face.'

'There,' Max yelled.

Danny used Zym's phone to deblur the image, and it was unmistakable.

'That's Mercedes,' Bobby said, 'and the M Bank logo is right behind her.'

Danny frowned. 'I don't get it? I thought...'

'Looks like your girlfriend hasn't been totally honest with us, Wheels,' Zym replied.

'I knew something wasn't right about her,' Danny snapped. 'And she's not my girlfriend.'

'He doth protest too much,' Zym laughed.

Danny glowered at Zym. 'We need to find out what she's up to.'

'What do you suggest we do next, Zym?' Max asked.

'We need to—'

There was a knock on the bedroom door before it opened a little, and Pat poked her head around it. Seeing Bobby out of bed and dressed, she quickly slipped into the room and closed the door. 'Bobby, your boss is here with Danny's dad.'

'Why is Nigel here?' Bobby asked.

'No, he isn't called Nigel. I think he said his name was Bill something,' Pat replied.

Danny opened the door slightly before closing it as quietly as possible. 'It's Big Bill!'

'He can't see two Bobbys,' Max said.

'Hide in the bathroom,' Adam suggested. 'Bobby, take your top off and get back into bed.'

A few seconds later, Pat opened the bedroom door and ushered in Danny's dad and Big Bill.

'Bobby, great to see ya,' Bill said.

'Hi, Bobby. I was worried when Danny told me you'd collapsed,' Paul said.

'Morning, Mr Wh—Paul, and you too, Bill,' Bobby said nervously.

'Non vediamo l'ora di rivederti,' Bill said.

'*What the heck is he saying*?' Bobby thought.

'*He said they can't wait to see you back*,' Max replied.

'Thanks, Bill. I hope I'll be back soon,' Bobby said.

'Danny said it was some kind of alien virus. Maybe you picked it up in Italy?' Paul said.

'Yeah,' Bobby laughed half-heartedly as he saw Danny smirk at the "alien virus" comment.

'How long they reckon you'll be outta action?' Bill asked.

'I'm not sure, sir. Maybe a week or so,' Bobby replied.

'Just make sure you're fighting fit before you come back to work,' Paul said. 'Bill and Jay agreed—your job's safe. Take as long as you need.'

'Thank you, sir. That means a lot,' Bobby replied.

'Gotta look after our future stars,' Bill smiled. He glanced at Adam and Zym and said, 'I'm sorry, fellas, don't believe I've had the pleasure.'

'I'm Bobby's boyfriend, Adam.'

'Pleased to meet ya'll.'

'I'm Danny. Bobby's chief minder,' Danny laughed.

'I think we all know you, Danny,' Paul replied.

'And you are, sir?' Bill asked, holding out his hand to Zym.

'I'm Bruno, and I'm just an old family friend passing through,' Zym said, gripping and shaking Bill's hand firmly.

Bill glanced down at his hand after Zym let go, and saw the colour start to return to his fingers. 'Mighty fine grip you have, Bruno.'

'Have they gone yet?' Max thought.

'Shh, not yet. I think Zym almost crushed Bill's hand.'

'That's one of his tricks. You don't need to be strong to crush someone's hand if you know the technique.'

'Bobby! Your boss is talking to you,' Pat scolded.

'Oh, sorry, sir. I, uh, felt a bit dizzy for a minute,' Bobby said.

'That's fine, lad. You take it easy,' Bill replied. 'Danny, you take care of him now, ya hear me.'

'Yes, sir,' Danny replied, giving his best American salute.

'I think it's best if we leave Adam to care for Bobby and keep Danny well away from him,' Paul laughed.

'Hey, Dad, you're supposed to be on my side,' Danny protested in mock indignation.

'I'm sure your ego can take it, son,' Paul grinned.

There was a crash from the bathroom as Max slipped and knocked a bin across the floor.

'Sounds like y'all have an intruder in there,' Bill said.

Bobby started to say, 'That's, uh, the—'

'Bobby's cousin, Max,' Pat said hurriedly. 'He's been staying for a few days, but he's...'

'He's been throwing up,' Danny shouted, hoping Max would hear.

Max let out a loud groan for effect.

'Should he be here?' Bill asked.

'The doctor checked on him and said it seemed like a twenty-four-hour bug,' Pat replied. 'He was leaving when you arrived.'

'That fella was the doc? He looked older'n me,' Bill laughed.

'Come on, Bill, we gotta get going if we're gonna make it to the Palace of Westminster for lunch. Good to see you again, Pat. If I can help in any way, just let me know,' Paul said.

'Thanks, Paul, and nice to meet you too, Bill,' Pat said as she escorted them out.

Max hurried out of the bathroom as soon as the bedroom door closed. 'Why did they come here?'

'To see how Bobby was,' Adam said.

'That's strange,' Max said.

'Why's that so strange?' Adam asked.

'How many CEOs of a multi-billion-pound company would take time out to visit an office junior in hospital?' Max challenged.

'Come on, Chief. Paul is my dad, and he's Bill's biggest customer,' Danny protested.

'Maybe,' Max conceded.

'I've got a more difficult question,' Bobby said. 'How can we still talk telepathically even though you've transmuted?'

'You can?' Zym asked.

'Yeah, we can, and you're right, I don't know,' Max replied. 'Has it ever happened to you, Zym?'

'Nope, and I've never known anyone it has happened to until now,' Zym replied. 'Maybe it's because you separated so recently, and your adrenalin is still pumping around your bodies.'

'Yeah, you're probably right,' Max agreed.

Bobby got out of bed and pulled the black jumper back on.

'Hang on, that's my jumper,' Adam challenged.

'Aww, bless 'em. They're even sharing clothes now,' Danny laughed.

'Never mind that. When are we going to Switzerland?' Bobby demanded.

The bedroom door opened, and Pat walked in. 'Who's going to Switzerland?' she asked.

'We are. Zym has some information about Dad's death, and it involves M Bank's Zermatt laboratory,' Bobby replied.

'Observatory,' Max corrected.

'Whatever,' Bobby replied. 'Either way, M Bank's place in Switzerland has a link to whoever killed Dad.'

'But we don't have anything over there,' Stephen protested as he approached from behind Pat.

'Danny, show that train logo on the...oh, it's still on the TV,' Bobby said.

They all looked at the screen and saw Mercedes in front of the train carriage, with the M Bank logo visible.

'Explain that then!' Bobby demanded.

'That's definitely our logo, but I've never seen that train in my life,' Stephen protested. 'Do you have any other pictures of the area?'

'Keep flicking, lad. There's plenty,' Zym said to Danny.

As Danny flicked through pictures on the phone, it showed side shots of the train, the view back down the train tracks, and two observatory domes on top of towers at either end of the front of a hotel.

'I thought you said it was a large observatory,' Danny challenged.

'It is. Their facility is behind the hotel, but access is restricted. If you scroll forward a couple more pictures, I did grab a shot before security moved me away,' Zym said.

Danny quickly found the picture of a large observatory dome. 'How tall is it?'

'I'd say twenty to thirty feet high for the dome. But a lot of the facility is underground,' Zym replied.

Max stood up and walked over to the screen, studying the image. 'Danny, can you find that place on Earth Mapped?'

'Sure thing,' Danny said, putting down Zym's phone and tapping away on his instead. After finding what he was looking for, he started streaming the image to the television. 'There's the hotel, but there's no observatory.'

'What's the Mapped date?' Max asked.

'Two years ago. There's no way that observatory was built in two years,' Danny said.

'My thoughts exactly. Mapped has been doctored to take it out,' Max said.

'I've stood in front of it, and I can guarantee it's there,' Zym insisted.

'That would have cost a billion dollars or more to build. How could that happen without the CEO signing it off?' Max challenged Stephen.

'I swear, Bobby, I've never seen or heard of this place,' Stephen insisted.

'So, you'll help me find out why my dad was killed and what's going on there?' Bobby asked sceptically.

'I'll do anything and everything to help you...' Stephen stopped and looked at Bobby sitting on the edge of the bed and then back to Max in front of the television. 'What the hell?'

There was an awkward silence before Pat said, 'Stephen, I forgot to mention—this is Bobby's cousin, uh, Max.'

'But they're identical,' Stephen said. 'Hang on, you and Simon don't have siblings.'

'Egg donor,' Danny blurted out.

'Whaat!' Stephen and Pat exclaimed in unison.

'Sorry, Pat, but you can't really hide it. Besides, Stephen deserves to know,' Danny continued. 'Stephen, technically, Bobby and Max are brothers. Max's mum, may she rest in peace, couldn't have children, so Pat and Simon donated a fertilised egg, which she carried as her own.'

'Uh, so, she was sort of like family then?' Stephen stammered.

'Yeah, Auntie Sue was lovely,' Bobby said, putting on his best sad face.

'I'm sorry to hear she passed, Max. I hope it was peaceful,' Stephen said.

'I'd rather not talk about it,' Max replied.

'Of course,' Stephen said, still looking confused.

'Okay, now we all know each other. Can we get back to my dad's murderers!' Bobby insisted.

Pat walked over to Bobby and sat beside him. 'Champ, I miss your dad too, but he died in a car crash. He wasn't murdered.'

'We need to tell her the truth,' Max said.

'Not with him here,' Zym snapped, pointing towards Stephen.

'I'll leave if it helps,' Stephen offered.

'You stay right there,' Pat snapped. 'I'm sick to death of everyone interfering with my family and my decisions. You're my partner, and Bobby's my son. Simon taught me the importance of families staying together when it gets tough.'

'But...'

'No buts, Zym. Simon said he always thought he was better alone, but having a family made him realise he'd missed out on so much because we're stronger together,' Pat replied. 'If we're going to deal with this, whatever this is, we're all doing it. Now sit down, everyone, and start talking.'

Bobby and Max explained what they knew with help from Danny, Zym and Adam.

'Can I ask a question?' Stephen asked.

'In a minute,' Pat said. 'So where is this Richard Roberts?'

Danny pulled up the picture of Roberts on Zym's phone.

'There,' Bobby said, pointing at the screen.

Pat got up, walked over to the television and studied it. 'He does look a bit like your dad,' she agreed.

'Show the next picture, Danny,' Bobby said.

'No, it's not possible,' Pat said, stepping back in shock.

'What is it, Pat?' Stephen asked with concern.

Pat looked at the screen in disbelief. 'Bobby, he's got your dad's eyes. I've looked into those eyes so many times. Apart from that scar above his eyebrow and the gaunt, haunted look, it could almost be him. They do look like twins.'

'What's next then?' Adam asked.

'That's easy. We're off to Switzerland. WestFi may have bought my company, but I'm still the CEO. If anyone can get us in there, it has to be me,' Stephen said.

18
Surprise

'Stephen, it's stunning,' Pat said. 'It's just like you expect it to be. Every building looks like a wooden Swiss chalet, even the shops and hotels.'

'It's better than Rome,' Danny agreed. 'At least the Swiss know that roads should be smooth.'

'So smooth it'd be perfect for a taxi to take us to our hotel,' Dazza moaned as he dragged his case while lugging his camera bag.

'Zermatt is car-free. Besides, after sitting all that time, the walk is refreshing,' Max said.

'But they had electric taxis,' Dazza protested.

'Stop moaning, big man. We're here on a mission; you're just here for work, trying to get your scoop when the IFFS descend in a couple of days,' Danny laughed.

'And here's me thinking you wanted my press card access,' Dazza smiled.

'Well, you do have your uses,' Danny said.

'Will you lot pack it up? Just look at that scenery,' Pat replied.

Dazza looked around at the views and said, 'Yeah, it's okay. That big hill with the snow on would make a great backdrop.'

'That big hill is the Matterhorn,' Max sighed.

'Well if it don't mind, I don't Matterhorn,' Dazza laughed.

'Dazza, you're a great photographer, but promise you'll never give it up to be a comedian,' Bobby said as they reached the entrance to their chalet complex.

'Guys, there's a problem,' Danny hissed.

'What's up?' Dazza asked. 'It looks quite decent here.'

'The place has Cranside Security,' Danny said.

'It's a WestFi complex, which was built by their subsidiary Brinkswell Construction, and they own Cranside, so that's inevitable,' Stephen said matter of factly. 'That's how I managed to get us this place. It was booked out to some politician, but when I asked Big Bill, he cancelled the booking and moved the politician to one of their old places up in the hills.'

'Uh, yeah, but, well, I know that security guard,' Danny said. 'I've seen him before.'

'We work for WestFi, you numpty,' Bobby laughed. 'Cranside does most of our security. You've probably seen him in our London offices.'

'Yeah, I guess so,' Danny said doubtfully.

The guard walked chirpily out of the gatehouse towards them, flicking his navy blue jacket back just enough to reveal his rifle.

'Identify yourself,' the guard said, his thin build and cheery smile overcompensated by his gruff tone.

'Stephen Marchent and guests,' Stephen said.

The guard grabbed a clipboard through the gatehouse window and ran his finger down the list before beaming broadly. 'Ah, yes, Mr Marchent, what a pleasure to meet you. I have you here with a Mr and Mrs Morris, a Mr Thomas, a Mr White, a Miss Moore, Mr Morelli, Mr Lee and Mr Turner.'

'It's Mrs Morris and Mr Morris,' Stephen corrected. 'I'm afraid Miss Moore couldn't join us, and Mr Lee has a football match, but he's hoping to join us tomorrow.'

'Of course, sir. I'll amend my records tout suite,' the guard replied.

'I think you'll find the French phrase is tout de suite,' Stephen said as the guard opened the gate.

'Absolutely, sir. I must apologise I don't speak the local lingo. I've been drafted in to support the IFFS event,' the guard said.

Stephen sighed, 'Would you care to tell us where our chalet is, Mr...'

'Williams, sir. Eric Williams. If you need anything, just let me know,' Eric replied with a smile.

'How about where our chalet is? These cases are heavy,' Stephen said.

'Oh, my goodness. I'm so sorry, sir. You are in the Matterhorn. It's that large chalet straight ahead and up the slope above the other buildings. It has a second perimeter fence and security detail, but they are expecting you. There's a vehicle just to your left, waiting to take you and your guests. Please leave your luggage, and it'll be taken up for you,' Eric said in a flustered tone.

Eric ensured everyone's luggage was accounted for and escorted the guests towards the waiting oversized golf buggy.

'Excuse me,' Eric said to Danny.

'I knew it, he's recognised me. Once seen, never forgotten,' Danny whispered to Dazza.

'Mr White, sir,' Eric insisted. 'Can I check something with you?'

Danny sighed, 'Yes, Eric. How can I help?'

'Mr Lee, the one who's coming tomorrow,' Eric said excitedly. 'Is he Adam Lee, the Watford goal machine?'

Danny hesitated before saying, 'Yeah, he is. Is that all you wanted to ask?'

'Thank you, Mr White. Yes, that's all. I'm sorry for being so presumptuous, but I'm a huge Hornets fan.'

As Danny settled into a seat by Dazza and his chair was loaded into a trailer attached to the vehicle, Dazza laughed. 'What did you say? Once seen, never—what was it?'

'Oh, shut up,' Danny muttered.

A short while later, they had unpacked and were relaxing, admiring the view.

'I've been in worse hotels,' Dazza laughed.

'Never mind that who's Mr Thomas?' Danny asked.

'It's me. I had to use my old name, Maxwell Thomas. I got my passport renewed a while back with a photo of Bobby,' Max replied.

'Uh, isn't Max Thomas sixty-five?' Danny challenged.

'Sixty-four, actually,' Max said.

'Close enough. How did you get the passport office to agree to change your picture from an older man to Bobby?'

'I've been studying a friend of mine. I tried his technique and took a little stroll through some computer systems, followed by a few edits on a database, and suddenly, it was easy to show the man at the passport office that they'd made a mistake by putting some old guy's picture on my passport,' Max laughed.

'Was that the night you stayed at mine, and I was showing you the legacy software the government still use, which gives you a backdoor into their entire system?' Danny queried.

'Might have been, buddy,' Max replied with a wink.

'Can we get back to business?' Zym grumbled. 'When can you get us inside M Bank's observatory?

'It's closed today as they're preparing it for the IFFS conference in two days,' Stephen replied.

'We can't wait two days to get in there,' Zym snapped.

'No, we don't have to wait two days. We can get in tomorrow. It's a construction site today, with riggers installing lights, cameras, video equipment, sound systems, and seating and staging,' Stephen explained.

'But that could give them time to clear the place,' Zym protested.

'Come on, Zym. If they've got an Exodus machine up there, they won't be able to take it away in a day. It would take weeks to dismantle it,' Max said.

'Well, I'm going up there to see what's happening,' Zym insisted. 'Are you coming, Junior?'

'Fine, I'll come too. It'll be useful to scope out the place anyway.'

'Let's all go. I can look for good picture positions,' Dazza suggested.

'Can we stay here and explore the town?' Pat asked.

'Of course, sweetheart,' Stephen replied. 'Anyone else want to join us?'

'I'll pass, thanks,' Bobby replied. 'I want to see that place.'

'I'd better go and keep an eye on Bobster,' Danny said.

'I've booked the restaurant for eight,' Stephen said.

'So make sure you're back, especially you, Champ,' Pat added, looking at Bobby.

'Yes, Mum,' Danny laughed.

'You can behave too, Daniel,' Pat replied, smiling.

Dazza started laughing, which resulted in Danny playfully punching him in the arm. 'What's so funny, big man?'

'I've just never thought of you as a Daniel,' Dazza replied.

'Says the ginger, six foot four, white guy called Darius!' Danny laughed.

'You've got five hours before we need to go to the restaurant. Just be careful,' Pat said.

Almost an hour later, Bobby, Max, Danny, Zym, and Dazza passed through the barriers at the top of the Gornergrat and looked up the path towards the imposing hotel. The flat-fronted grey stone four-storey hotel was bookended by two circular towers with telescope domes topping each tower. To the right of the hotel were steps leading up to a large open-air seating area, and beyond that, a footpath wound up to the back of the seating area before curling up to a viewing area at the top of the mountain. At the front of the hotel was a glass-walled single-storey extension positioned between the round towers, which served as the hotel's entrance, the reception, and an indoor seating area. The extension's roof provided another guest terrace, accessed from a door on the hotel's first floor.

'It's imposing, but I can see why so many attendees are staying down in Zermatt,' Max said.

'The train has M Bank's logo on the last carriage, but only a couple of people got off,' Bobby said.

'Yeah, I grabbed some pictures,' Dazza said.

'They headed towards the hotel, but where's the large observatory?' Max asked. 'Those two at the top of each tower aren't that big.'

'We need to go up the path and keep to the right of the hotel. Then it's ahead of us, up another path,' Zym explained.

'I did some checks on this place online, and it says there is a public viewpoint right where you say the observatory is,' Danny said.

'Don't believe everything you see online, youngster. You'll see for yourself if your chair can make it with this light layer of snow,' Zym replied.

'Ha, I laugh in the face of snow. Well, as long as it's not very deep,' Danny laughed. 'This shouldn't be too bad with my all-terrain tyres.'

As they started trudging up the path towards the hotel, Max asked, 'How long have they been working on this place?'

'From what I've found out, they've been working on the underground part for twelve years, but the overground part has had work done in the last four years,' Zym replied.

'That's only three years after M Bank Research was founded as a joint venture between M Bank and WJ Futures,' Max said.

'Who is WJ Futures? I've never heard of them,' Zym asked as they reached the front of the hotel.

'We don't know. The name came up during the due diligence. All we know is that somehow, they're owned by WestFi.'

'Couldn't Wheels find them?' Zym laughed, glancing back at Danny and the others trailing behind.

'Nope. He tried every way he knew and kept getting stuck in the Cayman Islands,' Max replied. 'Let's wait for them to catch up.'

'Danny, switch your chair off and let me push it,' Dazza offered.

'It's fine. It was just a patch of ice under that layer of snow,' Danny grumbled as the back of his chair skidded sideways again.

'Look, another ten feet and the path has been gritted,' Dazza said. 'Let me push you that far to Zym and Max.'

'I'll be okay, I'll just adjust the traction—' Danny was cut short as his chair spun round. 'Fine, okay, but just to that path.'

'Wow, Danny White agreeing to be pushed,' Bobby laughed.

'Don't push your luck, Bobster,' Danny replied in mock disgust.

'Dazza's the one doing the pushing!' Bobby laughed.

As Dazza pushed Danny the last few feet, Danny looked around, taking in the view while also examining the hotel ahead of them. The guest terrace above the glass-fronted ground floor was dotted with a few hotel guests chatting, drinking and enjoying the view.

As the others joined them, Max said, 'Don't make it obvious, but have you seen who's been watching us from the first-floor terrace?'

'Where?' Dazza asked, looking around.

'Max, haven't you learnt yet? Dazza doesn't do subtlety?' Bobby laughed.

'I spotted her when Dazza was pushing me up here,' Danny confirmed.

'Who?' Dazza asked.

'She was with you in Rome, and then I saw her here the last time I came. Now she's here ahead of us,' Zym muttered.

'Who was?' Dazza challenged, getting increasingly frustrated.

'Mercedes,' Bobby hissed.

'Where?' Dazza queried.

'The far end of the balcony, just above the hotel entrance,' Max replied.

'Oh yeah,' Dazza confirmed. 'Shall we see if she wants to join us?'

'Nooo,' the others replied in unison.

'But I thought she was our friend?' Dazza asked, frowning in confusion.

'So did we,' Bobby said. 'But it looks like she's involved.'

'We can't be sure of that. But she does seem to be cropping up in unexpected places,' Max said.

'Come on, we can worry about her later. Let's go and look at that large dome at the back,' Zym replied, heading off.

Max hung back as the rest hurried after Zym until they were forty to fifty feet ahead of him. He kept looking back at the reception entrance, but apart from a few tourists coming and going, he didn't recognise anyone or see anything untoward.

The path Zym and the others followed ran straight across the front of the hotel and then turned sharply to the left. As Max trailed them and turned the corner, he saw some steps leading up to a second hotel terrace. To the right of the steps, the path sloped upward, meeting the same terrace at the rear of the hotel. He looked up at the second terrace and saw Mercedes leaning over the wall, watching Bobby, Zym, and the others moving up the slope and chattering away. As the gang approached where the path merged with the terrace, he watched Mercedes flip up the hood of her coat and wrap a scarf around her lower face and neck.

'It's not that cold,' Max thought as he slowly walked up the steps.

The gang followed the meandering path up towards the viewing area at the peak, and Mercedes followed them. As the path doubled back and continued to rise, Max heard his friends shouting his name.

'*Bobby, if you can hear me, tell them to stop shouting,*' Max said.

'*Where are you? We thought you were right behind us,*' Bobby replied.

'*I am, but don't look for me. Just tell them I'll meet you at the viewing area, where Zym said the large observatory is,*' Max replied, ducking beside a wooden hut as he noticed Mercedes looking around.

As the gang stopped shouting, Max watched Mercedes switch her focus back up the path and she started following them again. From the safety of the side of the hut, he watched the gang reach the top of the footpath, with Dazza pushing Danny again. He laughed as he watched Zym gesticulate wildly, pointing to where Max presumed the observatory was. Glancing back down the path, he saw Mercedes sitting on a wall, swinging her legs like a tourist enjoying the view while carefully glancing over her shoulder, watching the gang.

He watched his friends disappear from view, then Mercedes stood, glanced around, and hurried after them. Max decided to break his surveillance and ran up the slope. As he reached the top, he noted Mercedes had gone to the far right-hand corner, sitting on a wooden bench near a large metal box that resembled a half-sized shipping container. To his left, his friends were standing near the edge, arguing.

He ran across to them, panting from the run up the slope. 'I said we needed to get you fitter,' he gasped to Bobby.

'I don't see why your desire to run up mountain paths is my problem now,' Bobby laughed. 'Where have you been anyway?'

'I've been following Mercedes.'

'Where did she go?' Zym asked.

'She followed you guys, and you never even noticed,' Max replied.

'We were busy helping Wheels make it up here,' Zym said.

'I could have made it. You guys were just moaning about me not being quick enough,' Danny huffed. 'Anyway, where is Mercedes?'

'I can tell you, but you can't see her because of the giant observatory in the middle,' Max replied.

'Very funny, Junior. You saw the picture; it was definitely here,' Zym protested.

'Maybe it was an inflatable one,' Dazza suggested.

'You could be on to something, Dazza. A bouncy observatory to keep the kids happy,' Danny laughed.

'Alright, you young'uns can laugh, but I know what I saw,' Zym insisted. 'So, where's Mercedes?'

'Over by that metal shed thing. She's wearing the khaki green long puffer jacket with a black scarf around her lower face and neck,' Max explained.

'She's watching us intently,' Zym said, spotting her as he tried to glance around the viewing area nonchalantly.

'I said she couldn't be trusted,' Danny grumbled. 'She's trouble.'

'You never did. You just protested that she wasn't your girlfriend when we could see you fancied her,' Bobby replied.

'Well, she wasn't my girlfriend, and she definitely won't be now,' Danny insisted.

'He's not denying he fancied her, though,' Dazza laughed. 'I think she fancies him too. I reckon she's staring at Danny, not us.'

'I'm going to have it out with her,' Danny said as his chair's wheels slipped on the snow before it shot forward.

'Danny, wait a minute,' Max said, dashing in front of him. 'Guys, let's have an argument, and Danny can storm off by that metal shed. Let's see if she makes contact with him.'

'What are you going to do?' Danny asked.

'I'm going to check out this disappearing observatory, and the others can stay here and be ready to come to your aid if need be,' Max explained.

'I'm coming with you,' Zym replied. 'I can show you the area it covered.'

'Fine. Bobby and Dazza, stay here and keep an eye on Danny and Mercedes, but try not to be too obvious. Zym and I will try to find evidence of the observatory,' Max said. 'Ready, Danny?'

'Ready when you are, Chief,' Danny confirmed.

'I SAID THAT WON'T WORK,' Max shouted.

'YOU DON'T HAVE A CLUE. IT'S THE BEST WAY,' Danny yelled, moving away from the others.

'THE BEST WAY TO FAIL, YOU MEAN,' Max replied angrily.

'FINE, DO IT YOUR WAY,' Danny replied, heading towards the metal shed as his wheels skidded and slipped.

'WE WILL,' Max yelled after him. 'Come on guys, let's go back over to the side. We'll give him a minute or two to get over there, then Zym and I will look for the incredible disappearing observatory.'

'You are heading towards slapping territory, Junior,' Zym laughed.

As Danny skidded towards the other side of the viewing area, Max and the others leaned against the wall, staring at the rear of the hotel with their backs to him.

'I never understand why hotels put so much effort into making the front so welcoming, but they leave the rest looking drab and uninviting,' Max mused.

'Yeah, but who cares about the hotel? Look at those mountains, they're stunning,' Bobby exclaimed.

'Is that the big hill we saw when we arrived?' Dazza asked, munching on a muesli bar.

'Yes, Dazza, that's the Matterhorn again,' Max replied.

'It's big, innit,' Dazza said, pushing the empty wrapper into his camera bag and pulling out another bar.

'Did you bring all that food from home?' Zym asked.

'No, there was a huge food hamper and bottles of champagne in my bedroom with this card,' Dazza said, handing a card to Zym.

'Welcome to our accommodation, Prime Minister McGivern. We are honoured to have you as our guest and hope that you enjoy this selection of local delicacies and champagne as a gesture of our warmest hospitality,' Zym read.

'It seems your mum's partner is more important than the UK Prime Minister,' Max said.

Bobby frowned angrily. 'She may be with him at the moment, but he's a creep. She'll real—'

Bobby was cut short by a scream behind them. They turned to see more than a dozen people diagonally opposite from them standing around the area where Mercedes had been.

They ran across the viewing area and spotted Mercedes unconscious on the floor.

'What happened? She's a friend of ours,' Zym said, kneeling and undoing her coat.

The crowd exchanged puzzled looks, with some shaking their heads.

'Maybe they don't speak English. Try another language,' Bobby suggested.

'Good idea, lad,' Zym replied. 'Cosa è successo? È una nostra amica.'

'Que s'est-il passé? C'est une amie à nous,' Max asked in French.

A couple of people looked at each other and shrugged in confusion.

'Was isch passiert?,' Zym tried in the local German dialect.

'Mir hei nume es Gschrei ghört und sie isch ufem Bode gläge,' a woman replied.

'What did she say?' Dazza asked.

'She said they heard a scream and saw her lying on the floor,' Max said.

'This doesn't make sense. There's fifteen to twenty people here, and nobody saw anything?' Bobby queried, looking around suspiciously while Zym checked Mercedes's pulse and breathing.

Zym looked up and said, 'She's alive, and her pulse and breathing seem fine. I think she's been drugged.'

'Did Danny see anyth—where is Danny?' Dazza asked, looking around.

'Wo isch de Maa im Rollstuhl gange?' Max asked.

'Da isch kei Maa im Rollstuhl gsi,' a man replied.

'They reckon there wasn't anyone in a wheelchair,' Max said.

Bobby looked around on the floor, 'I can't even see any wheelchair tracks. It's all scuffed.'

As Bobby, Max and Dazza searched the area, a team arrived from the hotel with a stretcher and started assessing Mercedes before putting her on the stretcher and heading back to the hotel.

'Come on,' Zym said.

'You guys go with Zym. I'll catch you up,' Max said, studying the footprints in the light layer of snow.

As the others headed towards the hotel, following Mercedes on the stretcher, Max looked around.

'*This doesn't make sense,*' Max said, moving away from where they found Mercedes and heading towards the metal shed. '*There's footprints everywhere except over here.*'

As he approached the shed, Max bent down and pulled on a piece of black material poking out underneath the door, which ripped free. He examined it and frowned like he was trying to recall something before he slipped it inside his coat. He tried to open the door, but it was locked and wouldn't budge.

'*This isn't right. It looks like flimsy corrugated metal, but there's no give,*' Max thought.

As he walked around the shed, he estimated it was around eight-foot square and fourteen feet high, like a corrugated steel rectangle on its end. He tried pushing and pulling on the panels, but they wouldn't budge. Eventually, he gave up and headed towards the hotel.

19
ROOM WITH A VIEW

'How is she?' Max asked, his voice full of concern.

'She's coming round,' Zym replied quietly, glancing back at her. 'The hotel doctor says she may have been drugged, but he's not certain. He thinks it's best if she sleeps it off.'

'Nice of the hotel to let us use this room. It's got a great view down the path to the train station. I could get some killer shots of the big names rolling up from here,' Dazza said.

'They told me it's Mercedes's room,' Zym said.

'So she's got a prime room to see the big names coming here,' Max said. 'When does the IFFS start?'

'The IFFS meeting starts here in two days,' Dazza replied, pulling out his camera and snapping shots of the approach from the train station.

'It's happening overmorrow?' Zym asked.

'No, the day after tomorrow,' Dazza said, absentmindedly adjusting the angle of his picture.

'That's what I said—overmorrow.'

Max chuckled, shaking his head. 'When's the last time anyone said overmorrow? Not been in an English-speaking country for a while, have you, brother?'

'I was in America until 1915, actually, and I don't see why I should stop using perfectly good words just because others decide they're not trendy,' Zym said grumpily.

Bobby scrolled on his phone and started laughing, 'Not trendy? It says overmorrow stopped being used in the sixteenth century,' he laughed.

'There you go, only a few years ago. A mere bagatelle,' Zym replied with a smirk.

'A what?' Bobby asked, confused.

'Look it up, lad,' Zym laughed before glancing at Mercedes. 'Oh, our friend appears to be waking up.'

'Mercedes, can you hear me?' Zym asked quietly.

'W-where am I?' Mercedes asked, her eyes flickering.

'You're in your hotel room. We found you unconscious,' Max replied.

Mercedes opened her eyes and looked towards the voice. 'Oh, hi, Bobby. I feel so tired.'

'That's Max. I'm Bobby.'

Mercedes opened her eyes again and looked over at Bobby. 'Oh, you've got changed. Are we going somewhere?'

'I think she's still struggling with whatever she was drugged with,' Zym said.

Max opened the door to the small hotel fridge and pulled out a bottle of water, which he poured into a glass before returning to the bed. 'Mercedes, here, drink this.'

Mercedes lifted herself onto her elbow, took Max's glass, and sipped it. 'Thanks, Bobby.'

Bobby laughed. 'That's M—'

Max held his hand up to silence Bobby. 'Not now. Dazza, did you get any chocolate-coated muesli bars and some salted peanuts when you raided the Prime Minister's welcome pack?'

'Uh, yeah, but I was saving them 'til later,' Dazza replied reluctantly, handing over both.

'I think I'm going to be sick,' Mercedes said. 'Everything feels like I'm in a thick fog.'

'Here, eat this muesli bar. It'll boost your energy levels, and then have some nuts; the salt will help,' Max said assuredly.

Mercedes bit into the muesli bar, then sipped some more water. 'What happened? I remember...'

'You remember spying on us?' Bobby challenged.

'I guess,' Mercedes said in embarrassment.

'So why are you here, and why were you watching us?' Zym asked.

Mercedes stared at Zym and frowned. 'I know you, don't I?'

'Yes, I'm Max's brother, Zym.'

'Oh yeah. Max,' Mercedes said, looking at Max. Then she turned and saw Bobby and added, 'If that's Bobby and Max, who's he?'

'I'm Bobby, and he's Max. We separated,' Bobby explained.

Mercedes looked at Bobby and then Max. 'But you're identical.'

'Which is why you never noticed I wasn't with them when they went to the viewing area,' Max said. 'Now, why were you following us?'

'Viewing area?' Mercedes queried before sitting up abruptly. 'Danny! Where is he?'

'That's a very good question. I hope you have an equally good answer,' Max replied.

'How would I know? One minute, we were talking, and the next, I woke up with you four asking me questions,' Mercedes replied defiantly.

'Maybe this will help jog your memory,' Max said, pulling the scrap of black material from his coat pocket.

'That's part of my scarf. Why is it ripped?' Mercedes asked with a confused look.

'You tell me. I found it trapped under the door of that metal shed near where you were sitting, spying on us,' Max demanded.

'Yeah, come on, why were you spying on us?' Bobby asked.

'Because I don't know who to trust. I told Danny that Chris keeps disappearing for days on end, and then I heard him mentioning he was coming to the IFFS meeting, so I booked a trip here to see why and who he was with. I was telling Danny...' Mercedes's voice trailed off, and her eyes widened.

'You remember something, don't you?' Max pressed.

'I was telling Danny when someone grabbed me from behind and held something over my mouth, which made me sleepy. I remember falling, and Danny tried to grab me, but he only caught my scarf. Then...'

'Then what?' Dazza asked, finding the conversation more interesting than camera angles.

'I'm not sure; I was starting to pass out,' Mercedes said quietly, her eyes downcast.

Zym sat on the edge of the bed. 'You're doing so well. Just tell us what you remember.'

'Someone was talking to Danny, and... he went off with them,' Mercedes replied, looking down like it was a memory she wanted to forget.

'So they drugged Danny and dragged him away?' Bobby challenged.

'No,' Mercedes replied, looking up. 'The last thing I remember was the door to that metal shed being open and Danny following someone inside.'

'Danny wouldn't just go along without a fight,' Bobby protested.

'Sounds like he did, lad,' Zym replied. 'You never really know how anyone will act under pressure.'

'Not Danny,' Bobby argued. 'They must have threatened him. Did you see a gun?'

Mercedes looked nervously from Zym to Max, then Dazza, and finally Bobby. 'I don't know. It was all so quick... but I don't remember any weapon.'

'See, there could've been a weapon. She can't remember,' Bobby said defiantly to Zym.

Max listened intently but finally interjected, 'Whether Danny was forced or went voluntarily, one thing's clear; that shed... isn't a shed. It's solid, and I think it's something like a lift,' Max said.

'What about a VIP entrance for IFFS delegates coming by helicopter?' Dazza suggested.

Bobby frowned. 'But if the IFFS is in the hotel, why would they need a lift going down the mountain?'

'Because,' Dazza explained, 'the conference centre is inside the mountain. The hotel had some building work done, and they discovered a large cave, which they turned into a convention hall and offices. The lift might go down into the hall.'

'And the offices aren't part of the conference centre. There's a separate entrance for M Bank Research,' Mercedes added. 'I tried to get in, but they said WestFi staff don't have clearance.'

Max leaned forward. 'What about the conference centre?'

Mercedes nodded, relieved that the focus had moved from her. 'Anyone can go in there. There's a large reception area leading to a massive round convention hall. I looked yesterday, but they hadn't finished building the stage.'

'We need to get down there,' Zym insisted.

Dazza's eyes widened. 'Great, I can check out the press facilities.' Then he muttered, half to himself, 'I wonder if they've got catering laid on...'

'Let's go then,' Bobby said.

'We can't all go charging in there. Zym and I'll go down. You and Dazza take care of Mercedes. With any luck, she might remember more about what's happened to Danny,' Max insisted.

'I'm coming. I want to check out the press positions. Besides, my press card might be useful,' Dazza replied.

'The lad's right. A press card could be handy,' Zym agreed.

After Max and the others had left, Bobby sat on the edge of the bed and said, 'Alright, what gives?'

'What do you mean?' Mercedes asked weakly.

'Cut the act. I saw the relief on your face when they stopped asking what you knew and switched to talking about the hotel.'

'I did not,' Mercedes protested, glancing towards the window.

'You can't even look at me.'

'I can,' she retorted, looking at Bobby briefly before glancing away again. 'I'm still recovering from being knocked out.'

Bobby's eyes narrowed. 'Your whole story doesn't stack. Hotel rooms around here are booked months in advance for the IFFS, yet somehow, you book a prime room at the last minute just to see what Chris is up to. Were you even drugged, or was that an act?'

'But—'

'Don't try and swerve this,' Bobby insisted.

'It's not like it looks,' Mercedes pleaded.

'Then tell me how it is.'

'Fine, but you can't tell the others.'

'Mercedes said anybody could wander into the conference hall,' Zym said, 'but there's security everywhere.'

'Let's see if Dazza can use his press pass to get in,' Max replied.

Dazza approached an armed security guard who said, 'Excuse me, sir, can I help you?'

Dazza smiled, flashing his press card, and said, 'I'm with Business Inside Out. I'm just checking the press facilities to see where I can set up my camera.'

'Press day is tomorrow, sir,' the guard replied flatly.

'Come on, mate. This is my first solo job. I'll be quick.'

The guard remained emotionless. 'Press day is tomorrow, sir.'

'Yeah, yeah, you said, but please? Just five minutes.'

'Press day—'

'Is tomorrow. Alright, fine,' Dazza sighed, turning back towards Zym and Max. 'Thanks for nothing, Mr Helpful,' he muttered, walking away.

'No luck, lad?' Zym laughed.

'Flipping jobsworth,' Dazza grumbled.

Max looked around and noticed workmen coming and going down a corridor carrying various pieces of equipment and sheeting and said, 'Come on, I've got an idea.'

Max led Zym and Dazza down a corridor. 'Put those hi-viz jackets on,' he said, pointing at a row of them hanging along the wall.

'It won't fit,' Dazza grumbled as he put the largest-looking one on, which promptly split down the back. 'Told you,' he added.

'It'll work,' Max replied.

'Junior, Dazza is six foot four with ginger hair. I don't think a ripped hi-viz jacket will confuse anyone,' Zym replied.

'Here,' Max said, handing Dazza a cap. 'Now pick up that roll of carpet and carry it on your shoulders with Dazza at the back.'

'It looks like a bloody ski slope,' Zym muttered. 'Can't you crouch a bit, Dazza?'

A minute later, led by Max, they walked back towards the guard, with Zym and Dazza carrying the roll of carpet on their shoulders.

'This way, and don't you dare drop that roll,' Max ordered flamboyantly.

As they approached the guard who had blocked Dazza, Max said, 'Excuse me, would you mind helping? These two are making it bow in the middle, and I'm not laying a carpet with a crease in it.'

The guard barely acknowledged them. 'Just get on with it.'

Inside the conference hall, Max noted the almost three-foot-high circle of mirrored glass running around the middle of the wall surrounding the entire room. 'Very useful for spying on what's going on,' he muttered.

'What do we do with this?' Zym grumbled, indicating the carpet.

'Just dump it. Come on, let's see what's going on,' Max replied, heading towards the edge of the hall.

Zym and Dazza dropped the carpet roll and followed Max.

'Excuse me,' a voice said behind them.

Dazza turned and looked down at a short man in a bright green jacket and turquoise trousers. 'You talking to me, mate?'

'Yes, I am, and my name is Tarquin, not mate.'

'Alright, Tarquin. What d'you need?'

'That carpet belongs on the stage, not down there.'

'Tarquin, can I tell you a secret?' Dazza half whispered.

'Please do,' Tarquin replied inquisitively.

'Do you need that carpet on the stage?'

'Yes, I do. Well, the event director does.'

'Then go fetch the event director, grab one end each, and carry it up there,' Dazza replied, heading towards Max and Zym.

As Dazza joined them, Max started muttering, 'This isn't right?'

'Looks normal to me. A big conference arena with a stage and I guess this mirrored wall is to allow the press to look in, without being intrusive,' Dazza replied, noting a doorway to the other side of the wall with a sign saying, "Press only."

Max glanced around the room. 'No, it's not right.'

Max walked back towards the entrance, muttering. 'Ten paces, fifteen, twenty.' He stopped and looked up. 'Hmm, no, that's not it.'

'What's he doing?' Dazza asked.

'He's in Max mode,' Zym replied. 'Any minute now he'll look around and—there he goes, now he'll pace from one side to the other, stopping to look up.'

As if directed by Zym, Max did precisely as described, but he stopped in line with the centre of the room and looked behind him towards the hotel. Then he glanced towards the stage before staring at the ceiling. 'No, it's too short,' he muttered.

Dazza and Zym watched in amusement as Max wandered around the hall, stopping occasionally to look up and from side to side. As Max approached the stage, he looked back towards them before looking at the main entrance.

'Where's the rest of it?' he thought.

'Have you lost something?' a woman asked, rigging some lights to a truss.

'Sorry, I just noticed this room looks like it should be bigger,' Max replied.

'Maybe it is. The wall behind that backdrop is metal, not stone,' the woman replied. 'Perhaps they're expanding it,' she said before yelling, 'Okay, Ricky, haul it up.'

Max walked to the back of the stage and pulled aside the black curtain. He tapped the metal wall and listened to the hollow resonance. 'Hmm, what are you hiding?' he mumbled.

Max slipped behind the black backdrop, running his hand along the wall. He emerged from the other side and rejoined Zym and Dazza.

'Well?' Zym asked.

'There's more of this hall behind the stage,' Max said.

'It's probably changing rooms. They use this venue for concerts,' Dazza explained.

'Look at the room. What shape is it?' Max challenged.

'Round,' Dazza replied.

'Look again,' Max said.

'It's more semicircle,' Zym noted.

'Exactly,' Max confirmed, 'and behind the stage is a large metal door running the full height of the hall and most of the width.'

'What's behind the door?' Dazza asked.

'I don't know. Let's see if—'

'That's them,' Tarquin shouted.

'We need to get out of here, Junior,' Zym said.

Zym, Dazza and Max ran towards the entrance with Tarquin and three security guards in pursuit.

Dazza flew through the entrance first, but Zym was lagging behind. Max turned and saw the guards were close to catching Zym, so he froze, saluted and said, 'Welcome, Mr President.'

The guards and Tarquin screeched to a halt and turned in the direction Max was looking. As they did, Max ran back, grabbed Zym's arm and dragged him away.

'What! Where is the President?' Zym asked.

'Shut up, you idiot, and run!' Max replied, half dragging Zym.

Max dragged them towards an opening lift as they entered the hotel foyer. 'This way.'

Max hit the first-floor button to head back to Mercedes's room and relaxed as the lift door closed.

'Besides that metal door behind the stage, did you find anything else about that hall?' Zym asked.

'Yes, it's missing something, and if you need a clue, it's where we are,' Max replied.

'A mountain?' Dazza asked, frowning.

'No! We're inside one,' Max laughed.

Dazza thought for a moment, then asked, 'Why would there be a hotel in the conference hall?'

'I think Max means a lift, lad,' Zym suggested.

'Exactly. If that metal shed is a lift, it doesn't come into the conference hall. In fact, if it did, it would have to travel diagonally because the viewing area on the top of here is over the area behind that metal door,' Max nodded.

As the lift doors opened, Max noticed Mercedes's door halfway along the corridor was slightly ajar.

He approached quickly, with Zym and Dazza close behind. As he reached the door, he held a finger to his lips, signalling the others to stay quiet.

He eased the door open but paused at the sound of shuffling inside. Spotting a shadow moving around, he backed out and whispered, 'There's someone in there rummaging around.'

'What's the plan?' Zym asked.

'Dazza, block the door. Don't let anyone out. Zym follow me. We need to see if they're alone and unarmed; on my shout, we jump them.'

'Nobody's getting past me,' Dazza replied, puffing out his chest.

Max and Zym crept into the room. Watching the intruder's reflection in the window, Max held up one finger to indicate only one person.

He cursed the modern room layout. Typically, there would be a corridor with the bathroom to the side before it opened out into the bedroom, giving them ample time to assess the situation, but this was just a small area with the wardrobe, then the bedroom, with the bathroom opposite the doorway.

Max knew there was no time for caution. He held up three fingers and counted them down before signalling the charge.

Zym reached the intruder first. Noting the person was unarmed, he swept their legs and dived on top, pinning them to the floor.

'Oww, get off me,' a young voice protested.

'What are you doing in here, lad?' Zym demanded as the intruder squirmed.

'Chris? Is that you?' Max asked, leaning over him.

'Bobby? What are you doing here?' Chris replied indignantly. 'And could you please get this—whatever it is—off me?'

'That "whatever" is my brother, Zym,' Max laughed. 'Okay, Zym, let him up. This is Mercedes's brother, Chris.'

Zym climbed off and Chris scrambled to his feet. 'Thank you. What do you mean he's your brother? I thought it was just you and Lily?'

'It is just Bobby and Lily, but I'm Max. Bobby and I have separated.'

'You weren't lying then—'

'Guys, we have visitors,' Dazza said, walking into the room, followed by Bobby and Mercedes.

Chris looked at Max and then at Bobby. 'You're identical.'

'Never mind that. What are you doing in my room?' Mercedes demanded.

'Looking for my HR pass,' Chris replied sharply. 'It disappeared just after I told you I was coming here.'

'I don't have your pass, you've probably lost it in a club. And why are you attending an event for the world's leaders?' Mercedes asked.

'I was invited by Big Bill. I could ask you the same question,' Chris replied defiantly.

'Mr White asked me to come and even arranged this room for me,' Mercedes said.

'Why would Danny's dad ask you to come here?' Max asked.

'That's why we've been looking for you. He told Mercedes we were coming here and asked her to follow us, and then he told her to let him know when Danny was alone,' Bobby replied.

'That makes no sense,' Max said. 'Danny lives with his parents. His dad could talk to him alone whenever he wanted to.'

'You're not listening,' Mercedes huffed. 'Mr White knew you were coming here but didn't know Danny was. He knew only when I saw you with Danny at the front of the hotel. After I told him, he said to follow you and try to get Danny alone.'

'But how could you be sure you'd get Danny alone?' Zym asked.

'I couldn't, but I thought if I acted suspiciously, I might be able to make you all separate. Once Max didn't go with you towards the viewing area and followed me instead, I knew I was onto something.'

'You saw me following you?' Max asked.

'Of course. I can count and when I saw one was missing from the group, I glanced around and saw you sneaking up the steps,' Mercedes laughed. 'Mr White suggested I go and sit near the metal shed and try to get Danny there. When I saw him start to come over, I thought it had worked, but then you stopped him and put on that silly argument charade.'

'It wasn't a charade,' Max protested before adding, 'Okay, it might have been, but why did Danny's dad want him alone?'

'He said he needed Danny to help with a technical problem. I told Danny, and he said he'd go and get you, and we could go together. That's when it all went weird.'

'In what way, lass?' Zym asked.

'The door to the shed opened, and Mr White, with a couple of others, came out. I saw Mr White say something to Danny, then they headed towards the shed,' Mercedes replied.

'Why did you pretend earlier that it was just someone rather than Danny's dad?' Zym asked.

'I was worried you wouldn't believe me.'

'I'm still thinking about that. Also, why didn't you go with them?' Max added.

'I tried to, but that's when I was grabbed from behind. I fell forward, and Danny tried to catch me. I remember he caught my scarf and I felt it tug. Then, I was dragged back to where I'd been sitting. I saw Danny and Mr White entering the shed, and then I passed out.'

'Where does the shed lift go?' Max asked.

'What lift?' Mercedes asked.

'The one in the shed going down into the mountain,' Chris said, noting Mercedes looked worried. 'Where does it go?'

'I didn't know there was a lift inside it.'

20
No Entry

'You're late, and where's Danny?' Pat asked as Zym, Dazza, Max, and Bobby arrived at the restaurant.

'Sorry, we missed our train. Danny's dad showed up, and we lost track of the time. Before I forget, Danny's stopping with his dad tonight,' Bobby lied.

'*Why not tell her the truth?*' Max thought.

'*Because she'll worry even more than I'm worried,*' Bobby replied.

'I didn't know Paul White was here. Big Bill said he was coming to the IFFS, and Jay might pop in for the final day, but nobody mentioned Paul,' Stephen said.

'Are you attending the IFFS?' Max asked.

'Me? I'm not important enough,' Stephen laughed. 'I can show you around the M Bank offices tomorrow, but even they are out of bounds to us when the IFFS starts the day after and the guests are arriving.'

'Not to me,' Dazza said, proudly showing his press card. 'Work emailed my access code and details of where I have to go.'

'So where do you go?' Zym asked.

'We have three locations. The patio area to the side of the hotel is for arrivals by helicopter and those coming up from the train station. To the left of the reception room, they've cordoned off an area and in the corridor behind that one-way mirror on the one side of the convention hall. Although that last one is only available for the opening and closing speeches and a couple of keynote speakers,' Dazza replied.

'What about the rest of the time?' Max queried.

'No press allowed,' Dazza said.

Pat sighed. 'I know we're here to find out what this place has to do with Simon's death, but can we just have a nice dinner?'

'Mum, this is important,' Bobby protested, pushing his food around his plate.

'I know it is, Champ. But I think you have something just as important to deal with right now,' Pat replied.

'Like what?' Bobby demanded before feeling a hand rest on his shoulder.

'Like, maybe... me,' Adam said.

Bobby sprang to his feet, flinging his arms around Adam. 'Oh, hun, I've missed you so much.'

'It's barely been a day,' Adam laughed as a waiter brought an extra chair and laid another place at the table.

'How was the match?' Bobby asked.

'Not too bad, and I had a reasonable game,' Adam replied.

'Listen to Mr Modest,' Stephen laughed. 'They won five-nil, and Adam scored three of those goals.'

'My goal machine,' Bobby said proudly.

Dazza chuckled. 'You used to hate football.'

'I just get confused by the rules, but I like watching—especially when my man's playing,' Bobby said, squeezing Adam's hand.

'What's up for tomorrow?' Adam asked, smiling at Bobby.

'As the biggest asset in my new football team investment, how about being my second guest of honour at a tour of our

Swiss offices—the ones I didn't even know existed,' Stephen suggested.

'Only the second guest of honour?' Bobby demanded, feigning indignation.

'Sorry, Bobby, but your mum comes first,' Stephen laughed.

'Can't argue with that, sweetie,' Adam smiled. 'Talking of arguing, where's Danny?'

'He's staying with his dad tonight,' Max replied.

The following morning, Pat, Stephen, and the others arrived at the hotel and headed to the M Bank offices adjacent to the convention hall. They passed through the hotel reception and towards the conference centre, before heading left and through a glass door with the M Bank logo discreetly etched into it. As they entered the office, their path was blocked by a wide, polished, dark wood reception desk stretching from one wall to a door beside the other.

'Mr Marchent, we are honoured to have you visit us,' the receptionist, Petra Siderius, said warmly. 'One of my colleagues will be here shortly to show you and your guests around.'

'It's fine. I'm quite happy for us to explore on our own,' Stephen replied.

'I'm afraid that won't be possible,' Petra said, quickly adding, 'It's because of the security next door for the IFFS, sir.'

'Is Mr White here? Perhaps he can escort us,' Stephen suggested.

'Mr White?' the receptionist queried. 'I don't know a Mr Wh—'

'Es ist schon gut, Frau Siderius,' a female voice calmly interrupted. 'Herr White ist beschäftigt, aber ich kümmere mich um unsere Gäste,'

A short, stocky woman in a black trouser suit with a turquoise blouse appeared from the doorway beside the reception. 'Mr Marchent, we are honoured to have our esteemed Chief Executive visit our little facility. My name is Brigitte, and I'll be your host.'

'*What did she say to the receptionist?*' Bobby thought.

'*She told the receptionist it was okay, that Mr White was busy, and she would take care of us guests,*' Max replied.

'*But it sounded like the receptionist didn't even know who Paul was,*' Bobby pointed out.

Brigitte looked into a camera beside the door and held it open when it unlocked, saying, 'This way, please.'

The group endured an hour of being shown one office after another, followed by visits to two laboratories. Brigitte explained that being inside the mountain provided a stable environment for tests.

'Where are the other laboratories?' Bobby asked.

'You've seen them,' Brigitte replied, smiling reassuringly. 'We're only a small facility.'

'But my friend, Danny White, is working here,' Bobby insisted.

'Danny White?' Brigitte queried. 'Oh, you mean Mr White's son. Yes, he helped his father with a project overnight, but they flew home this morning. He knew you were coming, so he asked me to let you know he'll see you when you return.'

Bobby protested, 'Danny wouldn't go—'

But he stopped abruptly when Max thought, '*Don't say anything.*'

'Are you alright, Champ?' Pat asked.

Bobby paused before replying, 'Uh, yeah, sorry, Mum. I was just surprised by Danny leaving early.'

'He did apologise for leaving unannounced. But he and Mr White said it was urgent,' Brigitte smiled serenely.

'That'll explain why it was so sudden,' Max smiled. 'By the way, Brigitte, I noticed a steel door further down the corridor. Where does that lead to?'

'That's just a service door into the mountain. Workmen use it to run facilities into here and the conference centre next door. Geologists also use it to examine the mountain,' Brigitte replied dismissively.

'I'm a bit of an amateur geologist. Can we have a look?' Zym asked.

'I'd happily let you, but unfortunately, I don't have the keys,' Brigitte apologised.

'Please?' Adam asked, flashing his best smile.

'I'm sorry, Mr...?'

'Lee, Adam Lee.'

'Oh, you're Mr Lee,' Brigitte smiled. 'I'm so sorry, but I really don't have access to that area. But while I remember, Mr Pierce asked me if you would do him the honour of being his guest at the IFFS tomorrow?'

'Who?' Adam asked.

'That's Big Bill. I've told you about him,' Bobby said.

'I'm not sure,' Adam replied before noticing Max behind Brigitte, nodding.

'Please, Mr Lee. Mr Pierce would be so grateful to have you attend. Obviously, you can bring your partner,' Brigitte added.

'In which case, how could I refuse,' he said, grabbing Bobby's hand.

'Excellent. I've left all the arrangement details with our receptionist. She'll give them to you when you leave,' Brigitte replied with a broad smile.

Bobby's phone pinged, and he glanced at the screen, showing a message from Mercedes.

Mercedes

> Call me when ur done w/ the tour. It's urgent

'So, this is our little bit of Switzerland,' Stephen said.

'Yes, sir. As I said, we're only small. Do you need me to sort some lunchtime refreshments?' Brigitte smiled.

'I think we've taken up enough of your time. Thank you so much,' Stephen replied. 'Has everyone seen enough?'

'I think I've seen all I need to,' Max replied.

As they left, Brigitte grabbed an envelope from behind the reception desk. 'Mr Lee, here are the passes for you and your guest and the details regarding your attendance tomorrow.'

'Thanks,' Adam replied politely, putting the envelope into his small rucksack.

'What did you make of that?' Zym asked as they headed back into the hotel.

'I think they're hiding something behind that metal door, and they wouldn't have opened it even if I'd ordered them to,' Stephen replied.

'I agree,' Max nodded. 'That door leads to right behind the metal door behind the stage in the conference hall.'

'Are you sure?' Dazza asked.

'Max mode never fails,' Zym laughed. 'Junior has an incredible ability to map out spaces in his mind.'

As they walked through the hotel, Bobby rang Mercedes.

'Hi, Merce—slowdown... you're *where*? Drop me a pin on Maps. But why—Danny? No, Danny's not—what do you mean he's there? Uh-huh, yeah, but if he was covered, how could you—yeah, I can't imagine anyone else with a chair like his. But what about his dad? Really? But why would they—no, they claimed Danny went home with his dad this morning. We're on the way. Just drop me that pin and be careful.'

'You can tell us on the way,' Zym said.

'Stephen, can you look after Mum, please?' Bobby asked.

'I'm not letting you go without me, Champ. I've seen the trouble you get into before,' Pat replied.

'Please, Mum. You and Adam go back to the chalet with Stephen. I promise we'll be careful.'

'Okay,' Pat replied.

'Seriously? Thanks. I promise we'll keep in touch the whole time.'

'No, I'm not serious. Whatever's happening, I'm coming with you,' Pat insisted.

'You're not getting rid of me either, sweetie,' Adam added.

'Sounds like you're stuck with us,' Stephen added as they rushed to the train station.

21
THE COLLECTION

'Where are they?' Bobby asked

'Inside that compound,' Mercedes replied as the group stood on the forest's tree line, looking at what appeared to be a series of Swiss-style cabins and buildings resembling a holiday complex.

'How did you spot them?' Zym asked.

'You'd mentioned what time you were coming, so I was by my window having a drink, dressed, ready to check out that shed again,' Mercedes explained. 'I watched you head into the hotel, and just as I was about to leave, I saw someone covered with a black-and-white chequered blanket being pushed in a wheelchair.'

'Why was that suspicious?' Stephen asked.

'Because their head was covered, it was Danny's chair, and it was being pushed,' Mercedes replied firmly.

'Are you sure it was Danny's chair?' Pat asked.

'I'd recognise that chair anywhere,' Mercedes insisted.

'It's pretty unmistakable,' Bobby agreed. 'All those pockets, the "DIG" and "A genius lives here" stickers and the motors that do all his tricks.'

'Anyway, as soon as I saw him being pushed—which I know he hates—I rushed after them. They put him in the M Bank carriage...' Mercedes paused, glancing at Stephen.

'I'm on your side,' Stephen assured her.

'Stephen's been helping us,' Zym added.

'Okay,' Mercedes continued. 'They put Danny in the M Bank carriage, and I dived into one of the others. When we got here, they wheeled him through that hotel compound behind us.'

'Didn't anyone see you following them?' Max asked.

'No, they were too busy cursing the snow and the wheelchair.'

'Which building did they take Wheels into?' Zym asked.

Mercedes pointed. 'That one just below us. Look, you can still see the wheel tracks in the light layer of snow.'

Max scanned the compound and then studied the building Mercedes had indicated. 'I can't see any security.'

'It's low-key, but it's there,' Mercedes replied. 'I saw a tourist wander up from the train station, and an armed guard quickly escorted him away.'

'Why don't we just storm it?' Zym suggested.

Stephen studied the buildings. 'There are M Bank logos everywhere. Why don't we walk in? I am the boss.'

Max shook his head. 'Hate to burst your bubble, but I don't think you've got any authority here.'

'I'm starting to realise how much of my business I don't control,' Stephen sighed.

'Dudes, we're being watched,' Dazza said, peering through his camera's zoom lens.

Max sighed. 'We need to leave. If they've spotted us, it's just going to be a trap.'

'Maybe I could go in,' Adam suggested. 'They're not going to hurt a celebrity. I could pretend I'm lost.'

'Have you never heard of celebrities dying in plane crashes?' Zym sighed. 'Nobody's safe if the elite are after you.'

'Besides,' Max added, 'you're of more use at the IFFS tomorrow.'

'How many guests are you allowed?' Zym asked.

Adam pulled out the envelope Brigitte had given him. 'It says Adam Lee plus two.'

'That's you, Bobby, and Pat, then,' Max said.

Pat nodded, knowing that whatever was going on, being with her son was her priority.

'Hang on, I've got to be there too. It's my job,' Dazza said.

'Sorry, buddy, I forgot,' Max laughed.

'That's settled then,' Stephen said. 'Pat, Bobby, Adam *and* *Dazza* go to the IFFS, and the rest of us come here.'

'You don't need to do that,' Max said.

'I know, but I'm going to,' Stephen insisted. 'We're still no closer to finding out the link to Bobby's dad's death, and I promised I'd do anything to help.'

'Hey, dudes, can we do this somewhere else? There's four guards talking in a group, and they keep looking this way,' Dazza said.

'Let's get back to the train station,' Max said, leading the group through the trees and down the combined footpath and tramway.

'What time should we meet in the morning?' Mercedes asked as they approached the train station.

'Adam, what time do you have to be at the IFFS?' Max asked.

'Um, around ten, I think. Hang on,' Adam checked the envelope in his bag. 'Yeah, it says the welcome address is at eleven, and I should be there by ten-thirty.'

Max nodded. 'Let's meet here around nine-thirty then. Bobby, Adam and Pat—'

'And Dazza,' Dazza interrupted.

'And Dazza can stay on the train and get to the hotel on time,' Max suggested.

The following morning, as Max got off the train, he turned to Pat, Adam, Bobby, and Dazza. 'If you're worried about anything, get out of there.'

'Don't worry, Max, nobody is hurting my boys,' Pat said resolutely, putting her arms around Adam and Bobby. Noticing Dazza's expression, she added. 'You too, Dazza.'

As the train headed up the mountain and the others started trudging up the footpath, Zym said, 'I think we should get off this tramway and cut through the woods.'

'That sounds like a plan,' Max replied. 'Looking at how steep the woods are on either side of the tramway, it's a plan which will probably kill one of us, but it is a plan.'

Mercedes glanced over the edge of the footpath, 'I could make it down there.'

'There's a tram coming. We all need to get down there,' Stephen said urgently.

The four scrambled over the edge and laid flat against the slope, peering over the edge as the tram trundled past.

Zym tugged Max's arm and pointed towards the front of the tram. 'That's Dr Fellowes.'

Max pulled out the pocket mirror Adam had given him months ago in Covent Garden and angled it to see the tram. 'Apart from her and the guy sat next to her with a gun, the others are all human, and I recognise that guy in the back.'

'It's Chris,' Mercedes said in shock. 'Why's he on there?'

'They look drugged, even Chris,' Max observed.

Mercedes started to stand, but Max quickly pulled her back down. 'Don't let them see you. Whatever's going on here, we need to work it out before we make a move.'

Once the tram had rounded a bend and disappeared, they scrambled back onto the tramway.

'There were sixteen people on that tram, and most were human,' Max mused.

'And one of them was my brother,' Mercedes fumed.

'You mean *is* your brother,' Stephen corrected.

'I know what I mean!' Mercedes snapped. 'If he is involved with them, then he is no brother of mine.'

'Come on,' Zym said, heading off.

As they approached the edge of the compound, the surrounding terrain levelled out, and they moved quickly into the woods. It was still early enough in the season for overnight snowfall to be light, but it still made the hard ground slippery.

'There's no wheelchair marks outside the cabin where Danny was taken,' Mercedes noted.

'Which either means he's not left the cabin, or he was moved before last night's snow,' Max replied.

'Get down.' Zym hissed. 'Someone's coming.'

'That's Paul White!' Stephen exclaimed.

Paul stopped by the door to the wooden chalet and looked around. He could have sworn he'd heard his name but couldn't see anyone. Moving past the door to the corner of the chalet, he inspected the fresh snow, but it was untouched, even by wildlife.

'Is anyone there?' he shouted, his hand sliding inside his jacket as he stepped forward.

Satisfied that nobody was around, Paul walked back to the chalet door and unlocked it. He took one last look around before opening the door. 'Morning, son. How're you feeling today?' he asked, closing the door behind him.

'Looks like we've found Danny,' Mercedes said.

Zym stood up. 'I'm going for a closer look.'

As Zym approached the front of the chalet, followed by Stephen and Mercedes, Max circled around the side and rear. As he crept towards a rear door, it opened outward, and he dived behind a small wooden structure.

Max watched a tall, well-built man in a black padded jacket step outside, stretch, and turn to talk to someone inside. 'Mr White's in there, so just make sure nothing kicks off with the guy in the wheelchair. Oh, and fix that Wi-Fi; the signal here is rubbish.'

'But we're supposed to have two guarding him at all times,' another man replied.

'There is. You're here, and so is Mr White. I'm just grabbing some food. Thirty minutes, tops.'

'You'd better be. I've been on for ten hours and need to sleep.'

Once the first man had disappeared toward the main complex, Max crept towards a window and carefully peered inside. He saw a younger but equally stocky man with blonde hair fiddling with wires going into a small electronic box and cursing.

As he crouched down, Max noticed the wooden structure was a wood store. He grabbed a log around the size of his forearm and a couple of smaller sticks before moving towards the rear door.

As he approached the door, he slipped on the snow, and the noise alerted the guard inside. 'Dirk? Is that you?'

Max quickly picked up some wood chippings and threw them at the window.

The guard muttered, 'Dirk, stop mucking around. Did you forget your wallet again?'

Max noticed the door was slightly ajar, so he carefully eased it open and let it swing shut. The guard cursed and strode toward the door, pushing it open and nearly hitting Max, who was hiding behind it.

'Dirk, I don't care if White is here or not. I'm giving you a pasting for this,' the guard growled.

As the guard stepped outside, Max tossed one of the small sticks over the door towards the wood store. The guard turned quickly toward the sound and pulled out a handgun. 'Dirk?'

Max waited for the guard's gaze to shift and threw the second stick harder so it hit the back of the chalet further away. The guard stepped forward, gun raised. 'Stay where you are, or I'll—nghhh.'

With a quick swing, Max knocked the guard out with the log and tossed it back towards the log store. He dragged the guard over and propped him up against the store. 'Enjoy your sleep. Sweet dreams,' Max said with a smile before picking up the guard's gun, heading inside the chalet, and quietly locking the door behind him.

Max scanned the kitchen, looking for surveillance equipment, before moving to the hallway door. He heard voices from the left, but he looked to the right first to ensure it was safe to move. After crossing the hallway, he crept along the wall towards the voices.

'But Dad, today's the big day. You even got me away from my friends to fix the fault in your machine,' Danny's unmistakable voice said, tinged with frustration.

'I know, son,' Paul White replied, trying to placate him. 'But with so many VIPs, the security is crazy. Besides, the doctor still hasn't worked out why you passed out.'

'Yeah, but I'm alright now,' Danny protested.

Max reached into his pocket and pulled out his mirror. He angled it carefully around the doorframe and panned around the room slowly. He stifled a laugh as he caught sight of Zym peering in through a window.

'*You were a great enforcer, but you suck as a spy, brother,*' Max chuckled to himself.

'What if I watched from the one-way mirror viewing area?' Danny suggested hopefully.

'I'll ask when I get there. I'll get our security team to bring you up if they agree. Deal?'

'Okay, deal,' Danny replied dejectedly.

'Come on, son. I'll do what I can.'

'I know. I was just looking forward to seeing it transmit energy food around the world,' Danny said.

Paul smiled and said, 'I'll record it for you. Is—'

He stopped mid-sentence, his eyes narrowing and glancing towards the front door.

'What's up?' Danny asked, confused.

Paul turned his back to the window and put his finger on his lips. He slowly backed towards the front door and said, 'It'll be fine. You just wait and see.'

Danny frowned but remained quiet as he watched his dad.

As Paul finished speaking, he reached into his jacket and pulled out a gun. Turning quickly, he yanked the door open, causing Stephen to crash into the room.

'Well, well,' Paul sneered, training his gun on Stephen. 'Hello, Stephen. Fancy seeing you here.'

Stephen rolled onto his back, looking up, 'Uh, hi, Paul.'

Paul looked outside and waved his gun. 'You two—get in here. Now.'

Zym and Mercedes trudged into the chalet. Paul slammed the door behind them, locking it sharply. Walking across the room toward Danny, he kept the gun trained on the three of them.

Paul stared at them coldly. 'Who's going to explain why you're spying on us?'

'We weren't spying,' Mercedes replied confidently. 'We were trying to find out what happened to Danny.'

Danny frowned, looking from one to another. 'I'm here. What do you mean "what happened to me"?'

Mercedes stepped forward.

'Stay right where you are,' Paul said, thrusting the gun forward.

Mercedes froze. 'We were chatting, and then I was grabbed from behind and drugged, and you went with someone,'

Danny's frown turned into a puzzled expression. 'Not quite. You were telling me about Chris when Dad showed up. I turned to talk to him when you passed out. I tried to catch you but only caught your scarf,' he explained, glancing at Paul. 'Dad needed me to fix a fault with the machine, but he left a couple of assistants to look after you. Didn't you, Dad?'

Paul smiled, nodding casually. 'I did, son.'

Mercedes scowled, 'That's not true!'

'No, it's not, is it, Paul?' Max said, walking into the room behind Paul and Danny. With his gun raised, he said calmly, 'Oh, and drop that gun. We wouldn't want anyone getting hurt.'

Paul lowered his firearm and turned slowly to face Max. 'Well, if it isn't Bobby. No, not Bobby—you're Max, aren't you? When did you transmute?'

'Drop the gun, *Deceptor*,' Max insisted.

'GUARDS!' Paul shouted.

'Guards,' Max repeated. 'Oh, hang on, I forgot. Dirk's gone for some food, and his mate is sleeping. Now drop the gun.'

Paul glowered at Max and threw his gun towards Danny's chair.

'Chief, it's Dad,' Danny protested.

'I don't know if your dad is hosting a Shadower or if this one has transmuted. But he is definitely a Deceptor.'

'He's lying, son. You'd know if I wasn't your dad after eighteen years,' Paul protested.

'Danny,' Max said, stepping closer. 'I know you can't see auras, but do you remember the mirror Adam gave me and Bobby in Covent Garden?'

'Yeah...' Danny hesitated.

Max pulled out the mirror and went to show it to Danny, but Paul lunged forward, knocking Max's gun across the room. As they rolled across the floor, Zym, Mercedes, and Stephen dashed toward them, trying to pull Paul off Max.

A shot rang out.

'Get back,' Danny shouted, pointing the gun towards them, his hand shaking.

They scrambled to their feet, backing away slowly.

Max pushed himself up, breathing heavily, 'Thanks, Danny.'

'Stay there, Chief. Don't touch that gun,' Danny warned, his voice firm but trembling.

Max raised his hands and slowly stepped back. 'Come on, buddy. The mirror proves he's a Deceptor.'

'Son, you've only got his word for that. We just see a normal reflection, don't we? Don't let him lie to you,' Paul insisted.

'If Max says he's a Deceptor, I'd believe him, Wheels,' Zym said.

Paul looked darkly at Zym. 'Of course, an Italian waiter who has appeared from nowhere is totally trustworthy.'

Danny's hand trembled as he looked from Max to Paul, torn by loyalty and doubt.

Paul glanced at his watch. 'Son, I'll send you a direct feed from the IFFS meeting, and if they agree, I'll get you up there.'

'Buddy, he's lying. He doesn't care about you. There's something bigger going on,' Max protested.

'Max is right,' Mercedes added. 'Come on, Danny, you're intelligent enough to see that.'

'Oh, look. Now they're saying you're stupid for not believing them,' Paul sneered. Softening his voice, he added, 'Son, your mum and I love you. We'd do anything to protect you.'

Danny hesitated, his gun wavering between his dad and the others. 'Get the gun and go. As soon as they agree, get the security team to take me up there,' he said, his voice uncertain.

'Danny!' Mercedes exclaimed.

Paul moved quickly across the room, picking up Max's gun. 'I swear, if they agree, I'll get you there. In fact, you watch this lot, and I'll tell the guards now. I don't care what the IFFS say. You're my son, and I want you there.'

Danny sighed, relieved he'd made the right decision. 'Thanks, Dad.'

'Danny, how could you?' Mercedes said.

Paul smiled at his son and picked up the gun. 'I really should have killed you, Max, when you were hiding in the hospital bathroom.'

Max frowned. 'How did you know I was there?'

'We were pretty sure you were transmuting in Bobby when that useless policeman tried to lure you with a Daxson. But you really gave the game away leaving that picture of Mercedes by the Zermatt train on the television in Bobby's hospital room.' Paul sneered as he walked towards the door and unlocked it.

'What do we do with this lot?' Danny asked.

Paul smirked. 'They'll be busy trying to save their friend.'

Danny frowned. 'Which friend? They're all fine.'

Paul's expression hardened as he pointed the gun towards Danny, 'You.'

Mercedes second-guessed Paul, and she dived forward as he fired, pushing Danny onto the floor. Paul didn't wait to see the aftermath of his shot. He stormed out of the chalet and locked the door behind him as he headed for the train station.

22
Starstruck

'Wow, that's the French President!' Bobby said excitedly.

'Never mind that there's the manager of the Brazilian football team,' Adam replied.

'You two are funny. So starstruck,' Pat laughed.

'Excuse me, who asked for an autograph and a picture on the way in?' Bobby chuckled.

'Yeah, but that doesn't count. She's a dame, and I've been a fan since I was young,' Pat protested.

'Okay, Mum, whatevs,' Bobby replied, winking at Adam.

Adam grabbed three glasses of fruit juice from the drinks table and handed them to Pat and Bobby.

'Well, if I'd known such a fine lady was comin' with her strappin' minders, I'd've dressed up,' Big Bill said.

'Mr Pierce—uh, I mean Big Bill, this is my mum,' Bobby flustered. 'Mum, this is Big Bill. He's our top boss.'

'Charmed to make your acquaintance, ma'am,' Bill replied warmly. 'Does your mum have a name, Bobby?'

'Oh, err, yeah, it's, uh, Mrs Morris,' Bobby replied, his face red with embarrassment.

'I think my son means it's Patricia, but please call me Pat.'

'The pleasure's all mine, Pat,' Bill replied. 'Call me Bill.'

'There's a lot of very important people here, Bill,' Pat said, glancing around.

'None more important than you and your boys, Pat,' Bill smiled.

'What's this event all about?' Pat asked, looking around the reception room. 'There's celebrities, politicians, billionaire business people, and even royalty.'

'It's about bringin' us all together to save the planet,' Bill said.

'Is that like climate change and things?' Adam asked.

'Sure is, young fella,' Bill replied.

'Your Majesties, Your Excellencies, distinguished guests, and honoured friends. Please take your seats for this year's historic gathering,' the voice announced over the tannoy.

'This way,' Bill said.

'We're not in the front, are we?' Pat asked nervously.

'Only if y'all's a head of state,' Bill laughed, leading them to seats five rows back. 'We're back here.'

'Don't forget to turn your phones off,' Pat told Adam and Bobby.

'Y'all's fine. There's no signal in here,' Bill said.

Adam sat down, greeting the person on his right, while Bobby took the seat to his left, followed by Pat, with Big Bill taking the aisle seat.

Pat glanced around before nudging Bobby with her elbow.

'Oww, what's that for?' Bobby winced.

'Don't be so dramatic—it was only a nudge,' Pat laughed. 'Have you seen who's sitting next to Adam?'

Bobby leaned forward, peering to his right. The woman smiled, and Bobby smiled back before turning to his mum. 'Yeah, a woman, and?'

'What do you mean "and" it's *her*,' Pat replied.

'Who's her?'

'The lady from that film,' Pat said excitedly.

'Well, that narrows it down to several hundred or maybe thousand,' Bobby laughed.

'Oh, you know, she's in that film about thingy. She plays the one who turns up and does that thing with him from whatsit,' Pat replied, waving her hand vaguely.

'Oh yeah, her,' Bobby lied, pretending he had a clue.

'Please welcome our retiring chair, Pietr Van den Berg,' the tannoyed voice announced.

The lights dimmed, and a spotlight focused on a thin, grey-haired man with a small, greying soul-patch beard and round, wire-framed glasses.

'My friends and honoured guests,' Pietr started, 'The International Federation for Fiscal Security was founded in 1735 by Jernail Shah, and it has been my honour to steer it over the last twenty-two years. Now, the time has come for me to pass on the baton.'

The audience groaned in disappointment.

Pietr laughed. 'Now come on, all good things come to an end. Besides, this gives me more time to beat Big Bill on the golf course.'

Bill let out a loud guffaw, which rippled across the room.

'But you're not here for me, so let's keep going. It's a delight to present to you someone I know will take the IFFS forward into an exciting new future. Please welcome your new Chair, the former Health Secretary of the United Kingdom, Andrew Daks,' Pietr said as Andrew emerged from the side of the stage to rapturous applause.

Although smartly dressed, Daks's ill-fitting suit hung awkwardly on his slim frame, giving the appearance of someone trying too hard to blend into a world more polished than himself.

'Thank you, Pietr,' Andrew said, shaking his hand before stepping up to the podium as Pietr walked off-stage.

Andrew gripped the wooden lectern with a mixture of glee and trepidation. 'My honourable friends. I take over the mantle from Pietr at an auspicious time. We've shared a common goal across the centuries: to create a planet free of hunger and war. We've strived to eliminate sickness and suffering while working tirelessly to protect this planet for *our* future.

'It is with profound gratitude that I welcome you to this historic gathering, where we will celebrate those bold aspirations and explore our latest achievements. Inside this grand chamber, we are joined by the greatest visionaries. Leaders who are shaping nations, entrepreneurs driving progress, artists inspiring generations and philanthropists redefining compassion. Everyone here represents the pinnacle of individual success and a shared passion for building a world of unity, a world of action, a unified, true and free world. A safe and secure world of love, peace and harmony.

'As the eyes of this ravaged planet look upon us, let us move beyond daring to dream. Let us innovate and create that one true world—together.

'Before we commence today's agenda, I want to thank our media friends for covering our opening ceremony and invite them back to review our conclusions, dreams and innovations at the end of the day. Centuries ago, the IFFS set out to bring about a new chapter of global unity. Our aim this week is to measure how far we've come.'

The conference hall erupted into applause, as the media present in the hall and those in the viewing gallery behind the one-way mirrors were escorted out.

As the conference hall doors closed, Andrew glanced at the Head of Security, who gave him a thumbs-up. He turned back to the audience with confidence.

'Now that we are alone, I have some exciting news. Tonight, you will witness the future—a future where hunger has been eliminated, war becomes unnecessary, and death is no more.'

Andrew paused as the audience applauded, causing him to smile in satisfaction.

'But this future isn't some distant dream. It's not next century or even next year. The future starts now, with our next presenter. So, please, be upstanding and welcome our friend and the one responsible for bringing this project to life—Paul White.'

Andrew turned to his right, extending his hand in anticipation. The applause faded as the seconds passed, and no one appeared.

'Paul?' Andrew prompted, looking desperately across the faces in the stage wings.

As the audience started to murmur, Pietr ran back onto the stage, pulling Andrew to one side, and sliding his hand over the microphone. He whispered something, causing Andrew's expression to shift from confusion to frustration. Andrew glanced towards the back of the stage, looking for some inspiration, then back at Pietr, shaking his head in disbelief.

As Pietr gestured insistently before subtly motioning to the audience, Andrew exhaled slowly, his shoulders dropping in resignation. With visible reluctance, he gave Pietr a short nod and watched the former Chair briskly exit the stage.

Andrew moved back to the lectern and smiled nervously. 'Unfortunately, Paul has been delayed, so I'll continue.'

Bill leant towards Pat and whispered, 'Excuse me, Pat. I just need to make sure everything is alright backstage.'

Pat glanced at Bill. 'Of course, Bill. That did look a bit strange up there.'

Andrew cleared his throat as he stared at the autocue. 'Thank you, A...erm, okay, well tonight I'm excited to show you the progress my team has made since I acquired, I mean since Paul acquired M Bank,' Andrew stuttered.

A snigger rippled around the conference hall at Andrew's awkwardness.

'Transporting food worldwide has been at the expense of a colossal carbon footprint. Tonight, that ends. Let me show you the future of food transportation. Stand back as the doors open,' Andrew read before realising the last statement was an instruction, not something to say.

As the stage started to split in half and move to the sides, Andrew steadied himself and turned towards the large metal door being revealed behind the stage.

'Read the autocue,' a voice hissed behind him.

Andrew jolted back into the present. The side of the stage he was on including the lectern and one autocue screen rotated ninety degrees leaving him side on to the audience to his left with the metal door to his right. He ran a hand through his receding hair before gathering himself. 'Esteemed guests and friends, I give you the Porter machine. Point towa—' Andrew stopped as he realised he was reading stage directions again.

The metal door slowly lowered into the floor, revealing a large machine which looked like a cross between a giant telescope and a powerful military weapon.

Andrew glanced at the autocue for guidance, but it just showed the instruction: *Point towards the Porter machine and walk towards it.*

'This is the Portal machine,' Andrew said, walking towards the machine. He hesitated, then corrected himself after someone stage-whispered the proper name. 'I mean the Porter machine.'

Crossing the threshold into the room with the Porter machine, Andrew turned back to face the audience. Drawing a deep breath, he noted the screens on either side showing the autocue. 'This machine can transport food to anywhere, uh...to anywhere in the, uh...world,' Andrew stuttered, struggling as the autocue scrolled clumsily.

'What the goddamn hell is goin' on,' Bill demanded.

'There's been a problem in the village,' Pietr said. 'Some issue with Paul's son.'

'Well, damn Pietr. I don't give a rat's ass what's up with that boy,' Bill growled. 'If the machine's workin', he's no use. Where's Paul?' His eyes narrowed. 'This is the culmination of centuries of work.'

'Yes, sir,' Pietr replied. 'Everyone else is ready, including your son.'

'That runt's nothin' more than a DNA experiment,' Bill snarled. 'Get Paul here. Now.'

'There's some angry voices over there,' Adam whispered to Bobby.

'I can hear Big Bill; I've never heard him so mad. What's going on?' Bobby asked as another commotion near the conference hall entrance grew louder.

The audience turned to see Paul White gesturing furiously at the guards. While his words were muffled, they were sharp and agitated. As he finished talking, a group of heavily armed guards emerged from a side door and headed toward the reception area.

Paul strode towards the stage, his eyes cold and darting around the room, as he grabbed a microphone from the side of the stage. 'Sorry I'm late,' he began with a thin laugh. 'If only I had a transport machine that could zap me from one location to another,' he added, glancing briefly at the Porter machine.

Andrew briefly closed his eyes and exhaled slowly in relief. 'Paul, it's great to see you. I was explaining to everyone that this machine can transport food anywhere in the world.'

Paul gave a strained laugh, the edge in it unmistakable. 'Thank you, Andrew, and congratulations on taking over from Pietr. You'll make a fabulous Chair,' his words were sharp, and his voice barely concealed his frustration as he took slow, steady breaths.

'That's very kind of you, Paul,' Andrew replied cautiously, edging towards the side of the room. 'I'll leave you to it.'

'Yes,' Paul snapped, his body tensing as he glanced towards the back of the hall before looking back at the audience as he picked splinters of wood off his jacket.

'What's annoyed Danny's dad?' Adam hissed.

'Maybe because he was late,' Bobby muttered, his gaze following Paul's towards the hall's entrance. 'It could also be because his jacket is filthy. Look it's covered in green streaks and bits of wood.'

Paul gathered himself as he began speaking, his voice relaxing into a steady rhythm. 'My friends,' he said, spreading his arms. 'This Porter machine, combined with our satellite infrastructure, can transport food to anywhere in the world in an instant.'

'Stay here and make sure nothin' goes wrong,' Bill ordered.

Pietr flinched at Bill's sharp tone. 'Yes, sir. Where are you going?'

'I'm gonna have a word with that guard. Need to find out what's got Paul so pissed,' Bill replied, marching away.

As he reached the guard, he growled, 'What's goin' on, soldier?'

The guard stood to attention. 'Mr White reckons we're going to get intruders, sir.'

'Looks like y'all's gearing up for an invasion, boy,' Bill laughed.

'Mr White said it's his son and his friends, sir.'

'We've got half of 'em in there with me. I reckon you'll manage,' Bill said, heading back toward his seat.

'Is everything okay?' Pat asked as Bill sat down.

Bill smiled disarmingly. 'Nothin' to fret over, ma'am. Just a few troublemakers outside, but they ain't gettin' in.'

23
SHOWTIME

'Mercedes, are you okay?' Danny asked, struggling to free himself

Mercedes opened her eyes and frowned as she registered what had happened. 'Well, apart from saving your life from your crazed dad and being shot at? Yeah, I'm perfect, thanks.'

'In which case would you mind getting off me?'

Mercedes glanced down and realised she was sprawled across Danny. Her face reddened as she slid off him and sat up, rubbing her shoulder. 'I thought your dad was one of the good guys.'

Danny pulled himself into a sitting position but avoided looking at anyone. 'He is. There'll be a reason behind this,' Danny replied. 'It's not like Dad actually tried to kill anyone. He only shot in my direction to keep us busy and away from whatever's happening at the IFFS meeting.'

Mercedes reached over and held one of Danny's shaking hands. 'Danny, you know what he did.'

'No, it's not true. He's my dad,' Danny replied defiantly, not pulling his hand free from Mercedes's gentle hold. 'Max, you know Dad. Tell Mercedes she's wrong.'

Max looked at Mercedes and then Danny, struggling to find the right words. 'Danny, I'm sorry, but—'

'No, you're all wrong. Dad has given me everything. He believed in me when the hospital said I'd never survive as a baby. He gave me the best education and has...' Danny ran out of steam and dropped his head to hide the tears.

Mercedes shuffled over and put her arm around him.

Zym pulled Danny's wheelchair forward and studied it. He put a finger through a bullet hole in the centre of the backrest, then turned to Max, his eyebrows raised.

Max clenched his teeth and nodded. 'Danny, it wasn't your dad who shot at you.'

Danny looked up, wiping his sleeve across his eyes. 'You mean someone else fired?' Danny asked, looking at the others.

'It was Paul who fired, but he has an aura. So he's either hosting a Deceptor, or that is a Deceptor in a shell,' Max said.

Danny went quiet as he processed what Max had said. 'You mean he's not my dad?'

Max shook his head. 'No, it might be your dad, but if it is your dad, he's not in control of his body. It was the Deceptor who pulled the trigger.'

'I knew my dad wouldn't shoot me,' Danny said. 'But we've got to rescue Dad. He needs us,' Danny growled as shock turned to anger.

Max nodded. 'And we will, Danny. In the meantime, Stephen, check the back door. I locked it when I came in. The key should still be in the door.'

'I'll see if there's any bandages in there, too.'

'I'm okay.' Danny replied. 'Dad, I mean that thing inside him missed me,'

'You might be, but it looks like he clipped Mercedes as she dived across to save you,' Stephen said, heading towards the kitchen.

'I've been shot,' Mercedes yelped, looking at the blood on her fingers from where she'd been rubbing her shoulder.

Max helped Mercedes into a chair, slid off her coat and studied her wound. 'It's only grazed your shoulder. I think you'll live.'

Zym turned to Danny. 'Can I give you a hand, lad?'

'Cheers, Zym,' Danny replied, grabbing Zym's arm with one hand and his chair with the other as he hauled himself into it.

'The back door is locked,' Stephen said, entering the room with a first aid box. 'The key is still there, but there's a pile of wood outside blocking the door.'

As Stephen bandaged Mercedes's shoulder, Max started searching the room. 'We need some tools to break through one of the doors.'

'What about exploding some aerosols to blow the door open?' Zym suggested, rummaging in a cupboard.

'Guys,' Danny said.

'Hang on, Danny,' Max replied as an idea hit him. 'One of the guards was trying to fix the WiFi. He must've had a toolkit.'

'Guys,' Danny repeated more forcefully.

'Yeah, in a sec,' Zym muttered, checking out a cupboard. 'We need to break out of here first.'

Zym picked up a poker by the fireplace and tried jamming it into the doorframe, but it bent under his pressure.

Max returned from the kitchen, carrying a small canvas tool bag. 'Not much in here, but the claw hammer might work.'

Danny sighed, moved over to the door, and unlocked it.

Max stopped in his tracks. 'You've got a key?'

'Yeah,' Danny replied matter-of-factly. 'I wasn't a prisoner. I blacked out, and Dad had me brought here to rest. I was probably exhausted as I'd worked through the night.'

'I bet if you'd tried to leave, those guards would've stopped you,' Mercedes said.

'Nah, Dirk and Klaus are great. Anything I asked for, they got,' Danny insisted. 'Although…I'm not so sure now,' he added uncertainly.

Zym looked at the bent poker with a wry smile. 'Well, I guess I don't need this,' he shrugged before throwing it back into the fireplace.

After Stephen had finished bandaging her shoulder, Mercedes explored the cabin. Several minutes later, she shouted from another room, 'Guys, there's an angry-looking guy with blood on his face trying to smash in the back door.'

'Has he got black or fair hair?' Danny shouted.

'Fair,' Mercedes yelled back.

'That's Klaus. He's a laugh, but Dirk's a nasty piece of work,' Danny replied.

Mercedes appeared in the doorway, carrying some weapons. 'Klaus doesn't look like he's laughing, and some of his friends will be here in a few minutes. I could see them in the distance.'

'Bloody hell,' Stephen exclaimed as Mercedes dropped three automatic rifles, a couple of handguns and a handful of magazines onto a table.

'Where did you find them?' Danny asked, frowning.

'Behind a bookcase in the hallway, Mercedes smirked. 'It's got a pin-code lock, but someone thought it a good idea to write the code on the back of the picture next to it.'

'That'll be Dirk. He'd forget his name if he didn't wear a name badge,' Danny replied. 'Show me what else they've got in that cupboard.'

There was a crash from the back of the chalet, and Zym grabbed a rifle and ran into the kitchen, firing at the creaking back door.

The bullet embedded itself in the glass, resulting in Klaus grinning, with the blood on his face giving him an evil look.

'The glass is bulletproof,' Zym shouted.

'Yeah, this is Dad's ski chalet. The walls can even take a direct hit from heavy artillery,' Danny replied as he grabbed a pistol and headed into the hallway, grabbing Mercedes's hand. 'Show me the weapons cupboard.'

Max ran to the front door and locked it before picking up two rifles and throwing one to Stephen.

Stephen caught it clumsily before fumbling and dropping it. 'I don't know how to use one,' he said, picking it up.

'I thought you went shooting?' Max said, walking over to him.

'That's shotguns, not military weapons.'

'There's not much difference. There's your safety, which goes between safe, single shot or rapid fire. After that, it's the same as a shotgun, point at your target and fire,' Max explained.

An explosion rang out from the back of the house.

'Hello! Is anyone else coming to play?' Zym shouted.

'Just stay here, point that at the door, and if anyone tries to break in, fire,' Max said as he ran to join Zym in the kitchen.

'Chief, we've got enough to start a small war here,' Danny shouted as Max ran past.

'That's great, but we need an escape plan,' Max replied.

'Thanks for sparing me some time, Junior,' Zym said, crouching behind a table as Klaus continued to batter the door.

'This place is like a fortress,' Max replied.

'Feels like the Siege of Rochester all over again,' Zym laughed.

'But we had two months of misery before losing to King John,' Max replied.

'Yeah, but it proved how important Magna Carta was,' Zym replied.

Max laughed. 'Until a year later, then two years later and—'

'Alright, King John was a bit slow on the—'

Danny appeared in the doorway. 'If you've finished discussing ancient history, you might want to see this.'

'Ancient history!' Zym muttered as they followed Danny.

They reached the ammunition cupboard, and Max whistled in admiration, looking around the small room crammed with weapons on the walls. 'Is your dad planning a war?'

'Yeah, it's quite a collection, but that's not what you need to see,' Danny replied excitedly. 'Okay, Mercedes.'

While grabbing some handguns and as much ammunition as they could stuff into their pockets, they watched the wall to their right slide away.

'Surprise,' Mercedes said, standing at the top of a steep sloping tunnel.

'Where does it go?' Max asked.

'I think it goes to the train station, but I can't b—' Mercedes was cut short by another explosion at the back of the chalet.

'Come on,' Zym pressed. 'I'd rather take my chances down there than stay here.'

'Get going,' Danny insisted.

They started running down the slope when Max screeched to a halt. 'I've forgotten something.'

'Leave it, we don't have time,' Zym replied.

'I can't. Keep going, and I'll catch you up.'

'Junior, what's so important?'

'It's Stephen,' Max replied, disappearing into the chalet.

As Max ran into the front room, he saw Stephen motionless, pointing the rifle at the door.

'Stephen, come on,' Max shouted.

'It's okay, they can't get through,' he replied, staring at the door as it creaked and groaned under the battering.

Max grabbed Stephen's arm and started to drag him away. 'Come on, we've found an escape route.'

A minute later, Max and Stephen reached the weapons cupboard. 'Danny, what're you doing?' Max asked as Danny came up the slope.

'Just leaving a surprise for anyone who tries to follow us,' Danny smirked.

Stephen noticed a wire hanging down and grabbed the end. 'What's this—'

'Don't pull that!' Danny shouted.

Stephen followed the wire up to the ring it was tied to. 'What the hell. It's tied to a *grenade*. Are you trying to kill us?'

'It's tear gas, not an explosive grenade. I'm not planning on killing anybody,' Danny insisted, closing the door into the arms cupboard and hooking the wire onto it.

A loud explosion shook the chalet, causing some weapons to fall on the floor.

'You might not be planning to, but I think they will,' Max said. 'We need to move, *now*!'

'Two secs,' Danny replied, hooking another wire to the door and putting the roll it was attached to over a rifle barrel, using it like a spindle. 'Let's go.'

As they raced down the corridor, Danny stopped to cut the wire. 'I left some explosives here, but they've gone.'

'Uh, there's something up here in a crack in the wall by the ceiling,' Stephen said.

Danny moved his chair into standing mode. 'Who put it up there? I left it by one of the struts holding up the ceiling.'

Another explosion from the chalet echoed down the tunnel.

'Danny, come on. Just plant the detonator,' Max screamed.

'Fine,' Danny huffed, working quickly before returning to sitting mode and chasing after Max and Stephen.

As he neared the end of the tunnel, Danny saw Max, Stephen, Zym and Mercedes waiting outside a large steel door.

'How did you know the code?' Danny asked.

Mercedes laughed. 'Whoever sets the codes needs to mix them up a bit. It was the same as the one into the arms cupboard: seven, zero, nine, dash, four, five.'

'Where now?' Stephen asked.

'We could wait for the train,' Zym suggested. 'After all, this is the train station.'

Danny nodded. 'I'll see if I can find the signal box to make sure it st—'

He was cut short by an explosion and a cloud of smoke billowing out of the tunnel.

'Looks like my booby trap worked,' Danny said smugly.

'I think you'll find it's because I put your explosives in the rock fault in the ceiling,' Mercedes retorted.

'They'd have worked where I put them by a vertical strut,' Danny insisted.

'That would have weakened it, but it could have taken ages to collapse,' Mercedes replied.

Danny folded his arms. 'No, it wouldn't. It—'

'Will you two pack it in,' Zym snapped. 'Danny, find that signal box.'

Danny moved across the platform, looking for the signal control box. 'I can't see anything. They probably control it from Zermatt.'

Max noticed some two-wheeled luggage carts near the platform and asked Stephen to help him. 'Turn it upside down and jam that end into the teeth between the tracks. Then we'll do the same with the other one.'

Paul strode confidently across the area in front of the Porter machine. 'Just imagine how this will change the world. In the face of famine, war or a natural disaster, we can get food there in seconds.

'But this isn't just any food. It's pure energy. All of the benefits with none of the calories. That'll get you in the good books of your lady wife, Your Majesty.'

The audience laughed as a glass cubicle around the size of a shop fitting room was wheeled out.

'So, how do we make this energy food?' Paul asked, smiling disarmingly. 'First of all, let me invite some guests out here.'

Paul glanced at the autocue and said, 'I would like to invite the star of Hollywood's latest blockbuster, Irwin Stern, and the newest star of international footballer, Adam Lee, to join me.'

Adam looked at Bobby, who shrugged, but he could see Big Bill encouraging him to go up.

'My friends, please give some encouragement to Irwin and Adam as they join me,' Paul said.

Adam and Irwin walked up to Paul, who shook their hands. 'Thank you both for coming up here. Now take a bite of these apples and tell our friends what they taste like.'

Irwin took a bite and smiled. 'That's a nice fresh apple.'

'Thanks, Irwin. Adam, how's yours?'

'It's a bit sweet for me, but it has a nice crunch,' Adam replied.

'Only Adam could call an apple a bit sweet,' Bobby jokingly whispered to Pat.

'Thank you, gentlemen. Now, Adam, place yours in the green container, and Irwin, put yours in the yellow one,' Paul said. 'And now I'll place them into this machine we're calling the Separator.'

Paul opened the door, placed the containers on the seat and closed the door. 'May I suggest you avert your eyes. The light won't damage your sight, but it is very bright,' he said.

A voice counted down from five before a bright light filled the room. Paul retrieved the two containers from the Separator and placed them under a camera.

He reached into each container and lifted the two apples, handing them to Irwin and Adam. 'If you'd kindly taste your apples and confirm if they taste the same,' he said.

Adam and Irwin bit into the fruit, and both said they thought the apples had no flavour.

'If you look on the screens, you'll see there are still two glowing apples in the containers. Adam, can you remove yours and taste it,' Paul smiled confidently.

Adam frowned. 'It tastes like it originally did, but it's so light.'

Paul grinned. 'Some of you may have already experienced energy food, but even organics can eat it now. How do you feel, Adam?'

'Amazing. I feel full of energy but not even slightly bloated.'

'Ready to play a full match?' Paul laughed.

'Absolutely,' Adam replied.

'If you'd like to return to your seat, this next part involves Irwin's energy apple,' Paul said, directing Adam away.

As the audience applauded Adam, Paul took the other container to Irwin. 'Irwin, please remove your energy apple and take another bite.'

Irwin bit into the apple. 'Adam was right. It tastes the same as the original apple but lighter.'

'If you could put it back in the container, I'm now going to place it inside the Porter machine,' Paul explained, carrying it to the machine, placing it inside and closing the door. 'But making it appear at the back of the room is easy. So, on the screens, we are joined by a special guest from the UK. Hello, Prime Minister.'

'Hello, Paul. I'm sorry I can't be there in person, but as you can see, I'm in my study in Downing Street.'

'Do you have a plate in front of you?'

'Yes, Paul,' the Prime Minister replied.

'Engineering, are you ready?' Paul asked.

A voice came over the tannoy saying, 'Yes, Paul. We are ready to start the countdown.'

Paul noticed he was still standing on the raised floor surrounding the Porter machine and skipped forward towards the audience. 'Then start the process.'

A siren sounded, and an electronic voice said, 'Caution, Porter machine rising.' The ceiling above the Porter machine curved into a dome shape, and the machine started rising. It slowed as it approached its height limit, and the dome separated to reveal the sky. As the machine stopped rising, it began to rotate until the electronic voice said, 'Target confirmed.'

'Fire when you're ready,' Paul said.

The electronic voice started counting down from three, and then a short blast of light shot out of the barrel of the Porter machine.

A few seconds later, the screens in the conference hall flashed before the image cleared to show the Prime Minister holding up the plate with a half-eaten energy apple on it.

Paul put his arm around Irwin and guided him towards one of the screens. 'Does that look like your apple?'

'That's amazing, and yes, it does look like mine,' Irwin replied.

'Thank you, Irwin, please return to your seat, and thank you, Prime Minister,' Paul said cheerily.

Bill leaned over to Pat. ''Scuse me, ma'am, but this here's my part.'

'It's incredible, Bill. You're transforming our world,' Pat replied.

'Y'all don't even know the half of it, ma'am,' Bill said with a wink as he walked away.

24
The Distraction

The train screeched to a halt, stopping just before the blockage on the track.

Max climbed onto the step at the front of the train and pulled on the locked door to the driver's cabin. He waved his gun at the driver, who immediately got up and opened the door.

Max entered the driver's cab and said, 'Ich tu Ihnen nichts, ich muss nur ins Hotel kommen.'

'You what?' the driver replied.

'You're English?' Max said, surprised.

'Yeah, they drafted us in to help with the bigwigs,' the driver replied.

Max laughed. 'I just said I wasn't going to hurt you—'

'I bloody hope not. I'm on holiday next week,' the driver said.

'We just need to get to the hotel,' Max said.

'Why all the drama? We stop here anyway,' the driver stated.

'You've not been told of any problems?' Max asked as Zym joined them.

'I just do me job, pal,' the driver replied.

'So you'll take us to the hotel?' Zym asked.

'If you shift that junk off the line, I will,' the driver said.

Zym climbed out of the cab and, with some help from Mercedes and Stephen, removed the obstructions before they all boarded the train and set off.

'Can't we go any faster?' Max asked after a while.

'Sorry, pal, but this thing can only do twenty miles per hour, and that's on the flat bits.'

'How much longer?' Zym asked.

'We're almost there. Maybe fi—bloody hell, what's that?' the driver said, pointing to a shaft of light going from the hotel into the sky.

Max's muscles clenched. 'They've started.'

Zym watched the light disappear before turning to Max. 'We've got to stop them before it's too late.'

'Too late for what?' the driver asked.

'Before it's too late and your planet goes the same way as ours,' Max replied, jumping off the train as it reached the station, quickly followed by Zym.

'I swear some people start the day drinking at these events!' the guard muttered.

'Come on,' Max shouted as Stephen, Mercedes, and Danny disembarked.

'What's up, Chief?' Danny asked, noting the urgency in Max's tone.

'They've fired the Exodus machine,' Max shouted as they ran off the platform and up the path.

'The what?' Danny asked as Stephen and Mercedes helped Danny's chair cope with the light layer of snow.

'The machine you were working on to transport things,' Zym said as Max pulled ahead.

'Oh, you mean the Porter machine. Dad named it that because it transports things,' Danny replied.

'I'm more concerned about it leading to the destruction of things,' Zym said.

'It's only turning food into energy and transporting it,' Danny insisted as they approached the hotel.

Stephen peered inside the hotel. 'Can it transport us past armed security guards?'

'Blimey, are they expecting a war?' Zym exclaimed. 'How the hell are we getting past them?'

'I'm a guest, so they can't stop me,' Mercedes said.

'Let's check the back of the hotel,' Max replied.

As they walked around the side of the hotel, Max climbed a few steps and peered over the wall.

'There's one guard inside the side entrance and a couple on the path leading up to the viewing platform where you saw the dome,' Max whispered.

'I've got an idea,' Danny said, looking around. 'I reckon I can keep all these guards busy and give you a chance to get inside the conference hall.'

'If you can just give Mercedes and me time,' Max replied. 'Zym, can you and Stephen try to get to the Exodus machine? Sorry, I mean the Porter machine up there.'

'That's even better,' Danny said. 'Zym and Stephen, go up the steps and hide by the side of the hotel. As soon as the guards move, make a run for it.'

'How'll we know when to go?' Stephen asked.

'You'll know,' Danny said. 'Give me a few minutes. Mercedes, you and Max go into the hotel reception, and I'll get the guards to follow me.'

Mercedes frowned. 'How are you g—'

'Will everyone stop asking questions and just do what they're told!' Danny replied in exasperation.

'Okay, Wheels, tranquillo,' Zym said.

'What?' Danny asked.

Mercedes laughed. 'Zym was just saying calm down.'

'I am calm!' Danny insisted. 'Can we get on with it now.'

'Good luck,' Zym said as he headed off with Stephen.

'Oh, Zym,' Danny shouted.

'Yes, Wheels?'

'Do you reckon you could chuck that large rock over the side of the mountain to make it look like someone slid over it?'

'Sure thing,' Zym nodded. 'Come on, Stephen. Time to flex those muscles.'

Max and Mercedes wandered into the hotel reception, pretending to laugh and giggle about something.

A guard approached them with his rifle raised. 'I'm sorry, but the hotel is closed to visitors.'

'I'm pleased to hear it. We're staying here,' Mercedes replied, waving her room card.

The guard looked at the card and said, 'Thank you. I hope you enjoy your stay.'

'There's a table over there past the archway and near the entrance to the conference hall. We could sit there waiting for Danny to do his thing,' Max suggested.

As they sat down, Danny entered the hotel reception at full speed and headed for the guard who had confronted Mercedes and Max. 'Come on, it's the people that tried to capture Mr White.'

Danny flew back outside, pulled out the handgun, and as he headed towards the side of the hotel, he fired over the side of the mountain. 'Quick, they're getting away,' he shouted, looking towards the guards near the rear of the hotel.

Max and Mercedes sat at the table, sipping water, as they watched the guards in the hotel spring into action at the sound of gunfire.

The guard Danny had spoken to took control. 'You three, over by those windows,' he ordered. 'Jacques, take another two and get to the side entrance. You take your team to the kitchens and ensure the trade entrances are on alert.'

'Do we sneak in now?' Mercedes whispered.

Max studied how the guard handed out orders and directed his team. 'Not yet. This could work in our favour.'

'You two, get either side of that arch. Nobody comes through it in either direction. This place is on lockdown. Anyone that side stays in the conference, those on this side stay in the hotel,' the guard ordered.

'Now?' Mercedes asked.

'No!' Max whispered. 'Just look relaxed. We don't want him to see us and remember we're in the hotel. Damn, he's head—'

Mercedes leant over, flinging her arms around Max's neck and kissing him passionately.

She pulled away slightly and whispered, 'Has he gone?'

Max glanced past her and replied, 'Yeah, I think that's him outside.'

Mercedes sat back and smiled.

'I'm sorry, but I'm seeing Avery,' Max said.

'Don't flatter yourself,' Mercedes laughed. 'That was just to distract the guard. After all, who wants to interrupt teenagers hooking up!'

'Oh, okay,' Max replied, blushing. 'I think we can try to sneak in now.'

They slowly strolled towards the now unguarded entrance to the conference hall's reception area, glancing back to ensure the other guards were still busy in the hotel foyer.

As they walked into the reception area, Max spotted a woman in her mid-thirties flicking through a magazine and sitting at a table with name badges on it.

'Come on,' Max whispered as they headed towards the entrance to the conference hall.

Max reached for the door handle when he heard someone shout.

'Excuse me. Can I help you?'

Max and Mercedes turned to see the woman hurrying towards them.

'It's okay. We just popped to the toilet, and now we're going back in,' Mercedes said confidently.

'Not without your badges, you're not,' the woman replied.

'We left them on our chairs,' Max explained.

The woman stared at Max with a puzzled look. 'I know you, don't I?'

Max shifted awkwardly. 'No, I don't think so.'

The woman kept looking at Max, and then her expression changed. 'Of course. You're one of Big Bill's guests. You're with your boyfriend, that footballer.'

Max seized on the opportunity to play along. 'Yes, that's right. You mean my man, Adam Lee.'

The woman looked through the glass doors and could easily make out Big Bill near the front. 'You're with your mother as well. Oh, look, there's Bill, your mum, your boyfriend, and you sat in between them.'

'Um...' Max hesitated. 'That's, uh, one of those people they use to fill seats when guests, uh...'

'Yeah, it's a seat filler for when you pop to the toilet,' Mercedes said.

'I was involved in planning this event, and we don't have seat fillers,' the woman replied. 'Who are you?'

'Come on, they've run down to Danny,' Zym said, heading off, with Stephen chasing after him.

As they ran up the path towards the observation platform, Zym heard voices approaching above and dived behind a rock outcrop. Instinctively, he grabbed Stephen, yanking him in and simultaneously smashing Stephen's face into the rock.

'Ow, by dose,' Stephen mumbled, grabbing his face.

Zym put his hand over Stephen's mouth and whispered, 'Sorry, my friend, but be quiet; the guards are coming.'

Stephen tried to resist. 'It hurts,' he muttered before hearing the voices and freezing.

'Did you hear something?' a guard asked as they came down the path.

'Like what? I can hear that commotion coming from down there by that guy in the wheelchair,' the other replied. 'Is that what you heard?'

'I thought I heard someone saying something like "It's Burt,"'

'Who's Burt?'

'I don't know. It's just what I—' another shot rang out, cutting the guard off.

'Burt's gonna have to wait,' the second guard yelled as he started running down the path, with the other close behind.

Zym pulled his hand away from Stephen's mouth and examined his face. 'You'll live. Now come on, I can see something.'

Zym jumped off the wall from behind the rock and started moving up the path, his steps getting slower and more circumspect as he edged towards the open platform.

Stephen followed but kept touching his face and studying the blood on his hand. As he caught up with Zym, he grumbled, 'That bloody hurt, and I'm bleed—what the hell is that?'

'That is the dome I showed you back in London, and inside it is a machine capable of bringing the end to your world,' Zym replied as they crept around the dome, wary of any remaining guards.

As they approached the back of the dome near the metal shed, Stephen spotted the barrel of the Porter machine sticking out.

'Is that a gun?'

Zym walked towards it and glanced inside the dome. 'No, that's a transport machine,' he sighed, shaking his head.

Stephen stood beside Zym and peered inside. 'Wow, that's huge. So the mineral we found is fuelling this machine to send food around the world?'

'That's the start, lad. It's going to get worse,' Zym snapped.

'What do you mean worse?'

Zym turned and grabbed Stephen roughly by the shirt. 'That mineral can separate energy from the physical. It starts with food, then it'll be animals to "save the planet." Next, it'll be humans to "eradicate diseases and make you immortal," except it doesn't do any of those things. It'll lead to the collapse of the natural order of your world, which will be the real cause of the destruction of your planet.'

'But we're just trying to make the world better.'

Zym pushed Stephen away, fighting the urge to explode. 'Nature has a way of making the world better. Everyone else meddles in things, leading to consequences.'

'But unforeseen con—'

Zym's eyes widened as he stepped close to Stephen. 'You really think they are "unforeseen consequences?" They know what they're doing,' he raged, while keeping his voice low. 'I've been tracking this lot for years; whatever their motivation is, they've planned this. Nothing is "unforeseen," and you've just given them the missing jigsaw piece.'

'I didn't know,' Stephen pleaded.

'I know you didn't. If I thought you did, I'd have thrown you down the mountain,' Zym replied, resting his hands on the side of the opened dome and peering inside.

'I'm sorry,' Stephen said.

'Not as sorry as you will be if we don't stop this,' Zym said, crouching to see past the Porter machine and looking into the conference hall where he could see the front few rows and the wall on the one side. 'No, that can't be right.'

Stephen crouched by Zym, trying to get a similar view of the audience. 'What's wrong? I can see Pat, Bobby, and Adam sitting next to Big Bill.'

'It's not them; it's the reflection in the mirrored glass!' Zym said, his hands clenching the sides of the dome.

'They went that way,' Danny said, pointing towards the side of the hotel.

The guard looked in the direction Danny indicated. 'There's nobody there.'

'They jumped over the wall,' Danny insisted, moving forward a little.

The senior guard moved slowly towards the wall with his gun raised. 'There's nobody here.'

Danny glanced around, noting where the other guards were and then fired towards the small wooden shed at the bottom of the path leading up to the observation area.

'One of them just peeked over the wall and fired,' Danny said.

A couple of guards ran to the shed, and after looking around, they shook their heads.

Danny moved his chair into standing mode and moved towards the wall. 'Look, you can see where they slipped after jumping over here.'

The guard peered over and saw the disturbed snow, where something had slid through it.

Two guards joined the group from the observation platform.

'Anything untoward up there?' the senior guard asked.

'Nothing, sir,' one replied.

'What about Burt?' the other guard whispered, laughing.

'Shut it,' the first guard replied.

'Will both of you shut it and search the area,' the senior guard snapped. 'We've got a lot of important guests inside, and if there are armed intruders, I want them caught. Head down towards the station in case they've gone that way.'

'Yes, sir,' they replied in unison before heading off.

'I don't get it?' the senior guard said, leaning over the wall.

'Get what?' Danny asked, looking around for signs of the nonexistent gun-toting intruders.

'You said they jumped over the wall around here.'

'Yeah, look, you can see the marks in the snow where they slid down.'

'But that trail goes straight off the edge of the mountain,' the guard noted.

Danny leant forward. 'Oh, yeah. Perhaps they died,' he suggested.

'Possibly. But if they did, then how did they manage to shoot.'

Danny paused, frantically thinking. 'Look, there's loose rocks and gravel to the side. They must have scrambled onto it.'

'Of course, and that explains why there's no footprints in the snow,' the guard mused.

'Yeah, I guess,' Danny replied, biting his lip to suppress a smile.

'Then they could have crept up the gravel to the wall,' the guard said. 'It was just over here, wasn't it?'

'Yeah,' Danny answered distractedly as he tried to see Zym or Stephen.

'Funny, isn't it?' the guard said.

'Yeah,' Danny muttered. 'Uh, sorry, what's funny?'

'There's no snow on the loose gravel. But up against the wall, there's quite a lot.'

'I guess the wind makes it drift,' Danny said.

The guard nodded. 'You're probably right. But it does raise another question.'

'Does it?'

'You saw someone peek over the wall here and fire,' the guard said. 'Although he never hit anyone. Oh, it was a man, wasn't it?'

'Yeah, yeah. Definitely a man. I guess he was a bad shot,' Danny said nervously. 'Anyway, we should check in with the other guards.'

'He must have been very light,' the guard said. 'To see over the wall from that side, he'd have to be up close and standing in that snow. But there's no footprints. In fact, it's pristine.'

'Yeah, well, come on. The other guards might have picked up his trail,' Danny said, heading towards the hotel entrance.

The guard raised his rifle. 'Stay right where you are and slowly drop your gun.'

25
Conference Time

'I'm Bobby Morris's brother,' Max lied. 'Mum said they'd be here, so I said I'd surprise him.'

'Come with me,' the woman ordered. 'What's your name?'

'Max.'

The woman picked up her computer tablet and scrolled through it. 'Are you Avery Moore or Abigail Jenkins?' she asked, glancing up at Mercedes.

'No, I'm...' Mercedes started before looking at Max, who replied with a nod. 'I'm Mercedes Medici.'

'There you are. Mercedes Medici, sister of Christopher Medici and a—'

'Ex-sister of Christopher Medici.'

Without looking up, the woman continued, 'And an employee of WestFi.'

'Why have you got all that information?' Max demanded, glancing around to see if any guards were near.

'I'm asking the questions, thank you,' the woman said. 'I can't find any mention of a Max Morris. What previous names have you used?'

Max frowned. 'What do you mean?'

'What names have you used in previous transmutations?' the woman said matter-of-factly.

'What's a transthingy?' Max asked, trying to look confused.

The woman sighed and pointed to a mirror on the far wall.

Max turned and saw the auras around him and the woman. 'Ah,' he replied.

'Yes, ah. Now, let's try again. What names have you used in the past?'

Max thought for a moment, then said, 'Maximilian Habsburg.'

'Hmm,' the woman muttered. 'Any others?'

'Of course, try Maximilien Robespierre,' Max replied.

'How about someone alive in the last fifty years?' the woman asked, tilting her head and staring at Max.

'Maxwell Thomas,' Max sighed.

The woman glowered at Max before looking back at her tablet. 'Maxwell Thom—oh.'

'No, Thomas, not Tommo,' Max replied.

'Maxwell Thomas, previously mistaken for Michael Thomas. Believed to have escaped inside a London teenager, possibly Robert Morris,' the woman said. 'No, that's not possible.'

Max shifted awkwardly, not liking this public revelation of his background.

The woman looked at her tablet and then stared at Max. 'It says that you're suspected of being Max Janus, who first came to Earth in 46 BC.'

'Sorry, I've never heard of him,' Max insisted.

'If this is true, then you're Maxoraxin,' the woman replied.

Max shook his head. 'Not me.'

'There's a lot of gaps in this list, but from what I remember when you left Zephyrion and based on my research since coming here several months ago, I'm sure it's you,' she insisted.

'I'm sorry, but you're confusing me with this Maxohal. I've never—'

'Got you. I knew it was you,' the woman replied.

'What do you mean?' Max asked, frowning.

'I never mentioned Maxohal.'

'Yes, you did!'

'I said Maxoraxin.'

'No, you definitely said Maxohal,' Max said firmly. 'I think I'd remember my...'

'Remember what?' the woman smiled. 'You were going to say remember your own name, weren't you.'

'No, I—'

'Max, it's me, Erzsi,' the woman replied. 'I was Jericesen's secretary and worked for Timezel, bless him.'

Max felt numb. A lifetime of memories flashed through his mind, taking him back to life on Zephyrion, his parents, the stormy night and the lottery that led to him chasing Jeric and others to this planet.

'You can't be,' he said.

Erzsi laughed. 'Timezel always said if I ever met you again, I should mention the bookcases in his office.'

'It really is you, Erzsi,' Max replied.

'I'm Erzsébet here,' Erzsi replied.

'But when—how?'

'I've been here about ten months, trying to find out what's going on,' Erzsi explained. 'We started receiving signals from a planet far away, and in one of them, it mentioned Jericesen.'

Max scowled. 'Jericesen? I've not heard that in a long time. What did it say about him?'

Erzsi glanced around nervously and lowered her voice. 'That he's looking for volunteers to help him build a new Zephyrion.'

'I think he's a bit late for that,' Max laughed bitterly. 'You built a new Zephyrion on Astral 5, Noton 3 and Tuscan 3 two thousand years ago.'

Erzsi smirked. 'Now who's quoting historic names? My planet is just Astral now. Noton is called Malvis, and the other planet was Tascun, not Tuscan, although it's called Androvir now.'

'Is Timezel still the supreme leader?'

Erzsi lowered her eyes, and her expression darkened. 'He died during the Great Ungathering more than a thousand of your years ago,' she sighed. 'My partner was... killed in the same war. The Ungathering tore our worlds apart. Androvirs and Malvinians have a trading treaty, but Astral split into three territories. While the wars have stopped, there is still a lot of tension between each territory, and they despise inhabitants from the other planets.'

'So much for one united world creating peace,' Max replied.

Mercedes coughed loudly. 'Mind if I ask what's going on here?'

'Sorry, Mercedes, this is Erzsi. She helped us uncover the corruption on our planet and chase the individuals to Earth,' Max explained.

'Nice to meet you, Erzsi,' Mercedes said. 'I'm confused, though. You said you've been here for ten months, but you also said you received signals from a planet far away.'

'That's right. I was living on Astral as a research scientist when we started getting signals from here, maybe about a year ago by your time,' Erzsi said. 'I've often wondered what happened to Max and the others, but I didn't want to risk coming here to find they were all gone and there was no way home.'

'But no spaceship could travel from even the nearest habitable planet in a few months,' Mercedes insisted.

Erzsi laughed. 'We don't use spaceships; we use travel hoppers.'

'WHAT?' Max exclaimed. 'Don't you use Exodus machines?'

'You really are out of date,' Erzsi chuckled. 'Technology has moved on. Every building has several travel hoppers. They're like a glass cubicle. You step inside them, say where you want to go, and a few seconds later, you arrive at your destination.'

'But surely not to other planets?' Max asked.

'They go to Malvis and Androvir, but you need a travel permit code before it sends you, and if you try to travel there without a permit code, it takes you straight to Leyton,' Erzsi explained.

'What's Leyton?' Mercedes said.

'It's a prison planet,' Erzsi replied. 'The only people there are Deceptors.'

'What?' Mercedes asked, frowning.

'Deceptors are what we call criminals,' Max explained.

'Oh. So, they serve their sentence on that planet,' Mercedes said. 'Or is it like a processing centre until their trial?'

'If you end up in Leyton, that's it. There's no escape. It's a one-way ticket. I assume you've seen Julirani?'

'Juli's here?' Max replied.

'Yes. She's been working on the inside—oh, they're moving. Quick, this way,' Erzsi said, hurrying them towards a side room.

'What's going on?' Max asked.

'They're separating the humans from Zephyrions,' Erzsi replied.

'What do you mean?' Max said.

'Look through this side window and tell me what you see.'

'No... that's not...but they're some of the most powerful people in some of the world's major countries,' Max gasped.

'What's wrong?' Mercedes asked, just seeing a room full of people.

'They're Shadowers,' Max said.

'Who is?' Mercedes replied.

'All of them!' Max exclaimed. 'The one-way mirror around the room is full of auras. It looks like only a few are human. I need to get in there.'

'Do you still use Shadowers?' Erzsi laughed. 'That's so old-fashioned.'

'We were called Shadowers before they rebranded us Zephyrions,' Max moaned.

'That's the Max I remember,' Erzsi smiled.

'Some of them are coming out; let's creep in,' Mercedes suggested.

'You can't,' Erzsi replied. 'The next part is for Zephyrions only.'

'Well that's a bit, erm, does racist count, or is it planeterist?' Mercedes asked.

'Why is it Shadowers only?' Max asked.

'I don't know,' Erzsi said. 'I was told to arrange something to keep the humans busy. They never let me see what they were organising.'

Max stared at the mirror on the far wall as people filed out of the conference hall. 'They're all human. Can you include Mercedes in your group while I go inside?'

'Sure, but here, you'll need one of these,' Erzsi said, handing over a delegate pass.

'Chester Price,' Max read on the pass.

'I could have given you Alastair McGivern, but I think they might've guessed you're not the UK Prime Minister,' Erzsi laughed.

Max headed towards the doors into the conference hall when Mercedes hissed, 'What should I do?'

Max turned and said, 'Find out why they're here and what they've seen. Bobby, Pat, and Adam should be amongst them.'

'Did you hear that?' Zym said, looking behind him.

Stephen tilted his head, listening intently. 'It sounds like machinery.'

'It's the lift in that shed, come on,' he said, dragging Stephen with him.

Stephen instinctively put his hand over his nose, wanting to avoid Zym smashing his face into another object. 'What're we going to do?'

'Haven't got a clue, lad,' Zym replied. 'I'm making this up as we go.'

'But what if they've got guns?'

'Duck,' Zym laughed, 'and move fast.'

The machinery in the shed ground away with the occasional squeak before coming to a halt. Zym put a finger to his lips as the shed door opened.

'You go round to the left, and you go right. If you see anyone shoot to disable,' the lead guard said as three armed guards emerged from the shed.

The guard kicked the shed door to close it, but it thudded against Zym's boot. Zym waited to see if the guard reacted before he edged forward and slipped inside the shed, followed by Stephen. The door clicked shut, and the lead guard spun around but relaxed as he saw nobody.

'Come on,' Stephen said, glancing at the door and then back to Zym.

'But there's three floors?' Zym replied. 'I thought it would be up here and down there.'

'Just press one before they open the door,' Stephen said, chewing his lip.

'Let's work our way down then,' Zym said, stabbing at the middle button.

The lift whirred into life and slowly descended.

'What if they heard us get in here?' Stephen asked.

Zym scratched his cheek. 'Do you worry about everything, lad?'

'But they might be waiting for us with guns.'

'They might be waiting with a glass of wine and a tray of chocolate,' Zym replied.

Stephen's face screwed up. 'You think so?'

'Nope. But it's just as possible. Never worry about what you can't change, lad,' Zym smiled. 'In the meantime, stay flat against the lift wall.'

Zym felt his heartbeat quicken as the lift came to a stop and the doors opened into a floodlit area. He peered outside and realised they were at the far end of the conference hall with the Porter machine between them and the audience. He leant back and pressed the lower button, and the doors closed before continuing the descent.

'A bit too much going on there,' he sighed.

The lift stopped again, and the doors opened to a dimly lit corridor.

Zym scanned the corridor with its grey walls, white ceiling, and dark grey floor. The only illumination came from low-powered LED ceiling lights and brighter beams of light escaping through the glass in a door near the far end. Satisfied that nobody was around, he stepped out of the lift. 'Come on, but keep quiet.'

'Where are we going?' Stephen whispered.

'Down to the far end of the corridor,' Zym replied.

'Why?' Stephen asked, repeatedly glancing back toward the lift.

'Because I need to get my steps up, of course,' Zym sighed.

'Oh,' Stephen replied.

They reached a solid metal door on their right, which was locked. Zym studied the keypad but realised they didn't have time to crack it. 'We could do with Wheels. He'd be in there in seconds.'

Zym moved to the next door, which opened to reveal a small cleaning cupboard. Zym closed it quietly, and they continued to move down the corridor.

'What are we looking for?' Stephen asked.

Zym rolled his eyes. 'I don't know, but if you see it, let me know.'

'Okay,' Stephen said, looking back toward the lift.

They reached the next door, which was partly glazed, and Zym peered through the glass, but the room was pitch black. He opened the door, turned on the light and walked inside.

'One, two, four, eight, twelve,' Zym counted. 'It's a dormitory with twelve beds.'

'Where's the bathroom?' Stephen asked, peering inside.

Zym walked past a five-foot wall. 'It's here,' he said, pointing at a metal toilet bowl with a small sink beside it.

'It's a bit basic,' Stephen replied as Zym returned to the doorway.

'I don't think it's des—' Zym flicked off the light and dragged Stephen inside before pulling the door to, leaving a small gap to look through.

'Will you stop dragging me around,' Stephen protested before Zym's dagger look silenced him.

Zym peered through the crack in the door, and it confirmed the creak he heard was a door opening. He watched as a man came through the door at the end of the corridor and walked towards them. The man stopped at the brightly lit door almost across from them and opened it.

'Are the new arrivals ready?' the man asked.

Zym couldn't make out the response, but the man replied, 'They better had be. We don't want anyone fighting back.'

'What new arrivals?' Stephen asked.

Zym held his hand up to silence him. 'Shh,' he said.

The man glanced at his watch and said, 'I'll be back in fifteen minutes.'

As the man headed back towards the door at the end of the corridor, he passed a room in darkness, and Zym spotted the man's aura in the door's glass. As the man closed the door behind him, Zym crept out and waved to Stephen to follow.

Zym approached the room where the man had been talking to someone and peered through the glass. 'This is weird.'

'It looks like a hospital waiting room,' Stephen said, standing in front of the door and looking inside.

Zym grabbed Stephen and yanked him to one side. 'What the hell are you doing, lad?'

'I was just looking like you were,' Stephen protested.

'But you stood right in front of the glass,' Zym hissed. 'What if they'd seen you?'

'The guard had his back to the door, and everyone else was sitting on chairs and staring like zombies,' Stephen replied.

'You saw the whole room?'

'Yeah, there's four rows of benches on each side. There's two more benches at the end and two in the middle,' Stephen replied.

'How many people?' Zym asked.

'I'm not sure. I was counting, but you pulled me away. I got to twenty, but I think I missed about four or five,' Stephen said. 'Oh, and the guard.'

'There's only one guard! Are you sure?'

'Yeah, he was stood facing them and waving his hand in front of one of them.'

Zym patted his pockets, but all he felt were rounds of ammunition, and he sighed. 'Got any change?'

'What're you going to buy down here? A sandwich?'

'I want something to throw that way when he comes out,' Zym explained. 'Well?'

Stephen raised an eyebrow. 'Who carries cash nowadays?'

Zym turned, scowling. 'Anyone who doesn't want the State tracking their spending. Do you have any or not?'

Stephen checked his pocket and pulled out a ten franc note. 'This do?'

'What do I do with this? Make a paper aeroplane to distract the guard,' Zym growled. 'I need coins.'

'Fine,' Stephen muttered, sticking his hand in his pocket and pulling out a handful of coins.

Zym grabbed them and turned toward the door. He tapped, waited, then tapped again.

'What're you trying to do?' Stephen whispered.

'Lure him out, then knock him out and shove him in that store cupboard.'

Stephen handed over his gun. 'Here, hold this.'

Zym grabbed the weapon, frowning as Stephen pulled the door open. 'Excuse me,' he said casually in his best received pronunciation. 'Is this the star's dressing room?'

Zym's jaw dropped as he watched.

The guard marched toward Stephen. 'You shouldn't be here,' he growled.

Stephen backed out of the room nervously. 'Where should I be?'

'One floor up,' the guard said, reaching the door.

Zym crouched behind the door as the guard moved forward.

'I can't get the blasted door open. I thought I'd jolly well come too far as soon as I entered the corridor, but the door's jammed,' Stephen explained, pointing.

The guard started to move, but Stephen walked in front of him, forcing the guard to step sideways, and Zym whacked him with the gun, sending the guard crashing to the floor.

Zym grabbed the guard's legs and started dragging him toward the store cupboard. 'You could give me a hand,' he snapped.

Stephen snapped out of a daze. 'Oh, sorry, yes, of course,' he stammered, running to the cupboard door and holding it open.

Zym dragged the guard inside, yanked the keyring off his belt and locked the door behind him. 'I meant helping me drag him in,' he muttered, glowering at Stephen.

'You should've said,' Stephen replied, following Zym back to the room full of people.

As they entered, Zym paused and scanned the room. 'Something's wrong,' he said.

Stephen tilted his head, puzzled. 'Some of these were on the tram when we went to rescue Danny, but they're very quiet.'

'It's more than that,' Zym replied, crouching in front of a woman. 'Are you alright, miss?'

'My name is Victoria Graham, and I'm so happy to be here.'

Zym pivoted to the person behind him. 'Are you okay, lad?'

'My name is Michael Studerus, and I'm so happy to be here.'

Stephen walked down the far side of the room. 'They're all staring straight ahead with their hands in their laps.'

'It's like they've been brainwashed,' Zym said.

'Look, it's Chris,' Stephen said, running across to the back of the room. 'Chris, it's me, Stephen,' he said, kneeling.

'My name is Christopher Medici, and I'm so happy to be here.'

A door banged in the corridor, and Zym glanced outside. 'Quick, sit down and act like them.'

Stephen turned to Zym. 'But—'

'Not now,' Zym hissed, squeezing himself onto the bench, putting his hands in his lap and staring forward.

26
THE TWIST

'You dullards are going to regret this,' Danny protested. 'Don't you know who I am?'

'Yes, Mr White, we know exactly who you are,' the guard replied coldly.

'When my dad finds out about this, you're all going to be in a heap of trouble.'

The guard smirked. 'Your father was the one who warned us about you. Schultz, disconnect the battery on Mr White's chair, and don't touch any metallic parts until you've done it.'

'Yessir,' Schultz replied, kneeling behind Danny's chair.

Danny twisted in his chair. 'Schultz, be careful back there. You'll need to release the kill switch before touching the battery, or you'll be fried.'

Schultz jerked back. 'Woah, I'm not going near it if it's that dangerous.'

The first guard rolled his eyes. 'Get out of the way. White warned us his lad pulled stunts like this. Look, the battery has quick-release levers. You just flick them off like th—'

The guard's words were cut short as an electric shock tore through him, sending him flying across the room.

Danny leaned back, smiling. 'I told you so.'

Schultz ran across to the guard slumped against the wall, and checked his pulse. 'He's dead.'

Danny smiled. 'I did warn you.'

Schultz glanced around the room as if looking for answers. 'But I never saw his energy soul leave his shell. Why didn't he move into another human when his shell died? You're close enough.'

Danny put a finger to his mouth as if in deep thought. 'Hmm. I wonder if, while working on the Separator, I accidentally set my chair's electrical defence system to the same voltage and frequency that I was told to test the Separator at.'

Schultz frowned. 'I don't get it.'

'No, but your friend did,' Danny smirked. 'You see, every object has a unique frequency. Dad kept telling me to test the machine at different frequencies for different objects, but there was one he was really insistent about. The funny thing is it never worked on anything from Earth.

'That's when I remembered the depletors the Chief said you used on Zephyrion. I figured that setting might be useful for my chair.'

Schultz's confused expression changed to anger. He clenched his fists, his nails digging into his palms so hard that Danny noticed a drop of blood fall from his left hand. 'You can't be allowed to get away with this,' he screamed, heading towards the door. 'Mr White needs to know.'

Danny shot across the room, blocking the exit. 'I'm the one who tells my dad my latest discoveries.'

'Let me pass, or you'll regret it,' Schultz snarled.

Danny tilted his head and stared at Schultz, smiling. 'Why didn't you say so before?' he said, backing away from the door.

'About time you realised you're not in charge here,' Schultz said, grabbing the door handle.

Danny edged forward, his head bowed and his arms hanging on either side of his wheelchair. 'I'm sorry,' he said.

Schultz froze, taken aback by Danny's remorse. 'It's not me you need to apologise to. Mr White isn't going to let you ruin today,' he snarled.

'I know,' Danny replied remorsefully. 'But I do have to apologise to you too.'

'It's him you need to say sorry to,' Schultz snapped, nodding towards the dead guard.

'That's my point,' Danny said quickly, flicking a switch that dropped a short metal pole on a wire into his hand. He swung the pole at Schultz and hit a button on the rubber end he was holding.

Schultz didn't have time to react before the electric shock sent him sprawling across the room. Danny moved across the room and prodded Schultz with the pole to confirm he was dead.

'Well, I did say sorry,' Danny smiled before heading to the door.

Danny cracked the door open and peered out. At the far end, he could hear the sounds of a busy kitchen. The other direction led past several glass doors before ending at the foot of a stairwell. With nobody in the corridor, he slipped out and headed toward the stairs.

As he passed the glass doors, he noted they led to a reception room with people milling around eating and drinking. He paused and noticed several people sleeping in chairs or staggering around. A crash from the kitchen reminded Danny to keep moving. He quickly reached the stairwell, where he saw a lift on the far side and a corridor leading to more rooms with a first aid sign by one of the doors.

'Psst.'

Danny stopped and glanced around.

'Psst, Danny.'

Danny scanned the stairwell to see who it was and how they knew his name.

'Dude, over here.'

Danny turned and saw a tall stack of flight cases with a hand waving at him. He approached cautiously before spotting who was crouching behind them.

'Dazza, what're you doing there?'

'Not so loud,' Dazza hissed.

'Shouldn't you be with the press pack?'

'I was. We covered the opening ceremony, and then we were brought down here for refreshments,' Dazza explained.

'You mean there's free food, and you're not there?' Danny laughed.

'It tasted funny. Then the lady from Alliance Press fell ill, followed by Andy Snap and Martin from Bulletin Weekly,' Dazza explained.

'There's a guy called Andy Snap?' Danny queried.

'It's not his real name. He's Andrew, uh...' Dazza frowned. 'Well it's Andrew something, but they call him Andy Snap 'cos he gets a lot of pap shots of celebrities.'

'But why're you out here?'

Dazza glanced over the flight cases. 'Guards came in and started putting people onto stretchers and carrying them away. They said they were taking them to hospital.'

Danny shrugged. 'Isn't that a good thing?'

'I followed one pair. When I say followed, I watched them walk down that corridor and go into another room, then come out a few seconds later with an empty stretcher.'

'Is that the room with the first aid sign?'

'I thought they were going there, but they went past it and into another room,' Dazza said.

'Did you look in the room?'

'Yeah. It's full of beds stacked in bunks. They were just putting people into them, but...' Dazza's voice trailed off as if unable to describe what he saw.

Danny grabbed Dazza's hands. 'Come on, mate. It can't be that bad. What did you see?'

'The beds had doors on the side. They put people into the beds and shut the doors to keep them in,' Dazza shuddered at the memory.

'Hospital beds have things like that to stop unconscious people rolling out,' Danny replied. 'It's for their safety.'

'No, you don't understand. Look,' Dazza turned his camera to show Danny.

'Those aren't hospital beds. They're cages!'

'We need to get out of here and get these to my editor,' Dazza said.

'Let's find the others. The Chief will know what to do,' Danny agreed.

'Mercedes, what're you doing here?' Bobby asked, sipping a glass of water.

'It's a bit complicated,' Mercedes hissed. 'Where's Adam and your mum?'

'Mum's nipped to the toilet, and Adam's having his picture taken with the president of some European country,' Bobby replied.

'I didn't know Adam was into politics,' Mercedes replied in surprise.

Bobby laughed. 'He's not. They wanted selfies with him.'

Mercedes led Bobby away from the main group to a quiet corner of the room. 'I'm here with Max.'

Bobby scanned the room. 'Where is he?'

'He's not in here. He's gone into the main hall with the Zephyrions,' Mercedes whispered. 'He told me to come here—'

'What do you mean with the Zephyrions?'

'Everyone still in that hall are Zephyrions. They moved all the humans into here,' Mercedes explained. 'Well, except for the woman organising everything in here, Erzsi.'

Bobby scanned the room until he saw the woman who had ushered them in and who seemed to be in charge. 'I've never seen her before, but her name is familiar. Like a distant memory.'

'Apparently, she was one of the ones who helped Max come to Earth all those years ago.'

'Maybe one of Max's memories is triggering me, but I'm not sure.'

'Anyway, Max said he'll investigate what's going on in there, and Erzsi sneaked me in here to find out what you saw,' Mercedes said, studying the room intently.

'Hang on, where's the others?'

'Danny caused a distraction so we could get in here, and Zym and Stephen could get up to the viewing platform to see the Exodus machine. We've not regrouped yet.'

'The Exodus mach...ah, the Porter machine,' Bobby replied. 'Yeah, they used it to send the energy apple to the Prime Minister.'

'They were able to send it into Downing Street?'

'Better than that. They sent it to the PM's desk,' Bobby replied admiringly.

Mercedes put her hand to her mouth.

Bobby looked concerned. 'Are you okay? Do you need a drink or anything?'

Mercedes shook her head as she struggled to find the words. 'Um, this is frightening.'

'It's incredible, isn't it,' Bobby said. 'It means if someone is trapped, they can send food directly to them.'

'Never mind food. If they can be that accurate, they could send anything or anyone in energy form anywhere. They could kill world leaders, fire weapons or anything. There'll be no safe or secure place on the planet,' Mercedes gasped.

'But why would they want to do—'

'Bobby, quick,' Erzsi gasped, running over.

'How did you know I'm Bobby, and what's wrong?'

'Because you look identical to Max,' Erzsi replied. 'Now come on.'

'Actually, I was here first, so it's Max who looks—'

'Sorry, but shut up and come on. It's Adam,' Erzsi said, grabbing Bobby's hand and yanking him as she ran off.

Hearing Adam was in trouble was all the incentive Bobby needed as he ran with Erzsi, closely followed by Mercedes. They approached a group of people stood in a circle.

'Let us through,' Erzsi ordered.

'Mum, what's happened,' Bobby cried as he saw his mum crouching beside Adam's body.

Pat looked up at Bobby, trying hard to fight back her emotions. 'I was looking for you both and spotted Adam. As I approached, he collapsed,' she explained.

Bobby felt Adam's pulse. 'It's slow but steady. Has anyone called a doctor?' he said before thinking, *How do I know how to do this?*

Suddenly, Max's voice appeared in Bobby's mind. *'Do what, buddy? What's happened?'*

'It's Adam. He's collapsed. I need you, Cowboy.'

'I need to find out what's happening. Have you met Erzsi?'

'Uh-huh, she's here.'

'You can trust her, buddy. Do what she says.'

'Bobby, we need to move him,' Erzsi said, breaking Bobby's thoughts.

'We need a doctor,' Pat demanded.

'Let's get him onto this stretcher, and we can take him to the hotel's medical room,' Erzsi replied.

One of the guards holding the stretcher grabbed Erzsi by the arm and dragged her away. Mercedes couldn't make out what they were saying, but the conversation was very heated. Only when Erzsi held up four fingers and pointed in their direction did the guard relent and nod in agreement.

As they rejoined the group, Erzsi smiled. 'Good, you've got him on the stretcher. Bobby, can you, your mum and Mercedes follow these two guards? They'll take you to the hotel's medical centre until the doctor arrives. I'll see you down there shortly.'

The last thing Mercedes heard as they left the room was Erzsi saying, 'Come on, ladies and gentlemen. There's plenty of food available. Help yourself to drinks.'

27
NEW BEGINNING

Max sat near the back in what he hoped was a vacant seat. From there, he could make out Big Bill on the far left near the front, several world leaders, international celebrities, and leading experts in science, medicine, and engineering.

'Excuse me, but you're in my seat,' a woman in a black dress said.

'Oh, I'm sorry,' Max replied, moving to the next seat.

'I didn't see you for the earlier sessions,' the woman said.

'No, my flight was delayed,' Max explained.

'Hi, I'm Doctor Juli Fellowes.'

Max hesitated. 'Hi, I'm Chester Price. Have you been on this planet long?'

'Only a couple of thousand years,' Juli laughed. 'How about you?'

'Could this really be Julirani, my former partner's sister?' Max thought. 'I've been here a long time too. Do you remember a guy called Maxohal?'

'No, never heard of him,' Juli replied, staring at the stage. 'Was he famous?' she asked, glancing briefly at Max.

'Uh, no, I don't think so. I met him years ago, and he said he'd been here that long too,' Max lied.

Juli glanced at Max and then looked back at the stage. 'What was he like?'

'Who?'

'That Maxohal person,' Juli asked without shifting her focus.

'A bit of a loner, to be honest,' Max replied. 'But he always looked after his friends.'

'Seems like a nice guy. Oh, they're starting again,' Juli said.

Paul White moved to the front and centre of the hall with Big Bill following behind.

'Folks, y'all seen a lot today, but this is just the beginning,' Bill said. 'Before Paul shows y'all what we got cookin', our president, Zara Shah, has a few words.'

A large screen rose from the floor, and a smartly dressed South Asian woman appeared on it.

'That's Jay,' Max whispered.

'You know her?' Juli asked.

'Sort of. She owns the company my former host works for.'

Juli laughed. 'That doesn't narrow it down much. Do they work for Bluestone or Spearhead?'

Max frowned. 'Neither. He works for Westbridge Enterprise Finance.'

'Oh, I thought he worked for one of her main companies.'

Max turned to Juli. 'I thought WestFi was one of her main businesses?'

Juli continued to stare straight ahead. 'God, no. She's the major shareholder in Bluestone and Spearhead. Between them, they control almost everything. Now, shh, I want to hear her.'

'My fellow Zephyrions,' Jay said. 'I want to apologise for not being there in person, but so much has happened in the last year or so, and I can't be everywhere at once.

'When I first came here two thousand years ago, I was promised a world of plenty. A planet that had all the modernity of our home but was ripe for us to conquer.

'Nico lied. This planet was backward. They had no technology, vision, or way of communicating beyond this planet. We've had many friends join us over the two millennia, but it's been a one-way ticket.

'When I founded the IFFS in 1735, its mission was to ride the wave of emerging technology until we could contact home. Last year we managed to do it, thanks to the technology we have been developing. This year, the discovery of luminae by a bungling group of humans meant we could finally return home.

'Unfortunately, home was hostile. Zephyrion has turned into a red desert, and Astral 5 is torn into three regions by infighting. While the other two planets are now called Malvis and Androvir, they are governed by dictators who send anyone who objects to their tyranny to a cold, desolate planet called Leyton.

'But the scouts we sent back discovered a force ready to rebel. A noble group of Zephyrions prepared to fight for freedom. Their planets are filled with corruption, but we can build a new beginning here.

'Our indoctrination of the local inhabitants is almost complete. We've slowly taken control of several countries by replacing their leaders with our own and with the United Kingdom being the latest, we now have access to nuclear weapons. You'll have noticed the remaining prominent world leaders who are not Zephyrions were among the humans who were with us, and we were also joined by some leading influencers from the world of social media, sport and entertainment. As these become Zephyrions, they will help spread the message that everything we do is to make the world safer.

'We've tried to take control of this planet before, but it always ended in war. This time, it's different. We are going to show you how we can bring enough of *our* kind to replace all of their leaders. This means we can take over this world not only without them knowing but with their support, as we end their infighting.

'We are also working to free us from these shells. We know this planet's atmosphere is too light, but we can resolve that. We have been adapting the climate to our needs for the last hundred years or more. The humans believe what we tell them and are helping us get it to where it should be. But now is the time to move to the next stage. Humans have overpopulated this planet, so we've launched a new drug that we are convincing them will make their food healthier, but in reality, it will reduce their breeding.

'Now, let's complete the process. We've been preparing our human guests and the press for our new Zephyrion friends, so I'll hand you back to Paul to start the proceedings.'

The screen slid back down, and the stage to the right moved partway across the opening to reveal Paul White standing and applauding. 'Thank you, Jay. Now, my friends, we have a little demonstration for you. Big Bill, please bring out our volunteers.'

'Sure thing,' Bill smiled, waving to someone hidden to the left.

A group of people shuffled onto the stage, with Chris Medici in second place and Zym and Stephen towards the rear.

'What the...' Max gasped.

'Are you alright?' Juli asked.

'Uh, sorry, yeah,' Max replied, looking at Zym and Stephen near the back of the line.

'Ma'am, can y'all introduce yourself,' Bill drawled.

'My name is Karin Metz, and I am so happy to be here.'

'Thank you, Bill, and welcome Karin,' Paul said. 'My friends, you know how restrictive it is having to build a new DNA shell every thirty or forty years to fit in with this planet's lifecycle. The hassle of finding a host and taking control until we can emerge and kill them off so we can adopt their life,' he added.

'We can coexist and don't have to kill them,' Max hissed.

Juli side-eyed Max but said nothing.

'But did any of you notice anything about the apples?' Paul challenged. 'Oh, come on, don't be shy. Think about it. We can't survive as energy souls without building a DNA shell, but...'

'The energy apple didn't dissipate,' an audience member shouted.

'Exactly,' Paul replied. 'But what if we did the same to humans? Karin is one of our human volunteers. Bill, please escort Karin to the Separator.'

Bill moved Karin by the arm to the Separator, helped her sit inside and then closed the door. 'She's ready, Paul.'

'Thanks, Bill. Let's countdown from three, two, one and go,' Paul said.

A flash of white light subsided, revealing a body slumped against the wall of the Separator and a healthy-looking Karin sitting upright, almost glowing.

Bill opened the Separator door, and Karin stepped out.

'How ya'll feelin', ma'am,' Bill asked.

'I feel wonderful, but where am I?' Karin asked.

'That's great. Now my colleague here'll take care of you and answer any questions,' Bill replied as someone ran on from the side and escorted Karin away.

'That's fantastic, Bill,' Paul smiled. 'As you've witnessed, this planet's atmosphere can't yet hold our energy souls together, but it is enough for the indigenous inhabitants of this planet,' he said to the audience.

'I've got to stop this,' Max said, gritting his teeth.

'I think you need to calm down,' Juli replied, glancing at Max.

Max looked to his right. 'Hmm, that's around forty-five feet to the side, which gives a better approach but more disruption getting past,' Max muttered. 'It's only ten feet to the centre aisle, but the approach is exposed.'

'But what if we could exist in our natural form?' Paul asked. 'Some years ago, there was an experiment to produce a hybrid Zephyrion and human.'

'No,' Max shouted as he tried to stand, but Juli yanked him back down.

'Our next volunteer is...' Paul glanced at the autocue. 'Christopher Medici. Who carries both Zephyrion and human genes. Bill, can you help Christopher—'

Max broke free of Juli and started fighting his way to the aisle. 'Stop this, now!'

Juli pushed after Max, trying to grab him. 'Max, not now.'

Bill pulled out a gun and fired towards Max. 'C'mon, boy. These walls are impenetrable by energy souls. So the only humans you can get into are these drugged-up fools.'

As Bill fired again, Zym dived forward, knocking him to the floor. A guard lifted his rifle to shoot Zym, but Stephen jumped on the guard's back, causing him to spin around, trying to shake Stephen off.

'You...give me your radio,' Paul shouted at a nearby guard, who nervously handed it over. 'Conference hall, code red. I repeat, code red, conference hall. Bring my box of tricks.'

Zym and Bill traded blows, rolling around on the floor as Stephen continued to pummel the head of the guard he was still clinging to.

As guards poured into the conference hall, Max battled through the audience, who were rushing for the exit. He reached inside his coat and pulled out a gun, firing into the air, causing the crowd to move away from him. All around the hall were dignitaries, protected by personal security, being hurried out.

As he reached the front of the hall, Max looked to his right, but there was no sign of Paul.

'Stand still, punk,' Bill snarled, pointing a gun at Max. Behind Bill were four guards restraining Zym and Stephen while another aimed a rifle at them.

'Drop your gun, Bill,' Max replied.

'You sound like y'all has the upper hand, boy,' Bill snapped. 'Guard shoot one of 'em. I don't care which.'

'Okay,' Max shouted, lowering his gun to the floor.

'Get over there with your buddies,' Bill ordered.

Juli started to back away slowly, but Bill spotted her. 'Where're you going, ma'am?'

Juli froze. 'I was chasing after that man to stop him hurting anyone,' she stuttered.

'Looked more like y'all was helpin' him,' Bill replied. 'Who are you?'

'I'm Doctor Juli Fellowes. I'm one of the scientists working on the Porter machine,' Juli said.

'It's true, Bill,' Paul shouted as he entered the hall from the far side. 'Doctor Fellowes was an important part of the team making it safe.'

'Then thank you, ma'am. I apologise for keepin' you,' Bill smiled, waving his gun for her to leave.

Paul watched Juli head towards the conference hall exit and started clapping. 'Well done. The mighty Max Janus and his bumbling friends have managed to cause the mass evacuation of the world's leaders.'

'I think you mean the world's dictators. So the plan is all about taking over the planet and wiping out humans!' Max growled.

'Max, you're jumping to conclusions. Jay warned me that when we finally got you, you'd be headstrong,' Paul laughed.

As the guard nearest them was watching Paul, Zym saw an opportunity and lunged for his gun, but Bill reacted quickly, shooting Zym in the arm.

The sound of gunfire made Juli jump, and she glanced back to see Zym twist away, clutching his arm.

Paul laughed. 'Nice shooting, Bill.'

'Hardly,' Bill replied. 'I was aimin' for his head.'

'Mr White, we're picking up incoming,' a voice shouted over the tannoy.

Paul lifted the radio he'd grabbed from the guard. 'Do you mean to collect our VIPs?'

'No, sir. Most of them have been moved to the secondary helipad and are being rushed away,' the voice crackled from the radio. 'I mean incoming from Zephyrion.'

'Damn, we'd forgot about them,' Bill drawled.

'More of your cronies, huh?' Max said. 'We'll stop you.'

Paul laughed. 'In your dreams. Guards, where are my box of tricks?'

'I don't care what tricks you're bringing out; we will stop you,' Max snapped.

'You're going to love these tricks,' Paul sneered.

A few minutes later, a guard pushed open the door, and Adam appeared, being pushed in a wheelchair by Bobby, followed by Pat and Mercedes.

'Sorry, sir. They'd been sent down to the train station to take the footballer to the hospital,' the guard apologised.

'Why the hell was he... never mind, just get in here,' Paul snapped.

'*What's up with Adam?*' Max thought.

'*I think they drugged him,*' Bobby replied. '*He collapsed at the buffet they laid on for us.*'

'*How are the rest of you?*'

'*We've been better, Cowboy. Where's Danny and Dazza?*' Bobby asked.

'*I thought they were with you.*'

'I said get over there,' Paul snapped at Bobby.

'What? Oh, sorry, yes,' Bobby replied, wheeling Adam across the hall behind his mum and Mercedes.

Big Bill glanced at Mercedes and shook his head but didn't say anything.

'Now push your boyfriend over to the group with the Medici boy,' Paul ordered.

'No, why would I do that?' Bobby protested.

'Because he is a more valuable host for our new arrivals than your mother,' Paul sneered. 'So do it, or I shoot your mother, and he still becomes a host.'

As soon as Juli shut the conference hall doors behind her, she looked around the foyer. 'Erzsi, where are you?'

'Excuse me, miss, can I help you?' a guard asked, heading towards the conference hall.

'I'm looking for the woman managing the event. Her name's Erzsi,' Juli said, scanning the foyer.

'She was in the hotel's medical centre. One of the young VIPs was taken ill, and I helped carry him down, but that was a while ago. I've been checking the hotel grounds since then, so she may have left,' the guard explained. 'Sorry, I've got to get in there,' he added, nodding towards the conference hall.

'Yes, of course, and thanks,' Juli replied. 'Oh, can I ask one more thing?'

The guard rubbed his finger around his collar. 'Sure.'

'Where is the medical centre?'

'Go to the hotel reception and down one level. You can use the lift or stairs,' the guard replied. 'Sorry, I have to go,' he added, rushing into the conference hall.

Juli walked through to the hotel reception and headed downstairs. Halfway down, she paused, tilting her head to listen to the voices. '*What do they mean cages?*' she wondered. She carried on listening and thought, '*Who's the Chief?*' Then she realised the voices were about to move. She grabbed the railing as she pondered running back upstairs before deciding to press on down.

'Hello,' she said, smiling at the incredibly tall ginger-haired journalist with his camera and bag. As she passed, she noticed someone behind him. 'Oh, hello, Danny. What're you doing here?'

'Hey, Juli. This is my friend, Dazza,' Danny said. 'He's with the press pack.'

Juli smiled. 'Nice to meet you, Dazza. I hope you're enjoying yourself?'

'I was, but it's getting a bit, ugh,' Dazza said as Danny discretely punched him.

'Are you alright, Juli? You look a bit lost,' Danny asked.

'I'm good, thanks. I'm just looking for the medical centre.'

'Don't go that way; it leads to the kitchens. The medical centre is over there,' Danny said.

'Okay, thanks,' Juli replied with a smile.

As she headed in the direction Danny indicated, Dazza hissed, 'Why did you punch me?'

'Because she's been working on the Porter machine with me, which means she works for Dad.'

'Oh, right,' Dazza replied. 'Um, I don't get it,' he added, scratching his head.

'Get what, big man?' Danny asked as he watched Juli open the door to the medical centre and disappear inside.

'Well, if she works for your dad, isn't that a good thing?' Dazza asked. 'I mean, well, it's not like he's a baddie, is he?'

Danny turned his wheelchair so he could look towards the kitchens and shook his head. 'I hope not, but after he tried to shoot me in the cabin, I'm not so—'

'Shoot you?' Dazza exclaimed.

'Shh, do you want the whole hotel to hear?' Danny hissed. 'Come on, we need to get upstairs and find out what's going on.'

'But your dad tried to shoot you, why would he do—'

'Because he's dangerous,' Erzsi said.

Danny and Dazza spun around to see Juli and Erzsi running towards them.

'Well, him trying to shoot me sounds pretty dangerous. But he might still be my Dad,' Danny replied, moving his chair into standing mode.

Dazza leaned over and whispered, 'Careful, that's Erzsi. She's one of the organisers.'

Erzsi laughed. 'You might want to practice your whispering. I've also been one of Big Bill's assistants for the last few months.'

'See, I said she was one of them,' Dazza said triumphantly.

'If "one of them" means a Zephyrion, then yes, I am. But we're trying to stop them, not help them,' Erzsi said.

'Is there anyone in that medical centre?' Danny asked, noticing a few people in the kitchens kept looking down the corridor towards them.

'There's a couple of people in there. But some of the other rooms should be free,' Erzsi said as they headed down the corridor past the medical centre.

'Not that room,' Dazza shrieked as Juli went to grab a door handle.

'I see you know about the battery cages,' Erzsi said, moving Juli's hand away from the door and pointing to a room opposite.

As they hurried inside, Erzsi glanced up the corridor before shutting the door.

'What do you mean, battery cages?' Danny asked.

Erzsi glanced around the room, which looked like an old hotel meeting room which was now used to store folded tables and spare chairs. 'They're a bit like battery cages for chickens, but these are for humans. Each cage has the nationality, name and background of the drugged human inside. The plan is to send them to their respective countries for storage in a host farm.'

Dazza scratched his head. 'I heard you speak, but I still don't get it.'

Danny's mouth opened and closed without saying anything as he looked back and forth between Erzsi and Juli.

Erzsi looked down and sighed. 'This event isn't about extracting energy food and transporting it around the world.'

'But Dad said...' Danny started to say before trailing off.

'That'll be the dad who shot you earlier?' Juli challenged.

'Hmm,' Danny muttered. 'Maybe the Deceptor in him has different ideas. But if this event isn't about food, what's it about?' he added.

'Your planet is being invaded,' Erzsi said. 'Coordinates for the host farms in each country are being collated to send back to Deceptors on our home planets. They will start sending Zephyrions here in the next few months, and the caged humans will host them until they can transmute into their own shells.'

'But it takes about six months for that to happen,' Dazza stated.

Danny slapped his hand to his mouth. 'Of course, it will. That gives them time to build armies in every country.'

'Armies which can support their country's leaders, several of whom are already Zephyrions,' Erzsi confirmed.

'But what happens to the caged humans after they've hosted?' Dazza asked.

'If they were a bad host, they'll probably be killed. But if they're reasonable or important, they'll be recycled for the next arrival,' Erzsi explained.

Dazza turned to Danny, his eyes blazing. 'And you and your dad are involved!'

'No. I didn't know anything about it,' Danny protested weakly. 'Dad never—'

'Dad said, Dad never, Dad blah, blah,' Dazza replied. 'Your Dad is working with them to destroy our world.'

Danny lowered his chair into a seating position, staring at his feet. 'I swear, big man, I never...'

'That's right. Call me big man, and make a joke of it. That's all we are to you and your super brain, isn't it? We're just a joke,'

Dazza snarled, walking away from Danny and kicking a chair out of his way. 'I've seen those people drugged in their cages.'

Danny slouched back into his chair, dropping his head into his hands. 'I didn't know,' he whispered.

'Oh, please, you were working with him. You even left Mercedes unconscious and crept off with him—'

'Dazza,' Erzsi hissed.

'What?' Dazza snapped. 'It's true. Danny only cares about himself—'

Juli grabbed Dazza's arm. 'Dazza, stop,' she said.

'Why should...' Dazza paused in shock. He'd never seen Danny cry, let alone sob in the way he was.

'I didn't know. I swear I didn't know,' Danny repeated, his voice weak and croaky.

Erzsi knelt to Danny's right with her left arm over his shoulder in comfort. 'It's okay, Danny. We know you didn't.'

'I didn't, I swear on my Dad's...on my life,' he sighed.

'But...' Dazza said.

'Dazza, look at him. He's your friend,' Juli replied, gently pushing Dazza forward.

Dazza glanced at Juli and then at Erzsi, who nodded back. He crouched down nervously in front of Danny.

'Hey, dude. C'mon, it'll be okay. I was just angry,' Dazza said. 'Let's sort this and get back home. Breakfast at Mike's café is on me.'

Erzsi rubbed Danny's shoulder as she hugged him. 'Danny, we're here for you. But we have to stop Big Bill, and we can't do that without you.'

'C'mon, Danny. I'm sorry I lashed out, dude,' Dazza replied.

'Danny, we need to move,' Juli said. 'They've got your friends and Maxohal.'

Danny lifted his head, and the tear tracks shined off his cheeks like fresh ski trails in the snow. 'Maxohal?'

'Our friend who transmuted in your friend Bobby,' Juli replied.

'You mean the Chief!' Danny said, wiping his eyes.

'Um, yeah. I think so,' Juli replied. 'and he had two other people helping him.'

'Were they our age?' Dazza asked.

'No. One was a middle-aged Italian, and the other looked like a cross between a country gentleman and a high school geography teacher,' Juli said.

Danny sniffed as he started to feel stronger in himself. 'That sounds like Zym and Stephen.'

'Bill shot the Italian in the arm,' Juli added.

'I think they've got Adam, Bobby and his mum too,' Erzsi said. 'Oh, and Mercedes. They should have been in the medical centre, but the doctor said some guards had collected them just before I got there.'

Danny wiped his eyes. 'So what's happening now?'

'I'm not sure. I wasn't involved in organising this section of the day,' Erzsi replied.

'I know,' Juli said. 'This is where Zephyrions start arriving, and the human slaves become hosts.'

'Oh, that's why Chris Medici and the others were brought up. I met his ex-sister, Mercedes,' Erzsi said.

Juli laughed. 'I don't know about ex-sister, but they definitely share the same parents. Big Bill is their father, and they have the same mother, Cinzia Medici. Her husband Francesco agreed to adopt them both when he married Cinzia, and they took his surname. Mercedes would have been around twelve months old at the time.'

'Do they know?' Erzsi asked.

I don't think so. Mercedes said her and Chris were adopted, but I don't think she knows about Big Bill being their father,' Danny replied.

'I've heard her say the same. I think she likes being Big Bill's favourite, but she's in denial about why,' Juli replied.

Erzsi nodded. 'Yeah, Big Bill does have a soft spot for her.'

'But if she's Bill's daughter and he defo has a soft spot for her, she's probably been telling him everything we've been doing,' Dazza said.

'I've always said I didn't trust her,' Danny snapped. 'I bet she's upstairs right now laughing with them.'

'Talking of upstairs, didn't one of you say Adam and the others are up there, and more Zephyrions are on the way,' Dazza said.

'Oh, hell yeah. We need to stop them,' Erzsi said.

'Let's get to the Porter machine control room,' Juli replied. 'I've got a little surprise.'

'Lead the way,' Dazza replied as they rushed out of the room.

As they headed down the corridor, led by Juli and Dazza, Danny grabbed Erzsi's hand.

'That man up there,' Danny started.

'Which one?' Erzsi replied.

'My da...' Danny sighed. 'The one we know as Paul White.'

'Yeah, what about him?'

'He's not my dad, is he?'

Erzsi stopped and turned to Danny. 'I don't know. He might be with a Zephyrion inside him transmuting. But it might also be a Zephyrion in a shell.'

'If he is just one of your kind in a shell...' Danny gulped, struggling to say what his mind was telling him.

'No, it doesn't mean your dad is dead,' Erzsi second-guessed. 'He might be in one of those host farms.'

'Wherever Dad is, I'm going to find him,' Danny insisted.

'And I'll help you,' Erzsi replied. 'Come on, we need to catch up with the others.'

28
HELLO OLD FRIEND

'Caution, Porter machine lowering,' an electronic voice said.

As the machine started to lower, the dome flattened out, forming a flat ceiling again, and the Porter machine rotated until it pointed to a flat open area near the group which included Adam and Chris.

Paul snatched up his radio. 'What's going on?'

'Oh, hi, Dad,' Danny's unmistakable voice said over the tannoy. 'Don't worry about using the radio. I can hear you all clearly up here.'

'Danny, son,' Paul said hesitantly. 'Is everything okay with the Porter machine?'

'It's brilliant, Dad,' Danny replied. 'I've just been told about some new features, so I thought I'd better test them for you.'

A female voice muttered something in the background, and Danny said, 'Apparently, your guests are about to arrive. Bobby, can you, Zym and the others grab Adam and those other humans and move them over near the auditorium seating? Oh, and be quick.'

'Y'all stay right there,' Big Bill said, waving his gun. 'Guard if anyone moves, shoot them.'

There were some muffled discussions coming over the tannoy before the Porter machine moved again, pointing towards the guard Big Bill had ordered.

'Drop the gun, Bill, and stand down your guard. My friends need to get on with it,' Danny said.

'Get down here now, boy, and I won't kill 'em all,' Bill snarled. 'Guard, kill that boy grabbing the wheelchair.'

A bright flash came from the Porter machine, and the guard fell to the floor.

'Anyone else want to keep waving their guns around?' Danny asked as the barrel of the Porter machine slowly moved across the guards.

The guards dropped their guns, and several ran out of the conference hall. Bill tightened his grip on his handgun and started shooting after them.

'Drop it, Bill,' Danny said, pointing the Porter barrel towards him.

Big Bill turned and fired at the Porter machine. 'Screw you, boy.'

Another flash of the Porter machine saw Bill collapse.

'Have you killed him?' Mercedes asked.

'He's still alive. And so is the guard,' Danny said. 'Juli explained a trick she'd put into the machine which reverses its firing mechanism. Instead of firing them from the launch platform to another location, it zaps them back into the platform.'

Max laughed. 'It's a good job you didn't zap their weapons with them.'

Juli leant toward the microphone in the control room. 'Come on, Max, you should know this technology can only move energy. We've pressurised and sealed the Porter launch platform, so their energy souls should be secure.'

Pat, Zym, Mercedes and Stephen had walked around the Porter machine to see the locked and sealed glass launch platform.

'They're here,' Zym shouted.

'Why do they look so different?' Stephen asked.

'Because that's how they really look. That is their energy soul shape. Bill's not a tall, wiry American. He's a five-foot-nine, dark-skinned Shadower. Although you can see his attitude is the same,' Zym replied.

Stephen looked at Bill, who was shouting and banging on the glass, but he couldn't make out what Bill was saying, apart from the muffled thuds from the banging. 'Why're they naked?'

'Because these machines can only transmit energy,' Max explained as he walked up between Stephen and Pat. 'Anything organic like their human shells, clothing, and guns gets left behind. And since you don't have energy clothes on this planet, they're naked.'

Pat looked at Bill and laughed. 'I think we should change Big Bill's name to Little Bill.'

'Why does he keep pointing at me?' Mercedes asked.

'Hang on,' Danny said. 'I'll turn on the intercom.'

Danny flicked a switch, and Bill shouted, 'Mercedes, you have to let me out.'

Mercedes noticed the change in his voice. He still had an American twang to his voice, but the assured, relaxed drawl had disappeared.

'Why would I do that?' Merecedes replied angrily. 'You told the guard to shoot us.'

Bill looked directly into Mercedes's eyes. 'Because I'm your father. Cinzia and I were due to marry, but your grandfather wouldn't give his blessing.'

'Then my nonno was right. Francesco is my dad and always will be,' Mercedes replied. 'Look at Chris. What sort of father drugs his own son? You're dead to me. Danny, cut him off'

Mercedes walked away, and Danny shut down the intercom, leaving Bill banging on the glass.

'Hey, where's Paul gone?' Dazza asked, looking at the monitors in the control room.

'No time for that. We've got arrivals,' Juli shouted.

Danny watched the Zephyrions appear and fired the Porter machine to move them into the launch platform. While he managed to capture all of them, there were a few misses as the Porter machine fired into the ground, causing some tremors.

'Welcome to planet Earth,' Danny said. 'Your departure to...yes, Juli, I know, sorry about that, now as I was saying, your transfer to planet Lend...Leyton will be happening shortly.'

Juli confirmed the last Zephyrion had arrived according to the machine, and Danny fired a couple of celebration shots from the Porter machine into the ground. But as the final shot hit the ground, the conference hall started to shake as if it was suffering from an earthquake.

'Danny, stop firing and meet us at the front of the hotel,' Max yelled.

'Max, the guard inside is waving at the camera like he wants to say something,' Danny yelled.

The ground shook again, more violently this time.

'We need to get out of here,' Mercedes said as a few small rocks fell from the roof.

'Bobby, take Adam, your mum, Stephen and Mercedes and get to the front of the hotel,' Max ordered. 'And take those humans with you. They look like the drugs are wearing off.'

'But what about you and Zym?' Bobby asked as another tremor started.

'We'll be right behind you,' Max yelled.

'I'm staying,' Chris said, slowly getting to his feet. 'I want to help.'

'What if Chris was involved? He's older than me so he must have known about Bill. How can we trust him?' Mercedes snapped.

Chris turned in shock. 'Mercedes? What's wrong?'

'You know,' Mercedes sniped.

The ground shook as Chris started to say, 'I've been drugged and held captive. I don't—'

'SHUT-UP!' Max yelled. 'We don't have time for this. Mercedes, help Bobby and the others get out. Chris, get over here, and Danny, use the intercom to the launch platform.'

Juli pressed the intercom button to the platform. The screams of around twenty people begging to be let out were deafening.

Erzsi leaned over and pressed the talk button. 'Everyone shut up, or we'll fire you into deep space. Now you...yes you, the one waving, what do you want?'

'I accept my fate, but please save the ones on level three. Most of them are innocent,' the guard pleaded. 'And if you find Astrid, tell her I love her.'

'There were only two levels,' Zym insisted.

'Tell him we know he's lying,' Max yelled. 'Zym found only two levels.'

Erzsi pressed the talk button again. 'We know there's only two floors. Nice try.'

The guard shook his head violently. 'No, I swear. Bill and Jay have been using it to hold all their enemies and anyone they wanted to experiment on. The first door by the lift leads down to it. Let me out. I've only been on this planet for about a year, so I only take a few seconds to come round in a host. I can get you down to them.'

'I saw that door i—' Zym was cut short as a large tremor struck.

'Max, this makes sense. We sent a few Zephyrions back, and they all seemed like they were drugged,' Juli said. 'There were rumours about a hidden jail.'

'Should I let him out, Chief?' Danny yelled.

'Yes, uh, no. Damn, we need a human host,' Max cursed.

'I'm on the way,' Dazza shouted.

'No need, Dazza. It looks like I can help after all,' Chris said, feeling better by the second.

'Guard, go and stand by the door and get as tight as you can to the metal wall. The rest of you stand back,' Danny ordered.

Juli pressed a button, and a glass wall isolated the door from the rest of the launch platform.

'Get ready, Chris,' Danny said.

Chris stood by the door to the launch platform.

'Opening in three, two, one,' Danny counted before Juli opened the launch platform door.

The guard came rushing out and straight into Chris, knocking him to the floor.

'Uh, what the hell just happened?' Chris yelled, scrambling to stand as another tremor shook. 'I suddenly feel amazing.'

'That happens sometimes,' Max said, helping Chris up.

'No, this is different,' a slightly deeper version of Chris's voice replied. 'I feel a lot stronger than in my first host.'

'Are you the guard?' Zym asked.

'Yeah, I'm Eron.'

The ground shook again, and a few more rocks fell from above.

'We need to get going,' Eron said.

As Max and Zym ran after Eron, Danny shouted over the tannoy, 'Hey, Chief, what about us?'

Max stopped and turned toward the Porter machine. 'Send that lot back, then get outta here.'

Max chased after Zym as Danny activated the roof mechanism, which creaked and groaned.

'It's not opening,' Danny said. 'What the hell do we do now?'

'You remember you just zapped a load of Shadowers who appeared inside the conference hall?' Juli asked.

Danny tilted his head. 'Hmm, and what has—ah, you're saying we don't need the roof open.'

'I'm saying if there's enough clearance to get the right angle, we won't need to,' Juli said. 'Right, let's get these coordinates in. Are you sure they're right, Erzsi?'

'That'll take them straight to Leyton,' Erzsi confirmed.

The Porter machine kicked into life as Juli pressed load on the screen.

'Caution, Porter machine rising,' the electronic voice said.

'No,' Juli screamed, hitting an override button.

The Porter machine stopped rising but started rotating, and the barrel began to point upwards.

'It's not going to make it; look, the bit of roof that moved is going to stop it,' Dazza exclaimed.

As they all stared at the monitor, Erzsi said, 'No, look, it's just going to clear—oh, maybe not.'

The barrel of the Porter machine hit the roof, and the sound of scraping metal reverberated around the hall as the barrel stopped rotating.

'Maybe if I fired the Porter machine, it'd free the door mechanism,' Danny suggested.

'Dazza, come on, there must be a manual mechanism somewhere,' Erzsi replied.

'I've got a better idea,' Juli suggested. 'Why don't we just lower the Porter machine by the small amount it lifted before I stopped it?'

'Oh yeah,' Danny said, pressing the button.

'Caution, Porter machine lowering.'

'Now upload the coordinates again,' Danny said as another tremor struck.

The Porter machine's barrel rotated, clearing where it had previously jammed and pointed higher. Stopping only a fraction away from the roof. 'Target confirmed.'

'Everyone ready?' Danny asked before pressing fire.

The electronic voice counted down from three, and then a short blast of light shot out of the barrel of the Porter machine.

A few seconds later, another tremor struck, freeing the roof mechanism, which finished opening.

'A bit bloody late,' Danny laughed.

Juli studied her monitor. 'Everyone is clear and heading towards Leyton.'

'Right, let's get out of here,' Danny said.

'Where are the stairs?' Zym asked. 'The lift was at the back of the conference hall.'

They ran out of the hall into the foyer area and headed towards the large mirror Max had noticed when he met Erzsi.

Eron scratched his head.

'What's wrong?' Max asked.

'I can't remember the code,' Eron sighed. 'It starts three, one, but I'm not sure.'

'There's not even a keypad,' Zym grumbled. 'It's only a mirror. Let's smash it.'

'It's solid steel behind that mirror,' Eron said, tapping the side of the mirror's frame as a keypad emerged.

Max looked at Eron and frowned. 'You did that without thinking. Talk to me and start tapping in the code.'

'How do you think that'll help?' Eron asked as he tapped in five numbers.

The mirror clicked and opened slightly.

'Hey, it worked,' Eron added, pulling open the door.

'Simple distraction technique to let your subconscious do the work,' Max replied as they ran down the stairs.

As they reached the bottom of the stairs, Zym opened the door and saw the lift at the far end. It seemed like a lifetime ago since he had emerged from the lift with Stephen, but this time, they rushed down the corridor as tremors continued to reverberate.

'What's the code?' Zym asked.

'Three, one, seven, five, four,' Eron replied. 'Hey, I didn't even think about it this time.'

'This feels so weird,' Chris said. 'I can see everything Eron is thinking.'

'You'll get used to it,' Max replied as they rushed through the doorway and down the stairs.

At the bottom of the stairs, a door opened into another corridor with two doors on either side.

'Shut the door,' Eron ordered. He grabbed a face mask from a cabinet. 'Put these on,' he said, handing them to Max and Zym.

'What're these for?' Max asked, putting one on.

'You'll see,' Eron said as he opened the door and followed Zym and Max into the corridor.

Another tremor hit, and Max looked up and watched as a crack formed along the length of the ceiling on the left side.

Zym ran to a door, but Max shouted, 'No, this side.'

Zym paused and frowned. 'What's up, Junior?'

Max pointed to the ceiling crack. 'We need to do this side first. If we open that side, it may weaken the ceiling further before we get everyone out.'

Zym darted to the other side and opened the door. 'They're not locked!'

'They don't need to; look, they're drugged,' Eron said, pointing to the ten people sat on their beds.

'The air!' Max exclaimed. 'The air is mixed with some sort of mind suppressant. They're catatonic.'

'As long as they stay here in this air, they remain compliant,' Eron explained.

'What if you need to move them?' Zym asked, looking around the room.

Eron patted his pockets. 'Damn. I keep forgetting I'm not in my body.'

'No, you're in mine,' Chris replied, and we don't have those on me.

'Sorry,' Eron said. 'We had darts we could inject into anyone we move out of here. They last for about two hours.'

'What if you don't inject them?' Max asked.

'It can vary. Some recover in a few minutes in normal air, and some can take ten to fifteen minutes,' Eron explained.

Zym walked over to a woman sitting on the nearest bed to the door. 'Stand up,' he said.

The woman stood up without saying a word.

'Lift your leg,' Zym ordered, but the woman didn't move.

'That wasn't specific enough,' Eron said, walking over to Zym. 'Lift your left leg.'

The woman did as instructed. 'It's an auto obedience drug,' Eron explained.

'Lower your leg,' Zym said, before adding, 'Lower your left leg.'

'I see what you mean,' Max said. 'Everyone, stand up, walk into the corridor, turn left, walk to the stairwell and stop.'

In unison, the remaining nine people stood up and followed the first woman, who was already heading to the stairwell.

As they passed, Max pulled out his mirror. 'They're all Shadowers.'

'They will be. The drug only works on our kind,' Eron said.

They moved to the second door, which opened into another room with ten people. Max gave them the same instructions, and as they shuffled out, Max rushed to the next room, followed by the others.

'Astrid,' Eron shouted, running towards the woman who turned at the mention of her name and flinging his arms around her.

'This is a bit awkward,' Chris said.

'Oh yeah, sorry, Chris,' Eron said, releasing Astrid.

Max gave the instructions again, and everyone filed out.

'No, Astrid,' Eron said, holding her arm. 'Stay by my side.'

Moving to the final room, Max opened the door and whistled. 'Wow, there must be thirty in here at least.'

'This is the punishment quarters,' Eron said with Astrid beside him. 'They had minimum rations and were always the ones Jay and Bill insisted we used for heavy labour.'

Max gave out his order and watched as they filed past. He held out his hand and grabbed one man. 'You, come with me,' he said.

Zym looked at Max and frowned. 'What's going on, Junior?'

'Not now,' Max replied. 'Come on, let's get these out of here. Eron, Chris lead the way.'

As they made their way up the stairs, another tremor struck, and part of the roof collapsed at the far end of the tunnel, causing Max to shiver.

'You okay?' Zym asked, noting Max's reaction.

'Yeah, fine. Just a touch of déjà vu.'

'That was a long time ago and literally a world away,' Zym replied. 'Let's go before this lot caves in.'

'Yeah, you're right,' Max sighed. 'Come on, old-timer. I'll race you to the top,' Max laughed as they playfully pushed each other up the stairs, with the man Max had ordered to stay with him following behind.

29
No, No, No

As they emerged into the open air at the front of the hotel, Max and Zym were still pushing and shoving each other.

'Where did they all go?' Max asked, trying to spot all the people they had released amongst the throng of hotel guests.

They moved through the crowds while hotel staff handed out free drinks to keep the guests happy.

'Max, Zym, over here,' Stephen shouted behind them.

Max turned to see Stephen waving from the raised patio at the side of the hotel.

'What're you doing up there?'

'Some of those people we released started to attract attention from the hotel guests. Guests were asking if they were zombies?' Stephen replied, following Max and Zym from above as they walked towards the steps to the upper level.

'Who's the chap with you?' Stephen asked.

Max glanced back. The childhood memories of running up the stairs with Zym had removed the man from his memory. 'Oh, umm... can you take Pat and Bobby to the back by the footpath and grab Danny and the others, too? We'll go round this way,' Max said, pointing to the path to the side leading up to the back of the upper level.

'They're already sat at a table back there,' Stephen replied. 'I'll grab some chairs for you.'

As Max, Zym, and the man headed toward the footpath, Max grabbed a glass of whisky from the waiter's tray.

'I think Pat's about to get a shock,' Max said.

'Is that for her?' Zym asked.

Max glugged the drink and dropped the glass onto a nearby table. 'Nope. If I'm right, I'm going to need several of them, never mind Pat,' Max replied.

Zym grabbed Max's arm. 'Max, what's going on?'

Max stopped and turned to the man following them. 'What's your name?'

The man stared blankly. 'My name is...' he paused and looked around, trying to find the answer.

'It's the drugs,' Zym said. 'Eron told us some take a while.'

Max glanced at Zym before turning to the man, 'Where are you from?'

'Z-Z-Zephyrion,' the man replied.

'So you're a Shadower,' Zym said.

The man shook his head and frowned as if starting to remember. 'No, I'm —'

'Hey, dudes. Come on, the gang's waiting for you,' Dazza said. 'Oh, wow, you found that Roberts guy. He looks even worse than on that online video.'

'Yeah, the drugs are taking a while to work off,' Zym replied.

Just before they reached the others, Max turned to the man. 'Wait here until I call you.'

The man nodded before scratching his head. '*Where was he, and why was he doing what this young boy was telling him?*' he thought.

'Chief, you're okay?' Danny asked as Zym and Max rejoined the group. 'When we heard part of the lower floor had collapsed, we were—'

'We're fine, Wheels,' Zym replied.

'Dazza, get some drinks,' Max said, sitting on one of the chairs Stephen had grabbed.

'And any food,' Zym shouted.

'What's going on?' Bobby asked. 'I got a mental image of you down there. I could feel your surprise at seeing all those drugged Shadowers and your concern about the place collapsing, but then it was like you were scared, no, not scared...uh...shocked. Yeah, that's it, you were shocked like you'd seen a ghost or something.'

Pat noticed Bobby was wringing his hands and seemed to be getting emotional. 'Are you okay, Champ?'

Bobby turned and looked at Pat, blinking rapidly. 'Huh? Yeah, I'm fine,' he replied, wiping his eyes.

'But you're crying, Bobster,' Danny added.

'No, I'm not...' Bobby wiped his eyes again. 'Yeah, I am. Why am I crying? I feel like I'm being overwhelmed.'

'I'm the same,' Max replied. 'Ever since that accident in Piccadilly Circus, transmuting in you has been different to any host I've had.'

'Can't help being special, can you, Bobster?' Danny laughed.

Max glanced at Danny but ignored his comment. 'Even since we've split, it's been weird.'

'Weird? Like how?' Adam asked, holding Bobby's hand.

'We can communicate telepathically, and as Bobby just said, we can feel each other's emotions,' Max said, wiping his eyes.

Zym frowned. 'What are you trying—'

'Pebble?'

Zym looked around in confusion, but with so many people around, it could have been anyone. 'Junior, what is—'

'Pebble?'

'Who the hell is—'

'Is it really you, Pebble?'

The crowd behind Zym parted as the man Max had rescued pushed through.

'Hey, look. I found that Richard Roberts guy wandering around,' Dazza said, putting a tray of various drinks and food on the table.

'Please tell me it's you,' Richard said, stumbling around the table, using the chairs and backs of Zym and Max to stay upright.

Danny moved his chair back and went into standing mode. 'Easy tiger, where do you think you're going,' he demanded, blocking the man's path.

Pat stood up, her mind racing, as she walked towards the man before resting a hand on Danny's shoulder. 'Thanks, Danny, but I don't think he's a threat.'

Danny returned to sitting mode and backed out of the way but stayed close enough to intervene.

Pat and Richard didn't move. Their eyes studied each other cautiously, taking in every detail. To the outside world, it looked like two people were conversing but without any sound.

'What's going on?' Dazza whispered to Mercedes.

Mercedes shrugged. 'They seem to know each other.'

'No, it can't be,' Pat said, reaching out and lifting one of Richard's hands and examining both sides.

'Mum?' Bobby said, standing and moving to Pat's side.

The man flinched hearing that term, and his eyes flicked to Bobby.

Bobby moved uncomfortably. Not since he came out as gay to his friends had he felt as awkward as he did now under the gaze of this vaguely familiar man. Adam noted Bobby's unease and quickly stood beside him, wrapping his arm protectively around Bobby's waist as a slight tremor struck.

Richard glanced at Adam and smiled weakly before looking back at Pat. 'We were right then,' he said.

Pat nodded, unable to speak for fear of bursting into tears.

Bobby looked at the man and then at Pat. 'What does he mean you "were right"?'

Pat looked at Bobby and smiled. 'Your dad and I always said you had so much love to give that one day you'd find someone special, and it wouldn't necessarily be a girl.'

'Oh,' Bobby replied, looking down at the floor as his mind raced.

Pat grabbed the man's other hand. 'It is you, isn't it?'

'I always said if the world was a beach, I'd still find my lucky pebble on it,' Richard smiled.

'Simon!' Pat exclaimed, pulling him towards her.

Simon yielded into her arms. 'I thought I'd never see you again,' Simon replied, tears rolling down his face.

Bobby looked up. 'What?'

'But it's been five years,' Pat stuttered.

'Five years?' Simon frowned.

'Yes. I identified your body after the car crash, and we had a funeral,' Pat said, hugging him tightly. 'How can you be here? What happened?'

'I was tricked by a police constable,' Simon said. 'He told me you and Bobby had been in a car accident. He rushed us to a hospital where a nurse said she needed a blood sample to see if I was a compatible donor for Bobby, but I think she injected me with something. Everything since has felt like an uncontrollable dream, except a few times when they moved me but forgot to dart me. I tried to run for—'

'Dad?' Bobby asked, staring at Pat and Simon, who were still embracing.

Simon and Pat stopped hugging, but he kept a firm grip of her hand. 'Hello, son. Blimey, you've grown.'

Bobby hesitated briefly before rushing to Simon and throwing his arms around him. 'Is it really you, Dad?'

'Yeah, it is, Bobby. I've missed so much of your life. I don't know what's going on here, but from now on, I'm never leaving you and your mum again,' Simon replied, hugging his son tightly and smiling at Pat, who joined in the hug.

Bobby looked at Simon, 'I've dreamt of this for so long. I've got a million questions.'

'So have I,' Pat added.

'I'll answer them as much as I can,' Simon replied.

'I think the questions will need to wait,' Max said. 'We need to sort out this mess first.'

'I'm confused. If that's Bobby's dad, who and where is Richard Roberts?' Dazza asked.

Max had been studying Simon with his mirror. 'I think Richard Roberts was Simon's last host, and it was Richard's body that Pat identified and buried.'

'Richard's dead?' Simon asked.

'It was a car crash. The police said he had your wallet and was wearing your work clothes,' Pat replied.

'And he had your watch, Dad,' Bobby said, releasing Simon from the hug. 'I've still got it. But you can have it back now,' Bobby added, starting to remove it.

Simon placed his hand over the watch strap. 'You keep it, son. You've earned the right to wear it.'

'This don't make sense,' Dazza said, scratching his head.

'What's up, big man?' Danny asked.

'Well, if Richard Roberts was Bobby's dad's host,' Dazza said, 'and he was a Shadower. Why was—'

'Simon is the Shadower, Dazza,' Mercedes explained.

'I'm a Psiorite, actually, but we're all from Zephyrion,' Simon said.

Pat looked at Simon, her head tilted. 'You're an alien?' she said, the colour draining from her face.

'I'm sorry. I did try to tell you so many times I wasn't from your world,' Simon said, his eyes widening.

'Yeah, but I thought you meant that as in not from a North London council estate because you were from South Yarra in Australia. Not because you're a flipping alien,' Pat replied.

Simon looked down at the floor as his mind raced. 'Oh!'

Adam put his hand to his mouth, trying to suppress a giggle.

'Adam!' Bobby said in a scolding tone.

Adam looked at Bobby, and Simon stood behind him, still looking at the ground. 'I'm sorry, Boo,' he sniggered, 'I can't help it. Your dad reacts just like you when he's thinking or losing an argument.'

Pat's gaze ran from Adam to Bobby before settling on Simon, and she laughed. 'You're so right, Adam. It's been so long, I'm used to Bobby doing that, but I'd forgotten his dad does it too.'

Simon glanced up at Pat.

'Don't you give me that look, Simon Morris,' Pat replied with a smirk. 'You've got a lot of explaining to do when we get home.'

'Dear guests, you may have noticed the tremors have stopped. We have received details from our local geological office, which says things have returned to normal. As a safety precaution, the conference centre will remain out of bounds, but the hotel is now safe for you to return to your rooms or any of the bars and restaurants,' a voice said over the tannoy.

As the crowds started to move back into the hotel, Max looked around. 'Where's Chris and Eron?'

Simon turned sharply. 'Did you say Eron?'

'Yeah, he was the guard who helped us find you. He was looking for his partner Astrid,' Max explained.

'It was quite moving when he found her,' Stephen added. 'He really loves her.'

'No! Eron doesn't love Astrid. She's a Psiorite, and he hates them like Big Bill does,' Simon said.

'Like Big Bill did,' Juli said. 'We dispatched him and all his new arrivals to Leyton.'

'Where?' Simon asked

'It's a prison planet we use for the most dangerous Deceptors from Astral, Malvis, and Androvir,' Erzsi explained.

'I've heard of those names. When they clean out the air filters, they let us breathe normal air for a while, and one of the newer prisoners said they'd renamed Noton and Tascun,' Simon said.

'So what's the situation with Eron?' Zym asked.

'He's a hunter. Bill used him to hunt down and kill Psiorites,' Simon replied. 'Because Astrid was a Psiorite, she could talk to other Psiorites and find out where they are, and the drugs meant she had to obey Eron.'

'Why did they hate Psiorites?' Max queried.

'Bill blamed Psiorites for being stuck on Earth. Bill came here following Zeryn's promise,' Simon replied.

'But why does Eron hate Psiorites?' Zym asked.

'Eron came when he heard the messages talking of Jericesen,' Simon said. 'From what I heard, he's a paid psychopath. He'll kill whatever he's told to as long as he's paid well.'

'But you said you're a Psiorite,' Mercedes said.

'I am, but male Psiorites don't have the telepathic or psychic skills,' Simon explained. 'So she wouldn't have sensed me.'

'Does this mean I'm a Psiorite too, Dad?' Bobby asked.

'Yep,' Simon replied.

'So that's why,' Max said.

Simon turned to Max and studied him. 'I've just noticed you're identical to my son. Who are you, Shadower?'

'I'm Max, and your incredible son was my last host,' Max replied.

'You're all Shadowers?' Simon asked, scanning the group.

'Not all of us. I'm Juli, and I came here two thousand years ago.'

'I'm Erzsi, and I've been here about ten months.'

'I'm Danny, and I've been super-human since birth.'

'In his dreams,' Dazza said.

'I'm Zym, and I've been here for a couple of thousand Earth years. That was Dazza; Adam is the guy holding your son's hand, the fella there is Stephen, and this is Mercedes, and they're all human.'

'No way,' Simon said.

'What is it, Dad?' Bobby asked.

'I've only ever met one Zym. It can't be.'

Juli frowned. 'That's a good point. I've only known one, too, Zymraxin, and he had a brother called Maxohal. I thought it was you in the conference hall.'

Zym laughed. 'I think we've been rumbled, Junior.'

The colour drained from Max. 'Juli? My late partner Lin's sister? It is you?'

'It's been a long time, Max,' Juli said.

'I thought you'd died in Pompeii.'

'I nearly did. I had a great life there. First of all, with Cornelius and Simonus, and just before the eruption, I owned a lot of land as Julia Felix and hosted parties. If I didn't have to visit an aged descendant of Cornelius's on Sicily, I'd have died.'

'This isn't happening,' Simon said.

'What's up, lad?' Zym asked.

'Max, Zym, Juli and Erzsi. No, no, no. Not after all this time,' Simon said.

Max looked at Simon, his mind whirring. 'Bloody hell. Simo?'

'The one and only,' Simon said, glancing around the group. 'I've found my family and my greatest friends.'

'Simon, are you okay?' Pat asked.

'Okay? That man there,' Simon said, pointing to Zym, 'made me feel like I actually belonged somewhere, and Max was like a brother. Well, Max and Zym were.'

Danny coughed. 'This is lovely, and everything, and Bobby getting his dad back is incredibucks, but I've lost my dad, and I'm worried about my mum.'

'Danny's right,' Erzsi said. 'Deceptors have done something with his dad, and it's our turn to help him now.'

'Let me make a call and get M Bank's jet on standby to get us back home. I'll arrange for our luggage to be collected and either meet us at the airport, or it can be sent later,' Stephen said.

'Just a minute,' Pat said to Simon, kissing him briefly. She turned to Stephen, saying, 'Thank you, Stephen. I know this must be hard for you. In another life, I'd be proud to be your wife, but—'

Stephen put a finger to Pat's lips. 'Don't say another word. You've found your husband and the father of your children. I promised you I'd always look after you and nothing has changed. Be with Simon and the kids, and let me do what I can.'

Pat gave Stephen a kiss on the cheek. 'You're a special man, Stephen Marchent.'

As Pat returned to Simon, Stephen turned away and strolled towards a table where hotel staff were handing out free drinks.

'Do you need to tell me something?' Simon asked.

'All you need to know for now is that Stephen has been an incredible support, and without him we might never have found you,' Pat replied, kissing Simon briefly.

Juli rushed after Stephen and put her arm around him. 'You're a good man Stephen Marchent.'

'No, I'm not. I want Pat to be happy, but I wish it was with me.'

'And yet you've let her go,' Juli replied.

'I've got no choice. I love her,' Stephen's head drooped. 'That means my feelings have to come second to hers.'

'One day you're going to be a wonderful husband to somebody,' Juli said.

As he looked up, Juli wiped a tear off his face with a finger.

'Why is love so painful,' Stephen asked.

'Because if it wasn't then it wouldn't be real,' Juli replied.

Stephen smiled weakly. 'We'd better rejoin the others,' he said as they turned with two fresh drinks and headed back to the group.

'Do we know where Paul White's gone?' Max asked.

'I want to get Mum safe first,' Danny replied. 'Then we can look for those host farms where Dad might be.'

'What about Eron?' Mercedes asked.

Simon shook his head. 'He's obsessed with hunting for female Psiorites. He won't be involved with White.'

Bobby muttered something to Adam, who nodded.

'What's up, Champ?' Pat asked.

'Dad, as I'm your son, you said that makes me a Psiorite, right?' Bobby asked.

'Yes, son, it passes down through the family,' Simon replied. 'But us males don't normally have any of the Psiorite abilities.'

'But your daughter would?' Max said, realising where Bobby's questioning was going.

'I guess so,' Simon replied. 'But it's irrelevant as I don't have a daughter.'

'Lily!' Pat screamed. 'Stephen, we need to get to the airport *now*.'

30
THE DIVERSION

'What was Australia like?' Bobby asked.

'It was great, although Rich Roberts made life difficult at times,' Simon replied.

'How did you end up transmuting inside him?'

'Bobby, you've been questioning your dad the whole flight,' Pat said firmly.

'It's fine, Pat. We've got a lot of catching up to do, and I've got a feeling that when I see Lily for the first time, this will seem tame,' Simon laughed.

The pilot emerged from the cockpit and approached Stephen and Max. 'Sir, air traffic control is asking us to divert to RAF Northolt.'

'What do we do?' Stephen asked Max.

'Captain, have they said why we need to divert from London City?'

'They said London City is closed due to a major incident,' the captain replied.

'Why Northolt and not somewhere like Luton, Southend or Cambridge?' Max muttered. 'I don't like this.'

'It's true,' Dazza said. 'My boss has asked me if I'm still landing in London City and to get some pics. So something is going down there.'

'But why Northolt? It's used for royalty, government officials and VIPs,' Max mused.

'Adam's a VIP,' Bobby said.

'Not that important,' Adam laughed.

'Pat, have you got hold of your neighbours?' Max asked.

'Yes. They've gone to Mary's sister's home,' Pat replied. 'She said everything is normal, except the news about the crisis in Zermatt.'

'Where's her sister?'

'Newmarket,' Pat replied.

'Captain, can you tell air traffic control we'd rather divert to Birmingham?' Max said.

'Of course,' the pilot replied.

'Oh, and make sure you plot a route taking us just south of Cambridge,' Max insisted.

'Chief, I can't go to Birmingham,' Danny said.

'Neither can we,' Max replied. 'Have you reached your mum?'

'Yeah. She's not heard from Dad—that Deceptor.'

'Have you told her to get out?' Zym asked.

'No, our house is like a fortress, Chief. You've seen it. Nobody can get in if it's locked down.'

'Nobody except those authorised,' Max replied.

'I thought of that,' Danny said. 'I've removed him from the security system, and her sister and brother-in-law are there.'

'You mean your Uncle Jimmy?' Bobby asked.

'Yep. I messaged him and Auntie Jane as soon as possible after *he* disappeared in Zermatt,' Danny replied. 'They left Hereford straight away, and Uncle Jimmy said he'd bring some friends.'

'You're trusting farmers to protect your mum?' Dazza said.

Bobby laughed. 'Have you seen Danny's uncle?'

'Yeah, he's a short, thin guy with an afro. I think he's from Johannesburg originally,' Dazza replied.

'He also retired last year as an officer in the twenty-second,' Danny added.

'The *what*?' Dazza asked.

'I think Danny is referring to the twenty-second Special Air Service,' Mercedes explained.

'I could still have him,' Dazza replied, laughing.

The pilot walked down the cabin towards Max and Stephen. 'I'm afraid ATC has refused the request to divert to Birmingham and insists we go to Northolt.'

'Interesting,' Max replied. 'Captain, what are our nearest options if we had to do an emergency landing?'

'We could divert back to Southend, or else there's North Weald Airfield or Cambridge Airport,' the pilot replied. 'But we don't have an emergency.'

'No, no, of course not. But just theoretically, what about Duxford?'

'We could land at Duxford if required under a theoretical emergency,' the pilot agreed.

'Thanks, Captain, I guess you'd better go and confirm Northolt then,' Max replied. He watched the pilot return to the cockpit before saying, 'Danny—'

'Already on it, Chief. Any second now,' Danny replied.

'That was so strange,' the pilot said to Max as everyone disembarked. 'We suddenly appeared to run out of fuel and had a warning of decompression in the cabin.'

'Very peculiar,' Max replied, looking around nonchalantly. 'Where did we land?'

'Duxford,' the pilot replied. 'As it was an emergency landing, you don't need your guests to complete a General Aviation Report immediately, but if they can, as soon as possible. Also, everyone is a UK citizen, aren't they? I noticed two Italian surnames on the list.'

'Oh, you mean Medici and Morelli. No, they're both as English as tea and biscuits. They're grandchildren of Italian immigrants,' Max lied.

'Hey, there's a bus stop,' Dazza said as the group left the airfield.

'I've never caught a bus before,' Stephen said.

'Why doesn't that surprise me,' Danny replied.

'Oh, listen to little Lord Moneybags,' Mercedes smirked. 'When did you last catch a bus?'

'I've been on a bus before,' Danny insisted.

'That minibus in Rome doesn't count,' Mercedes snapped back.

'Guys, will you pack it in,' Max replied. 'When we get to Cambridge, we can get some vehicles from my garage.'

'Your country place is outside Cambridge, Chief,' Danny said.

'It is, but I store my vehicle collection in a warehouse in Cambridge,' Max said.

A bus pulled up, and Max boarded, followed by the others. 'Twelve adults to Cambridge, please.'

'Hey, we're both senior citizens; don't we get free bus travel?' Zym asked as Max paid.

Max glowered at Zym and hissed, 'I look eighteen.'

'Is it our fault we've got good genes?' Zym said, smiling.

Thirty minutes later, they were standing in the middle of an industrial estate, staring at a compound called Hal's Hold. The front area was littered with old shipping containers, while a large red brick warehouse stood at the back. To the side of the entrance was a fenced-off area containing a small electricity substation.

'You need it, we'll hold it for you,' Dazza read.

'Catchy sign,' Danny smirked.

'I wonder what gave you the idea for the name, Maxohal?' Simon said.

'It's a mystery, Simohal,' Max laughed as he punched in a security code and stared at a camera.

The main gate swung open, and Max turned to the others. 'Follow me to the main building and stay within the yellow lines.'

'What happens if we don't?' Mercedes asked.

'The defence system rotates its methods. You'll get a verbal warning; if you ignore it there'll be a warning shot.'

'And then?' Juli asked.

'That's where it gets random. It could give you a taser-style electric shock, shoot you to disable you, or if it still sees you as a threat, it'll get a bit more terminal,' Max explained.

'Is that legal?' Pat asked.

'That sign saying there's a substation plus the high voltage and danger of death signs means I've never had to find out,' Max replied.

As they reached the main roller door to the warehouse, Max repeated the security code and camera procedure, but this time, a gruff male voice said, 'We're closed.'

'Maxwell Thomas to collect my hippo.'

There was a pause before the roller door started to rise, revealing a solid steel plate sinking into the ground.

'Blimey, Chief, what're you hiding in here?' Danny asked.

'Just a few cars and things,' Max replied.

'Nice Saab convertible,' Stephen said as they started to see the vehicles behind the door.

'Why've you got a London taxi?' Danny asked.

'Great for avoiding taxes going into the city, and you get some breaks on parking, of course,' Max replied, frowning as if his reply was obvious.

Pat pointed to the right. 'Is that a—tank?'

'It's a 1944 Comet with a 75mm gun,' Mercedes said.

'Very impressive,' Max replied. 'But it's the later 1945 version with the 77mm gun.'

Danny started laughing. 'Let me guess. That's good for parking, too.'

'Something like that,' Max said, walking to a five-year-old grey SUV.

'But what's wrong with the Rolls Royce?' Dazza asked, pointing to the deep purple saloon.

'We want to blur into the crowd, not shout over here,' Max replied, starting the car.

'Chief, you leave the keys in the car?' Danny said in surprise.

'It saves looking for them,' Max replied, turning the ignition off and wandering over to a plain blue Ford people carrier.

'Aren't you worried about someone stealing them?' Adam asked.

'Not really. If someone gets past all the security, I reckon hiding the keys in a lockbox would be too easy for them, so why bother? Besides, I've got four—no five of these around the country. I almost forgot Glasgow,' Max said, starting up the Ford.

'Something is going on,' Erzsi said, staring at her phone.

Juli looked across to Erzsi's phone. 'Max, you need to see this. It's all over the mainstream media.'

As the others started pulling out their phones, a look of shock spread around the group.

Max turned off the Ford, grabbed his phone from his pocket and pressed a button. A screen lowered from the ceiling and started to mirror his phone. A few clicks on breaking news brought up the story everyone had been looking at.

A newsreader stared at the camera in shock. 'As you've seen, the events in Switzerland have been devastating. The tremors we've felt across Europe have been confirmed as being centred around the Swiss village of Zermatt.

'The beautiful hamlet, which was playing host to the annual International Federation for Fiscal Security, was rocked by a series of Earth tremors in the last twenty-four hours, which geologists described as highly unusual. However, footage from the press gathered at the global gathering has confirmed the government statement that our planet is being invaded. Let's see that statement again from the UK Prime Minister.'

The image changed to a tall, thin, dark-skinned man at a lectern with UK flags draped down two poles on either side of him.

'Good afternoon. We are facing unprecedented times. In the last twenty-four hours, Switzerland has suffered from repeated Earth tremors. At first, we believed these to be natural but unusual tectonic movements, but we now know they are far more dangerous.

'Our planet is being invaded by aliens from a different world. We don't know their intent, but we have seen them use advanced technology to kill our people.'

The screen changed to show the Porter machine firing at Big Bill and Eron and their shells collapsing without revealing their trapped energy souls moving into the Porter machine launch platform.

The image cut back to the Prime Minister looking shocked. 'I'm sorry to show you that, but I'm sparing you the full horror. We don't know how many aliens are already here, but we have been tracking those responsible for killing the respected American businessman, William J Pierce and several others. After their killing spree and trying to start earthquakes with that weapon, they fled the country. But we know where they are.

'After killing Mr Pierce, they hijacked his corporate plane and came to Britain. We tried intercepting the flight, but unfortunately, they forced a crash landing at Duxford Airfield. After killing the pilot, they torched the plane before killing two border control guards and escaping in stolen vehicles.'

The image on screen changed to show the plane they had recently been in, sitting at the end of the runway on fire. It then moved to show two heavily blurred images of what looked like bodies lying on the ground by the entrance to the car park.

Dazza frowned. 'We didn't do that!' he exclaimed.

'Welcome to the world of propaganda press, bro,' Danny replied.

The screen switched back to the Prime Minister. 'I have spoken to the leaders of the other parties in Westminster, and we have formed a council of war. All political differences have agreed to be forgotten, and we will be a unity party of governance.

'I have already received messages of support from the President of the United States and the President of Russia, and other nations have pledged to do all they can to capture these aliens.

'At this stage, we are trying to keep life as normal as possible, but we must introduce some restrictions. Gatherings of more than twenty people are prohibited, and we are introducing a national digital currency to stop the alien invaders from trading. This new currency will be introduced in the coming weeks.

'The plans to introduce a digital identity card will also be accelerated. We know you have already seen the advantages of a digital ID card over carrying a physical ID, like a driving licence or passport. Speeding up their introduction will close the loop on these murderous invaders of our planet by restricting their movements.

'I am also introducing a complete ban on international travel. No flights or boats will be allowed to enter or leave Great Britain until further notice, except for military craft. That means the Isles of Man and White are off-limits, as are Northern Ireland and the Channel Islands. Only smaller islands, dependent on Great Britain for supplies, may continue travelling to and from the mainland. Only British citizens currently abroad who wish to return will be allowed into the country.

'We must show solidarity and take mutual responsibility for protecting not just our family and friends but also our nation and planet. Each and every one of us must, at all costs, be vigilant. We are not introducing martial law at this stage, but we cannot rule it out if these aliens are not captured quickly. Anybody caught sheltering or assisting these aliens will be immediately imprisoned and charged with treason.

'Now is the time for all of us to stay calm. Please do not panic and beware of fake news. Do not circulate false rumours or believe pseudo-experts. We, your government, will continue to provide clear and transparent information, but be under no illusion that we are at war with these aliens.

'Your government is totally focused on combating these invaders. I am calling on all political, economic, social, and religious stakeholders to join our national unity alliance and overcome this crisis as quickly as possible.

'We have overcome adversity before, and we shall again. I know we can collectively rise to this challenge and emerge victorious.'

The screen switched back to the newsreader. 'That was Prime Minister Alastair McGivern ten minutes ago. Our government have since released pictures of the aliens.'

The screen displayed pictures of Max, Bobby, Pat, Stephen, Danny, and Dazza.

'If you have seen any of these individuals, please contact the emergency services immediately. Please, do not be fooled by their appearance. These are dangerous aliens. Do not approach them,' the newsreader said. 'According to the police, the aliens were seen fleeing Duxford in two vehicles. Unfortunately, we don't have any images of the vehicles, but eyewitnesses say they were dark grey and silver.'

'We caught the flipping bus,' Dazza insisted.

'Never mind that, you dullard, they've just shown our faces. We're screwed,' Danny replied.

'Not all of us,' Simon said.

'How can we get Lily now?' Pat demanded, glowering at the screen.

'Send your friend a message saying we'll get her,' Juli suggested.

Pat shook her head. 'She won't go with strangers.'

'I'm her dad. I'll go with Juli,' Simon said.

'I know you are, but she's never met you. You died before she was born,' Pat replied, before adding, 'I mean disappeared.'

'They didn't show my face, and Lily knows me,' Adam said.

Zym looked at Adam, his mind racing. 'That's a good point. Why didn't they include you? They knew you were there. You were one of the celebrity guests, and they had Pat and Bobby on the screen.'

Max pulled out the mirror Adam had given him when he was in Bobby. He angled it to see Adam.

Adam spotted Max and shouted, 'I'm not one of you; I'm *human*!'

'Sorry, Adam. I had to check,' Max replied.

'Well, how about checking everyone else who wasn't mentioned?' Adam insisted.

'What's the point? We know Simon, Zym, Erzsi, and Juli are Shadowers,' Mercedes said.

'Yes, but you're not, and they knew you were there,' Adam snapped.

Max turned his mirror towards Mercedes. 'She's human.'

'*See*!' Mercedes replied.

'Can we get back to Lily?' Pat insisted. 'Who's coming with me to get her?'

'You can't go, Mum,' Bobby replied. 'Our faces have been on national telly.'

'Bobby's right. I'll go,' Simon said. 'I could do with a couple more in case we run into problems.'

Pat folded her arms. 'But—'

'Pat, let me go with Simo and Adam. I swear on my life we will protect your daughter,' Juli said.

'*Simon*,' Simon replied.

'What?' Juli asked.

'I'm Simon. Simo died years ago when that woman finally made me realise I could love someone without them leaving me,' Simon said, smiling at Pat.

'Fine,' Pat replied. 'But you tell me the second you're on the way back with Lily.'

'Of course, Pebble,' Simon replied, kissing Pat lightly. 'The people carrier or the SUV, Max?'

'Neither; take that grey MG ZT385.'

'But that's a tatty, old, funny-looking Rover,' Adam said.

Max smiled. 'Actually, it has a four-point-six-litre V8 Mustang engine, a former factory test model that came with 385 horsepower.'

'Still sounds a bit slow by modern standards,' Simon said.

Max folded his arms. 'That's why I've upgraded the injectors and fuel system and added a boosted supercharger. Overall, I reckon it's close to 700 horsepower.'

Adam crouched down to look at the wheels. 'Wow, are those carbon ceramic brake discs?'

'Since when have you been into cars?' Danny asked.

Bobby laughed. 'Since he started watching The Man, The Machine.'

Simon noticed Pat's look and said, 'Come on, I need to fetch my daughter.'

As Juli climbed into the front passenger seat and Adam got in the back, Simon sat in the driver's seat and ran his hands over the steering wheel. 'I've not driven a car for over five years,' he sighed.

'I can drive if you want?' Adam suggested.

'It's fine. I used to drive in the Southern Cross Rally and would have won in '66 if I hadn't clipped that tree on the last night in my Volvo,' Simon replied, turning the ignition key and smiling as the V8 roared to life.

'You'd better drive carefully. I've only just got you back, and once you've got Lily, my life will be in that car,' Pat said.

'I know,' Simon replied out of the window as he drove slowly out of the warehouse, the car growling like an angry lion.

'Uh, excuse me, I am your son, you know,' Bobby said, folding his arms.

'I know, Champ. But I can keep you safe here. They're going to be out there, exposed,' Pat replied.

'Not entirely,' Max said as he opened an app on his phone, which was still paired to the large screen hanging from the warehouse ceiling.

'Blimey, Chief,' Danny said admiringly. 'When you asked me to adapt a car tracker, I wondered what you'd use it for. But what are those options down the side?'

'Oh, nothing much. It's a bit like a racing car where I can change the settings remotely,' Max replied.

31
COMING HOME

'When's Mummy coming?' Lily asked, staring out of the window.

Mary Nobbs sighed. She loved looking after little Lily for her neighbour Pat, but it was usually for a few hours, not a few days. She had never been so reminded of her rapidly approaching seventieth birthday. 'Not long now, petal. Mummy said she's sending Adam to pick you up.'

'Yay. Adam is funny,' Lily replied excitedly.

'You're such a bundle of energy, young lady,' Mary's husband David said. 'How long did Pat say before they'd be here?'

'She said they were about twenty-five minutes away, and that was around fifteen minutes ago, so Janet will miss saying goodbye to this little one,' Mary replied.

'Why your sister spends so long at the hairdresser never ceases to amaze me,' David laughed.

'Says the man who uses polish as shampoo,' Mary replied, smiling.

'It takes hours to maintain this look,' David replied, folding his arms in mock disgust.

'Is Daddy coming?' Lily asked.

Mary looked at David and mouthed, 'Her dad died before she was born. What do we say?'

'He is, isn't he?' Lily added excitedly.

David glanced at Lily before whispering, 'Message Pat. Or nip into the kitchen and call her.'

'Good idea. Keep an eye on the little one, and I'll give her a call,' Mary said, smiling at Lily before heading into the kitchen.

'Simo, will you slow down?' Juli shouted, gripping her seat.

'I told you it's Simon,' Simon replied, downshifting as he exited the Newmarket bypass. 'Did Pat say the address was in Newmarket?'

'No,' Adam replied from the back of the car. 'You need to turn left. It's just on the edge of Newmarket.'

Simon glanced to his right before swinging left onto the A142 and accelerating.

'We need to go left,' Adam screamed as they almost missed the next turning.

Simon yanked the handbrake and spun the steering wheel. 'At least this thing has a proper handbrake,' he said as the car squealed into the turn, clipping a plastic road bollard and sending it flying.

'We need to turn left in three-quarters of a mile,' Adam said, staring at the maps app on his phone while trying not to slide around the back seat.

'Simon,' Juli said, being careful to say his name, 'why are you driving so fast?'

'Because there's been a black BMW following us since we merged with that other road about six miles ago,' Simon replied.

'And I can hear a helicopter approaching, although I'm not sure it's locked onto us yet. Juli, ring Pat and get Mrs Nobbs to bring Lily into the front garden, if they've got one, or wait by the front door.'

Adam looked out of the rear window. 'I can't see any—oh, there is something back there going as fast as us.'

'He's staying back the whole time. Which way?' Simon shouted.

'What?' Adam said, glancing forward. 'Oh, yeah, um, left, yeah, left by that pub.'

Simon yanked the handbrake and spun the wheel, causing the car to fishtail. As the vehicle straightened, he floored the accelerator.

'Pat said it was by a pub,' Juli said.

'No, it's that pub just down there and the white house after it,' Adam replied.

'Tell me if you see that BMW,' Simon said urgently as he pulled on the handbrake as they passed the house, leaving the car sideways across the road. He slammed the car into reverse and shot up onto the forecourt of a garage, the car hidden from the road by a wall.

'Juli, you and Adam go and fetch Lily. I'll—' Simon was cut short by his driver's door being pulled open.

'What the hell, mate,' said a scruffy mechanic in his early forties, wearing overalls smeared with oil.

Simon climbed out of the car and smiled. 'I'm sorry, mate. This thing is a bit temperamental. The brakes locked and sent me sideways, so I thought I'd better get off the road.'

'Yeah, sure. Folks drive like lunatics down here,' the mechanic said, walking around the front of the car as Juli and Adam hurried off.

Simon glanced up the road and noticed the BMW had stopped. Two men dressed in black combat gear got out of the car before it moved off, slowly accelerating. By the time the

BMW passed, Simon and the mechanic were standing in front of the MG, blocking most of it from the road.

'It looks like an old ZT, but that engine sounded like a V8,' the mechanic said.

Simon kept looking at the car while noting the BMW speeding past. 'Yeah, it's one of their limited-edition models before they went bust.'

'It sounded awesome. I can't fit it in now, but if you want to leave it here, I can check what's causing the brakes to lock first thing tomorrow,' the mechanic said.

'We need to get Lily out the front,' Mary said, returning to the living room.

'Daddy's almost here,' Lily said excitedly, heading towards the door.

'Excuse me, young lady, but aren't you forgetting something?' David said.

Lily turned awkwardly. 'Sorry, erm, thank you for having me.'

David laughed. 'You're very welcome, but I meant, don't you need to put your shoes and coat on?'

Lily giggled and flopped to the floor, pulling her shoes on with David's help.

Mary picked up Lily's coat and small suitcase. 'Come on then, let's go and see Daddy.'

'But he's dead,' David hissed as Lily darted out the door.

'Long story,' Mary replied. 'I'll tell you after.'

Despite the six-foot hedge hiding the road, Lily looked towards the sound of a noisy car engine drawing closer. 'That's Daddy.'

'Sounds like a lunatic to me,' David said as the sound of screeching tyres filled the air.

Lily ran towards the gate, but Mary grabbed her before she managed to open it. 'No you don't. Just wait here. Daddy and Adam won't be long.'

Lily crossed her arms in defiance but didn't move.

'She's got her mother's fire,' Mary said.

A dark-skinned woman opened the gate, followed by Adam.

Lily strutted across to Adam, who swept her up in his arms, which made her laugh. 'Have you been behaving yourself?' he asked.

'Yes,' Lily replied curtly, looking over Adam's shoulder for Simon.

Juli smiled at Mary and David. 'I'm Juli. Sorry, we need to go, but hopefully, we can catch up soon.'

'Nice to meet you, Juli. Pat said you were an old family friend. Where's Simon? We've not seen him since...well since the accident,' Mary said.

'He's by the car. He thinks we're being followed,' Juli replied as Adam kept Lily distracted by swinging her around.

David nodded. 'Yes, we saw the propaganda about Pat, Bobby, and the others being aliens.'

'You'd better get going. Give Pat and Bobby our love,' Mary said.

Adam carried Lily out of the garden, followed by Juli, carrying Lily's coat and case.

A bullet clipped the hedge near Adam, followed by a shout, 'Stop there.'

Juli looked up the road and saw the two men in black combat gear running towards them. 'Run,' she shouted at Adam.

'What the hell's going on?' the mechanic said, hearing the gunshot.

Simon noticed the commotion and said, 'Can you get me a business card?'

'Uh, yeah, okay, hang on,' the mechanic said, heading towards his office.

Simon jumped into the car, fired it up and pulled forward as Adam yanked open the back door and jumped inside with Lily. Juli was just seconds behind, scrambling into the front passenger seat.

Simon swung the car to the left, lowering the passenger window. 'Mary, David, get in,' he shouted.

'Good grief, it is you,' David exclaimed.

'Get in quick,' Simon said as a bullet ricocheted off the car.

'Just go,' Mary said. 'They're not going to bother with two pensioners.'

'I'm not—' Simon was cut short by another bullet hitting the car.

David leaned forward and said, 'Go before they hit us with a stray bullet.'

Simon needed no further convincing and set off, the car shooting forward at speed but controlled with all the skill of a racing driver. As the MG sped past the two armed men, they fired several rounds at the car, but they made hardly any impact.

'What the hell is this thing made from?' Simon muttered as he swung the car right, ignoring the painted mini roundabout.

'Transparent aluminium windows and a boron carbide and Ultra-High-Molecular-Weight Polyethylene body,' Max's voice sounded in the car.

'Max, what is this thing?' Simon yelled.

'Just an old MG with a few little extras,' Max replied. 'I'm scanning wavebands, and those guys with the peashooters have called you in. That BMW is heading back to them, but the helicopter hasn't found you yet.'

'How can you be sure?' Juli asked.

'Easy, I've hacked into their surveillance system, and we're watching the feed from the helicopter,' Danny replied.

'Have you got Lily?' Pat yelled.

'Wow, there's no need to shout,' Simon laughed. 'Yes, she's safe and sound.'

'Hey, Mummy. Look, Daddy's back,' Lily said in excitement.

'Yes, munchkin, it's exciting, isn't it,' Pat replied.

'Stealth mode engaged,' an electronic voice said.

'Woah, what just happened?' Simon asked.

'Sorry, I should have warned you. The car is now using cooling systems to ensure its external temperature matches the surroundings, making it invisible to thermal image cameras, and projection panels make it look like a different car to external observers. It currently looks like a red SUV,' Max replied.

'Blimey, Chief. I've been underestimating you,' Danny said.

'You may be a genius on computers, but I've been an engineer for a long time,' Max replied.

'You always denied being an engineer when I said it,' Zym grumbled.

'You're my brother. I'm legally obliged to disagree with you,' Max laughed.

'Dudes, flick to the news,' Dazza said, his face ashen.

Max flicked the television to the news channel.

'Repeating our breaking news, there has been a double fatal shooting near Newmarket,' the newsreader said. 'The police said they were called to a reported sighting of some of the wanted invading aliens, and on arrival, they discovered the aliens holding two elderly people hostage. During negotiations, the aliens stole a car from the neighbouring garage. The police have confirmed the garage owner is in a critical condition with head injuries from where they ran over him during their escape.'

The television image changed to show the house Simon and the others had recently collected Lily from. In front of it was a white plastic tent.

The newsreader said, 'The victims have been named as husband and wife, David and Mary Nobbs from Haywood in North London. The aliens brutally shot the elderly couple at point-blank range before speeding away in an old grey Rover 75.'

'It's an MG,' Max muttered.

'Never mind that. Simon, what happened to Mary and David?' Pat screamed.

'Nothing, they're fine,' Simon replied. 'They insisted on staying, saying they'd be alright.'

'Well they're not now. They've been k—,' Pat stopped herself, remembering Lily was with Simon.

Juli whispered something in the car, but it was unintelligible to those listening from the warehouse.

'Bloody hell. I swear they were fine when we left,' Simon replied, the shock in his voice almost visible.

'Simon, don't come back here. I'm sending directions to another compound,' Max said. 'When you arrive, you'll enter a tunnel and go down a red route. At the end is a parking lot. Leave the car there and pick another vehicle. I'd suggest the Ford or the Bentley. I'll be notified what you're driving. Follow the blue route. I'll send directions to the car to take you to a safe house.'

'Why didn't you say this car had navigation?' Simon moaned as the central section of the dashboard lowered, replacing the dated-looking radio front and dials with a large map displayed on a touchscreen.

'You never gave me chance,' Max replied.

'Can we concentrate on getting my family back together?' Pat protested.

'You will, Pat. We'll all meet up there,' Max said reassuringly. 'Zym, you take Stephen, Dazza, and Erzsi, and I'll take Pat, Bobby, Danny and Mercedes.'

'Any recommendations on transport, Junior?' Zym asked.

'Most of the normal cars are bulletproof and have weaponry built in. But the two hybrid Hyundai SUVs are the latest additions,' Max replied.

'And that means?' Zym said.

'And that means I'm taking the black one,' Max replied.

'Looks like we've got the silver one,' Zym said.

'I can't believe they killed Mary and David,' Pat said, fighting back tears.

'I know,' Max said, trying to sound comforting. 'But we need to concentrate on our safety at the moment. I swear we will avenge their deaths.'

A few miles away, Simon was following the directions Max had sent to the car. He had turned off the main road back to Cambridge and was heading down a country lane before screeching to a halt when he reached a tractor blocking a farm entrance.

A man in the tractor looked at Simon and then down at the car as if scanning them both. If it weren't for the slight jerk in the man's movement, an observer would have thought he was human rather than mechanical. A second or two later, the tractor backed up, and the road behind lowered to reveal a ramp into a tunnel.

Simon set off rapidly down the ramp. Glancing back, he saw the tractor driving back into place just before the ramp behind him lifted to close the tunnel entrance. Simon followed the tunnel as Max had instructed, noting the red line running along the wall on both sides until he reached a small open area at the bottom with a Lister Knobbly, a Bentley Mulsanne, and a Ford SUV parked up.

As Adam, Juli and Lily clambered out of the MG, Simon couldn't stop himself from admiring the Lister. Its black bodywork absorbed the light, making the central gold stripe running its entire body length appear to be floating.

Out of the corner of his eye, he spotted Lily running towards him, and he swept her up in his arms. 'Well, young lady, I guess this is hello,' Simon said, staring lovingly at his daughter. This was the first time he'd ever seen her, yet it felt like he'd known her his entire life.

'Silly Daddy. We've seen each other lots of times,' Lily giggled.

'Have we?' Simon asked, his head tilted as he studied his daughter.

'Granny Shaz introduced us in our dreams ages ago,' Lily replied, looking at the funny-looking black car.

Simon felt a tingle run through his body. He knew he'd started dreaming more of his mother over the last few months, and he suddenly remembered seeing a little girl in some of his dreams. 'Was it only Granny Shaz?' he asked as Lily squirmed free of his grip, dropping to the floor so she could inspect the car.

'And GeeGee Kazi,' Lily said, trying to find the door handle.

'She really is a Psiorite,' Simon thought aloud. 'She can talk to my mother and grandmother.'

'Bentley or Ford?' Adam asked, interrupting Simon's thoughts.

'Huh?' Simon replied, not taking his eyes off Lily.

'Earth to Simon. Have you forgotten we're on the run?' Juli said.

'Hmm,' Simon said, mesmerised by his daughter exploring the car.

'Simon, come on,' Juli said, shaking him.

'What? Oh, hell, come on, everyone in the Ford,' Simon ordered. 'You too, munchkin,' he said, sweeping up Lily.

'What's wrong with the Bentley?' Adam asked.

'Nothing if you want to be easy to spot,' Simon said, noticing the child seat on a nearby shelf. 'You always were ready for anything, Max,' he muttered as he grabbed it and put it in the Ford.

'You really have been gone for over five years. There's so much CCTV in the UK now; they can track you anywhere and in anything,' Adam replied grimly.

'Even so, I think something more common is likely to be less noticeable,' Simon replied as he strapped Lily in and jumped into the driving seat.

Twenty miles away, Max watched the road and glanced in the mirrors as he sped along the back lanes while Danny studied the car.

'I can't believe you had the front passenger seat engineered for a wheelchair, Chief,' Danny said.

'I didn't. I had both front seats engineered. A flick of the button and they fold into the floor, leaving the wheelchair anchor points,' Max replied. 'The car Zym's driving is the same.'

'Chief, your phone has a message,' Danny said.

'Jeeves, read my message,' Max shouted.

An electronic voice sounding like an English butler said, 'Zone twelve, Ford SUV grade 4 active.'

'Jeeves, forward destination from this vehicle to that Ford,' Max ordered.

'Certainly, sir. Destination sent and acknowledged.'

'Jeeves off.'

'You call your control system Jeeves?' Danny laughed.

'I happen to like P.G. Wodehouse,' Max replied.

'Not long ago you hated this sort of technology,' Danny said.

Max smiled. 'I know then some smart Alec differently-abled fella showed me how to embrace it securely.'

Danny glanced at the navigation screen. 'Chief, why're we heading to your place near Upper Wheatstone Power Station?' he asked.

'We're not, but we are going past it,' Max replied, glancing in the mirror to check Zym was still following.

'I still have nightmares about that place,' Pat added.

'Tell me about it,' Bobby grumbled. 'I was the one being shot at.'

'Actually, that copper was shooting at me,' Max insisted.

'Yeah, at you inside my body,' Bobby snapped.

'Excuse me, but I lost my first vision control chair—' Danny was cut short by his phone ringing. He answered it and hit the speaker button.

'Danny? It's Uncle Jimmy.'

'Hi, Jimmy. Is everything alright? Has something happened to Mum?'

'Yes, we're all fine. We've relocated from your place and are using the emergency protocol Delta, November, Alpha. Did you get that?' Jimmy asked.

'Yep, Delta, November, Alpha, confirmed. We're still in transit, but I'll let you know when we reach our destination,' Danny replied. 'Anything else?'

'Don't go home. According to my surveillance team, your place is still secure, but there's a lot of armed presence around it,' Jimmy said. 'Gotta go. Use this number if you need any of us.'

'Can I speak to Mum?' Danny asked.

'She's in another vehicle, but she's okay. She's still shaken up about what you said about your dad. If I can help, let me know. Gotta go,' Jimmy replied before hanging up.

'Is your uncle normally like that?' Mercedes asked.

'Like what?' Danny replied.

'Not saying much, and isn't not letting you speak to your mum a bit weird?'

'Nah. Jimmy's never been a big talker, and he didn't stop me speaking to her. She's just not in the same car as him.'

Danny's phone rang again with a withheld number. 'See, that'll be her now,' Danny replied, answering the video call.

'Hi, son, it's Dad here.'

Danny stared at the image of the man as his emotions twisted. 'You're not my dad!' Danny snarled.

'You always were a smart lad,' Paul smirked. 'Now come back to London and bring Max with you...' Paul paused and muted his phone as someone spoke to him. His face reddened, and his gesticulations made it clear he was angry. He turned back to his phone and unmuted it, taking a deep breath simultaneously. 'It seems your mother has evaded us, but it's alright; we have an alternative.'

'Aww, I'm sorry to disappoint you, Father,' Danny said sarcastically. 'Mum is well out of your reach, so you can't shoot her like you tried to kill me, you sicko.'

Max glanced at Danny in surprise.

Danny muted his phone. 'I'm not stupid, Chief. I saw the bullet hole in the backrest of my chair, he didn't shoot towards me, he wanted me dead, and if it wasn't for Mercedes, I would be.'

'We all make mistakes,' Mercedes replied with a little smile.

Danny turned back to his phone but couldn't suppress a smile himself.

'Now come on, Danny, there's no need for name-calling,' Paul said.

'I'm going to do more than call you names when I see you, you sick shit,' Danny snapped. 'What've you done with Dad?'

'Oh, don't worry, Daddy is nice and safe, look,' Paul replied, turning his phone to show a TV screen with the real Paul White in white overalls shuffling along in a queue for food. 'He's such a good host and so intelligent, it would be a shame to remove him permanently from our hosting programme.'

'You touch him, and I swear I will wipe you and your kind from this planet,' Danny replied.

'Danny, you always were such a hothead. I'm not going to hurt your dad; I just want a trade,' Paul said with a twisted smile.

'Deal. I'll come in, but you let my dad go.'

'That ego of yours, Danny. I don't want you, I want Max. It's always been about Max. My boss has some scores to settle,' Paul smirked. 'I'm going to send you some coordinates. You need to be there by eleven o'clock tomorrow morning. I'll then send you directions to where to meet. You'll have an hour to get there. Bring Max, his brother Zym and those traitors Juli and Erzsi. If you do as you're told and hand them over, I'll return your dad.'

'How can I force all four of them to agree?' Danny asked.

'Not my problem, son. See you tomorrow,' Paul replied before hanging up.

'We have to rescue, Dad,' Danny insisted.

Max glanced at Danny. 'We will, Danny.'

'You swear?' Danny asked.

32

It Takes Two

'You realise we're walking into a trap?' Juli said.

'We've got no choice,' Max replied as the group sat eating their takeaway pizzas in the two farm worker cottages Max had knocked into one.

'I think we had a choice not to order these awful pizzas,' Zym moaned.

'They're not bad,' Bobby replied.

'Says the boy eating pizza with pineapple on it!' Zym muttered. 'I thought you'd have tried to improve the lad's taste buds, Max.'

'I did. He used to eat crisps for breakfast,' Max replied.

Adam put his hand to his mouth to catch the food he was spraying out with laughter. 'He still does, given the chance.'

'Looks like he's been snacking already. Aren't you hungry?' Simon asked, noticing Bobby wasn't eating.

'I've had two slices already,' Bobby replied, patting his stomach.

'No you haven't,' Mercedes said. 'You've only had one. You reached out for another slice but then didn't take it.'

Bobby glowered at Mercedes. 'Yes I did. You just didn't notice.'

'Champ, are you still skipping meals?' Pat asked.

'No!' Bobby yelled as he stood up. 'Will you all leave me alone,' he added, storming off.

Adam went to stand, but Simon was already up and put his hand on Adam's shoulder. 'I'll go,' he said, heading after Bobby.

'Are you alright, son?' Simon asked when he found Bobby sitting on a bench looking out across fields of farmland and trees.

'Yeah, I guess so,' Bobby replied.

Simon sat on the bench and looked out across the fields, enjoying the unusually mild, late autumn evening. They sat like that for several minutes, just watching the slow, lazy breeze rustle through the few remaining leaves on the trees.

'Dad, did you think of us while you were gone?' Bobby asked, still staring straight ahead.

'Every waking moment, son.'

'I always knew you'd come back someday.'

'I'd still be there if it wasn't for you, Bobby.'

'It's them you need to thank,' Bobby replied, nodding back to the cottage. 'I was just a passenger.'

'What did I tell you about lying, young man?' Simon said jokingly. 'We've had a hectic time, but your mum and Max have told me what's been happening. None of this would have happened if you hadn't saved Max after that Deceptor tried to kill him in Piccadilly Circus.'

'I didn't do anything. I just did what anyone else would have.'

'That's my point. Not everyone else would have, but you did. You went to help an elderly man that you'd never met.'

'Well, you and Mum always said we should help people in trouble.'

'Saying it and doing it are worlds apart. Your act of kindness started a chain of events that saved me and brought me home,' Simon said, putting his arm around Bobby and hugging him. 'You are my hero, and never forget it.'

Bobby studied his Dad's face. The last five years had taken their toll on him. Aside from no longer having a beard, his dad's hair was heavily flecked with grey, wrinkles and lines covered his face, and a thin, almost gaunt frame now replaced his formerly muscular build. 'What did they do to you in that place?' Bobby asked.

'Enough to make me realise surviving to see you all again mattered more than anything they could do to me.'

'I wish I could be brave like you, Max and the others,' Bobby sighed.

'Bobby, you were just thirteen when you were told I had died.'

'Twelve. I was twelve.'

'There you go, twelve and yet your mum told me you became the man of the house. Helping her with chores and even more, you had a baby sister to deal with just a few months later. And I wasn't there to help you grow up into the fine man I see. You're one of the bravest men I know.'

'Thanks, Dad. I've missed you so much.'

'And I've missed you too, kiddo. Now let's go back inside and find out how we're going to kick ass tomorrow.'

As they stood up, Simon froze and scanned the fields in the evening gloom. 'Did you hear something?'

Bobby looked around but shook his head.

'Hmm,' Simon mused. 'I guess I'm not used to being outside anymore. Come on, let's join the others,' he said, putting his arm around Bobby's shoulders as they strolled back inside.

'I've already said we've got no choice,' Max protested.

'Junior is right. Wheel's dad is our priority,' Zym said.

'So we just turn up and hand ourselves over,' Erzsi said bitterly.

'What the hell's going on here?' Simon asked as he walked into the kitchen. 'We came here two thousand years ago to defeat Zeryn and Jeric, and now we just give up?'

'We're not giving up, but we have to save Danny's dad. We've come here uninvited and brought Zephyrion's battle with us. What happens next is our responsibility,' Max replied.

'Agreed,' Simon said. 'But I say let's prepare to win, not surrender and lose. They don't know I'm amongst you, so we have an element of surprise.'

Bobby reached for a slice of ham and pineapple pizza while they were arguing. Pat went to say something, but Simon grabbed her hand and shook his head.

'But one person isn't much of a surprise,' Zym replied.

'What if there were two?' Bobby said, munching on the pizza.

'I've got a little surprise for them too,' Danny replied; turning to Simon, he added, 'Can you pass me a coke, please?'

As Simon handed Danny a can of coke, a door creaked behind Dazza, and he stood up to investigate. As the door slowly opened, Dazza stepped to the side and watched as someone started to enter. As soon as the person was clear of the doorframe, Dazza punched them squarely in the face, sending them crashing to the floor.

'I've been waiting to do that. These alien folks are getting on my nerves,' Dazza said.

Erzsi coughed nervously.

Dazza laughed. 'No, you dudes are cool. It's these invaders that are getting on my brainwaves.'

Suddenly, chaos erupted as several armed soldiers entered the room, followed by Eron and Astrid.

'Stay where you are. We just want the Psiorite,' Eron said.

'I'm a Psiorite,' Bobby said.

Eron looked and sneered. 'I can see from Chris's memory that you're just a nobody from WestFi. No, that's not right, you're Max Janus, you helped me rescue Astrid, but you're a lot thinner.'

'I'm Max.'

Eron turned towards Max. 'Ah, yes, Janus. I never managed to thank you for helping me save Astrid. Now, where is the Psiorite girl?'

'There isn't one here,' Max replied.

'Liar,' Eron replied, lashing out at the person nearest him and sending Mercedes flying across the room.

'Chris, why are you doing this?' Danny asked, dropping his hands either side of his chair.

'Chris Medici is dead. Or at least he will be when I've transmuted. Now, where's the Psiorite? Astrid, where is she?' Eron asked, gripping Astrid's wrists tightly.

Astrid was staring at the floor, but she pointed towards the stairs.

Pat stepped between Eron and the stairs leading to the bedrooms. 'You'll have to kill me first,' she said, crossing her arms.

Stephen rushed to Pat's side, adding, 'Me too,'

Eron looked at Pat and Stephen in bemusement. 'Okay, kill them both.'

As the soldiers lifted their rifles to shoot, Danny shot forward. 'Come on, dullards, you don't need to do this. All you want is the girl, right?'

'Give her to me,' Eron demanded.

'She's just a five-year-old girl. There's what, eight or nine soldiers here to take care of this lot; why don't you, me, and your girlfriend go and sort this girl out ourselves? No hassle, just nice and simple,' Danny suggested.

Simon turned and lunged at Danny, grabbing him by his top. 'You touch a hair on her head, and you'll need more than a wheelchair.'

Danny winked and whispered, 'Shake me and don't let go until I say, then run for Lily.'

'I'm going to kill you,' Simon raged, shaking Danny.

'It's better than us all dying,' Danny shouted, manoeuvring his chair to face the stairs. 'Can someone get this dullard off me?'

Eron nodded at two soldiers. 'Grab him, and if he resists, kill someone.'

The soldiers moved towards Simon, and Danny whispered, 'Now.'

Simon dived for the stairs as Danny raised his right hand, brandishing a pole. He swung it at the first soldier, and a quick flash saw the soldier go flying back, hitting the wall motionless. He quickly did the same to the second attacker, spurring the others into action.

Dazza swung his elbow into the face of the soldier behind him as Max and Zym lunged for two others, followed by Bobby and Adam on another. Stephen dived for another soldier, knocking him into Eron and sending them all sprawling on the floor. Two soldiers grabbed Juli and Erzsi, but they twisted the soldiers' guns and used them to shoot each other's soldiers.

'Don't kill them,' Max shouted, 'or they could leap into the humans here.'

Pat grabbed Astrid and pulled her away.

Astrid flinched. 'Please, don't hurt me. He forces me to do this.'

Danny shot forward, jabbing the soldiers Juli and Erzsi had shot, plus two more soldiers. Max grabbed a gun and shot two more, wounding them both. Stephen was now straddling the soldier he'd knocked over and was punching him repeatedly as the soldier tried to push him off.

Eron scrambled to his feet, and noticing Danny with his back to him, he picked up the gun from the soldier Stephen was attacking and aimed it at Danny.

'Danny, behind you,' Pat shouted.

Danny spun round, hitting what he thought was a soldier with the pole, and seeing the gun, he pressed the button on the pole's grip. '*No!*' he screamed as he realised it was Chris's body flying back against the wall and sliding down into a sitting position with his head slumped forward.

With Eron and six soldiers dead, thanks to Danny, and with two soldiers shot and injured, the remaining three soldiers lost the will to fight. Max and Zym, helped by the others, bundled the soldiers together with Erzsi and Stephen pointing guns at them, while Adam and Bobby rushed over to Mercedes, who was starting to come around. Meanwhile, Danny, Dazza and Juli rushed to Chris's body.

'I didn't realise it was Chris. I thought it was one of them,' Danny said, indicating the remaining soldiers.

Juli put two fingers against Chris's neck. 'There's a pulse.'

'Are you sure?' Danny asked.

'Yes, look, he's breathing,' Juli replied.

'What happened?' a dazed Mercedes said, looking up at Adam and Bobby.

'We were attacked by Eron and his group trying to get to Lily,' Bobby replied.

'Oh, yeah, I remember now, Chris came into the room and—where is he?' Mercedes said, standing up and going dizzy. 'I owe him one,' she added, swaying slightly before getting her bearings and spotting him against the far wall.

'Hey, take it easy. You were knocked unconscious,' Adam said, grabbing Mercedes's arm to steady her.

'I'm fine, but what's happened to Chris?' Mercedes asked, staggering across to him.

'Ten seconds ago, she was ready to punch him!' Adam exclaimed.

'Why do you think I date guys? They're less complicated,' Bobby laughed.

'Chris, can you hear me?' Juli asked, gently shaking him.

'What's wrong with him?' Mercedes asked, trying to crouch down before half falling to her knees.

'Danny zapped him with his pole,' Dazza replied, pointing to the metal pole Danny was still holding.

'What the hell is that?' Mercedes demanded.

'Yeah, what is that thing?' Max asked.

'It delivers an electric shock,' Danny replied.

'By the looks of those soldiers over there, it's more than just a shock—bloody hell, if their shells are dead, it means they're in two of you lot,' Max said, scanning the room.

'Calm down, Chief. Their energy souls are dead too,' Danny said reassuringly. 'When we were developing the Separator machine, I kept thinking about my dad...I mean that thing's insistence about a certain frequency, so I set my chair to the same one. It turns out that is the right level to kill energy souls from your planet,' he said.

'Blimey, it seems Wheels has only gone and developed a depletor,' Zym laughed. 'At last, we have proper weapons from home.'

'Actually, it sounds like it dissipates energy rather than depleting it,' Mercedes said.

'I can live with dissipators,' Zym replied. 'How many have you got, Wheels?'

'Including this, uh, one,' Danny replied. 'No, hang on, I've got two.'

'Where's the other one?' Max asked with a sense of foreboding.

Danny tapped the left side of his chair. 'Here.'

'Great, all we need is a few months to mass-produce some, and we'll be ready for tomorrow,' Zym sighed.

'Where am I?' Chris groaned.

'Never mind that where's Eron?' Max asked.

'Um, I don't know,' Chris replied. 'I can't sense him.'

'Lily's gone,' Simon screamed, running downstairs. 'I've looked everywhere for her.'

'Lily!' Pat yelled.

'Erzsi, Stephen, keep an eye on them,' Max said, indicating the soldiers. 'The rest of you split up and look everywhere.'

'Can I help?' Astrid mumbled.

'Are you sure you checked under the beds?' Pat yelled at Simon.

'Of course I did,' Simon said.

'She's in that cupboard,' Astrid muttered, pointing to a small wooden door in the far corner of the room.

'Bobby, you and Adam check the garage, and I'll check outside,' Max ordered.

Astrid started to walk across the room as Bobby and Adam ran to the garage.

'Where the hell is she going?' Zym asked.

'That door doesn't open,' Max said.

Astrid tried the door handle, and when the door didn't budge, she tapped it. 'Lily, your mummy and daddy are worried.'

There was a metallic scraping sound, like an old bolt being moved, and the door creaked open to reveal Lily sitting on a wooden step.

'Lily,' Pat screamed, running over and sweeping her up in her arms.

'I'm okay, Mummy,' Lily said.

Zym studied the door before saying, 'I thought you said the door didn't open? It was just locked from the inside.'

Max looked and replied, 'The builders reckoned it was a blocked-up cupboard, but there's stairs.'

Max ran up the stairs, and after some bumping and scraping from above, he came down the main staircase. 'It comes up to a trapdoor in the bedroom Lily was in.'

'And you've never noticed it, Junior?' Zym said.

'It's under the bed!' Max exclaimed. 'I paid builders to knock this place into shape and an interior designer to furnish it.'

'For someone so precious about security, that's not like you,' Bobby said, returning from the garage.

'I only had this place finished last year, then I had a little accident, so I've been a bit busy,' Max retorted.

'Hmm, I'll let you off,' Bobby replied with a smile.

Simon turned to Lily, still held tightly by Pat and said, 'How did you know to hide there?'

'Granny Shaz told me,' Lily replied. 'I heard all the bad men down here, and she showed me the place.'

Pat frowned. 'She's been on about Granny this and that for months. Wasn't Shaz your mum?'

Simon sighed. 'I think we need a family meeting. It's about time Bobby and Lily learned about my family, and I need to tell you a few things, too.'

'You guys need to talk. Use the bedroom while we plan for tomorrow.' Max said.

As soon as they had gone upstairs, Zym said, 'I still think this is a mistake. This couldn't be more of a trap if it had party balloons and a sign saying 'trap this way.''

'I agree, but if we can save Danny's dad, we have to try,' Max insisted.

'But we don't even know how many of them there are?' Zym grumbled. 'There could be hundreds or even thousands waiting for us.'

'I'm not so sure,' Juli said. 'I've been working on the inside for a couple of years, and they like to keep things low-key. But they won't be happy about you gatecrashing the IFFS.'

Zym frowned and turned towards Juli. 'Why were you working there when they'd faked your death, taken you away from your family and friends and killed your previous host?'

'I don't have any family or friends, or at least this shell doesn't. I'm a member of a group monitoring the rise in Zephyrions on Earth in the last fifteen years,' Juli replied. 'The real Juli Fellowes passed away several years ago from a genetic terminal illness.'

'But she was your host,' Zym said.

'Yes. I was her boss when she started in laser technology. We worked together for years, and as both her parents had died when she was young, I virtually adopted her,' Juli replied. 'She offered to be my host when my last shell was getting frail. Then, when I was transmuting inside her, and she found out about our group, she insisted on helping.'

'But if she died so long ago, who died in that interstate crash?' Danny asked.

'Nobody. We'd spotted a trend of hosts being killed, and Juli suggested that two of us transmute, one after the other. Then, if they came after us, the one they killed could jump into a new host,' Juli explained. 'When I transmuted, I took over Juli's work and the group arranged for her to live out her days in a luxury villa in California.'

Danny filled in the blanks. 'And the lost sister story was—'

'Was just that. A story,' Juli laughed. 'We recruited Erzsi not long after she came to Earth.'

'I wish we'd known before,' Zym said.

'We didn't know if you were alive,' Juli replied. 'You, Max and Simo had disappeared. We never linked Simon Morris to Simo, and we only found out about Max when that power station incident happened.'

'It was a bit more than an incident,' Bobby insisted.

'Can your group help us? Max asked.

'I've been messaging them the whole time. They're pulling together a force, and as soon as we know the final location, they'll be ready to fight,' Juli replied.

'Another element of surprise. I'm starting to feel like we have the makings of a plan that isn't going to kill us,' Max said.

33
THE FACE-OFF

'Five minutes to go,' Zym said. 'At least Junior's place on the edge of the Cotswolds was close.'

'We need to trust the plan,' Danny insisted, gripping the steering wheel tightly, his eyes focused on the car's clock.

'Are your friends ready?' Zym asked.

'Yes, they've come together about ten minutes away, so they won't attract any attention,' Juli replied.

'I hope this works,' Bobby said.

'Hope is all we have, lad,' Zym said.

Danny's phone bleeped. 'Here we go,' he said, punching the coordinates from the message into the car's satellite navigation.

'That's almost fifty minutes away, and we only have an hour to get there,' Zym said.

'Get going,' Juli said. 'I'll message my group and let Pat and the others know.'

'I'll message Max and Simon,' Erzsi said.

'Good idea. Wheels, get going and pass me your phone,' Zym said.

'Here, but what're you up to?'

'I'm going to annoy our narcissistic Mr White,' Zym said, smiling.

Zym messaged:

'Okay, it's a trap,' Zym said.

'How can you be so sure?' Erzsi asked.

'He dismissed Danny and his dad as irrelevant,' Zym replied.

'Let's see what he says to this,' Zym said, tapping away on Danny's phone.

'He's good,' Zym said, replying,

'Simon and Max said they'll be there more than ten minutes ahead of us,' Erzsi replied.

'My group will get there just before us, too,' Juli said.

After an otherwise uneventful journey, Danny approached the barrier to the site they had been directed to. 'It's an airfield,' he said.

'There's two armed guards on the gate, but it does seem strangely quiet,' Zym agreed.

Danny stopped as they reached the barrier, and a guard approached the vehicle.

'Can I help you, sir?' the guard asked cautiously while keeping a hand on his assault rifle.

'Danny White to see, uh,' Danny paused, unable to say the name. 'I'm expected. I've got Max Janus and others.'

The guard lifted a computer tablet before replying, 'Danny White, yes. Follow the road down to hangar C. It's the second on your left.'

'Where are all their military? I expected armed guards, soldiers, the works,' Zym said, looking round the almost deserted airfield as Danny followed the signs to hangers A to E.

'I said they liked to keep things low-key,' Juli said. 'They may be controlling the elite, but they need to rely on the human military to support them.'

'Has anyone got a signal?' Zym asked. 'I can't get one on Danny's or my phone to find out where Simon and Max are.'

'I can't get one either. I've been trying to find out where my group are,' Juli replied, scanning the surrounding buildings and the faces of people going about their business.

'We're out of time, folks,' Danny said, pulling up at the back of hanger C.

Two soldiers dressed in black with assault rifles approached the car.

'Out now,' one ordered, waving his rifle to reinforce the instruction.

While Zym, Juli, Erzsi and Bobby got out, Danny sat behind the wheel.

The guard tapped the driver's window with the rifle. 'Get out.'

Danny opened the door and shrugged. 'I can't go anywhere until you release the catches holding my chair, dullard.'

The soldier bent forward to look at the catches when the other shouted, 'Don't touch his chair. I heard what he did in Switzerland.'

The soldier jumped back and pointed at Bobby. 'You, get over here and undo his catches.'

As Bobby bent down, he hissed, 'No funny stuff. Not yet, anyway.'

Danny smiled and nodded. Once Bobby had released the catches, Danny said quietly, 'Stand back. I wouldn't want the ramp hurting anyone.'

'Why are you using the ramp when your chair can get you in or out?' Bobby whispered.

'You'll see,' Danny smirked.

As Bobby stepped to one side, Danny hit the ramp release button sharply, causing it to shoot out, hitting the soldier in the ankle and making him swear.

'Sorry, did it catch you?' Danny sniggered. 'This thing can be temperamental.'

'Get round there with the others,' the soldier snarled, rubbing his ankle.

The soldiers frisked the others for weapons, but when left with Danny, they looked at each other and shook their heads.

'I'm not touching him,' the injured soldier said.

'Nor me,' the other replied. 'Let's just get them inside.'

'Aww, guys. I understand. This is our first date after all,' Danny said, winking.

The first soldier opened a door into the hangar and waved everyone inside. Danny deliberately took his time, making it look like his chair only just fitted through the doorway.

'You okay?' the soldier asked his colleague, who kept rubbing his ankle.

'I'm going to enjoy making that disabled kid suffer,' the soldier replied, limping.

'I'm not disabled, I'm differently-abled,' Danny muttered. 'And you're gonna discover how differently soon, dullard.'

The hangar was vast, with a large curved roof running from left to right. As they entered the hangar, they passed a small office complex on the right, in front of which was a large television screen mounted on wheels, followed by a large grey private jet half out of the open hangar doors with its air stair door open. To the left were three turboprop planes, all angled slightly towards the open door, with more than a dozen armed soldiers in the same black uniforms, with black hoodies covering their heads, standing in front of the planes.

'Get over by those old planes,' the limping soldier ordered.

'Where's my dad?' Danny demanded, scanning the hangar.

'You're not giving the orders, boy,' the soldier said, raising his rifle towards Danny.

'Nor are you, soldier,' Paul White said, coming out of the office complex. 'Hello, son,' he added.

Danny shot forward but was blocked by the soldier. 'You're nothing to me,' Danny replied. 'You said to bring them here, and you'll give me my dad.'

'Hmm,' Paul smirked. 'I did say that, didn't I.' Paul rubbed his chin and walked towards the open hangar doors, glancing at the jet as he passed it. 'But you've given me a problem.'

'I've done what you asked,' Danny snapped, flexing his fingers by the sides of his chair.

Paul stopped just outside the hangar and turned. 'You might have brought them here, but you didn't plan to play fair, did you?'

'I don't know what you mean?' Danny replied, edging slightly closer to the limping soldier.

Paul waved to someone out of sight, and a group of thirty people came trudging into sight with twenty armed soldiers behind and to the sides of them. 'I assume this lot belongs to you?'

Danny shrugged. 'Never seen them.'

Behind Danny, Juli shifted awkwardly.

'Is this your group?' Zym hissed. 'Not exactly a task force, are they?'

'It was very short notice, and we're mainly based in Switzerland and Italy,' Juli protested.

Paul noticed the exchange between Juli and Zym and laughed. 'Looks like your friend knows them.'

'Let them go,' Juli protested.

'I don't think so,' Paul replied. 'Take the Zephyrions off to the Porter machine for transport to Leyton, and the humans can go to the Cotswold host centre for grading,' he said to the soldier leading the group.

'*No!*' Juli screamed as she ran forward before a soldier grabbed her.

'Enough!' Paul shouted. 'The deal is off. From now on—'

Paul was interrupted by a guard running up to him from the offices he'd emerged from earlier. 'Sir, she's ready.'

Paul strolled across to the television and turned it on. 'Hello, Jay. Can you hear me?'

The image on the screen showed Zara Shah, WestFi's owner, sitting in a large, pale grey, corporate-style armchair.

'Hello, Paul. Have you managed and neutralised all risks?' she asked, sipping iced lemon water.

'Hi, Jay. Yes, we've captured their pathetic ambush squad, and they're under armed guards.'

'Bring Max and his annoying brother forward,' Jay demanded.

'Stay there, Max. You too, Zym,' Danny shouted as he yanked one of the poles from his chair and hit the soldier with a limp, sending him sprawling across the floor.

The soldiers behind Danny raised their guns as the soldier who had escorted Danny and the others in went to check on his friend.

'What happened?' Jay asked angrily.

'Just checking, Jay,' Paul replied. 'Well, what's up with him?'

'His shell is dead, sir.'

'Strange thing to do, Danny. As the only human in this hangar, you've just become a host,' Paul smirked. 'Relax, soldiers. We can wait for your guy to take control of the boy, and this will all be over.'

'Bring out my dad!' Danny demanded, moving his chair slightly sideways so he could see some of the soldiers behind his friends.

'You can't win, Danny,' Paul replied. 'Go ahead, hit one of them with your stick. They'll just jump into a nearby civilian, maybe even your dad.'

'So he is here?' Danny snarled. 'I want to see him.'

Paul sighed. 'Fine. Soldier, leave that shell and fetch the other Paul White.'

Danny bristled at his father being referred to as "the other Paul White" but he fought the temptation to lash out.

'Apart from the clothes, they look almost identical,' Bobby whispered as the soldier appeared dragging Paul by the arm.

'Plus, the real Paul is a lot thinner,' Erzsi replied.

Bobby looked down at himself and, thinking of Max, puffed out his chest to look bigger.

'Can you hear that hum?' Zym asked.

'Now you mention it, yeah,' Juli replied.

'Dad, are you okay?' Danny shouted, worried about his father's dishevelled look in the oversized white overalls.

Danny's father stared blankly.

'What have you done to him,' Danny snapped, pointing the pole at the soldier standing by his father.

'Calm down, Danny. He's just a little tranquilised. We find hosts are less likely to hurt themselves like this,' Paul said. 'The drugs wear off in a couple of hours when they're needed for hosting.'

'You mean they're unable to fight back,' Danny snarled.

'Let's get back to business,' Paul replied. 'Have you come to trade or to wave that cattle prod around?'

'Bring Dad to me first,' Danny ordered.

Paul smirked. 'You're not giving the orders—'

'Just bloody do it, Trim,' Jay shouted from the television screen. 'And bring Max and Zym forward.'

Paul nodded at the soldier to take Danny's father across to Danny and waved at some soldiers at the back to bring Max and Zym forward.

Zym frowned, looking from the television screen to Paul and then to the jet. A second later, he felt the barrel of a gun in his back, shoving him forward with Bobby beside him.

'I can't see them clearly; move them towards the sunlight,' Jay ordered.

'Where's Max and my dad?' Bobby whispered to Zym as they were shoved towards the hangar's entrance.

'They'll be here, lad,' Zym replied reassuringly, glancing back at their friends and the soldiers behind them. As they passed the back of the jet, he added, 'Can you see that heat shimmer from the engines?'

'Yeah, perhaps it landed just before we got here because if the engines were on, we'd be blasted, wouldn't we?' Bobby said.

'*Don't look round, Bobby, but I'm closer than you think,*' Max thought.

'Stop talking and stay there,' Paul ordered.

'Turn them round,' Jay shouted.

'You heard the lady,' Paul said. 'Turn around.'

Zym and Bobby started to turn when Jay screamed, 'You bloody idiot, Trim. That's Zym, but the other is Max's old host, that boy.'

Paul stormed in front of Zym. 'Where's Max?'

'He's right here. But did Jay call you Trim? As in Trimhal?' Zym asked.

Paul laughed. 'You always were stuck in the past. Yeah, I used to be Trimhal a long time ago, back on Zephyrion when you and your useless brother were playing at being enforcers,' he said. 'But where is Max?'

Zym smiled. 'If you're such a hotshot enforcer, Trim, you'd know Max is here.'

'This boy isn't Max,' Trim snapped, shoving Bobby so hard he fell back onto the ground.

Zym crouched down to check Bobby before turning his head to look up at Trim. 'I never said Bobby was Max, did I?' he added before swinging a punch as he quickly stood up, connecting right in the middle of Trim's face, sending him sprawling backwards.

As Zym sprang into action, the two soldiers in the middle of the group near Juli, Erzsi, Danny and Paul, turned in opposite directions, dropping their rifles and pulling out strange-looking handguns with a wire trailing from each. As they fired, arcs of electricity discharged from the weapons and as each soldier was hit, they flew backwards and crumpled to the floor. Juli turned and saw that the two soldiers were Max and Simon. Max moved at incredible speed and quickly killed the soldiers on his side before helping Simon.

The two soldiers that had pushed Zym and Bobby forward turned towards the group, but before they could open fire, Danny aimed his pole towards each of them and fired, sending them crashing to the floor.

In the mele, Trim had dashed towards the jet, but the door closed before he reached it. Suddenly, the air in the hangar started to warm as the engines whirred into life. The sound moved from the hum of the auxiliary power unit to a whine and then to a deep roar from the turbines as the engines ignited.

Trim kept banging on the side of the plane, but as the pilot slowly increased the thrust and the aircraft rolled forward, the television and other objects behind it started flying backwards, smashing into the offices.

'Everybody out, *NOW*,' Max shouted.

Zym helped Bobby stand, and they ran after Juli and Erzsi.

Danny pulled his father onto his lap and chased after the others, but the sound of a rifle firing stopped his wheelchair as the bullet crashed into the electronics under the seat.

'Help,' Danny yelled as Trim lifted the rifle to take a better aim.

Max ran back to push Danny's chair out of the hangar, with Simon struggling to keep up.

'Take one more step, and the disabled kid gets it,' Trim shouted, shooting just ahead of Danny's chair.

As they swerved to avoid the bullet, Max and Simon span Danny's chair around, pushed by the tail end of the jet's engine wash as it cleared the hangar and headed towards the runway.

'Perfect,' Trim said, walking towards them. 'Now drop those depletors and kick them over here.'

Simon and Max dropped their handguns, while Danny dropped the pole on the floor with a loud clanging sound.

'Kick it over here,' Trim demanded.

'Uh, hello, dullard, it's wired to my chair,' Danny replied, lowering his left hand, hidden by his still unresponsive dad lying across the chair. 'And their guns are wired to battery packs.'

'You know that mouth of yours is going to shorten your life, kid,' Trim sneered.

'You're not the first person to say something like that,' Danny replied. 'Probably won't be the last either,' he grinned.

A jet engine roaring made them glance outside to see the grey jet tearing off into the sky.

'Looks like your boss is leaving you here alone, Trim,' Max said. 'Not the first time he's done that, is it?'

Zym frowned. 'What do you mean him? That was Jay on the plane. I worked it out when she shouted Trim's name. I heard it on the TV and from the plane. Then I noticed the movement of the shadows on the TV matched the clouds casting shadows on the plane.'

'Sorry, old timer, but youth wins again. Are you going to tell him who Jay is, or do I?' Max said, staring at Trim.

'When did you work it out?' Trim asked, laughing sarcastically.

Max never broke his stare away from Trim. 'She kept talking about managing and neutralising risks. It was one of Zeryn's favourite phrases and of course...'

'Jericesen,' Trim said.

'Jay is Jericesen?' Zym asked.

Trim couldn't hide his smirk. 'You always were slow, Zym.'

'But what I don't understand is, if you were always working for Jeric and Zeryn, why did you send enforcers to help me track Dronin back on Zephyrion?' Max asked.

'They were all traitors to our cause. It was the perfect way to cleanse the squad,' Trim replied. 'But it's time to go. Zym go outside and get the others back in here, but stay in sight. But before you do, drop the battery pack to that weapon and kick it over.'

Zym undid the battery pack belt and kicked it across the floor before slowly walking out of the hangar, glancing in both directions.

As Trim bent to pick up the battery belt and dissipator, Danny grabbed the pole on the left side of his chair, pointed it at Trim and fired.

Trim picked up the belt and gun and smiled, fastening the battery belt around his waist and pushing the handgun into his pocket. 'Oh dear, it looks like the disabled kid's batteries are dead,' Trim smirked as he lifted the rifle. 'Now say g—'

Trim was cut short as a green and yellow two-seater convertible slammed into him, sending him flying over the top and landing behind it.

As Adam skidded the Lister to a halt, Mercedes stood up and pointed her dissipator at Trim.

Dazed and confused, Trim tried to reach the rifle near him, but Mercedes fired. 'Danny is differently-abled, thank you,' she said as Trim fell back, dead.

'What the hell are you doing here?' Max asked.

'Danny's uncle turned up and said their safe house was compromised. When he heard what you guys were up to, he left Danny's mum with Pat and the others and said he was coming here with some friends to help,' Adam explained. 'There's no way I was missing the chance to save Bobby, and I saw this in your garage last night, along with some of the dissipators you were building overnight.'

Zym smiled at Mercedes. 'Let me guess, you felt the same about saving Danny?'

'Hell, no,' Mercedes insisted, glancing at Danny before looking away.

'Hey, Danny, how's your old man?' Jimmy asked, strolling into the hangar and glancing around at the dead bodies.

'Hey, Uncle Jimmy. I could do with a hand. Dad's still not very responsive,' Danny replied.

Max and Zym helped lift Paul off Danny's lap, and Adam grabbed a chair for Paul to sit on.

'Area secured,' Jimmy said into a walkie-talkie. 'So, have you guys been busy faffing around in here?' he asked.

'What the hell's faffing?' Zym asked.

Max sighed. 'Faffing around is like messing around. Sorry, Jimmy, my brother's English is stuck in the nineteenth century. It's nice to see you. I'm Max, and this dinosaur is Zym.'

'Nice to meet you both,' Jimmy replied. 'I finally get to meet the guy Danny never stops talking about.'

Danny went to protest but changed his mind.

'All clear to bring them in, Major?' a soldier asked from the hangar doorway.

'Yep, bring them in,' Jimmy replied. 'Did you lose any of your team?' Jimmy asked Max and the others.

A few seconds later, Juli's friends appeared, followed by ten soldiers in combat gear.

'There were eleven of you?' Zym said, surprised.

Jimmy laughed. 'Yeah, we were a bit heavy-handed. If I'd known, I'd have just brought a couple of the team.'

'We failed to get the ringleader, though. Jeric, or Jay as he's called now, escaped on that jet,' Max said.

'I saw it leave,' Jimmy replied. 'But we've got a bigger challenge coming.'

34
THE TAKEOVER II

'You're wrong,' Danny insisted. 'Technically, it may be stronger per kilogram, but it's more fragile if it's hit at an angle, making it impractical.'

'Not if you layer it in sheets in opposing directions and then wrap it,' Mercedes protested.

'That might work,' Danny mused. 'But the wrap would need to be thin. Otherwise you lose the weight saving.'

'Well, yeah, I'm not as daft as you look,' Mercedes replied.

'Morning,' Paul said as he walked past them.

'Hey, Dad,' Danny replied.

'Morning, Paul,' Mercedes said. 'How are you feeling?'

Paul rubbed his temples. 'I feel like I've been to one hell of a party but can't remember a thing.'

'Where's Mum?' Danny asked.

'She's still asleep,' Paul replied. 'Where's everyone else?'

'Lily's watching a cartoon, and most of the others are in the kitchen,' Danny replied.

'That's a good place to be. I need coffee,' Paul replied. 'I'll leave you lovebirds to your debate.'

As Paul headed towards the kitchen, he smiled as he heard Danny and Mercedes protesting about any romantic involvement.

'What's next then?' Simon asked, watching through the doorway into the living room as Lily jigged around, watching some new dance cartoon on the television.

'We need to get Jeric and stop him,' Max replied. 'We know he's got a lot of control over the elite.'

'You guys have certainly stumbled into something big,' Jimmy said. 'Stirling Lines is in lockdown, and they're trying to persuade a lot of us recent retirees to come back.'

'You have no idea,' Paul White said, strolling into the kitchen. 'The SAS HQ in lockdown is just the start.'

'Great to see you up, Paul,' Jimmy replied. 'But damn, you look awful.'

'Cheers, Jim. Trust you to be blunt with the truth,' Paul replied, pouring a coffee.

'You know me, no messing or endless chat. Say it like it is and move on,' Jimmy replied.

'How's Danny taking things?' Max asked.

'You know Danny. Nothing keeps him down for long. He's currently arguing with Mercedes about which material provides the best tensile strength per kilogram for his next wheelchair,' Paul said.

'Nothing says true love than a good intellectual argument,' Max laughed.

'I'm glad you're not still inside me and making claims like that,' Bobby replied.

'Talking of hosting, how long ago did Trim jump into you, Paul?' Max asked.

'It was not long after you're little power station incident. From the start, he took full control of me and kept me suppressed. In the end, he let me broker the deals, but he wouldn't let me communicate with anyone who knew me. The first time I was free of him was when he transmuted, which was when I bought Innovest, and then I was drugged and put into that host centre,' Paul replied.

'So they let you do the business deals but stopped you revealing Trim was inside you?' Zym asked.

'Yep. Almost as soon as Trim jumped into me, I found out that Jeric was Jay. I didn't know how big her plans were because she keeps everything to herself and only reveals what she needs to,' Paul sighed.

'With Jeric having control of Bluestone and Spearhead, he holds the world's purse strings,' Juli said.

'He also seems to own the UK Prime Minister,' Erzsi added.

Paul sipped his coffee before saying, 'Jay doesn't seem to own McGivern; she does own him. She was blackmailing him over indecent images before making him a host for one of you lot. She uses blackmail a lot.'

'If McGivern is one of Jeric's men, then he now has control of a nuclear power,' Max said.

'We've lost before we start,' Simon exclaimed.

'You're overthinking this. It doesn't matter who they are or what they've got. You've got a job to do. We need to control the tempo, plan, build the team and execute,' Jimmy replied.

'We could have done with you in 1667. The Dutch destroyed us in Medway,' Zym said.

'All battles are the same,' Jimmy said. 'Just remember to plan and execute, and there should be no loose ends. Oh, and never let them see you sweat.'

'We've got the mother of all loose ends with Jay out there,' Paul said.

'How many countries does Jay or Jeric control?' Max asked.

'Mate, rule one, agree on your enemy. Is it Jay or Jeric, she, he, they or even it?' Jimmy said. 'If you keep using multiple terms, it'll overcomplicate things.'

'Then it's Jeric and he,' Max replied.

'Rule two, know the extent of his power,' Jimmy said

'That's back to my question. How many countries does Jeric control, Paul?' Max asked.

'His financial clout through Bluestone and Spearhead means he can have personal meetings with anyone,' Paul replied.

'Too broad, mate,' Jimmy replied. 'Which countries are totally under his control?'

Paul finished his coffee, still standing and leaning against a worktop. 'I'm trying to remember when Trim was using me as a host.'

'Just take your time, Paul. This is important,' Zym said.

'I know the UK was seen as the best place to start. Recent compliance with propaganda scare stories had shown Europe to be susceptible to manipulation by the elite. As an island country, the UK was selected as an easier option to lockdown,' Paul replied, pouring more coffee.

'You said the Prime Minister was already a host. Has Jeric got any other country leaders?' Max asked.

'I'd say the alien in McGivern must have transmuted around the time of the IFFS,' Paul replied. 'So he's not even a host now, he is one of you.'

'That'll be why they didn't risk him coming to Zermatt,' Max said. 'They wouldn't want the UK Prime Minister collapsing in public.'

'Any other countries?' Zym asked.

'They're infiltrating the whole of Europe, but I think the only other country they're close to taking control is Switzerland, where they've replaced two members of the Federal Council,' Paul replied.

'At least Switzerland doesn't have nuclear weapons,' Zym said.

Max shook his head. 'They have something even worse. They're the bankers to the world.'

Paul sighed. 'Can it get any—'

Adam ran into the kitchen. 'We've got a problem.'

'Yeah, we've been talking about it,' Zym said.

'You've heard the news about martial law then?' Adam asked. 'It's all over socials.'

Paul turned and flicked on the small television on the wall by the kitchen window.

'We interrupt this broadcast for an emergency statement from the Prime Minister,' the newsreader said.

Simon heard Lily whining from the living room about her television programme being interrupted and saw Pat trying to calm her down.

The screen changed to show Alastair McGivern standing outside 10 Downing Street.

'My fellow citizens, I'm afraid we have seen a dramatic escalation since my last press conference. The aliens who are invading our planet and who have started with our democratic and free nation have escalated events. Two elderly citizens were gunned down in a horrific attack in Newmarket, and a garage owner was also killed in their escape.

'Yesterday, they attacked a military airport in Oxfordshire in an attempt to gain control of our airspace. We were able to rescue people from the base, and while they managed to take control of parts of the base for a short time, we managed to regain control,' McGivern said, pausing for effect.

'What's he on about? We drove away from the camp without any fight?' Adam said.

'Propaganda never needs to be fed the truth,' Jimmy replied.

'As a result of these latest developments, I have been to see His Majesty the King,' McGivern continued. 'With immediate effect, we are now at war with these aliens, and the United Kingdom is under martial law. Parliament has been replaced with a council of war headed by me and supported by the Cabinet and key business advisors.

'We have circulated images of all known aliens and ask you to be vigilant. Please do not confront them; just make a report using the number or website shown on your screen or download the UK war app from your phone supplier's store. God save the King.'

The screen changed to a series of scrolling photographs with a message saying, "If you see them, report them."

'They've included all of us!' Bobby said. 'Even Adam.'

'Not quite everyone,' Max replied. 'They obviously don't know about Jimmy or his team, and they've not included Paul.'

'I guess they don't know Trim is dead yet,' Zym said.

'What do we do?' Adam asked.

'We give up, or we fight back,' Max replied.

'Looks like we're in a war then,' Zym said.

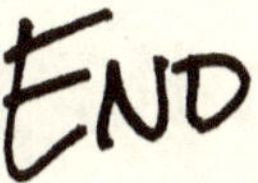

Max and the Corporate Takeover is the third book in the Max Janus series. Max and the Hidden Visitor is where the journey between Max and Bobby Morris begins.

The Regent Supreme is the prequel, and it explains how and why Max came to Earth over two thousand years ago.

The Corporate Takeover picks up from where The Hidden Visitor ends and brings the first two books together in a fight to uncover the truth, which could become the ultimate fight for survival.

About the Author

D.P. Bowkett qualified as an accountant in 1997, auditing a diverse range of businesses and preparing the accounts and tax returns for people as varied as builders to military leaders and the landed gentry. A career in the automotive industry and financial services saw him become a Group Chief Financial Officer for a multi-billion-dollar multinational business before starting his own management consultancy business. He now advises companies across Europe in growth and expansion, managing risk and working on due diligence for investments, acquisitions and divestment.

His love of writing stemmed from creating articles for numerous websites and producing regular reports for clients who use them for marketing and business intelligence.

This love of writing and reading science fiction culminated in his latest project, documenting the life of an alien, Max Janus, who came to Earth over two thousand years ago.

Outside his professional endeavours, Dean cherishes moments with his family, which includes five grandchildren.

www.ingramcontent.com/pod-product-compliance
Lightning Source LLC
Chambersburg PA
CBHW050610170726
48283CB00001B/190